Praise for *An Uncommon Grace*

"A truly riveting read from first to last! Serena Miller immerses readers in the world of the most conservative Amish sect, the Swartzentrubers, with authenticity and depth. *An Uncommon Grace* is aptly named as it showcases the chasm between two cultures that can be bridged only by God's grace and truth. If you pick up this book, prepare to not put it down till the last page!"

—Laura Frantz, author of *Courting Morrow Little* and *The Colonel's Lady*

"Set in the heart of Amish country, *An Uncommon Grace* is the perfect mix of page-turning suspense and poignant love story. I was so captivated by the characters that I stayed up way too late reading their story. I couldn't put this novel down!"

—Melanie Dobson, author of *The Silent Order*

"Miller takes you from war-torn Afghanistan to the Shetlers' farm in Amish country Ohio in *An Uncommon Grace*. This story will make your heart pound in fear for a community terrorized by a killer and cause your heart to beat with hope for two lives in turmoil. I guarantee you will love these characters along with a story that will keep you turning pages and rooting for love despite the strict laws of the Swartzentruber Amish."

—Jillian Kent, author of *Secrets of the Heart*, The Ravensmoore Chronicles, Book I

"Serena Miller's latest offering, *An Uncommon Grace,* is a captivating story populated with fascinating characters, an unpredictable plot, and a memorable setting. Miller's attention to cultural detail sets this book apart. With gentleness and respect she invites readers into a unique and rarely viewed world. I became so involved in the characters and emotionally invested in their story, I was truly reluctant to reach the last pages of the book. Definitely a recommended read."

—Annette Smith, author of
A Town Called Ruby Prairie

"Serena Miller breathes such life into her characters they almost leap off the page into your imagination. From the first paragraph of *An Uncommon Grace* to the final page, you are caught up in the story of Levi and Grace. Miller paints their very different worlds in wonderful, eye-opening detail. A great read."

—Ann H. Gabhart, author of
Words Spoken True and the Shaker series

AN UNCOMMON
Grace

A NOVEL

SERENA B. MILLER

 HOWARD BOOKS
A DIVISION OF SIMON & SCHUSTER, INC.

NEW YORK   NASHVILLE   LONDON   TORONTO   SYDNEY   NEW DELHI

Howard Books
A Division of Simon & Schuster, Inc.
1230 Avenue of the Americas
New York, NY 10020

First Howard Books trade paperback edition April 2012

HOWARD and colophon are trademarks of Simon & Schuster, Inc.

For information about special discounts for bulk purchases, please contact Simon & Schuster Special Sales at 1-866-506-1949 or business@simonandschuster.com.

The Simon & Schuster Speakers Bureau can bring authors to your live event. For more information or to book an event contact the Simon & Schuster Speakers Bureau at 1-866-248-3049 or visit our website at www.simonspeakers.com.

Designed by Kyoko Watanabe

Manufactured in the United States of America

10 9 8 7 6 5 4 3

Library of Congress Cataloging-in-Publication Data

Miller, Serena.
An uncommon grace : a novel / Serena B. Miller.
    p. cm.
I. Title.
PS3613.I55295U53 2012
813'.6—dc23   2011035334

ISBN 978-1-4516-6030-2
ISBN 978-1-4516-6034-0 (ebook)

To my lionhearted husband, Steve.
Thank you for fighting your way back to us.
Now . . .
"The winter is past. The rains are over
and gone. Flowers appear on the earth.
The season of singing has come."
—SONG OF SOLOMON 2:11–12 NIV

Acknowledgments

My sincere gratitude to:

The incomparable Dr. Tsuyoshi Inoshita, oncologist and friend who, along with his competent and caring staff, helped save my husband's life this year. My Old Order Amish friends who corrected my Pennsylvania Deutsch, provided me with the hospitality of their peaceful farm, and sent me home with elderberry plants and enduring memories. Eli and Vesta Hochstetler, owners of Gospel Book Store in Berlin, Ohio—for introducing me to valuable Amish research resources. Editor Holly Halverson, for making this a better book. Agent Sandra Bishop—for flying all over the United States using her God-given gifts to promote Christian fiction. Kristi Cordle, RN—for medical information. Eli, Adam, and Ethan Cordle—for allowing their nurse-mommy the time to review this manuscript. Kim McCray and Kendra Cram—for information about Children's Hospital. Dewey Cordle, former dairyman—for calving information. Don Coriell—for insights into the challenges of running a family farm. Gabe Coriell, horseman—for explaining about various equine breeds and stamina. Brenda Kallner, grant writer—for in-depth proofreading. Velva and Pete Hunter—for years of faithful encouragement. Phyllis Stevens, Vivian Woodworth, Sharon

Hardin, and Ruth Miller, my sisters and mother-in-law—for understanding and support during difficult deadlines. Caleb Miller, son—for making me laugh when there was little to laugh about. Jacob Miller, son—for tech support and unwavering patience. Derek Miller, son—for on-site technical advice about Bagram medevac teams. Meaghan Mattiuz Miller and Julie Gardner Miller, daughters-in-law—for holding our family together these past difficult months. And to the women of our church—who astonish and teach me daily with their spiritual wisdom, dedication to their families, and love for one another.

Author's Note

During a recent trip to Holmes County, Ohio, I met an Old Order Amish man who was offering buggy rides for a small fee. While we rode around town, I peppered him with questions about his people—which he good-humoredly answered.

At the end of our trip, I asked if there was anything he would like me to include in this book. Something about his people. Something he would like my readers to know.

Like most Amish, he didn't answer quickly but paused to give my question consideration. His answer, when it came, surprised me.

"Tell your readers that we appreciate them coming here to see us. They bring much-needed revenue into our county. Without them and my buggy-ride business, I would have nothing."

I promised that I would indeed put that in my book.

A few moments later, I entered a small bulk-food shop in the same village. The elderly Amish clerk and I spoke of the terrible rains they had been having. She told me that the creek behind her house had risen so high that it had washed out a large portion of her fence. She said she had "lost her man" ten years earlier from a heart attack, and now she and her sister were trying to keep the farm going. I judged her age as past eighty, and as she totaled my purchases, it occurred to me that this was probably the only income she had besides what she could manage to wrest from their farm.

The next day, I purchased a basket from an Amish teenager with cerebral palsy who was sitting beside his father alongside the road. The boy proudly showed me his basket, with his name painfully scribbled on the bottom. My nephew also has cerebral palsy, and I know the struggle it must have been for this boy to weave that basket. I bought it, of course. It now sits on my writing desk. I smile when I look at it, because it reminds me of the boy's pride in the work of his hands.

There are tiny "stores" in the basements and sheds and spare bedrooms of Amish homes down every road you travel in Holmes County. The handmade signs at the end of their driveways say:

> Eggs for Sale
> Rag Rugs
> Bluebird Houses
> Hickory Rockers
> Maple Syrup
> Honey
> Quilts
> Wall Hangings
> Homemade Baskets
> Baked Goods

More often than not, when you enter one of these Amish homes, you will be met with friendly women in prayer *Kapps* who are as curious about your world as you are about theirs. They will want to know where you are from, and if you've had much rain, and how your garden is doing, and if there are any of their people where you come from.

These valiant, flawed, hardworking people—the Amish—take no government handouts, no food stamps, no Social Security, and they even hire teachers and educate their children at their own expense, all while supporting our own public schools and welfare programs with their tax dollars.

So for those reading this who, like me, once thought that the Amish must bitterly resent the tourists who descend upon their countryside every summer—I'll repeat the words of the Holmes County buggy-ride man. "Tell your readers that we appreciate them coming here to see us."

For my yoke is easy, and my burden is light.

—MATTHEW 11:30 NIV

I t was ninety degrees in the shade, but Grace Connor was not sweating.

This was not good.

Dehydration came swiftly in the Afghanistan desert. She needed to find something to drink—and fast.

She rolled out of her cot, pushed open the door of her ply-wood B-hut, and stared out at the heat waves shimmering off the packed earth of Bagram Air Base. It was going to be a long walk to the dining hall.

A jet roared in for a landing as another blasted off—the rumble of engines reverberating through her skull. The noise of jets and the thup-thup-thup of military helicopters were a constant in her life, along with the fumes of the medevac choppers each time she flew a rescue mission.

Sometimes rocket fire punctuated the sounds. Sometimes she heard gunshots in the distance—never knowing if it was the firing range or terrorists trying to make another pointless point. Sometimes she heard the rattle of bomb-proof bull-dozers nosing around the perimeter, deliberately setting off homemade Taliban mines.

Bagram Air Base was decidedly not a restful place. In addition to the noise, there always seemed to be some ragtag band of terrorists determined to penetrate security. The Taliban had not had a lot of luck yet, but every day the gates opened to the civilian Afghans who risked their lives, by NATO agreement, to work alongside the soldiers and civilian support staff who constituted the biggest military base in Afghanistan. The possibility of an attack inside the gates was a threat of which every soldier was constantly aware.

It was not the safest environment in the world, but safety wasn't what she had signed up for when she volunteered to become part of the elite Dustoff medical team.

As she trudged through the heat in search of something cool to drink, her parched throat choked on the dust kicked up by all the MRAP (Mine Resistant Ambush Protected) and other vehicles. The weird-looking desert ants, long-legged to keep their bellies off the hot sand, scurried out of her way.

In the direct sunlight it was a brain-baking 100 degrees. Come July, the temperature would climb higher than 130 degrees in some areas of Afghanistan. How the soldiers on patrol endured it, she did not know.

She scanned her CAC (Common Access Card) at the entrance and practically fell into the coolness of the dining hall. Bins of Gatorade were iced and ready. The military had learned to take the need for electrolytes seriously. She dug out a bottle of the orange, life-giving nectar, utterly annoyed with herself. She had served in Afghanistan for four years, and she knew better than to allow herself to become dehydrated. She guzzled the whole bottle of Gatorade before catching her breath.

The problem was, she had been so exhausted after last night's struggle to rescue three wounded soldiers pinned down by enemy fire that, once they were safe, she had fallen fully clothed into a sleep so deep it had felt a like a coma.

Grabbing a second bottle, she sat down at a table and pulled a paper out of her pants pocket. She took another mouthful of Gatorade—lemon-flavored—and read the paper for the umpteenth time.

One signature, and she would be committed. That's all it would take. One signature and she would reenlist for another two years.

Her decision should be a no-brainer. She hated it here. She hated the heat, the danger, the sand, the dirt, and the cobra that she had found tangled up in the glue strips she had placed beneath her cot to catch mice. With her nurse practitioner's license, she could make a heck of a lot more money back in the States at a top-notch hospital—and relax in a Jacuzzi in some air-conditioned apartment complex at the end of each day.

It *should* be a no-brainer. Except that she was an excellent nurse. She was fast and smart, and had a hair-trigger ability to make solid medical decisions while under fire. Her training had helped save many soldiers' lives.

There were only a few other people in the mess hall, all of them busy with their own conversations or watching a day-old baseball game on the Armed Forces Network. The noise of voices and jets and the clatter of kitchen staff preparing supper faded into the background as she closed her eyes and prayed for wisdom, for guidance, for a clear-cut answer.

None came.

She opened her eyes, wishing she was one of those people to whom God seemed to give a personal directive for every decision they made, but her experience had been quite different. It always felt as though whenever she asked for wisdom, God sat back, folded His arms, and said, "I gave you a good brain and a great instruction manual—use it."

She had always made the best Bible-based decisions she could and hoped for the best, but this time, she was truly torn. The soldiers needed her. Perhaps she should give them another two years of her life.

She took a pen out of her pocket and clicked it. Her hand hovered over the paper. She hesitated. Drummed the pen on the table. Clicked it. Put it back in her pocket.

Come on, God, just tell me what to do. This is important. Can't you send me a letter or an e-mail? I'll do whatever you say if you'll give me a definite sign. Just this once, Lord, please?

She smiled at her audacity. Who did she think she was—asking God to send her an e-mail?

Like that would ever happen!

And yet . . .

She left the dining hall and walked over to the MWR (Morale, Welfare, and Recreation) facility, which had a bank of computers where soldiers could check their e-mails. She wasn't surprised when she found over a dozen in her in-box, but the one that screamed out to her was a message from her younger sister. The subject heading was a disturbing "Come home!"

Grace clicked on it. Something must be terribly wrong. Becky was only seventeen and had been living with their grandmother for the past eight years—ever since their parents had died in the boating accident. Becky usually filled her e-mails with high school chatter about grades and ball games and clothes, but this e-mail looked different from what she usually sent. The body of it wasn't punctuated with Becky's usual smiley face icon after every other sentence.

> Grandma was taken by ambulance to the hospital last
> night. It's her heart. They've done surgery, but the
> doctor says she's going to need a lot of care for a while.
> I can be with her at night, but I have school during
> the day. If there's any way you could come home for a

couple of months until I can graduate, it would make
things a whole lot easier around here.

Her grandmother was ill? Elizabeth Connor had been
the spiritual rock of their family as long as Grace could remember. Her farm in Ohio had been the sanctuary to which
Grace and her sister had fled after their parents died. The
last time she was home, her grandmother had seemed tireless
and ageless—but now it hit her that Elizabeth might not be
around as long as she had hoped.

How bad was the heart attack? How much damage had
been done? Her medically trained mind wanted answers. She
wanted to meet face-to-face with the doctors and hear Elizabeth's prognosis firsthand. The first few weeks after heart surgery could be critical. There was no way a seventeen-year-old
should be handling that alone.

Grace wrote a quick, affirmative answer and logged out,
not bothering to open any of the other e-mails. They could
wait. For the first time in her life, she had received a very personal answer from God, and it was loud and clear.

There were other competent nurses who could take her
place in the Dustoff unit, but no one could take her place at
her grandmother's side. There *was* no one else. For a moment, she closed her eyes, blocking out the noises and heat
of Bagram, and remembered the soothing clip-clop sound
of Amish horses and buggies and the cool greenness of her
grandma's Holmes County farm.

She grabbed an extra Gatorade and headed back to her
B-hut.

It was time to pack.

chapter ONE

The moment Levi Troyer caught sight of his family's farm he knew something was wrong. The yard, which had been filled with activity less than two hours ago, was now empty, and it looked as though it had been abandoned in a hurry.

Even though it was not his mother's routine to wash clothes on a Thursday, she had wanted to take advantage of the sunny spring weather. When he left this morning, she had been pouring gasoline into the small engine that powered their wringer washing machine. He was concerned to see that the long wire line was empty, even though it should be heavy with wet laundry by now.

During his entire twenty-five years, he had never known his mother to leave her laundry unfinished. In fact, she prided herself upon having it on the line by eight o'clock in the morning at the very latest. Now it was almost nine.

He clucked his tongue and with his heels nudged his horse into a faster trot, but as he drew closer, he saw that not only was the drying line empty, but dirty clothes still lay in piles on the back porch where Sarah, his four-year-old sister, had been helping their mother sort as he had trotted past them this morning on his way to deliver a special-made basket to a customer.

A bucket of water lay overturned upon the porch, the water within it spilled, staining the porous wood. No voices called to him from the house. No slamming screen doors broke the quiet of the lovely spring day.

He glanced up at the clear blue Ohio sky, checking for a threat of rain. Not a cloud in sight. *Maam* had not canceled her plans because of the weather.

"Guta Myah!" he yelled.

No voices greeted him.

"Good morning! Is anyone home?"

The only answer was the caw of a crow rising from a corner of the cornfield. There was not even the scritch-scratching of his stepfather's handsaw coming from the workshop to cut the oppressive silence. Always before, whenever Levi came home from the nearby village of Mt. Hope, his two little brothers and sister would be watching for him. They would come running, excited over the small treats they knew he would have tucked away in his pockets.

Not today.

Of course, there was always the possibility that his stepfather could have cut himself in the woodshop. His mother might have slipped and hurt herself carrying the heavy buckets of water from the well for her laundry. Or one of the children might have been hurt by the new vile-tempered rooster who had a zeal for flying at whoever came near the hens. If that were the case, he would make certain the rooster ended up in his mother's stew pot before nightfall! There were so many potential accidents waiting to happen on a working farm. Sometimes he felt as if he spent most of his waking hours watching out for his family, trying to keep them safe.

He dismounted, flipped the reins of the horse over the side porch railing, and strode through the back door, hoping to find his mother in the kitchen busy cooking dinner—ready with an easy explanation to dispel this feeling of dread that had come over him.

The kitchen, too, was empty. The only sound greeting him was the tick-tock of the old regulator clock. There was no music of his mother's singing or his stepfather calling out to her for some small thing. No teasing. No laughter. Absolute silence except for the clock and the creaking of his own work boots as he walked across the wooden floor.

He hurried into the front room, the feeling of sick dread thickening with every step. Everything looked exactly the same as when he left this morning—except for the pile of old clothes in the corner. For a moment, he thought it was nothing more than misplaced laundry. Then his brain processed the fact that it was his stepfather's crumpled body.

He crossed the front room in three long strides and knelt at *Daed*'s side. There was no pulse in his wrist or his neck. Abraham Shetler's life had drained out into a pool of blood, saturating the rag rug that *Maam* had painstakingly made one winter.

Levi's own pulse hammered in his ears as he took the stairs two at a time to the bedrooms.

He found his mother lying on her right side in the hall, directly outside the doorway of her bedroom. One arm was outstretched and her eyes were closed. Her choring kerchief had come undone and her blond hair spilled out. Blood saturated the front of her dark green dress. She was curled up as much as her pregnancy allowed. Somehow she had managed to ball up her work apron and press it against her right side before losing consciousness.

He fell to his knees and placed his fingers against her neck. Unlike his stepfather, she still lived. He pulled the stained apron away and saw a bullet wound in her right side, almost grazing her rounded belly. To his eyes, the bullet wound seemed much too small to have caused so much blood.

She was only a few weeks away from giving birth. His mind recoiled from the possibilities of what the bullet might have done to the unborn babe. What kind of person shot a woman heavy with child?

"The children"—his mother opened her eyes at his touch—"are hiding in barn." She began to cry softly. "Thank *Gott* you are here!"

His gentle mother was a noted healer in their tight-knit society—a woman who had absorbed as much knowledge as possible with the eighth-grade education their faith allowed. He had often helped her tend her medicinal herb garden while she patiently taught him the healing properties of each plant.

One thing he knew—no plant or herb could treat a bullet wound. He had to get her to the hospital as fast as possible. She needed an ambulance. Now.

Resentment flared within him over the fact that, unlike the Old Order Amish, his Swartzentruber Amish church did not allow them to keep a phone of any kind—not even a telephone shanty at the end of their driveway for emergencies.

He had no way to call for help.

His mind went into overdrive, evaluating his options. By the time he could harness and hitch the driving horse to the buggy, then carry his wounded mother out, load up the children, and drive the ten miles per hour the horses could sustain all the way to Pomerene Hospital—nine miles away in Millersburg—it would be too late. Suddenly her belly tightened, her body convulsed, and she cried out—much as she had cried out when his little brothers and sister had been born here in this house.

She could *not* be in labor. Not now. It was too early.

"Hold on, *Maam*." He pressed her work apron tightly against the bullet wound and raced back down the stairs. He plunged through the door, leaped upon his startled horse, and galloped to the barn.

"Are you all right?" Levi called up to the hayloft as he paused at the giant doors of the barn.

"*Jah,*" he heard a small voice responding.

"Stay where you are. I am going for help." He wheeled his horse around.

"But, Levi . . ." Albert's frightened face appeared above him. "Can we come down now?"

"Do not step foot out of this hayloft until I return. *Verschtehsht du?*" He looked Albert straight in the eyes. "Do you understand?"

The little boy nodded.

Thanking God for the obedience his good mother had instilled in her little ones—they would stay put until he returned for them—he urged his horse into its fastest canter as he shot out onto the road, racing for his mother's life, eating up the distance that separated him from their closest neighbor, and thanking God for their *Englisch* neighbor who had no prejudice against telephones.

He also thanked God for the brokers who brought their less-than-perfect racehorses from Kentucky up to Ohio to the Amish auctions. He had purchased Devil Dancer only a month before—in spite of *Daed*'s insistence that the name was a bad omen. Levi did not believe in omens. He believed in strong, well-muscled lines and the gentle willingness he saw in the lovely mare's eyes. After one week, delighted with his purchase, he had changed her name to Angel Dancer.

He rarely let her run flat-out. She was too valuable an animal to risk a broken leg on the uneven ground of their fields. There was no telling when a hoof might accidentally bury itself in a gopher hole or trip over a rock. Now, on the graveled back road, with the reins slack enough to allow her all the headway she needed, it seemed as though she sensed the urgency of his mission and wanted to live up to her new name. She seemed to grow wings as she raced toward their neighbor's home—running like the champion she had been bred to be. It felt as though her hooves barely touched the ground as they flew toward help for his mother.

"Good girl!" he whispered.

As his horse skittered to a stop in front of the neighbor's house, he prayed that someone would be home. Anyone. If not, he would access their telephone by himself—even if it meant kicking in a door or breaking a window to do so. He could repair the window or door. He could not repair his mother. Even the Amish knew the magic of the numbers 911.

"Hello! Is anyone home?" He leaped off his horse and ran up the porch steps.

To his relief, a young woman flung open the door. She was dressed in white shorts and a red tank top and her dark blond hair was cut as short as a boy's.

"What's wrong?" She put a hand up to her eyes to block out the bright morning sun.

"I am Levi Troyer. We live over there." He pointed to his home. "My mother has been shot. She needs help."

He hoped that this woman was Grace—the *Englisch* granddaughter his mother had met while visiting Elizabeth Connor a few days earlier. When *Maam* heard that their neighbor had finally come home after her heart surgery, she had taken the lady some freshly dug sassafras root, all washed and ready to be made into medicinal tea.

When she returned from her visit, *Maam* told them that Elizabeth was being well cared for by her oldest granddaughter, a nurse just back from the strange land of Afghanistan. The two of them had a wonderful good time, she said, talking about the healing of sick people.

Levi's stepfather, like most Swartzentruber men, was wary of unnecessary contact with the *Englisch* and had warned her not to spend too much time with this granddaughter of Elizabeth's. *Daed* had reminded her that they were to keep themselves apart from the world.

The woman—this Grace Connor—did not hesitate now or pepper him with questions. She jerked a slim cell phone from her pocket and punched in numbers.

"Claire Shetler has been shot at her farm, two miles west of Mt. Hope. We need an ambulance here immediately!" Grace gave her name and the location of the Shetler house, then shoved her phone back into her pocket and without another word disappeared into the house.

Levi saw Elizabeth Connor making her way slowly onto the porch, steadying herself with a walker. She was wearing a cheerful pink sweatsuit, but she was pale and shaky, hardly recognizable as the hearty, active woman he had seen working in her garden with a rototiller less than a month ago. He had waved and called out a greeting. She had laughed and challenged him to a contest to see who could produce the first tomato of the season.

"What's going on, Levi?" Elizabeth said. "Is Claire okay?"

"Someone shot her and she is going into labor."

"Oh, my goodness!" Elizabeth's hand flew to her mouth.

Grace emerged with a large black leather bag slung over one shoulder. In her hand she clutched keys. "Go inside, Grandma, and lock the door. Call Becky at school and tell her to come home until I get back."

"I'll be fine," Elizabeth said. "You concentrate on helping that poor woman." She made a shooing motion with her hand. "Go!"

The granddaughter jumped into a small red car. "Do you want to ride with me?" she asked.

"No. I will be right behind you."

She spun gravel as she took off toward Levi's home.

There had been few times in his life when Levi had been as grateful to another human being as he was at this moment. He had hoped only for the use of a telephone and a quick response from the ambulance people. Having a trained nurse already speeding toward his mother was a gift from God.

His strong horse was fast, but the car was faster. As he urged Angel Dancer on, his broad-brimmed straw hat blew off and landed somewhere in the field beside him. He barely noticed. A summer hat was nothing. It could be replaced with a few dollars and a quick visit to the home of the Swartzentruber woman down the road who wove them. The value of his mother's life was incalculable.

Sometimes the *Englisch* could try his patience—like when loud rock music tumbled out of their open car windows and frightened his horse, or when they insisted on taking pictures of a people who hated being photographed. Not now, though. He was grateful that Elizabeth's granddaughter with the too-short hair and the immodest clothing lived so close.

He rounded the curve and saw Grace's car slide to a stop directly in front of the porch, crushing a portion of the mint garden his mother raised each year for tea. As she mounted the porch steps, he flung himself off Angel Dancer and ran into the house behind her.

Grace was already bent over his stepfather, checking for a pulse. She glanced up at him, her expression grim. "He's gone."

"I know."

"Where's your mom?"

"Up there." He nodded toward the stairwell. Grace ran for the stairs and bolted them in front of him, taking them two at a time, as he had done earlier. He had never seen a woman do that before. Of course, she was not wearing long skirts. Even under the circumstances, he was a little embarrassed by her shorts and skimpy top.

All thoughts about the woman's clothing were erased by the sight of his mother, still crumpled on the hallway floor. Her breathing was shallower than when he had left, and the labor pains that wracked her body seemed to have grown weaker. She appeared barely conscious.

"Claire, what have they done to you?" Grace knelt and placed two fingers against the side of his mother's throat. She scanned *Maam*'s body with narrowed eyes. "How far along is she?" Grace grabbed latex gloves out of her black bag and snapped them on.

"Not yet eight months."

Grace gently rolled his mother onto her side. "There is an exit wound. Good. It looks like the bullet passed straight through the fleshy part above her hip. If the shooter was trying to kill her, he was a bad shot. I don't think the uterus was compromised, but there's too much blood on the floor to be coming from this one wound."

She pulled Claire's skirt above her knees and made a clucking noise in the back of her throat as she found and inspected a second wound high on her right leg. "I'm afraid this bullet must have hit the bone. It's still in there." She grabbed a length of rubber tubing from her black bag and wrapped it around his mother's upper thigh, pulling it tight, creating a tourniquet.

His mother would be mortified if she knew he had seen her like this, and yet modesty mattered little when the life of someone so precious hung in the balance.

Levi had never felt so helpless or as useless. Give him a saw and a hammer, and he could create a fine table or build a sturdy house. Give him a young black ash tree from the north side of the hill, and he could turn it into work baskets that would last for generations. Give him a hoe and a plow, and he could feed a family. But standing here over his wounded mother was so alien to him that he was practically paralyzed by the enormity of it.

"What can I do?"

Grace's green eyes flashed as she twisted the tourniquet tighter. "Pray!"

Instead of praying, he slammed his fist against the wall, welcoming the pain. From afar off he heard the ambulance siren as he silently cursed the *Englisch* person who had brought this terrible evil to his family.

chapter TWO

"**D**o you want me to ride with your mother to the hospital?" Grace asked as the ambulance siren wailed closer. "Or do you want to?"

Levi was torn. He hated to leave his mother completely in the hands of strangers, but he knew *Maam* would not want him to leave his little siblings frightened and alone.

"There are *Kinner* to care for."

"*Kinner?*"

"Children."

"You have children?" Grace pressed his mother's balled-up apron tighter against the bullet wound in her side.

"Two little *Bruders* and a sister. They are hiding in the barn. I cannot leave them alone."

"It would be best if I went with her anyway. Some EMTs are great, some . . . not so great."

"Please, then." His voice broke. "Go with her."

The ambulance was now so close that he wondered if the noise would make Angel Dancer bolt and run. He had not taken the time to secure her reins.

"Does your mother have any allergies?" Grace shouted.

"I don't think so."

"How old is she?"

17

"Forty-one." It gave him a small bit of comfort to have one correct answer to give. Nothing else in his life seemed to have an answer right now.

The siren stopped abruptly. He heard voices down below, and Grace answering them. He heard footsteps on the stairwell and then he watched as two men expertly loaded his mother onto a stretcher, rejecting his attempt to help.

He grasped the porch railing as the ambulance bumped across the yard, its lights flashing. It was nearly impossible to believe that this terrible thing was happening. Not on a brilliant day like today when the sun was shining so brightly. Not on a day like today while a yellow warbler sat singing his cheerful song from the top of the wild cherry tree.

The driver flipped the siren on as they drove away. Levi watched until the ambulance was no longer visible, wondering if he would ever see his mother alive again.

Levi knew that his yard would soon fill with police cars. He knew that a second ambulance and crew would probably be sent for his stepfather's body. But before he spoke to anyone else, before he dealt with one more thing, he needed to get to the children huddled in the barn and try to comfort them.

As he strode to the barn, he wondered—just how did one go about telling a four-, eight-, and ten-year-old that their father had been murdered? How did one also break it to them that their mother's life was hanging by a thread?

He passed Angel Dancer cropping grass in their front yard, grabbed her reins, and took her with him into the barn. He secured her to an inner post and then climbed the ladder to the huge hayloft.

The children were not there.

For a moment, he panicked. Had the man who had killed

his stepfather done something with the children while he was riding for help? Had the evil that had entered his home been lurking in the barn while he watched the lights of the ambulance recede?

Then he noticed a small pile of hay in the farthest corner shift slightly.

"Is the bad man gone, *Bruder*?" Ten-year-old Albert popped out from beneath the hay. His face was sticky with tears. Bits of chaff clung to his skin.

The children had been hiding by burrowing into the hay like little field mice.

"I think so," Levi answered. "Did you see him?"

"No." Jesse's head emerged beside Albert's. "We only heard him. He was shouting at *Daed*. *Maam* told us to go hide in the hayloft until she came for us."

"Where is Sarah?" Levi looked around, but the little girl was nowhere to be seen.

"She cried herself to sleep." Albert lifted some hay, revealing his little sister. She was hiccuping in her sleep from having cried so long. "I tried, but I could not get her to stop."

Levi thought his heart would break as he lifted the little girl into his arms. Her precious face—usually wreathed in sunny smiles—was puffy and red.

How terrifying it must have been for these children to be up here, listening to gunshots, not knowing whether to try to run for help or to stay hidden.

"You did well, little brother—keeping our sister safe. No one could have stopped her tears."

"Did the bad man run away?" Jesse asked.

"I think so."

Albert frowned. "Where are *Daed* and *Maam*? Why did they not come out here, also?"

"*Maam* was hurt. She is on her way to the hospital."

"Did *Daed* go with her?"

Levi tried to answer, but his throat closed up. He coughed to clear the tightness, and it took every bit of willpower he had to say the brutal words.

"No. *Daed*'s dead. The bad man shot him."

They were little boys. Nothing in their lives had prepared them to absorb this kind of information. They sat in stunned silence.

"Who will take care of us?" Jesse's freckled face was creased, already trying to puzzle things out.

That was one question Levi had no trouble answering. "With God's help, I will take care of you."

Sarah awoke at that moment, disoriented, and called out for her mother. When Levi told her she could not come for her—that *Maam* was in the hospital—it took a long time to calm her down. He wished he could take all three of the children into the house, feed them, and then rock each one of them in *Maam*'s rocking chair. But he could not take them into the house without them seeing their murdered father, and that was definitely not a picture he wanted emblazoned upon their innocent minds.

"There you are." A middle-aged man in a sheriff's uniform climbed off the hayloft ladder. He was a large man, and his hair was cut flat on top.

The two younger boys shrank away from him. A wide-eyed Sarah buried her face in Levi's shirt.

"I'm Gerald Newsome—the county sheriff." He squatted beside Levi. "I got a 911 call from the dispatcher. Then I got a call from your neighbor, Elizabeth Connor, telling me all about the trouble you people were having. I've already been inside the house, Levi. I've seen your stepfather. Another ambulance is on the way. Are all of you okay?"

Little Sarah pulled away from Levi and took a good look

at the strange man. Her chin began to quiver. None of them had ever been this close to a lawman.

"No," Levi said. "We are not okay."

Sheriff Newsome shifted his weight to the other knee, picked up a piece of hay, and stuck it in his mouth. "You got a place you can go stay for a while? Get the children away from here?"

"We have many within our church who would welcome us."

"Good." Sheriff Newsome chewed the piece of hay for a few more seconds. "I hate to ask right now, but I have to. Did you or the children see anything?"

"No. I was gone. The children heard the man's voice, but they did not see him."

"Was he *Englisch*?" The sheriff glanced at the two little boys.

Both Jesse and Albert nodded vigorously.

"What did he say?"

"He wanted *Daed*'s money from the auction," Albert explained.

The sheriff looked a question at Levi.

"My stepfather had a two-year-old foal that brought a good price at the Mt. Hope auction yesterday," Levi explained. "Many would have known."

"That would explain a robbery, but not a . . ."

In his mind, Levi heard the word that the sheriff was kind enough not to say in front of the children.

In his world, raised among people so pacifist that they did not believe in so much as putting up a hand in one's own defense, absolutely nothing could explain a murder.

The ambulance had barely stopped beneath the portico of the Pomerene Emergency Room before Grace was out the back door, helping release the undercarriage of the gurney upon which Claire lay. She steadied the IV pole that held the lifesaving liquid they had started flowing into Claire's veins moments after they had lifted her into the ambulance.

As she helped maneuver the gurney through the door, she heard her name being called.

"Grace? Is that you?" It was Karen, an ER nurse she had bumped into in the cafeteria while her grandmother was in the hospital. Karen, a vibrant redhead, was a beautiful woman, but she had served in Iraq and had the bearing and no-nonsense attitude of a staff sergeant. After Grace had helped her clean up the lunch tray she had accidentally knocked out of Karen's hands, they ended up bonding over war stories.

"What's going on?" Karen asked.

"My neighbor, Claire Shetler. Age forty-one." Grace gave the information in short, clipped sentences. "Gunshot wound to the upper right thigh and lower abdomen. According to her son, she has no allergies. Is there a surgeon on call?"

"Yes. Dr. Allen." Karen rounded the desk. "I'll page him. Follow me. Room two is open."

As Karen and other staff members crowded around and took over Claire's care, Grace found herself backed up against a wall. It felt strange not to be in the thick of the battle for Claire's life, but this wasn't her turf.

"We've got this, honey," Karen said over her shoulder. "Go help yourself to some coffee."

Grace watched for a few more minutes. They seemed competent and there really wasn't much space. Reluctantly, she left the room as the familiar adrenaline rush began to drain away, leaving her limp and shaky. She leaned her forehead against the coolness of the hallway wall for a moment and then found her way to the waiting room.

As she passed the coffeepot that Karen had mentioned, the smell of scorched coffee made her stomach churn. She had practically lived on the stuff during her first year in Afghanistan and had permanently lost her taste for it.

Instead of coffee, she chose an empty chair in the far corner of the waiting room and closed her eyes, still trying to quiet her spirit and the pounding of her pulse. This was *not* what she had planned for the day—but this is what God had apparently planned for her.

She prayed for Claire, for the unborn baby, and for those now working to save their lives. Prayer came easily for her, but leaving things in God's hands did not.

That was her grandmother's strength.

Speaking of which . . .

She pulled out her cell phone and dialed, breathing a sigh of relief when she heard her grandma's voice.

"Are you okay, Grandma?"

"Right as rain, sweetheart. I've just been sitting here in the living room on the couch behaving myself and waiting for your call. Is Claire all right?"

"So far."

"Do you think the baby will make it?"

"Possibly, but that family could really use your prayers right now."

"Oh, honey. I haven't stopped since the moment Levi rode into our yard."

After their brief conversation, Grace picked up a magazine and flipped through it. Someone had thoughtfully dropped off their private stash of *People*—but only after carefully cutting off the address. She wondered what, exactly, they expected someone to do with those addresses—drive up to their homes and stare? Knock on their front doors and complain that they had not donated a higher-quality magazine?

The country she had fought for was getting more paranoid every day. After what had just happened to her neighbor,
she couldn't say she blamed Americans for their fear. There
was a lot of crazy floating around.

She tossed the magazine back onto the table. Movie stars'
divorces and personal dramas felt unimportant in the cold
light of an emergency room. Besides, she had been out of the
country so long, she didn't even know who most of the people
in the magazine were—and furthermore, she didn't care. Her
efforts to watch TV since coming home had been met with
little success. It was just too hard to concentrate on the silliness
of a sitcom after all she had seen.

She closed her eyes again and leaned her head back. The
disconnect between the reality of an Afghanistan battlefield
and the culture to which she had returned was not something
she had been able to bridge in the two short weeks she had
been home. Outside of her grandma's farm, she felt like an
alien in her own country. She couldn't help but wonder if that
feeling of alienation would ever go away.

"Does my mother live?"

Her eyes flew open. The sudden sound of Levi Troyer's
voice startled her so badly that she almost dove for cover.
Struggling for equilibrium, she took a deep breath and studied the small family group standing before her. Levi, in his
dark blue pants and sweat-stained blue shirt, towered over
her. In his arms, he held a towheaded little girl wearing a
dark gray dress and a black bonnet. The child's eyes were as
blue as the sky but also red from weeping. A piece of straw
clung to a wayward curl in the process of escaping the bonnet. Standing solemnly beside Levi were two small boys who
were near-replicas of their older brother. Both had the same
gold-streaked brown hair and dark eyes. She judged them to
be somewhere between eight and ten years old. They wore

identical straw hats, with brims so wide, the hats looked too big.

"Your mother is with the surgeon right now, but I haven't heard anything." Because of the worried-looking children, she forced a cheerful note into her voice. "Who do we have here?"

Levi laid his free hand on the smaller boy's hat. "This is Jesse." Then he rested his hand on the older boy's shoulder. "And this is Albert—my *Bruders.*"

"Hello, Albert and Jesse." She solemnly shook the boys' hands.

Levi noticed the straw in the little girl's hair and plucked it out. "This is Sarah, our sister. She spent too much time in the hayloft this morning."

"Hello, Sarah," Grace said. "You have pretty eyes."

The little girl gave her a shy grin before laying her head against her big brother's shoulder.

"Sarah does not have many *Englisch* words yet," Albert informed her.

"I do," Jesse volunteered. "I have many *Englisch* words."

She had no idea what they were talking about.

"Our children usually speak only German when they are small," Levi explained. "They don't learn *Englisch* until they go to school." He gently tweaked the little girl's nose. "I think Sarah understands some of what you said, but she is being bashful."

"Oh." She absorbed that information. That would explain why the few small Amish children she had spoken to on the street since moving here had given her sweet smiles but not answered.

"How did you get here?" she asked.

"The sheriff came after you left. He called a driver for us after he finished asking questions." Levi looked worried.

"I—I did not refuse. It would have been hard on our horse to come so far and it would have taken a long time."

At that moment Dr. Allen entered the room. He was an older man and his face was gray with fatigue. He did not look happy.

"Are you Claire Shetler's family?" he asked.

"We are." Levi swallowed hard. "Does my mother live?"

"Yes." Dr. Allen glanced at the children clustered around Levi and forced a smile. "She's . . . fine."

"And the babe?" Levi's voice sounded strained.

"We are airlifting him to Children's Hospital in Columbus."

"My mother had a boy?"

"She awoke long enough to name him Daniel. We had to do a C-section because of . . . complications, but he does have a fighting chance."

"Did the bullet—?"

"If I were you"—Dr. Allen threw a glance at the children— "I would concentrate on caring for these little ones for now."

"Can we see our *Maam*?" Jesse asked.

Karen approached them with a clipboard in her hand. "Mrs. Shetler is asking to see"—she gave Grace a strange glance—"you."

"Me?"

"Yes. She specifically asked for you, even though I told her I thought her family had arrived."

"Then I'll go see what she wants."

As Grace got to her feet, Karen handed Levi the clipboard and a pen.

"While he fills these papers out, I'll take you to her," Karen said.

After they had walked far enough away for Levi and the children not to hear, Karen filled her in.

"The bullet managed to miss the uterus," Karen said. "But all the trauma compromised the pregnancy. Dr. Allen had no choice than to take the child by C-section. We had to use three units of blood to stabilize the mother. It was very close. If you hadn't been there to help . . ." Karen shook her head. "I've lived here my whole life and I admire the Amish for so many things—but those ultraconservative sects that don't allow any type of telephone at all . . ." Again Karen shook her head. "None of my business, of course. It's a free country."

"None of my business, either," Grace said. "Except that today it suddenly became my business."

When Grace arrived in the recovery room, Claire was so pale that she nearly blended in with the white sheets. Even her blond hair, still pinned closely to her head, seemed colorless, harshly illuminated by the hospital lights.

"How are you feeling?" Grace took hold of Claire's hand lying limply on the sheets. It was ice cold.

"The babe . . ."

"Dr. Allen says he has a chance."

"A chance." Claire gave a great sigh.

"Children's Hospital is one of the best in the world. He should be there soon. They will take good care of him."

"My Abraham is gone?"

"Yes." Grace's heart broke for the woman. "I am so sorry."

"I thought that is what I heard you say in the ambulance."

"We thought you were unconscious."

"The words got into my mind anyway." Tears silently crept down Claire's cheeks and neck, dampening the front of her hospital gown.

"Was there something you wanted me to do?" Grace grabbed a tissue and handed it to her. "Is there some way I can help?"

"I wanted you to come because I cannot yet be strong for my children." Claire took the tissue and wiped her eyes. "I need more time before they see me."

"I don't think anyone is expecting you to be strong. You have been through a terrible ordeal today."

"A mother must be strong for her children, and I—I cannot be strong. Not yet."

"Do you want Levi to come in to see you? I can stay with the children."

"No," Claire said. "My Levi does not need to see me like this."

Grace was at a loss. "Then what do you want me to do?"

"You own a vehicle?"

"I do."

"Could you take my children to my sister's home? Levi will tell you how to get there. They will be well cared for if they are with Rose. And then, please take Levi to my little Daniel. The babe will need someone beside him as he fights for his life. He should not be alone."

"I'll be happy to do that, but your baby won't be alone. There are wonderful doctors and nurses there."

"The babe will need someone who loves him—someone whose voice he knows."

"What about you? Don't you need someone to stay here with you?"

Grace vividly remembered recovering from the broken arm and collarbone, fractured ribs, and internal injuries she had sustained when the MRAP in which she was riding had taken a direct hit. Those mine-resistant vehicles were good at absorbing the blow of a homemade bomb, but if the explosion was a large one—and the roadside bomb Grace's MRAP triggered had involved nearly three hundred pounds of explosives—they sometimes overturned with troops inside.

That hospital stay had felt awfully lonely with no family beside her.

"You are not familiar with Amish ways." A wisp of a smile crossed Claire's face. "I will not be alone for long."

"I'm glad to know that."

A fresh-faced young deputy entered the room.

"I'm sorry, Mrs. Shetler, but I need to find out what you can tell us about the person who shot you and your husband. Did you see his face?"

"No. He wore a mask, and gloves." Her eyes were haunted, remembering. "Somehow he knew about the horse that Abraham had taken to auction the day before, and even though we gave him everything we had, it wasn't enough. He thought we were holding back."

"But why you?" Grace asked. "Why on earth would he shoot a pregnant woman?"

"I had a little money upstairs in my purse. Not much. I told him I would go get it. He followed me up there, but when he saw how little it was . . ."

"He shot you because there wasn't enough money in your purse?" Grace wished she could get her hands on the man— whoever he was.

"He was disappointed." Claire's voice sounded weary. "And very angry. I think *er is weenich aub*—he's a little off in the head. Or perhaps that is what people act like when they are on drugs?"

"I don't know what the man's problem was." The officer's voice was grim. "But we're going to do everything we can to find him."

"I'll take your children to your sister's and Levi to be with little Daniel," Grace said. "Don't worry about a thing. Just concentrate on getting better."

It wasn't until she was passing the nurses' station that she remembered she didn't have a car. She had left it back at the Shetlers'.

"Is everything okay?" Karen stopped typing and looked up from her computer.

"As okay as it can be. She asked me to take her younger kids to her sister's and her oldest son to Children's, but I came here in the ambulance. Is there a car rental place here in Millersburg?"

Without missing a beat, Karen reached into an oversized purse sitting at her feet and pulled out a ring of keys. "Here. Take mine. It's the blue minivan in the side lot. Hit the button and it'll beep."

"I can't take your van," Grace said.

"Sure you can." Karen jingled them in front of her. "Welcome to Holmes County—a place where people help each other."

"How will you get home if I take your car?"

"I can catch a ride. One of the other nurses lives near my house." She jotted a number on a slip of paper. "Call me when you get back and I'll give you directions."

"Are you sure you don't mind?"

"From one former Dustoff nurse to another—I absolutely don't mind."

"I really appreciate it. I'll call you as soon as I get back."

"Before you go"—Karen handed her the keys, then leaned forward and lowered her voice—"how well do you know this Amish family?"

"Not well. Why?"

"I don't know if this could be important to you, but I know a little about Claire Shetler. I heard about her when I did a rotation in obstetrics."

"I know she considers herself a healer. Is there a problem with that?"

"No. As Amish healers go, Claire is one of the better ones."

"So—what does this have to do with taking her kids to her sister's?"

Karen looked uneasy. "It's not the children." She nodded toward Levi. "It's him."

"Him?"

"The oldest son." Karen leaned closer and lowered her voice even further. "These people are Swartzentrubers."

"I thought their name was Shetler."

"It is Shetler. Swartzentruber is the name of their religious order."

Grace shifted the strap of her black medical bag to her other shoulder. "I just thought they were Amish."

"They are Amish."

"Okay. I'm lost."

"That's why I'm telling you this. If the Amish had a caste system, the Swartzentrubers would be at the bottom. They are the most conservative of all the branches. They are also the poorest. The Swartzentrubers are so conservative, they even sets limits on how much money a man can make. If they make more than a certain amount, they are required to hand it over to the church to be used for no-interest loans to others within their church. And sometimes teenagers from the other Amish sects call them names."

"Like what?"

Karen glanced over at Levi in the far corner of the waiting room to make certain he wasn't listening. *"Gnuddel vullahs."*

"You speak German?"

"It helps around here to learn a little. It means 'woolly lumps.'"

"I don't get it."

"They milk by hand, not machine. Some of them get lumps of manure and dirt matted in their long beards." Karen bit her lip. "I don't mean to speak ill of anyone, but they don't allow indoor plumbing, so some of them can't bathe all that often."

Grace looked over her shoulder at Levi. He was sitting, quietly entertaining the three children. Aside from his odd haircut and Amish clothes, he looked fairly normal to her. "He doesn't even have a beard to get matted."

"That's because he isn't married," Karen said. "They usually don't grow one until then."

"Why are you telling me this? Am I supposed to be afraid of him?"

"It isn't you who has reason to be afraid, it's him. A single Swartzentruber man being seen alone with someone like you could get him disciplined by his church."

"What do you mean—someone like me?"

"I think you look fine," Karen said. "You're cute as a button in that outfit. But in a Swartzentruber man's eyes—especially in their bishop's eyes—you are dressed like a harlot."

A bubble of resentment caused Grace to press down a little harder than necessary on the accelerator as they left the hospital. She couldn't help the way she was dressed. She had been inside her grandma's house, minding her own business, washing breakfast dishes when Levi had come galloping up. She had reacted quickly—like the professional she was. The last thing on her mind was what she was wearing. In her opinion, she was dressed completely appropriately for someone on a warm spring day inside a farmhouse with no air-conditioning.

Karen's words were not meant to hurt, but they stung anyway. A harlot? Grace couldn't remember the last time she had even heard that old-fashioned term. Somehow, the archaic aspect of it made it sound even dirtier.

Now, here she was, painfully aware that Levi was studiously staring out the passenger-side window—no doubt to avoid the sight of her bare legs.

She hadn't asked for this job. She didn't *want* this job. Trying to be a good neighbor in this area obviously could be a pain in the neck.

She tugged at the hem of her shorts, trying to make them cover just a little more flesh. No luck. They covered what they covered, and deep down she had to agree with Karen—that wasn't much.

"Are you sure you don't want to go back to your house to pack some things for the children before we take them to their aunt's?" she asked.

Levi's eyes stayed fixed on the acres and acres of fields filled with broken cornstalks, as though they were the most fascinating thing he had ever seen. "It is not necessary. Our aunt Rose has *Kinner* of her own—she will have what they need."

"But it would only take a few minutes to turn around."

"I do not want to go back to where our father died. It would not be good for the children. Not until our people have . . . cleaned."

How right he was—and how wrong she had been to suggest it. She was used to dealing with soldiers, not children.

"You're right. I'm sorry. I was just wishing I had a minute to run into my own house and change clothes before we drive all the way to Columbus."

"Why?" He turned his attention away from the broken cornstalks and looked at her.

For the first time since he had galloped into her life, she gazed directly into his eyes—and nearly ran off the road.

His hair was a variegated flaxen color that would cost the earth to duplicate in a salon. It was an unflattering cut, chopped off directly below the ears, but the color of it softened the starkness of the cut. His clean-shaven face was decidedly handsome, but it was his eyes, a dark shade of hazel flecked with gold, that were so arresting. She had never seen eyes like his before, and she felt as if they were looking right through her—and not liking what they saw.

She took in all of this in a glance before jerking the mini-van back into her lane.

"I just thought—"

"Your clothing is not important," he interrupted. "The children's clothing is not important. The only thing that matters now is to get to little Daniel and let him know that he is not alone."

"He's less than an hour old. He won't even be aware you're there."

"You know this to be true?" Again those eyes studied her.

"Well, no, I guess not." Something about the directness of his gaze and voice unnerved her.

"He will know the sound of my voice. It will calm him."

She had no reply. Science had shown that newborns were much more aware of their surroundings than people had once thought. Levi might be right for all she knew. Her expertise was not in pediatrics.

He dismissed their conversation by staring once again at the countryside whizzing past. The children, in her opinion, were unnaturally quiet. "Everybody okay back there?" She glanced into the rearview mirror. They were sitting as still as statues. "They're awfully quiet, Levi."

"Being inside a vehicle is not common to them."

"Were you and your stepfather close?" Grace wondered if his reticence might be coming from deep grief. She knew a thing or two about grief herself.

"What do you mean—close?"

"You know—did you get along well?"

It took him longer than she thought the question warranted for him to answer.

"Abraham was a good provider," he said.

"But were you close?"

"He was a dutiful father."

She was about to probe a little more when suddenly he stiffened. "Turn here."

Grace jerked the wheel and abruptly turned into a long lane that led to an idyllic rural scene. A lovely white farmhouse with a wraparound porch, built upon a gentle hill, rose before her. All around it were neatly maintained fields. A large, freshly painted black barn sat behind. A slender woman, dressed in a blue Amish-style dress with a kerchief tied around her hair, was trimming the fence line nearest the house with a gasoline-powered Weed Eater. A small girl about Sarah's age slid down a brightly colored slide that was attached to a nice jungle gym. Three boys jumped up and down on a trampoline. An older girl was working in a vegetable garden.

Grace couldn't help but compare it with the rather ragged and poor appearance of the Shetler farm.

"Are you sure this is the place?"

"It is."

"This is your mom's sister?"

"Rose is *Maam*'s twin." He leaned forward, apparently drinking in the sight of this farm.

As Grace drove closer, the woman turned and shaded her eyes against the sun. Grace could see the strong resemblance between her and Claire. She stopped the van and Rose suddenly recognized who was in the car. She dropped the Weed Eater and covered her mouth, her eyes wide and frightened. Then she broke into a run. She reached Levi just as he climbed out of the car.

"What's happened?" She grasped him by the shirt. "Where is Claire?"

"She is . . ." Levi suddenly choked up. He shook his head, unable to speak.

Grace saw that he couldn't do it. He couldn't say the awful words to this woman who looked so much like his mother. She climbed out of the car and came around to where Rose and Levi stood.

"I'm Grace Connor," she said, "a neighbor of the Shetlers. Your sister is going to be okay, but there was a shooting . . ."

Rose's face drained of color. She swayed slightly. Then she pressed her lips together, lifted her chin, and straightened her shoulders.

"The baby was taken to Children's Hospital in Columbus, which is where we're headed."

"The baby?" Rose asked.

This puzzled Grace. Rose and Claire were sisters. Twins. It seemed odd that Rose wouldn't know about her sister's pregnancy. Grace glanced at Levi and saw that his attention had been caught by a man striding toward them from the barn.

"What is going on?" he demanded. The man was barrel chested and formidable looking in stained work clothes and boots. He barely glanced at Grace but stared at Levi as though at an apparition.

"Henry!" Rose exclaimed. "My sister has been shot. Someone came into their house."

"What of Abraham?" Henry asked.

Levi found his voice. "*Daed* was killed by the intruder. *Maam* would take it as a kindness if you would care for the three *Kinner* while I go to be with the babe."

The three children had managed to take their seat belts off, and their faces were pressed against the van's windows. Rose lifted her hand in a wave.

"We will care for the children," she said. "It will be good to finally get to know them."

Levi lifted the children out, one by one, giving each an admonition to be good and to respect their aunt and uncle. Sarah showed signs of bursting into tears, but Rose cuddled her in her arms and spoke soothingly to her in soft German. The uncle, solemn and solid, laid a comforting hand on each of the boys' shoulders.

There were no hugs, no tears, none of the awkward pats on the back that men tended to give each other in times of crisis. As Levi and Grace got back into the van, the uncle motioned for Levi to roll down the window. Levi fumbled with the unfamiliar button. Grace managed it with the controls on her side.

"Your mother will be in our prayers," the uncle said. "And the babe. And you."

Through the window, the men clasped hands. Grace guessed it was as close to a hug as either of them would get.

As she turned back onto the main road, many questions crowded together in her mind. Why had Rose not known of her sister's pregnancy? Why were the children strangers to an uncle and aunt who lived less than five miles away? There was much she wanted to know, but Levi was so stone faced, she hesitated to ask.

He leaned forward as though to urge the minivan onward. "I would not mind," he said, "if you drove faster."

chapter THREE

I t was obvious that Levi was completely out of his depth.
As the young farmer stood gazing at the high ceilings
and the acres of brightly carpeted floor of Children's Hospital,
Grace could tell that he was overwhelmed by the enormity of
the place.

She inquired at the front desk for directions and Levi followed close behind as she made her way to the NICU—the
Neonatal Intensive Care Unit. When she stopped in front
of an elevator, he was so engrossed in looking around, he
bumped into her.

"I'm sorry."

"That's okay, Levi. It's a big place. There's a lot to see."

As they waited for the elevator, a nurse walked by pulling a crippled child in a red wagon. Another child whizzed
along, pushed in a wheelchair cleverly designed to look as if it
belonged to NASCAR.

"Jesse would like that chair," Levi observed.

"Let's hope he never has to be in one," she said. "These are
sick children, even if the staff does everything in their power
to make this place cheerful."

"Look." He pointed upward.

She glanced up. Suspended high from the ceiling, designed to look as though they were soaring free overhead, was a flock of metal birds.

The elevator doors opened. As they began to go upward, Levi acted startled and grabbed hold of the handrail.

"First elevator ride?" she asked.

"I did not know that this room was going to start moving."

"It will stop soon."

She heard Levi give a small sigh of relief when the doors opened.

As they walked through the halls, she realized, for the first time, how many curious stares the Amish had to endure in public places.

Her medical training had not been in pediatrics, but after they had scrubbed and donned hospital gowns, and after the nurse ushered them into the neonatal ICU, even Grace could see that Claire's baby—a tiny scrap of humanity lying in a clear plastic bed—was fighting for his life. She heard Levi's quick intake of breath when he saw the baby. He recovered quickly and approached the infant.

The rapid heartbeat displayed on the heart monitor grabbed her attention. She knew what a normal heartbeat should look like—and that electronic line was decidedly not normal.

"Hello, Daniel," Levi said softly, oblivious to the ominous lines of the monitor. "Our mother has given you a good strong name." He carefully caressed the infant's tiny arm. "You will grow up to be a fine man. Someday I will teach you how to plant and harvest and how to recognize the meadowlark's call. We will milk cows together—you and me and your *Bruders*. You have a sister, too, and she will be a little mother to you. You must get better, *Leiben*. You have a family who needs you."

Grace watched, transfixed, as this man who had been a

complete stranger to her until a few hours ago began to sing softly. It was a strange-sounding song, and she didn't understand a word, but his voice did not waver or go off-key. He acted utterly unembarrassed by his singing, seemingly unaware that anyone else was in the room except him and the struggling infant. The song sounded as though it came from the depths of his soul as he allowed the baby's tiny fist to curl around one of his work-worn fingers.

The neonatal nurse was also listening and watching. She elbowed Grace and nodded meaningfully at the heart monitor.

Grace's eyes widened at what she saw. The heart rate, which had been erratic when they entered the room, had become regular and steady.

She looked at the nurse questioningly.

"I've seen this before," the nurse whispered. "Sometimes the sound of a father or mother's voice can make a huge difference in a newborn's response."

"Levi is the child's older brother, not his father."

The nurse gave Levi an appraising look as he continued to sing the strange-sounding song. "Then that is one lucky baby."

"Are you hungry, Levi?" Grace asked. "I'm going down to the cafeteria. I'll bring you back something—or you can come with me if you want."

He sat on a stool the nurse had brought in for him. Daniel seemed to be resting more comfortably now. Levi had stopped singing, but his throat was dry. The nurse had pointed out the lines to him on the monitor that showed the baby's heartbeat. For now it was beating steadily, but he would watch it closely.

"I'm thirsty," he said. "But I do not want to leave."

"I'll bring you something," Grace offered. "What do you want? Coke? Sprite? Coffee?"

"Water."

"Just water?"

"Yes."

"No food?"

"No."

Her face registered disappointment as she walked away. This puzzled him. He was trying to be as little trouble to her as possible. It was bad enough that she had been forced to drive him here. It was one thing to depend upon fellow Amish. It was an entirely different thing to have to rely upon an *Englisch* woman—and a virtual stranger at that.

He liked what he saw as she walked away—perhaps a little too much.

He reminded himself that it was a shameful thing for a woman to dress so immodestly, but he knew in her world she was dressed more modestly than many of the women he had seen around town, especially the young tourists who came in the summer.

He still didn't like her short hair. Privately, he did not agree with the Swartzentruber expectations that a woman never cut her hair. His mother's long hair caused her many headaches, and the washing and drying of it was an ordeal for her, but he did think that a woman should wear her hair longer than Grace did.

He tore his eyes away from her and gazed down at his baby brother. This was whom he had come for. This was who was important. His family. Not the *Englisch* woman who had come so quickly and efficiently to their aid.

As he held the tiny fingers that he believed would some-day do so many good and productive things, he hoped that coming here with her today would not bring more trouble down upon his head. Spending time in the company of a young *Englisch* woman could earn him a tongue-lashing from Bishop Weaver.

The question Grace had asked on the drive here still haunted him. Were he and his stepfather "close"?

He still did not know how to answer that question. Abraham had taken pains to teach him how to work, which was a valuable thing to give a boy. Sometimes his stepfather's methods had been what many would consider brutal. However, solely because of Abraham, Levi possessed the knowledge, skills, and discipline a man needed to work a farm and support a family.

For these things he would be eternally grateful, but the fact remained, Abraham had been a harsh disciplinarian, and a difficult man to please.

Still, they had spent all day every day working together, eating meals together, living beneath the same roof together, worshipping together for many years. He had spent the biggest part of his life in his stepfather's presence. The vacuum Abraham's death would leave in all of their lives would be huge.

But were they close?

He did not think so. At least not in the mushy, *Englisch* way that Grace had meant.

Levi could hardly believe all that had happened in the past few hours. He had discovered *Daed*'s body, ridden to get help for his mother, made arrangements for his brothers' and sister's care, made his first trip to the city of Columbus—so many tall buildings!—and had to answer too many questions from a sheriff's deputy.

Answering the deputy's questions had made him extremely nervous. His people tried hard to avoid law officials. Allowing *Englisch* deputies to poke their noses into their business was a worrisome thing.

Except that now, he had no choice. The *Englisch* law had to get involved. They had even taken his stepfather's body away for an autopsy. He did not understand the need, but the deputy had patiently explained that it was a legal necessity in cases of murder.

The deputy had spoken to him slowly, as though to a child, enunciating carefully, evidently thinking him dense in the head. There were those who acted like that around his people, but it was a sign of ignorance on their part. Just because his people were Swartzentruber did not mean they were dummkopfs.

It occurred to him that Grace had not done that. She had spoken to him as naturally as though he were just another *Englisch* person. That was rare and he wondered at it.

Which reminded him—he would have to remember to pay her for the car trip. At fifty cents a mile, which was the going rate for hiring an *Englisch* driver, he would owe her a little under forty dollars one way. Even though he had no intention of leaving Daniel and riding back home with her today, he would pay her for the return trip as well. He still had five twenty-dollar bills on him from a delivery of several specialty baskets he had made last week. Giving her eighty would leave him with only twenty dollars in his pocket, but he did not need a lot of money to sit beside his brother.

His mind fastened on the many chores he had waiting on him back home. Hopefully by now, word would have spread, and his Amish brethren would be taking care of everything.

Once they knew his family was in trouble, they would find the time to care for his farm and livestock, along with their own heavy labors, and it would continue—without question—until he could leave Daniel's side and his family could get back on their feet. That was the Amish way. No one was ever left alone during times of crisis. From boyhood on, he had helped with others' chores during family emergencies. It was one of the many things he valued about his people.

"Here." Grace handed him a chilled bottle of water. He had expected her to bring him a paper cup of water instead of this blue bottle that she had obviously paid for. He wondered how much this fancy water had cost. This worried him. He hoped that the extra amount he planned on paying her for the trip would cover the cost.

"You're back quickly." He unscrewed the lid and took a long drink. It was delicious, much cleaner tasting than the water they drew from their well back home. "You didn't eat?"

"There was nothing there I wanted."

Daniel stirred and Levi glanced at the heart monitor. The baby's heartbeat continued strong. Levi relaxed slightly and allowed himself to look more closely at Grace's face. Dark circles were forming beneath her eyes. She looked weary. Today had been hard on her. He had not realized.

"You should go home now." He dug out his wallet. "Will eighty dollars be enough?"

She looked perplexed. "Enough for what?"

"Enough to cover the miles you drove—and the water you bought."

"What are you talking about, Levi?"

"*Englisch* drivers charge fifty cents a mile," he patiently explained. "I watched the numbers as they changed beneath your steering wheel. We traveled seventy-five miles to get here."

He extracted the four twenties and tried to hand them to her, but Grace backed away and looked at him with a hurt expression on her face.

"I'm not taking money from you."

Again, he was puzzled. She had provided a service that an honest man should pay for. It was a business transaction.

"I owe you eighty dollars." He again tried to hand the money to her.

"I'm your neighbor, for pity's sake!" She put her hands behind her back and shook her head. "I wasn't doing this to be paid. I did it because you needed help."

He saw the determination in her eyes and knew that this was a fight he would not win. At least not now. For whatever reason, this *Englisch* woman was determined to give him this trip as a gift.

Daniel stirred again, as though bothered by the loudness of their voices. Levi glanced at the monitor, and his own heart lurched. The baby's heartbeat was becoming irregular again.

Grace saw it at the same time he did. "I'll be outside in the waiting room."

"But you are tired. You should go home."

"Yes, I'm tired." She was already heading out the door. "But for now, I think I'd better stick around. I wouldn't feel right leaving you here alone." She glanced meaningfully at the monitor. "And you'd better hurry up and start singing that weird song again."

Weird song? The *Loblied* was not weird! He had sung this song from the *Ausbund* hymnal while sitting on his grandfather's lap during worship Sundays. He had sung the words at group singings as a teenager. This song with which he had been encouraging his little brother had been written by a Mennonite minister over four hundred years ago—and it was a good song.

What did she expect him to sing under such circumstances? One of those silly songs with repetitious words like he had heard coming from some of the *Englisch* church buildings he had passed on Sunday mornings? He wondered how they managed to hear themselves think—let alone worship—over the din of guitars and drums.

In his opinion, it was much better to worship in a freshly cleaned barn, or a friend's home, or a neighbor's workshop while joining with his spiritual brothers and sisters in lifting up the ancient words of their church.

The song he had sung to his little brother was *not* weird.

Grace was surprised to see Rose walk into the waiting room. She had removed the kerchief from her hair and donned a black bonnet along with a fresh dress that was a lovely sky blue.

Grace put down the ragged *Better Homes and Gardens* magazine she had been trying to read and stood to greet her.

"Hello, Rose," Grace said. "Levi is with—"

"How is the baby?" Rose interrupted.

"Stronger."

"Thank *Gott*." Rose's shoulders slumped in relief. "You say Levi is with him?"

"He hasn't left Daniel's side since we got here," Grace said. "Are the children here, too?"

"My married daughter is at my home caring for them. They will be fine with her."

"Have you spoken with Claire?"

"For the first time in ten years, yes—I have been to the hospital and talked with my twin sister."

"If you don't mind my asking . . ."

Rose put up a hand to forestall her question. "I know this must seem strange to you, so I will explain as quickly as I can. I was raised Swartzentruber Amish the same as my sister. When my husband and I chose to join with the Old Order Amish, we were banned from fellowship with anyone in our Swartzentruber church—even those who were our blood kin." Rose smiled ruefully. "In my world I am considered the black sheep of the family."

It was hard for Grace to imagine this lovely, modestly dressed Amish woman being the black sheep of anything.

"Then why is the rule suspended now?"

"It isn't. But in times of family emergency, leaders will sometimes relax the rules for a very short while until the crisis lessens. I intend to help my sister and her family as much as possible until Bishop Weaver insists that I leave."

"I'm not sure I'll ever understand the Amish."

"That's one of the nice things about being *Englisch,* don't you think?" Rose smiled. "You don't have to."

"That's true."

"I'm going to stay with Daniel now." Rose was suddenly all business. "Levi should go home. My *Englisch* driver is waiting to take him. You must go, too. I will handle this now."

"I can take Levi home," Grace offered. "I'm headed home anyway."

"No." Rose cocked her head to one side and gave her an appraising look. "I think it would be best if you did not."

"They are the strangest people," Grace said later to her grandmother as she set out her evening pills and helped her prepare for the night.

"Not when you truly know them."

"You've mentioned the Shetler family in the past, but I don't remember ever meeting them when I would visit you." She helped her grandmother climb into bed and then pulled the handmade quilt over her.

"Claire respected our time together and never came when any of my family was here. I deeply value the Shetlers' friendship. They have been good neighbors to me."

"In what ways?"

"Claire gave me this quilt one year." Her grandmother

smoothed her hand over the dark-colored fabric. "Do you have any idea how much a hand-quilted Swartzentruber quilt is worth? This one is so intricately stitched it would probably sell for over a thousand dollars. It took her one whole winter."

"It's beautiful."

"I should probably have it framed and put behind glass like they do in museums, but it makes me feel good to sleep beneath such a loving gift. Down through the years, they have tended to their own business while I tended to mine, but I always knew that if I needed them, they would come. So many times Claire has appeared when I was feeling poorly, carrying soup or a batch of herb tea. Often her concoctions helped. And then there was Levi."

"What about Levi?"

"He was the loveliest little boy." Elizabeth frowned. "Don't you remember me ever talking about him?"

"Vaguely, but you've talked about a lot of people down through the years, including a whole bunch of long-dead relatives and most of your students. After a while everyone kind of blended together in my head."

"Have I been that tedious?"

"Not at all." Grace laughed. "You're the only person I know who can walk into a grocery store and come out an hour later with no milk and no groceries, but worried sick about a new best friend you had just made."

"The deli-counter woman was going through a nasty divorce and I was concerned," Elizabeth said. "They patched things back together, you know. She still calls me from time to time to let me know how things are going."

Grace grinned. "What about the man you met on the airplane with whom you still exchange Christmas cards?"

Her grandmother sniffed. "He was a lovely young musician and we enjoyed our two-hour talk tremendously."

"I'm sorry I wasn't paying as much attention as I should have down through the years. Tell me about Levi. This time I'll listen. I promise."

"He reminded me of your father when he was a child. So curious and smart. I had an illustrated book on birds and we would sit together on my porch for hours studying it together and matching the pictures with the birds we saw around the farm. Of course that ended as he grew up and took on a man's share of chores around the farm, but he still comes when he notices something that needs to be done around here. I never have to ask."

Elizabeth gave a little sigh. "I always thought it was a shame that Levi was not allowed more than an eighth-grade education. There was a real brilliance in him. He could have been anything he wanted. Of course, it takes a very smart man to make a living on a small farm, and he seems content."

Elizabeth yawned.

"You're tired." Grace kissed her forehead. "Call out if you need me. I'll be on the couch."

"Oh, honey," Elizabeth said, "I don't want you having to sleep there. I'll be fine tonight. Go on up to your bedroom, child."

"I'm not comfortable being so far away from you," Grace said. "I hated leaving you alone this morning."

"I was fine," her grandmother protested. "Becky came home for lunch and when she saw I was alone, she stayed. Oh, I forgot to tell you, I had some company."

"Who?" Grace positioned a glass of water so it would be easier for her grandmother to reach.

"One of the sheriff's deputies came by."

"Did he have any news?"

"No, but he asked if I had seen or heard anything suspicious."

"What did you say?"

"I told him that if I knew anything about Abraham's death, I would not have waited around for a deputy to come to my house. I would have called the sheriff's office immediately."

"Did he tell you if they had any suspects?"

"They don't, but he assured me they wouldn't give up until they found out who did it."

"I hope they find whoever did it soon."

Elizabeth yawned again. "Me, too."

Grace turned out the light, left her grandmother's door ajar, and then walked around the house making certain every door and window was locked. Not that it would really make any difference. A determined man could easily break into this farmhouse—but not without making noise. The doors were sturdy and the windows had the old-fashioned frames that would be nearly impossible to open without breaking both wood and glass.

She shook out an afghan and got as comfortable as possible on the living room couch. She was grateful that her grandmother's bedroom was downstairs, opening directly off the living room. With Elizabeth unable to climb stairs, it was so much easier to care for her here on the main floor.

As she waited for sleep, she tried to picture the little boy Grandma had described. It was hard to imagine the taciturn, work-hardened Levi ever having been that child.

And, yet, her grandmother had been a principal for an inner-city elementary school in Columbus for thirty-five years. If Grandma said a child was brilliant, he was.

The couch was lumpy, and the unaccustomed quiet of the country was unnerving. Sometimes in Afghanistan, quiet could be deceiving. Sometimes it was merely a precursor to an attack. Try as she might, Grace couldn't seem to stop being on constant alert for the next missile whistling overhead—readying herself for the next run for the nearest bunker. Even though Bagram was huge and well secured, the Taliban loved making her and the rest of the personnel jump, and sometimes the terrorists just plain got lucky.

Unlike people who lived near a railroad track and got so used to the clatter of the trains that they didn't even notice when they went by, the sound of rockets or gunfire never lost its ability to thrust Grace into immediate action. Even when she was so exhausted from a mission that her sleep resembled a coma, the shout of "Incoming!" could propel her out of bed with her legs already moving at full speed. Her training and experience had made her hypervigilant, and she didn't know how to find the necessary switch to flip that hypervigilance off. She got back up, peeked in on her grandmother, and checked all the locks again.

She had just gotten settled back beneath the afghan when she heard footsteps coming down the stairs. Every muscle in her body tensed, ready for fight or flight.

"Sis?" Becky called softly.

She relaxed. "Over here, Becky. What's wrong?"

"It's creepy being upstairs all by myself."

"You can sleep down here on the other couch if you want to keep me company."

"Sounds good to me."

Even though Becky was seventeen, she was carrying her blanket and her favorite pillow along with her—just as when she was small and had crept into Grace's bed when she was afraid.

Becky made herself a nest on the other couch. In spite of the adjustments she was having to make, Grace was filled with gratitude that she had been able to come home. There was a killer on the loose and she was grateful that she was here to watch over the two people she cared for most in the world.

"I'm glad you could come home." Becky fluffed her pillow and doubled it beneath her head.

"I'm glad, too. Good night, Becky."

Instead of the roar of fighter jets overhead and the rattling gunfire of distant fighting that had permeated her sleep for so long, Grace heard the sound of her grandmother having a quiet conversation with God. Elizabeth had done that for as long as Grace could remember.

It gave her a feeling of peace even now, just as it had when she was little. The comfort of her grandmother's prayers helped her to temporarily switch off the feeling of unease with which she lived. She allowed herself to nod off as she listened to her grandmother standing sentry for their family, asking the God she had served for over six decades to surround their family with the strength of His mighty angels.

chapter FOUR

G race tossed her keys into the large wooden bowl that
sat in the middle of her grandmother's kitchen table.
She remembered Claire expressing admiration for the well-
crafted article the first day she had met her. Claire had shyly
informed her, during her one short visit, that the bowl was designed for kneading bread. It was obvious she was dismayed
to see such a fine culinary tool being used as a mere receptacle
for car keys.

Grace had chosen not to spoil the visit by telling Claire that
she had no earthly idea how to make bread, nor did she have
any particular desire to do so. The thought of herself elbow-
deep in bread dough almost made her smile.

Almost. Because even though she and Claire were worlds
apart in many ways, she felt a connection developing between
them that day. Claire had been fascinated by the fact that she
was a nurse—and had asked many questions. She, in turn,
had discovered that Claire had a great deal of knowledge
about healing plants. Grace had been too long in a primitive
country with poor medical resources not to respect those who
tried to relieve what pain and sickness they could with whatever tools they had.

In her hand was a box of handmade candy she had

purchased at Coblentz's chocolate factory over in Walnut Creek. Mother's Day was coming soon and she had picked up an assortment of her grandmother's favorites.

She was trying to figure out a safe place to hide the box when she heard Elizabeth exclaiming, "You brought chocolates!"

Grace turned around and saw that her grandmother had taken it upon herself to advance from a walker to a cane this morning.

"Are you sure that's a good idea, Grandma?"

"Chocolate is almost always a good idea."

"No, I mean the cane. Shouldn't you be using your walker?"

"Not when a cane works just as well. I'm feeling much stronger. Now—about those chocolates you are hiding behind your back."

"They are supposed to be for Mother's Day."

"Lovely." Elizabeth reached out her hand. "I'm declaring an early Mother's Day."

"I'm not sure you're allowed to do that, Grandma."

"I'm seventy-eight years old. I have just survived triple bypass surgery. In my opinion, I have earned the right to do pretty much anything I want—within reason. And in my opinion, eating a little chocolate is definitely within reason."

Grace reluctantly sat the box of chocolates on the kitchen table.

Elizabeth leaned her cane against the chair and eased herself down. "Did you get any of their Swiss-style truffles?"

"Of course."

"Caramels?"

"Would it be a box of Coblentz's without caramels?"

"Not in my opinion." Elizabeth lifted the lid. "Oh, you got pecan clusters, too."

"And buckeyes."

"*And* buckeyes! Be still my beating heart."

"It won't be beating long if you eat all this candy," Grace warned.

"Then am I to assume," Elizabeth said, "that you brought all this lovely chocolate home merely to hasten my demise? Have you been coveting my collection of butter dishes again?"

"Your collection of butter dishes?" Grace scoffed. "I would pay to have someone come in and carry most of this stuff out of here."

Elizabeth pretended offense. "Just because you lived in a tent with nothing but a duffel bag doesn't mean the rest of us can't have our comforts."

"It wasn't a tent, it was a B-hut. They're built out of plywood."

"Ah—so you lived in a box. Big difference." Elizabeth daintily selected a truffle and sank her teeth into it. Her eyes rolled back in ecstasy.

Grace watched with amusement. It was nice to see her grandmother enjoying herself again. Grandma had always been fun, but illness had taken much of the starch out of her these past weeks. The fact that she could exchange banter again was a good sign that her body was getting stronger.

"Hey, sis!" Becky came in, flopped down beside her grandmother, and eyed the candy box. "Ooh. You've been to Coblentz's!"

The older Becky got, the more she reminded Grace of their mother—a beautiful brunette with smoky blue eyes.

"I was trying to hide her Mother's Day gift, but she already caught me."

Becky lifted the box lid. "Can I have a buckeye?"

"One." Elizabeth held up a finger.

"What have you been up to this afternoon?" Grace asked. "Homework?"

"Uh-huh." Becky popped a chocolate in her mouth and spoke around it. "I have a report due."

"Chocolate should be savored," her grandmother admonished. "Don't cheapen the experience by talking with your mouth full."

"I'm going to start supper before you two stuff yourselves with candy," Grace said. "Spaghetti sound good?"

Just then, a knock on the door brought all three of them to a full alert.

"Were we expecting anyone?" Grace asked.

Elizabeth and Becky shook their heads.

Ever since the murder, they had been keeping the doors locked all the time, and Grace deeply resented the fact that they felt the need.

She peered out the window nearest the door. It felt odd to be so careful in broad daylight, but the Shetler murder had taken place in the middle of a gorgeous spring morning.

She relaxed when she saw that it was Levi and unlocked the door. He stood on the porch, his feet planted far apart, with what appeared to be a new broad-brimmed straw hat on his head. His expression was so serious, it worried her.

"Is your mother okay, Levi?"

"She will be home soon."

"How is Daniel?"

"He is doing well. Rose is with him now."

"Wonderful. Have the police discovered who the shooter was yet?"

He frowned. "If so, they have not told me."

She realized that she was keeping him standing on the porch.

"Would you like to come in?" she asked. "I was just starting dinner. It won't take long. You're more than welcome to stay and eat with us."

"Thank you. No." He glanced over his shoulder at the road, as though worried someone might pass by and see him standing there.

She was glad that she was wearing baggy jeans and a loose button-down shirt today. No one in his right mind could consider her outfit revealing.

"I have brought you a gift."

"Really?" This was unexpected. "You don't have to give me anything."

Again those dark hazel eyes studied her, as though trying to figure her out.

There was a leather strap slung across his chest. He pulled it up over his head, and she realized that it was attached to a basket he carried behind his back—the most cunningly made basket that she had ever seen. She didn't know a lot about basket-weaving, but it was easy to see that Levi was a master.

It was slightly larger than the black leather bag in which she kept her emergency medical supplies but much lighter. The leather strap, which had been a little tight across his chest, was the perfect length for her.

"This will hold your things more securely." Levi opened the curved woven lid and held it open so that she could see inside. "There are some compartments within."

She was amazed. Everything she carried in her medical bag would nest in that basket perfectly. Had she ever seen one like it, she would have bought it immediately, regardless of the price.

"When did you have time to do this, Levi?" she asked. "This must have taken days."

"Not days. Two evenings."

"It's beautiful."

"I thought it might be useful." He seemed uncomfortable with her praise. "It should be lighter than that big black bag you carry."

"It is light." She hefted the basket in her hand. "I can't imagine it withstanding all the abuse I give that bag."

"It is made with small strips from a black ash tree from our land. It will last many years."

She thought she heard just a hint of pride as he said that.

The basket was so unusual, so obviously crafted specifically for her, that she wondered if she had somehow—despite her *Englischness*—made a friend out of this solemn Amish man.

"Thank you so much, Levi, I—"

He interrupted her by turning on his heel and calling back over his shoulder as he strode toward his horse. "You would not allow me to pay you for the miles, so now we are even."

He didn't turn around or so much as wave as she stood at the door with his exquisite gift in her hand. He mounted his beautiful black horse and rode away without once looking back.

She had met a lot of men in her life, but this young Amish man—with his calloused hands and a concern for his family so intense he had hovered over his baby brother for hours—was not like anyone she had ever known.

chapter FIVE

L evi carried a sturdy side table, one he had just finished making, in from the workshop to place beside the heavy oak bed that his friend and cousin Timothy had helped him carry downstairs from his mother's room yesterday morning. They had placed the bed in a corner of the front room for his mother. She would be coming home soon—she and the babe—praise God!

Just in time for the funeral.

The doctor said she should not climb stairs for several more days, so Levi was making a place for her on the first floor. It would be good to have his family home again.

The house was too quiet. He did not like it. A home should be filled with children and conversation.

And it was clean. Uncomfortably clean. So clean that he was almost afraid to sit down. The women from his church had taken over, washing each room from top to bottom just as *Maam* always did in the weeks leading up to their turn at hosting church in their home.

It had felt strange coming home from the hospital and finding women working inside and out, including finishing the laundry his mother had begun. Several men from church were feeding the livestock and tending to the other numerous chores around the farm. It appeared that the only chore left for him to do before the funeral, besides carry down his mother's bed, was to gather the eggs and brave the bad-tempered rooster who was all ruffled up and annoyed over the comings and goings of so many people.

On his way to the house, he stopped. A handful of hermit thrushes were thoroughly enjoying the warm weather, fluttering and twittering among the branches of a young apple tree. It was nice to see that the little things had survived the winter. He inhaled the sweet fragrance of the snowy white apple blossoms and tried to calm his mind.

Whenever his heart was heavy, he had found that it helped to focus on natural things. Things that he had grown up with. Natural gifts from the hand of God. Things that reminded him that there truly was a God.

He missed his mother, his sister, his little brothers, and his stepfather. Abraham had come into his life when he was only ten years old. His widowed mother's new husband was a fair man who had taken his role as a father seriously and had taught Levi much about the practical aspects of making a living.

Basket-weaving was one of the things Abraham had taught him, patiently and in great detail. It was an occupation plied by many Swartzentruber families. The tourists each summer would buy almost any amount they could make over the winter, but Abraham was especially skilled.

As was Levi—thanks to his stepfather.

He wondered if it had been a sin to create such an intricately woven basket for Grace. As he pondered it, he decided that it was a prideful thing he had done. He had sketched it out on paper first, taking great pleasure in losing himself in creating a design that he had never made before. It had taken all of his skill in design and execution, but the look of amazement in her eyes when she had seen it had been worth every second.

As had the look of respect.

It was hard—this thing of being Swartzentruber. But it was all he knew how to be. Every relative he had was Swartzentruber except Rose, who had made the decision to cross over into Old Order Amish. It had been a terrible thing at the time. It was still a terrible thing, in his opinion. Because of the ban, Rose and her family had not been welcome at his mother's table for a little over ten years.

He still marveled that Rose was the person his mother had wanted to care for the children. She had told him later that it was because she knew that in Rose's household the children would be loved, and they would need all the love they could get after what they had been through. She had been afraid, she said, that they would simply be tossed in with the other children in any of the other Swartzentruber homes—some of which had as many as seventeen children in them.

Being a member of his church was decidedly not easy, but the preachers said that the road to heaven was narrow and the hardships his people chose to endure would someday be worth it. What bothered him most was not the extra work, or the restrictions on how much he could charge for his work, or even the lack of conveniences that other Amish got to enjoy. The thing that rankled him the most was the contempt in which his people were sometimes held by some in the less conservative Amish sects.

In some ways, he understood. His aunt and uncle's Old Order farm fairly sparkled with new paint and a well-kept lawn and gardens. In the summer he was certain it would be bursting with flowers. Their driveway had been well covered with a thick layer of gravel.

The Shetler farm looked shabby by comparison. The

house was in need of a coat of paint. The driveway was only packed dirt that turned into mud each time it rained. The yard was small and unkempt.

His church believed that it was wrong to take pride in the appearance of their farms and homes. It was one more way they chose to keep themselves apart from the world.

But in Elizabeth's granddaughter's voice, there had not been even a hint of contempt for him or his people. Grace was the kind of person he wished he could know better, but he was a baptized believer and should not allow himself to even think about someone like Grace Connor.

Still, the look of admiration he had seen in her eyes because of the special basket he had woven had felt sweet indeed.

"But I don't want to take a nap." Elizabeth sat on the side of her bed.

Grace set out a glass of water and two pills. "Grandma, you need your rest."

"I feel fine."

"You won't feel fine if you don't rest."

"I didn't make you take naps!"

Grace considered. That was true. It had been one of the many perks of her too-brief visits here as a child. No naps. Lots of stories. Picnics on the back porch. Visits to the chocolate and cheese factories.

"I'll read," Elizabeth wheedled. "And I'll stay in bed while I read. Would that make you happy?"

"Having you get well is what will make me happy."

"I think I've done pretty well—all things considered."

"I think you've done wonderfully," Grace said. "Is there a specific book you want?"

"Yes. It's in the top drawer of my dresser."

"This?" Grace pulled out a paperback. "*Love's Savage Heart?* Are you sure?"

It had a lurid cover, with a man so well muscled that she could not imagine him doing anything except working out twenty-four hours a day. The woman was apparently having a button crisis, from the looks of her blouse.

"You don't read these kinds of books." She glanced at her grandmother. "Do you?"

"I believe I am old enough to read any kind of book I want."

"Okay." Grace handed it to her. "If you're sure this is the one you want."

Elizabeth chuckled. "I was just rattling your chain. One of the nurses at the hospital gave this to me after she finished. She was such a doll-baby I took it to keep from hurting her feelings." She adjusted her glasses and reached for the book, scanning the cover. "The problem is, I'm afraid she's going to be disillusioned if she thinks she's going to find a husband who looks like that with his shirt off. It isn't possible, you know, although your grandfather came close."

"Grandma!"

"Well, he did."

"I wish I could have known him better."

"I wish I had, too." Elizabeth laid the book down. "He died so young. We had only been married forty years."

"He was sixty."

"That's entirely too young. You'll realize that once you pass forty."

"Is missing him the reason you keep all this stuff?" Grace gestured around her grandmother's cluttered bedroom. Fishing rods and wooden fishing lures covered most of one wall. "I don't understand this. None of us fish."

"He didn't fish much, either."

"Then why . . . ?"

Her grandmother scooted further back onto the bed, pulled off her house slippers, and dropped them on the floor. "He just loved collecting those things. We used to go down to Kentucky to the longest garage sale in the world. It went on for miles. I collected antique toys, old dishes, and anything else that struck my fancy. He would look for these old lures and fishing rods. We had wonderful times together." She gazed around at the room. "To you it's clutter. To me it's a room filled with good memories."

"But the big bedroom upstairs is chock full of things, too, and there's barely room in the kitchen cabinets for drinking glasses."

"Are you worried that I'm becoming a hoarder like those people on *Oprah*?"

"Grandma, I hate to say this—but I think you're getting close."

"Do you see any piles of old newspapers?"

"No."

"Do you have trouble walking through my house?"

"No."

"Then don't worry about it." Grandma picked up a small figurine from her bedside table. "Some of my things actually have value, you know—I mean beyond my memories. Your grandfather and I weren't completely foolish about what we purchased."

"Perhaps, but there's a lamp in the extra bedroom upstairs that is the most hideous thing I've ever seen."

"Now that was a wedding gift. Your great-aunt Hazel gave that to me. I never cared for it." Grandma's eyes twinkled. "I never cared much for Hazel, either. She's gone now, so you have my permission to get rid of it. Does that make you feel better?"

"A little." Grace traced her finger over the paperback. "Are you really going to read this while you rest?"

"Oh, heavens, no. From the looks of the cover, it might give me another heart attack. Hand me that volume over there on the table beneath the window. The one with note cards sticking out of it. I started that one before I got sick. I think I'm feeling well enough to start in on it again."

Grace brought her the book. It was a new volume on biblical archaeology discoveries.

"Hand me a pen, will you?" Elizabeth sank back into the pillows that Grace had piled onto the bed. "There's a chapter in here I think might interest our ladies' class when I start teaching again."

"You said that Levi used to come and read books with you," Grace said. "Did you ever study anything together besides birds?"

"Now that's an interesting question." Elizabeth laid the book back down on her lap. "Do you know what textbooks the Swartzentrubers use in their schools?"

"No."

"Reprinted *McGuffey Readers*. The kind my grandmother used. They have a couple of other textbooks, but only those printed specifically for Amish schools."

"You're kidding." Grace pulled a chair over to the bed and sat down.

"I'm not kidding. I'm not even exaggerating." Elizabeth removed her glasses and rubbed her eyes. "It was hard for someone like me—an educator—to watch without saying something. Levi zipped right through those *McGuffey Readers* and was hungry for more. The young teacher—she couldn't have been more than sixteen—knew little more than some of her students. I bought Levi a book once, as a gift. It was a large volume of Bible stories for children—just something for him to read at night before he fell asleep. I couldn't imagine anyone finding fault with a children's Bible storybook."

"Did he like it?"

"He loved it. He took it straight home to show Abraham and Claire. Came back the next day, all upset, to apologize."

"For what?"

"For the fact that Abraham had thrown it into the wood-stove and burned it."

"Bible stories?"

"Abraham was upset. He was afraid I was trying to corrupt their family's Swartzentruber view of the Bible."

"Which is . . . ?"

"If it isn't their High German Bible—the one that Martin Luther penned five hundred years ago—they don't trust it." Elizabeth shrugged. "Of course in the book I gave Levi, there was the problem of the illustration of Adam and Eve wearing fig leaves. I thought they were quite tasteful myself, but Abraham disagreed."

"That was a terrible thing for them to do."

"It seems that way to you, but in Abraham's eyes, he was simply being a good father. He was not a deliberately cruel man, but he was a careful one—and sometimes a very strict one."

"What happened then?"

"I was afraid they would stop Levi from coming to visit me at all. With you so far away, I cherished having an occasional visit from a child. So the next day, as soon as Levi had left for school, I gathered an armful of books I thought he might enjoy and took them down to show Abraham and Claire. I apologized for the Bible storybook and told them it was never my intention to go against their wishes. I asked them to go through the books I had brought and see if there was anything they felt Levi could safely enjoy."

"How many did they choose?"

"Three. Birds, insects, and one on identifying plants."

"That's it?"

"That was it. I had taken some storybooks with me just to see if any would pass their inspection. Abraham rejected them all. Fairy tales are strictly forbidden. Westerns are also forbidden because of the presence of guns. The only thing I did in addition to the books they allowed was to play little games with him that involved math problems. A piece of paper and pencil—no book. He caught on like lightning."

"As strict as they were, I'm surprised they let him come at all."

"Claire lost her first two children with Abraham—miscarriages—and she was sick much of the time when I first moved here. Of course, I was widowed by then and they felt sorry for me. Actually, I was feeling quite sorry for myself. That's one of the reasons I moved to Mt. Hope—after your grandfather's death, I thought it might be nice to live in a place with such an optimistic name."

"I always wondered why you chose to retire here."

"Well, it helped that it was beautiful, and that the crime rate was so low."

"Did things go okay after that?"

"Like I said, Claire didn't feel well for a couple of years and I think she appreciated my keeping her son entertained on evenings when he had finished his chores. Even though I was using only a pencil and paper, Levi became quite a whiz at math. Claire made this quilt for me a couple of years after she recuperated. I think it was in thanks for looking after her son. I think she might also have been glad for the bit of extra education I gave him. Claire tended to be more interested in book learning than Abraham."

Elizabeth glanced down at the book. "Would you take

this, Grace? I guess I was more tired than I realized. I think I would like that nap now. And here, please set my glasses on my nightstand."

"Of course." Grace placed the large book back on the table. Then she pulled Claire's quilt over her grandmother and left, leaving the door open a crack.

She grabbed a Coke out of the refrigerator and headed to the front porch, choosing a rocking chair close by her grandmother's window. The dogwoods were magnificent this year, and the perfume of Grandma's lavender blossoms was heady. As she rocked, she gazed down the road at the Shetlers' farm and pondered everything she had just heard.

What an alien people they were—burning a child's Bible storybook, using antiquated *McGuffey Readers,* and accepting sixteen-year-olds as teachers. She wondered what it would have been like to know Levi as a child.

Her father had been a career army officer. With all the moves that the military required, they had not come here all that often. Instead, Elizabeth had come to them. Whenever she got homesick for her family, she would pack a bag and buy an airplane ticket.

Grace popped the tab on her Coke and settled back in her chair. The dishes were done. There was a roast simmering in one of Elizabeth's many Crock-Pots. For a little while, she had absolutely nothing to do. It was a strange feeling. It seemed as if she hadn't stopped running since the day she had graduated from high school.

All she had ever wanted once was to be a great nurse. But being a military nurse in Afghanistan had meant having an inhuman toll taken upon her heart and soul. Not only were there soldiers, men and women, whose screams she had deadened with medication long enough to life-flight them to the hospital, but there were the beautiful, precious Afghan children who too often became victims and pawns in the terrorists' arsenal.

There had come a time, only a few weeks before she returned home, when she realized that in order to endure all the suffering, she had hardened herself emotionally to the point that she was feeling almost nothing at all.

She didn't want her life to be that way. She wanted to feel again.

She glanced around to make sure no one was nearby, then pulled *Love's Savage Heart* out of her right pants pocket where she had slipped it before tiptoeing out of the bedroom.

Perhaps Grandma didn't want to read it, but Grace had once possessed a romantic streak a mile wide. She didn't mind reading *Love's Savage Heart* one bit.

chapter SIX

"What in the world?" Grace nearly dropped the pitcher of orange juice. The view outside the kitchen window was most definitely not something she had ever seen before.

"What is it?" Elizabeth grabbed her cane, pushed up from the breakfast table, and made her way over to where Grace stood.

A long line of plain black buggies was snaking down the road as far as the eye could see—in both directions.

"Abraham's funeral must be today. I didn't know," Elizabeth said. "Do you notice something odd about that line of buggies?"

"No." Grace moved closer to the window. "Nothing except that it feels strange to see this in the middle of the twenty-first century."

"Look harder."

"I don't see anything except buggies."

"Exactly. There aren't any cars."

"Of course not. They're Amish. Why would there be cars?"

"Because there are almost always cars sprinkled among the buggies at the funerals of other Amish sects," Elizabeth explained. "Sometimes it's family members who have become

Mennonite. Sometimes it's someone who has become a car-owning Beachy Amish. Sometimes fellow factory or shop workers come. But Swartzentrubers seldom have *Englisch* friends."

Grace pointed. "There's one."

Sure enough, there was a lone white van coming into view.

"Someone must have hired an *Englisch* driver." Elizabeth craned her neck to see it. "I'll bet that's some of Abraham's relatives. Several migrated to upper New York State a couple of years ago. Land is less expensive there. Their bishop must have given them permission to come."

"You're telling me they would have to get permission from their bishop to go to a relative's funeral in another state?"

"Swartzentrubers do, yes. They don't allow what they consider a frivolous use of vehicles."

"Have you ever been to an Amish funeral?"

"A couple of them." Elizabeth went back to the table and sat down. "I wish I could go to this one."

Grace put the pitcher of orange juice back into the refrigerator. "You aren't strong enough yet."

"I know, but would you mind going in my stead?"

"I would stick out like a sore thumb."

"Of course you would. So?"

"The only thing I have fit to wear to a funeral is a pair of black dress pants and a good white blouse."

"That will do. But no jewelry, Grace. No high heels. And I'd suggest wearing no makeup. You'll feel out of place enough when you get there. And you won't understand a word the minister is saying. They preach only in German. You'll need to hurry so you can speak to Claire before it starts."

"Okay." Grace rinsed out her orange juice glass and put it in the sink.

"You should take something to contribute to the funeral

dinner." Elizabeth glanced around the kitchen. "I wish I had known when it was going to be. I would have had you bake something. Oh—I know."

Elizabeth dumped out the keys Grace had tossed into the wooden bowl that sat on the table. "Wash this out and fill it with some of that fresh fruit you bought. They seldom purchase out-of-season fruit. Tell Claire the bowl is a gift from me. She's always admired it."

Levi and his brothers pushed his mother's borrowed wheelchair into the barn, which the men had prepared for the funeral service. Claire held little Daniel in her arms. The three other children followed close behind. The benches were all set up as they were for church: the women's side facing the men's. The only difference was that Abraham was now dressed in his church clothes, lying in a handmade casket that one of Levi's cousins had built out of some poplar lumber that Levi had cut last season.

There was a small, hinged door cut into the lid of the casket that, when opened, showed only the top part of Abraham's body.

The circumstances of Abraham's death, and the delay in the funeral because of the autopsy, had given people plenty of time to hear about it, and there seemed to be a larger turnout than usual. He estimated there were around three hundred people there, perhaps more.

Ezra Weaver, their bishop, stopped him on his way into the barn. "This is a sad day."

"Truly sad," Levi replied.

Ezra had been bishop for only three years, but he was even more conscientious in performing his duties than the elderly bishop he had replaced. Their particular church district, already ultraconservative by anyone's reckoning, was becoming even more rigid under Bishop Weaver's oversight. Some of the congregation was pleased over this. Others, like Levi, were worried.

He waited for the bishop to move aside and allow him to get his family seated. Instead, the bishop seemed intent on having a chat with him.

"*So an shlim ding* to happen to your family," the bishop said.

"Yes. A very terrible thing," Levi agreed.

"At least your stepfather is no longer part of this sinful world anymore. But a man should live long enough to raise his children."

Levi nodded. "Our *Daed* would have wished to do so."

The bishop gave him a stern look. "It is your duty now to be a father to these little ones and to help your mother."

"A duty I willingly accept."

"You intend to work your stepfather's eighty acres by yourself?"

"I will, with Albert and Jesse's help."

"Good. It would be a shame for such fine land to grow into weeds."

Levi wondered what the bishop was getting at.

"It would be a great help to your mother if you were to select a *gute Frau*." The bishop stared at him meaningfully. "Most Amish men your age already have a *gute* wife and two or three children by now."

"True." His voice was steady, but inside, Levi was beginning to seethe. He now understood why the bishop had led the conversation down such a path. Land in Holmes County was at a premium. Eighty prime acres was a prize. A steady man who could farm as well as Levi was an even greater prize to a man with an unmarried daughter. The bishop was such a man.

The bishop bent over Claire. "That is a fine child. Holding him will comfort you in your sorrow."

"God's will," Claire said.

"Yes," the bishop agreed. "God's will."

It was as it always was. Any tragedy—no matter how major—was attributed to God's will. In Levi's opinion, this murder was the work of a vindictive Satan instead of a loving God. But he said nothing. His people's way of accepting tragedy and going on with life was admirable. The Amish could not afford to sit down and stop living because someone they loved had died. There were children and grandchildren to care for. Livestock to be fed. Crops to be harvested. The sound of a herd of cows bawling to be milked did not stop from respect for grief.

The bishop moved aside while Levi maneuvered his mother's wheelchair around a root sticking out of the ground. He would get a mattock tomorrow and grub that root . . .

"Hello."

He glanced up, surprised to see Grace standing nearby. She was holding a walnut bowl filled with fruit, apparently for the funeral dinner later. The children would love that. It had been a long winter and there would be many more weeks before the fruit trees began to bear.

As a growing child, he had made himself sick every spring eating green apples and raw rhubarb straight out of the garden—both so sour they made his eyes water—simply because his hunger for something fresh would be so great.

It was obvious that Grace was trying hard to be sensitive to the situation. She had made a real attempt at dressing appropriately. The blouse she wore was more form-fitting than he was comfortable with, but for an *Englisch* woman it showed restraint.

It was almost time for the service to start, but Grace didn't seem to realize. She crouched down beside his mother's wheelchair, the wooden bowl balanced against one hip.

"Grandma wanted to come, but she's still pretty feeble. She sends her heartfelt condolences and says you are to keep this bowl as a gift."

"When I am better, I will make some bread in this kneading trough and bring it to your grandmother."

"She would love that."

Levi saw Grace's face as she looked up at his mother, and his heart lurched at the compassion he saw there. This was not an *Englisch* person coming to sightsee—a problem they sometimes had to endure at funerals. Grace actually cared.

"Is there any way I can help you in the coming days, Claire?" Grace asked.

Levi was certain there was no way his mother would allow this *Englisch* girl to help her. He doubted Grace even knew which end of a wringer washer to shove the wet clothes through, let alone any of the other myriad chores his mother did each day.

"Could you come tomorrow?" Claire asked, much to Levi's surprise. "Daniel is not feeding well, and I think there is something wrong."

Grace's face registered immediate concern. "Have you told the doctor?"

Claire shook her head.

"Why not?"

The bishop had noticed the holdup. He looked pointedly at Levi, and then at Grace, as though to instruct Levi to shoo the *Englisch* woman away.

Levi pretended not to see. Bishop Weaver did not realize all that Grace had done for their family.

Grace laid a hand on his mother's wrist. "Why haven't you said anything to the doctor, Claire?"

His mother leaned forward and whispered something in Grace's ear. It was embarrassing to see all the heads turned their way, watching this strange exchange between Claire and this outsider. Suddenly, he wished Grace had not come. This was not her world. She did not belong here. Even if she was only trying to be kind, this was not a place she should be.

With everyone still watching, and the bishop impatiently waiting, Grace sat the fruit bowl on the ground, pulled the baby blanket away, and gave Daniel what appeared to be a quick examination. The baby, disturbed, howled in protest.

"He certainly has a healthy set of lungs." Grace wrapped the baby back up and laid him in Claire's lap. "I think he's okay for now. I'll come by tomorrow and check on him."

"Thank you," Claire said.

For the first time, Grace seemed to realize that a hush had fallen over the crowd as over approximately three hundred people watched her and waited for her to finish.

"Um, I'll just go put this someplace and . . ." She glanced around and saw all the faces turned toward her.

"You may put the bowl in the house," Levi said. "It is time for us to get started."

She seemed unsure whether to go or stay. He decided to help her make the decision.

"There will be no *Englisch* spoken here today," he said. "But my mother and I thank you for coming."

"I am so sorry for your loss," she said.

And then Grace Connor walked away while a barnful of people watched.

Except for him. He kept his eyes conscientiously facing forward. It would never do for the bishop to observe him—a baptized, single man well into marriageable age—gazing after a young, female, *Englisch* neighbor.

chapter SEVEN

"How did it go?" Becky was stretched out reading, taking up one entire couch. Elizabeth, on the other couch, moved some dark blue knitting and a how-to book aside as Grace fell onto the couch beside her.

"When did you take up this hobby?" Grace pulled a stray knitting needle out from where it had been sticking up from between the cushions.

"While you were gone."

"I was gone less than an hour and you took up knitting? Why?"

"I've had this yarn for ages and I figured this is as good a time as any for me to figure out how to be a really good old woman. That's what old women do, isn't it? Knit?"

"Not you. You don't even sew."

"I've let you down. A grandmother who doesn't sew. Shocking."

"Seriously. Why are you doing this?"

"I need a hobby, and this seems more productive than crossword puzzles. Now, tell me how it went at the funeral."

Grace sighed. "How do you know if you've made a complete fool of yourself in front of a bunch of Amish people?"

This caught Becky's attention and she raised her head

from the book she was reading. "What did you do, Grace?"

"Nothing, except try to give my condolences to Claire."

"And?" Grandma prompted.

"There was this big barnful of people sitting around on benches. Kids milling about. People talking. I saw Levi pushing Claire along in a wheelchair. She had the baby in her arms. I stopped and said hello. She asked me a question about the baby. I bent over to take a look at him, and when I straightened back up again, no one in the place was talking, Levi was red in the face, and everyone was staring at us."

Becky closed her book. "What happened then?"

"I gave them my condolences and got out of there. Levi—very pointedly, I might add—informed me that the funeral would be not be in English." She traced a seam on the couch with her finger. "It was obvious that he wanted me out of there as quickly as possible. I wish I hadn't gone."

"The Amish are hard to read sometimes," Grandma said, "the Swartzentrubers especially. For all you know, the women might have been wondering where you bought your shoes and all the single men wishing you were Amish." Elizabeth compared her handkerchief-sized piece of knitting to the picture in the how-to book.

Grace lifted one foot and inspected her burgundy, oiled-leather Birkenstock clogs that she had ordered over the Internet in a fit of "retail therapy" after one especially bad night patching together wounded soldiers in Afghanistan. "You really think the women wanted to know where I got these?"

"Are they comfortable?" Grandma asked.

"Extremely. That's why I bought them."

"Well, I'm sure you've noticed that Amish women don't exactly wear pointy-toed high heels. They go for comfort and durability—intelligent women that they are."

"I doubt they were admiring my shoes. I think I just looked utterly out of place."

Becky giggled. "Well . . . you were."

"You should have gone instead of me, Becky. You're the one who's been living here all this time."

"I was busy trying to find Grandma's yarn and knitting needles in the storage room upstairs—which wasn't exactly a picnic."

"I just remembered something else that puzzled me," Grace said. "All the men were still wearing their hats, although they were at a funeral—even Levi. I thought it odd that they didn't take them off."

"That would be paying too much respect to the dead. The Swartzentrubers take their hats off only to honor God. If you ever drive by the Shetlers' on a Sunday morning when they are hosting church, you'll see a huge pile of black hats near the entrance."

"They pile all those identical hats together? How can they tell them apart?"

"I asked Claire that once. She gave me a very common-sense answer. They write their names inside the brim."

"Well, that makes sense. But they don't take their hats off inside buildings or for the national anthem or anything?"

"Only for God," Grandma said. "Did Claire like the bowl?"

"She was very pleased. She said she's going to make a batch of bread in it and bring it to you when both of you are better."

"What did you say?"

"That you would love a visit."

"Good." Grandma shoved her glasses higher on her nose, unraveled two rows of stitches, and took another stab at her knitting. "I think you did well, all things considered. Your mission was to let Claire know that we cared about her and you accomplished that. You didn't go to impress everyone else at the funeral."

"I guess you're right, it's just that . . ."

"Just what?"

"Levi seemed downright annoyed that I came."

Grandma laid the tangle of blue yarn down on her lap. "He probably *was* annoyed."

"Why? Claire wasn't. She was glad to see me."

"It doesn't take much to start the Amish gossiping. You're a neighbor, unmarried, and lovely. Levi is a catch. You spent several hours with him the day Claire got hurt. You will probably be the subject of many conversations today and for several more days until something more interesting comes up. Levi knows that."

"Then why did you send me up there?"

"Because this wasn't about you and it wasn't about Levi. It was about Claire. She was burying a husband today, and I wanted her to know we cared."

"Then I guess I did the right thing," Grace grumbled. "I just wish it didn't feel so . . . messy."

"Life is messy, Grace." Grandma began to unravel the nest of yarn again. "Because people are messy. The sooner you accept that, the easier your life will become."

"Why?"

"Because you'll stop expecting perfection." She examined her how-to book again and restarted her knitting. "From other people and yourself."

Levi wanted to mourn his stepfather. He really did. He had come into Abraham's house as a ten-year-old boy and had been treated like a son. But that in itself had been a problem. To be treated like a son by Abraham Shetler had been to absorb a great deal of unnecessary discipline. It had been a rocky start between them until he had toughened up and learned to obey his stepfather without question. Over the years, they hammered out a working relationship.

He felt no overwhelming grief for Abraham, but he did feel the weight of responsibility. Abraham had been a worker. Now it would be his job to provide for the family.

He tried not to think about the hospital bills that would soon come due. There was no way he could pay them. It had taken two years just to save up enough to purchase Angel Dancer. He knew that soon one of the oldest men of their church would make the rounds to all the Amish farms in the area, asking for donations. Every family would give as much as they could—just as Levi and his family had always contributed all they could each time others had needed help. After that, there was the existence of the Old Order Amish relief fund that was set up for this sort of extreme expenses, and into which Swartzentruber families sometimes had to dip. Also, the hospitals often reduced the bills of the cash-paying Amish. Levi had watched other Amish deal with medical bills, and by the grace of God, he would also have access to enough help to pay their medical debts.

He positioned his mother and Sarah on the women's side, beside Rose. He took Albert and Jesse with him across to the men's side. Albert sat ramrod straight like the little man he was becoming. Jesse, at eight, slipped his hand into Levi's and leaned his head against his shoulder.

He looked down at Jesse's hands. Already they were showing the calluses of farm work and a couple of barely healed cuts from the sharp wood strips they used for baskets. He remembered his own hands, still tender from childhood, trying to weave well enough to win Abraham's approval.

Albert was becoming competent with the basket-weaving.

Jesse, however, was hopeless at it. The child couldn't sit still
for the long hours required to craft a fine basket. He clearly
hated the feel of the wet, slippery wood. Abraham had gotten
angry many times at Jesse's inability to weave well. There had
been quite a few spankings.

Levi knew that Jesse's palms were marked with crisscross
scars from wrestling with the sharp edges of the weaving
strips. He felt sorry for the little guy.

And then the strangest thought struck him. With Abraham gone, Jesse would never have to weave a basket again.
Not if Levi didn't make him—and Levi had no intention of
making him. Jesse was simply not cut out for it. Not this sweet
child who would rather watch the aerial acrobatics of a barn
swallow than pay attention to finishing off yet another badly
made basket.

Jesse was fascinated with everything that walked and
crawled or galloped. As much as he fidgeted when he was
forced to weave baskets, the child could lie still and watch a
lizard for hours. He could already name most of the birds that
nested around their farm.

Levi turned Jesse's palm over and traced the cuts. No—his
little brother would never sit and cry over making baskets
again. Levi was the head of this family now, and he would
get to make those decisions. The idea pleased him, but then
he remembered his mother's grief and plunged into remorse
over the way his mind was straying.

God's will be done. Just as the preacher was saying.

Suddenly, everyone stood up. Levi had been so deep into
his own thoughts he had not heard the cue for prayer. He
scrambled to turn around and kneel on the ground with his
elbows on the bench as everyone else did.

Then he heard a quiet sob and shot a glance over his shoulder at his mother, who, unable to kneel, was bowed in prayer

in her wheelchair. Rose had taken little Daniel into the crook of one arm. Her other arm rested around her sister's shoulders. *Maam* sat with her arms wrapped around her stomach, her head bowed—shaking with sobs.

There was a rustle as the group finished their prayer, rose again as one body, and sat down upon the benches for another two hours of preaching.

Levi forced himself to concentrate on the service. Despite his own issues with his stepfather, Abraham had done the best he could with what he knew, and the man deserved a decent funeral and a respectful family.

Why was it so hard to focus today? Through the open barn door, he could see the woods behind their house where the dogwood trees were in bloom. Their white blossoms were the size of a squirrel's ear now. The weather had been quite warm and humid, which meant that the morel mushrooms his mother loved would be springing up from the spongy ground. Hunting morels was one of his favorite things.

But it was not the time to think about gathering morels. It was time to listen to a couple more hours of preaching. Then the sad ride to the *Graabhof,* the modest cemetery where four generations of Abraham's family had been laid to rest.

The preacher finished and the church broke into song, their voices rising as one. They sang the songs *shlow*—very slow. They did this because prison guards had once mocked his people by dancing to the hymns they sang while awaiting execution. Those long-ago martyrs had deliberately slowed their hymns down until it was impossible to dance to them. That practice had lingered. Levi had been told that Swartzentruber singing was even slower than in the other Amish orders.

There was comfort in blending his voice with the others.

Becoming one with his church family in spirit and in voice. Levi felt the holiness of it penetrate his soul.

And then he caught sight of Zillah Weaver, the bishop's daughter, staring at him from the women's side. She was watching him intently, as though hoping to catch his eye. When she saw him looking at her, she smiled.

Zillah was blond and pretty, and she had been blessed with dimples that she never missed a chance to flash. In fact, the smile she used in order to show off those dimples best was a little odd. Even though his people were not allowed to hang mirrors on their walls, he would be very surprised if Zillah didn't have a hand mirror tucked away in a drawer somewhere with which she had spent time practicing the art of smiling. She was that kind of girl.

He quickly looked away. Zillah could be as sweet as sugar, but she had a mean streak. He had seen it more than once. When one truly knew Zillah, she did not seem so pretty anymore.

He had always been careful never to give any indication that he was open to courting her, but she was one of the few girls in his church district close to his age and still single. Having to marry within the Amish faith, and specifically within the Swartzentruber sect, limited one's options.

He wondered if her father, the bishop, was beginning to worry that she might never marry. That might explain his admonition for Levi to soon choose a wife for his mother's sake.

The preaching began again, a fresh preacher this time. Jesse fell asleep against his shoulder. Albert had his head down, twisting and untwisting two pieces of straw he had picked up from the floor.

Levi scanned the faces of the other women seated across from him. Were there any here for whom he could muster any enthusiasm? He knew of men who had chosen their wives the way a man chooses livestock, evaluating each woman's health and ability to bear plenty of children. Levi wanted more than that. He wanted someone with whom he could talk about things other than how many bushels of corn he had taken to market or how many quarts of peaches she had canned.

Deep down, he wanted someone with a good mind who would help him become a better man. And he wanted—truth be told—someone he would not mind lying down beside at night.

At that instant, his mind took flight in a direction that he absolutely did not want it to go. A very dangerous direction: Grace Connor.

She had impressed him with her competency and her compassion. He found himself wondering what went on in that *Englisch* head of hers. His mother said that before Grace came to stay with her grandmother, she had lived halfway around the world, riding in helicopters, going into battlefields, saving wounded soldiers. He wondered if she ever had nightmares about what she saw.

Jesse stirred against him. He put his arm around the little boy and held him close. His family would be depending upon him for their survival. He could not allow himself to think about Grace for even one second. He wasn't some Old Order teenager on *Rumspringa* sneaking around dating *Englisch* girls before he settled down. At twenty-five, he was a grown man with a family to support.

Getting to know Grace Connor as more than a nodding acquaintance was simply not an option.

chapter EIGHT

Grace's internal alarm clock nearly always rang a little before six o'clock in the morning. Her father had believed in awakening a child at the same time every morning, and the time he chose was six o'clock. Weekends as well as school days. And it had stuck. At least with her—maybe not so much with Becky.

Grace didn't mind. It helped her get a lot accomplished. Rising from her grandmother's couch where she had spent the night, she went over to the window and opened it. A cool morning breeze wafted in, rich with the scent of honeysuckle. The feel of the air on her T-shirt–clad body was so enticing, and the smell of honeysuckle so thick, she almost felt she could waft out upon it like one of those cartoon characters floating toward an enticing scent.

One thing she was not going to do with this morning was let it go to waste. If there was ever a morning made for running, it was today. She checked on her grandmother, who was still sleeping soundly, then went upstairs, threw on some sweats and running shoes, and came back down. She considered running shorts but abandoned the idea. She didn't want to cause some Swartzentruber man to drive his buggy into a ditch.

Becky was sleeping with a couch pillow over her head. Grace lifted the pillow and shook her sister's shoulder.

"Becky?"

Her sister sat straight up and looked around wildly. "Is Grandma okay?"

"Grandma is fine. I'm going for a run. I just wanted you to know where I was."

Becky rubbed her eyes. "What day is it?"

"Saturday. You can go back to sleep."

Becky didn't argue. She burrowed back under the covers.

Grace grabbed a piece of cheese and an apple and ate them on the back porch while she read a couple of chapters in the Bible that her grandmother usually left lying in the swing. Even in Afghanistan, she had tried to read at least something from the Bible every day. Sometimes she made it and sometimes she didn't—but living here, it was as easy as breathing.

Ecclesiastes—one of her favorite books—was where she was reading today. She had always thought it quite thoughtful of the ultrawealthy writer of the ancient book to have tried everything under the sun, only to later record that absolutely nothing of a material nature had brought him happiness—that all of his efforts had eventually felt like just a striving after the wind.

As far as she was concerned, the writer of Ecclesiastes was spot on. In her opinion, nothing really mattered in life except the people who loved you and those you loved. That and enjoying the gift of God's creation while serving Him to the best of one's ability.

She finished her Bible reading, did her stretches, and felt sorry for anyone who was sleeping in on a beautiful morning like this. As she took off on a gentle trot, she marveled over the fact that she still could not manage to take for granted the fact that she was waking up morning after morning to pleasant, cool weather.

Enduring the summer heat of Afghanistan had been a battle all by itself. The winter was a nightmare of freezing temperatures. That country had seemed to be a place of extremes in everything, from weather to geography to the zeal of its religious adherents.

She shook off the memories of broiling while trying to make a run for a medevac helicopter beneath an Afghanistan sun. This was Ohio. The weather was gorgeous and it was going to be a good day.

There was definitely something wrong with Daniel. The child had wailed nearly all night long. Levi worried about his little brother as he finished his morning chores. Breakfast sounded appealing right now, but he dreaded going back into the house to the gut-clenching sound of his baby brother's cries. Putting off entering the house for a few more minutes, he walked to the top of the hill behind his house to enjoy the sunrise.

As the sky turned into a panorama of color, his eyes automatically traced a line from the pond to the house. It would be so easy to filter the pond water, put in a pipeline, and create an indoor bathroom for his mother. What a burden of work that would lift off her shoulders! If he was honest, he also sometimes wished for a shower for himself. He had never experienced one, but he was certain it would feel wonderful to have the grime so easily washed off his body at the end of a hard day's work.

He stood on top of the hill, gazing over his fields. The earth was warm enough for him to sow oats. Very soon he could plant the acreage that, in a four-year crop rotation, was ready for corn.

There were still several acres of old cornstalks that had been left untouched by the men of the church. He was glad. Plowing the land with his four well-trained workhorses was something he enjoyed. Tractors were more efficient, perhaps, although that was hotly debated in some circles. Horses' feet didn't compact the earth like heavy tractor wheels and their "emissions" only added to the fertility of the ground. To a frugal farmer, it was no small thing that a horse had the ability to replace itself.

But what he personally disliked about tractors was that they drowned out the music of spring—like the song of the horned lark and the sound of horses snorting with excitement over being back in the fields after a long winter. A tractor caused one to miss the music of harnesses creaking and the satisfying popping of alfalfa roots as the sharp plow blades cut through the rich earth.

As he looked out over his farm, he took a deep breath, savoring the smell of honeysuckle. Then the faint sound of a baby's cry came to him through the air, and his bubble of satisfaction broke. Thank goodness Rose was planning to stay another day. Although women from their church came and went, he knew that his mother was most comfortable with her only sister. Rose would not be allowed to stay much longer. If she lingered, Bishop Weaver would have some pointed things to say about it.

At the funeral, it had not escaped anyone's attention that Rose wore a black bonnet smaller and less cumbersome than a Swartzentruber woman would wear and Rose's dresses were shorter, showing a few inches of ankle. The Swartzentruber women's dresses always modestly brushed the tops of their shoes.

It must appear strange, he supposed, to the few *Englisch* who knew of the schisms between Amish orders, how much stock was put into things like whether the buggies the church members drove had steel wheels or rubber tires. Or whether the members could purchase factory-made underwear or had to make it all by hand. The list went on and on. Sometimes it was hard to keep it all straight.

Personally, he didn't see the reason behind half the things they did—but he didn't have to. That was what bishops and preachers were for: to keep all the rules of their *Ordnung* straight in their heads and make certain everyone was following them. As long as he could plant and harvest and work in his workshop, he could be content.

Or at least he would be if little Daniel would just stop crying.

The sound of shoes slapping against the road startled him. Who was running? And why? Was there another emergency? He whirled to look.

As the figure came closer, he realized from the steady pace that it was someone running for exercise, not in desperation as he had feared.

And then he saw that it was Grace. Well, that figured. What other woman on this road would waste her time out running on a perfectly good Saturday morning when there was so much else a person could be accomplishing? He wondered if she had any idea how strange this behavior was here. How out of place.

She spotted him, waved, and to his discomfort headed right toward him. This was not something he welcomed, but at least it was early enough that perhaps no one would pass by and see him talking to this *Englisch* woman. He was torn between ignoring her by going straight back inside the barn or standing where he was and dealing with whatever it was she wanted. He opted for the latter.

When she reached him, she stopped, leaned over, grabbed

both of her knees, and panted. He waited for her to catch her breath.

"Sorry about that. I had no idea I was so out of shape," she gasped. "This is ridiculous. I've only run to the main road and back—a couple of miles—and this is how out of breath I get!"

To his eyes, she was not out of shape at all. In fact, quite the opposite. His eyes sought the horizon.

"How are your mom and the baby? Are they up yet? I promised her yesterday that I would stop by."

"They are awake."

"Is it too early to stop in?" she asked.

"No."

He had answered her questions. He wished she would leave now, but the woman seemed determined to hold a conversation with him right here on top of this hill.

"How did things go with him last night?"

"Not well."

She waited for him to explain, and when he didn't, she smiled. "You don't have much to say, do you, Levi?"

And then she was gone. Trotting down the hill to his home.

Her comment stung. There was much in his heart that he wanted to share with someone. He had a great deal to say. But it would be highly improper to share it with her.

Grace was used to being around men. As a former soldier, she basically lived year-round with a horde of them. She was used to the sight, the smell, and the sound of great numbers of men. She had heard all their corny jokes and most of their dirty ones. Some were brave, some were silly, some were practically certifiable. But none of them were like this Amish neighbor of hers.

The sight of him on that hill—silhouetted against the sunrise, his feet planted firmly in the ground, his chin lifted as he surveyed the fields laid out before him—had been a picture she almost wished she could hang on a wall. There was something timeless about the stance of his body, a farmer surveying his land, a man determined to pit will and sinew against a plow or whatever implement it took to provide for his family. It was—in her opinion—a picture too few women got to see.

She had felt a compulsion to go talk to him, to see if there was something behind his eyes besides Amish stoicism, but obviously there wasn't. Talking to Levi was a little like talking to a stump. The man was easy on the eyes, and he could weave a heck of a basket, but he certainly didn't bring much to the table when it came to conversation.

She brushed aside thoughts of Levi and started to worry about the baby. Hopefully Claire wouldn't be too put off by her running outfit. She had intended to go home and change before paying a visit, but if Levi was concerned enough to actually verbalize the fact that things were not going well, she'd better not wait.

The door was standing open, so she knocked on the frame. "Claire, it's Grace. Can I come in?"

Rose came to the door. "You are Claire's neighbor, the nurse who brought the children to me."

"Actually, I'm a nurse practitioner." She didn't usually make a big deal about it, but there was a difference. One for which she had worked hard.

"I'm glad you are here." Rose ushered her in. "The baby will not quit crying. I have never seen such a bad case of colic. We have tried a tincture of fennel seed and some other herbal remedies that have helped with our other children, but nothing works."

Rose sounded as though she was on the verge of tears

herself as the distinctive cry of a newborn in distress filled the house.

The inscrutable Levi and the three more miles she had fully intended to run this morning were forgotten. "Let me see him."

Claire's home was pleasant, in spite of its austerity. Or maybe because of it. It felt so very different from her grandmother's overstuffed house. The main impression was of wood. Wooden floors beneath her feet. Wooden chairs and tables. Rose led her into what appeared to be a living room, where Claire rested in a bed that had been placed in one corner.

The baby was lying on his back beside his mother, kicking his little legs and crying. Claire was wearily patting his tummy. Grace could see that the baby was squirming with pain, its pitiful cries going on and on. She also noticed that there were no baby bottles visible, so she supposed Claire was trying to nurse. Her mind sifted through the possibilities for so much unease in a newborn.

"It looks like Daniel is a little unhappy. Do you have enough milk, Claire?"

Claire showed no surprise at Grace's sudden appearance. She cupped one breast with her hand and grimaced. "I think so, but he acts so unhappy—I don't know."

"May I hold him?"

"You may as well. I cannot seem to do anything to help him." Claire sank back onto her pillows, exhausted. Grace was impressed that the poor woman was able to even hold her head up. C-sections were difficult enough to recuperate from, but add a couple other wounds, grief for a husband, and a colicky baby—and it's a wonder she was able to function at all.

And then there was the blood loss. Grace knew that with the bleeding Claire had experienced, there was a chance she would not be able to produce enough milk.

Grace was itching to give Daniel a thorough examination, but he began to cry even harder when she picked him up and cradled him in her arms.

Seeing that a horizontal position did not agree with him, she put him up over her shoulder, tucked his downy head beneath her chin, and began to pace the floor, crooning softly.

It wasn't immediate, but the cries slowly subsided until he fell asleep. She had once watched a staff pediatrician at an ER do this very thing. The mother had come in, wild with worry that her infant wouldn't quit crying. The pediatrician, wiser than most, had simply walked the ER floor with the child until it calmed down.

The visceral connection between a mother and baby was a strong one. Claire was dealing with enough grief and pain that it was quite possible that some of the trauma was being transferred to the baby.

Grace figured that Rose, as a twin, was probably reacting to her sister's grief to such a strong extent that she might be having the same effect when she held him. At least that was a theory. On the other hand, there might be something really wrong. As the cries quieted, she saw Rose sit down at the table and lay her head upon her crossed arms.

"Did either of you get a wink of sleep last night?"

"Not much," Rose said.

The child felt cozy tucked beneath her chin. She knew she could happily hold him like this for quite a while—or at least long enough to give these women some rest.

"When was the last time he ate?" she asked.

"About fifteen minutes ago," Claire said. "But he spit most of it right back up again. I think part of the problem is that he's hungry, but he cannot seem to keep anything down for long."

"When was his diaper last changed?"

Rose spoke from the table, her face still buried in her arms. "I changed him right after she fed him."

"Was the diaper wet?"

"Yes."

"Not just damp, actually wet?"

"Yes."

"That's good, then." Grace was relieved. "That means something must be getting into his tummy." She kissed the top of his head. "Why don't you two get some rest while I watch after him?"

Rose lifted her head and looked at her with something like hope in her eyes. "You don't mind?"

"Not at all. I'll sit outside in the porch swing for a while."

"Oh, that would be wonderful!" Claire said.

Rose looked meaningfully at Grace. "*Denke*. Thank you."

"You're welcome."

The swing was wide and sturdy. Sitting here, on a beautiful spring morning with a sweet baby in her arms, was not exactly a big sacrifice.

Grace settled herself into a corner of the swing and began to talk to the sleeping child.

"You are a sweetie. Even if you don't have any respect at all for your poor aunt and mother. I bet you kept your big brother up last night, too. Maybe that's why he was in a bad mood when I saw him. You'll have to let him get his beauty sleep from now on, little one."

A slight sound made her look up. Levi was standing on the porch, looking down at her and the baby.

"He is not crying." There was the sound of relief and wonder in his voice.

"Apparently you didn't get much rest, either," Grace observed.

"Our Daniel has strong lungs."

It occurred to her that she hadn't seen the three other siblings. "Where are the children?"

"Daniel has been taking so much care that Rose has left them a while longer with her married daughter. Henry will bring them back when Daniel calms down."

He disappeared without another word and she resumed her gentle swinging. She was surprised when he reappeared a moment later carrying a glass of lemonade and a plate of cookies.

"You have been running." He sat the refreshments down on the swing beside her. "You will be thirsty."

"Thank you, Levi."

What a strange man. She took a bite of a homemade buttery sugar cookie. *And a surprisingly thoughtful one.* The last thing she had expected was for him to show her this kind of consideration.

"This cookie is delicious. Did Rose make them?"

"No. Women from our church have brought much food."

"You are lucky to have so much support."

He looked ill at ease. "I have work to do." Without another word, he strode to the barn.

A half hour later, a buggy came trotting up the driveway. As it pulled slightly past her, Grace noticed that, like most of the buggies at the funeral, it did not wear a reflective orange safety triangle on the rear. She had meant to ask her grandmother about that. She had thought all buggies were required by law to have those safety devices mounted on the back.

The man who climbed down from the buggy looked vaguely familiar, but in her eyes, there was so much sameness about the older Amish men, it was hard for her to discern between them. They all wore the same clothes and the same beard, and most seemed to wear the same solemn expression.

The man's face, though, when he caught sight of her

wasn't just solemn, it registered extreme disapproval. She couldn't imagine why. All she was doing was holding a baby—and she wasn't wearing shorts.

"Hello," she said softly. She made no move to get up. She couldn't get up. Any jostling would awaken little Daniel.

The man looked as if he were in his midsixties, but she was only guessing. He might be much younger. A long, un-trimmed beard tended to make a man look old.

"You are the *Englisch* woman from the funeral," he said. "What are you doing here?"

"Please keep your voice down," she whispered. "You'll awaken the baby."

"Babies need to get used to the sound of voices." He did not lower his. "It is foolish to talk softly to keep from waking them."

She decided she did not like this man.

"Then I hope you won't mind babysitting him when he starts to howl," she said. "Claire and Rose are worn out."

His eyes widened. She could tell that he was not used to being spoken back to.

"Bishop Weaver." Rose had come to the door. "Please come in."

"You are still here?" he asked.

"Yes." Rose's voice was resigned. "I am still here."

"Our people can care for Claire."

"But she is my sister."

"She is Swartzentruber. You are not."

Rose's chin lifted. "I am aware of who and what I am."

He made a disgusted sound in the back of his throat. "I will see Abraham's wife now."

"I'm sorry," Rose said, "but she is asleep. This is the first rest she's gotten in two days." Then Rose firmly closed the door.

The bishop apparently did not know how to respond, so he scowled at Grace. "The funeral is over. You have no business here."

He still hadn't lowered his voice. Bishop Weaver was beginning to get on her last nerve.

"Are you telling me that there is something wrong with a nurse checking on a woman and child whose lives she helped save?"

"Only *Gott* can save lives."

"I agree," she calmly said. "But God had a little help from Levi, who rushed to get help, and the ambulance driver who broke the speed limit getting here, and the medical team that was waiting at the emergency room." She paused for a breath. "Like the good Samaritan in the Bible, we all functioned as the hands of God on that terrible day."

It was then that she saw his eyes glaze over as he shut out her words. She had seen the same look in the eyes of a mullah whom she had once made the mistake of speaking to in Afghanistan. It was the look of someone who believed that his way was the only way—and anyone who believed differently should remain silent.

She really should have kept her mouth shut. She was in way over her head with these people. She didn't understand the difference between the Swartzentruber Order or the Old Order or the New Order or the New New Order or any other order they wanted to create.

How many "orders" were there of these people anyway?

"Can I help you, Bishop?" Levi seemed to materialize out of nowhere.

"Yes," the bishop answered. "You can start by telling this *Englisch* woman to stay home where she belongs. We are to keep ourselves apart from the world."

It seemed to her that when Levi glanced at her, it was with

apology. "Grace Connor is a neighbor who has given my family much help."

"Hmmph!"

"Is there a reason you came, Bishop?"

"I came to see what your family needs."

"My family's needs have been met," Levi said. "The church has been a wonderful good help."

"If your family has no more needs, then it is time for your aunt to leave."

"My mother has found comfort in having her only sister with her."

There were so many undercurrents in the men's conversation; Grace didn't even pretend to understand.

"I will see you at church Sunday," the old man stated. "And I will expect to be told that your aunt is gone. I will send my daughter to live here until your mother heals. Unlike the other women of our church, Zillah is still unmarried and childless, so it will be no sacrifice for her to come."

"Zillah?" Levi's voice rose.

"Yes," the bishop said. "She knows what it is to run a Swartzentruber household." He glared at Grace. "You will no longer be needed. My Zillah will take care of this family from now on."

In silence, Grace and Levi watched the bishop step into his buggy and leave.

"So," she said, as his buggy trotted out of sight, "who put antifreeze in his oatmeal this morning?"

"I don't understand." Levi did not so much as smile at her attempt to lighten the mood.

"It's just an expression," she explained. "One my sergeant used to say when one of us was in a foul temper."

"Foul temper," Levi mused. "I don't think the bishop is in a foul temper, but he is overburdened with worries about his flock. It is a great responsibility to be the shepherd of over forty families."

"If he is so overburdened," Grace said, "why did he take the job?"

"It is not a job," Levi explained. "He was chosen by God."

"You mean he didn't have a choice?"

"Once a man has become a baptized member, he has a responsibility to serve in any way God chooses."

"And how do you know that the Lord chose him?" Grace asked.

"If a man picks up the *Ausbund,* our songbook, and it has a certain piece of paper in it—that is a sign from God that he is to be bishop, or preacher, or deacon."

It was the longest string of words she had ever heard come out of Levi's mouth. The man could actually communicate. Who knew?

"So where does the paper come from?"

"No place special." Levi's voice sounded slightly irritated. "Whoever is in charge of placing the paper in the hymnals gets to choose the kind of paper they use."

"What does the paper say?"

"How should I know?" Levi said. "I've never been chosen."

"You mean to tell me that you let these people tell you what to do, but you don't even know what the paper in the hymnal says?"

"What the paper says is not important." Levi was beginning to sound truly exasperated. "Why must you ask all these questions?"

"Because I'd really like to know what that paper says."

Levi gave her a long, level stare as though evaluating whether or not she would shut up and leave him alone if he told her. "What the paper usually says is 'You have been chosen.'"

"Why didn't you just tell me that in the first place?"

He sighed. "Because it is none of your business."

"That's probably true," Grace conceded, "but do you want to know what I think?"

Levi sounded resigned. "What do you think?"

"He may be your bishop. And he may be chosen by God. But frankly, I don't like him."

At this, Levi finally smiled. "I don't think the bishop cares much for you, either."

chapter NINE

Daniel stirred, snuffled, and began to root against her arm. The little guy was hungry. When he didn't find anything to eat, he started to cry again, a wail that penetrated all the way to the marrow of her bones.

"I had hoped your mother could rest a little more," she told Levi. "I wish I had a bottle so we wouldn't have to awaken her."

Levi considered. "We have some bottles of formula they sent home from the hospital."

"Has he had any?"

"Yes. Rose tried. He spits up formula, too."

"And you haven't taken him to the doctor?"

"*Maam* thought he would soon recover." He shrugged. "We do not easily go to the doctor."

"Warm up a bottle for me, if you don't mind," she said. "I would like to watch how he takes it."

Levi disappeared and came out a few minutes later with a small baby bottle.

She sprinkled some drops of formula on the inside of her wrist, testing the temperature. Cradling the baby in her left arm, she carefully inserted the nipple into his mouth. He immediately quit crying and drank greedily until about an ounce of formula was gone. Then he squirmed in her arms, made a face, and spit out the nipple, and a stream of formula shot out of his mouth, soaking the sleeve of her T-shirt.

"I'm sorry." Levi surprised her by going inside and bringing out a diaper, which he used to wipe off her sleeve.

"That's okay. I've had a lot worse on me than baby's puke. Is this how he reacts when he nurses?"

"Yes."

"That must have been what your mom had on her mind yesterday at the funeral when she said she wanted to talk to me."

She tried the bottle again. This time, the baby drank about half an ounce, sucking greedily, as though starving—then pulled away, squirmed as if in pain, and another stream of milk shot out of his mouth. Grace was quicker this time, and the liquid spilled upon the porch floor.

Again, she lifted him upright over her shoulder and in a few moments he stopped crying.

"Has your mother been keeping him in her bed with her a lot?"

"She has."

"I think I might know what is wrong."

"What?"

"I need to do a little research before I can say for sure, but I think this child might have infant gastroesophageal reflux. It happens frequently among preemies."

"And what does this long word mean?"

"Have you ever experienced heartburn, Levi?"

"No, but Abraham suffered from it."

"Think of this as baby heartburn. Some babies' esophagus sphincter muscles aren't developed enough to keep the stomach acid down. Instead, it comes up into the esophagus. That's the . . ."

"I know what the esophagus is, Grace."

"Okay, then. If a baby with a poorly developed esophagus spends a lot of time horizontally, or with someone holding him around the belly, the stomach acid won't stay down. That plus the upset Daniel is picking up from Rose and your mom might explain all this crying. At least it's a theory."

"You have no children. How can you know more about this than my aunt and mother?"

"A whole lot of medical schooling, Levi."

The baby had quit crying again. Enough liquid had dribbled into his stomach, in spite of the regurgitation, that she thought she could leave long enough to go check her facts.

"Would you take him?" she asked. "I need to go back home."

"You are coming back?"

His voice actually sounded hopeful. It was truly amazing what quieting a screaming child could do to raise a woman's value in a man's eyes.

"I'm coming back."

She transferred the infant into Levi's arms. As she made the transfer, the back of her hand came in contact with Levi's biceps. She was surprised. Beneath the loose-fitting shirt, the man had muscles that were as hard as rock. The few people she had ever known who had bodies like that worked out in fancy gyms every day, whereas this Amish man, from what she could see, simply worked hard around the farm.

"I'll be back as soon as I can." She took off running toward her home, but the image of Levi cradling the tiny infant in his strong arms was going to be very hard to forget.

He couldn't help it. No one was looking, and so he allowed himself the luxury of watching her run. He put his little brother over his shoulder, patted his back, and enjoyed the sight of the lovely *Englisch* woman with her long legs racing toward her home.

There was something about her pace that reminded him of the thoroughbred horses he had watched being put through their paces at the auctions. She was spirited, smart, and sleek—like some of the more expensive fillies he had seen galloping around the track, the ones who were far beyond the ability of a young Amish man to purchase.

He had admired those thoroughbreds' glistening health and good breeding, knowing he would never own one, but content to know that such magnificent creatures existed in this world.

That was what it felt like now to him, as he watched Grace lope toward her home. She came from a different world. Her life in the military alone was enough to make her alien to him. Her ignorance about his people and their ways was incalculable. But he could watch her from a distance and appreciate the magnificent woman she was.

But one thing she had said echoed in his ears.

A whole lot of medical schooling.

What would the weight of such an education feel like? No wonder she knew the long name of his brother's illness. If he were a betting man, he would lay money on her being correct in her diagnosis. He doubted that Grace was often wrong when it came to medical things.

As he turned to take Daniel back into the house, he remembered that Zillah would be coming to stay with them and felt half sick at the thought. Zillah might be competent enough to run a household while *Maam* recuperated, but it was going to be extremely awkward for him to have this girl, who had plagued him from childhood, living in his home.

One thing he knew for sure: He could not turn down the

bishop's offer. It was a reasonable thing for the daughter of the bishop, a young woman with no family of her own, to volunteer to come help a mother recuperate from surgery. It would look strange to their religious community if he refused. This was a thin line he would have to walk.

He patted Daniel's tiny bottom, careful to keep the infant upright over his shoulder. "Women are a blessing from God, Daniel. But some of them can be a sore trial."

The baby squirmed and passed gas—loudly.

"Oh!" Levi laughed out loud. "Is that your opinion of the whole thing, is it? Then you and I are going to be great friends, little *Bruder*."

As Grace entered the back door to the kitchen, the sour smell of the baby's throw-up made a shower an absolute necessity, but it would have to be a short one. She wanted to dig into some medical websites for more information about Daniel's colic.

She glanced at one of the many clocks her grandmother had hanging on the wall. With Becky home to watch over Grandma today, she had a long list of errands to run, but taking care of little Daniel was her first priority.

She found Becky and her grandmother watching Saturday-morning cartoons together. Elizabeth had a tray in front of her and was spooning up oatmeal. Becky was lounging in the armchair, one leg flung over the arm, eating an energy bar and petting a bedraggled-looking gray kitten.

"When did you find him?" Grace asked.

"I found *her* meowing on the front porch this morning when I went out to get the paper for Grandma. I have no idea where she came from." She held the kitten up for Grace's closer inspection. "Her name is Tabby."

"If you live here long enough, Grace, you will discover that Becky has a penchant for rescuing strays," Elizabeth said. "You came home during one of the extremely rare intervals when we were without four-legged companions. Now we have been blessed with a scrawny kitten."

"He'll fatten up," Becky said. "And you forgot about Bonzo."

"Bonzo?" Grace asked.

"Oh, yes. How could I have forgotten? Bonzo the turtle. Becky's roommate. I'm certain he will outlive us all. I've given up fighting it, Grace. Don't be surprised if you come home someday and find Becky cuddled up to a stray coyote."

"You like animals, too, Grandma," Becky said, "and you know it."

"True." Elizabeth leaned over and scratched behind the kitten's ear. "I've met several with personalities preferable to various people I've known, but you have to admit, Becky, our experiment with raising goats did not go well."

Grace was intrigued. "What happened?"

Becky laughed. "They escaped their fence and got into our yard, where Grandma had just hung up a week's worth of laundry."

"What clothing they didn't eat or chew to pieces," Grandma said, "they apparently tried to wear. You haven't lived until you've seen a billy goat prancing down the road wearing an old woman's panties on its horns."

"Well, it definitely looks like you guys are enjoying yourselves," Grace said.

"Tremendously," Elizabeth said. "At the moment, I am testing a theory that the demise of our civilization rests firmly on the shoulders of Bugs Bunny."

Grace noticed that the knitting Grandma had been working on was lying in a heap beside her.

"How's the knitting going?"

Grandma held up the tangle of yarn for her to admire. It was the most misshapen piece of knitting Grace had ever seen.

"What's it supposed to be?"

"A sweater for you, dear." Grandma sounded hurt. "Can't you tell? Don't you like it?"

Becky spluttered with laughter. "Don't let her mess with you. It was supposed to be an afghan, but she's given up on it."

Grace was relieved. "You had me scared there for a minute."

Elizabeth sighed and tossed the offending knitting into the corner of the couch. "I think I'm going to stick with crossword puzzles from now on."

Becky swallowed the last bite of the energy bar. "How was your run? You've been gone a long time."

"I was at the Shetlers'," Grace said. "That baby is having some issues I want to check on this morning. After I've done what I can for him, I think I'll go stock up on food for the week."

"Could you pick up some movie DVDs?" Becky said. "TV with Grandma is getting a little old."

"Preferably something with Cary Grant," Grandma said, "or Fred Astaire." She held one hand up to her mouth and whispered loudly, "Becky's taste in movies is a little odd."

Becky rolled her eyes.

"I'll try to find something you both can enjoy," Grace said.

After a short shower and clean clothes, Grace came back downstairs and found Grandma taking a midmorning rest in her room and Becky in the kitchen, coaxing the kitten to drink some milk. She was lying on her stomach with her chin resting on her fists, verbally encouraging the tiny thing to take laps with its pink tongue.

Becky looked up at her. "I think Tabby is going to be okay."

Just then Becky's cell phone buzzed with a text message. She sat up and read it and her face grew pale. She stared down at the phone as though she were holding a snake coiled to strike.

"What's wrong?" Grace asked.

Her sister shot her a fearful glance, cleared the screen, and nonchalantly slipped the phone into her pants pocket. "Nothing."

"What kind of a text did you get? You looked like you saw a ghost."

"Just one of my friends telling me that we have a big test Monday."

Grace was unconvinced. Becky was a good student. She would not be that upset at the idea of an unexpected test, especially since this was only Saturday morning and she would have two days to prepare for it.

It had to be something else. The problem was—what? Something told her that she wouldn't find out by prying. Whatever it was, perhaps Becky would eventually confide in her.

In the meantime, she had a sick baby to take care of.

After checking some sites on the Internet, she called Karen at the ER to confer about Daniel's problem. Karen, a mother of three, validated her suspicions and told her about a store in Berlin that carried slings for babies.

She was just fishing her keys out of the yellow soup tureen that had replaced the kneading bowl when her grandmother came into the kitchen.

Grace noticed that Elizabeth was walking without her cane today, and doing a good job of it. "You're doing better, Grandma."

"I have a good nurse. Are you leaving again already?"

"Do you mind?"

"Oh, I don't mind—I just wish I could tag along. Where are you headed?"

"Berlin, to pick up something for Claire and Daniel."

"Could I come with you?"

Grace considered. A short drive might do her some good. "I don't see why not."

"The last time I was in Berlin at the German Village, Schloneger's was selling a home-cranked sugarless ice cream that was out of this world."

"But you aren't diabetic."

"Maybe not, but I do watch my figure."

"You just finished off that pound of Coblentz chocolate I bought you."

"Some things"—Elizabeth sighed in frustration at her granddaughter's ignorance—"are just worth the calories, Grace."

"So, you're telling me you want to go get some ice cream."

Grandma cocked an eyebrow. "What do you think I've been telling you? Just let me go put my face on."

"I don't think we have time for you to put on makeup. I really need to get back to the Shetlers' as soon as I can."

"Well, then, do you mind if an old woman puts on her shoes?"

"Go put your shoes on, Grandma. I'll wait."

Becky had listened to the entire conversation while lying on the floor. "You don't have to say a thing, Grace. Ouch!" Becky extricated the kitten from her shoulder where it climbed with its tiny claws. "It looks like I'll be the one getting the groceries today."

"Do you mind?"

"No. You're the one taking Grandma out for ice cream."

"I'm all ready!" Their grandmother came out of the bed-room wearing a new lavender sweatsuit and a slash of red lipstick.

She had forgotten her shoes.

"What are you girls looking at?" She glanced down at her feet. "Oh, shoot."

chapter TEN

"That's my car," Grandma said.

"Where?"

"There." Grandma pointed with her plastic ice cream spoon.

They were passing Troyer's Country Store and Grandma's car, the blue Honda that Becky had been driving this past month, was parked in front.

And then Grace saw something that caused her to do a sudden, illegal U-turn. Becky was in the car, and a man had his head and shoulders pushed through her open window. As Grace pulled in beside them, she could see that Becky was leaning as far away from him as she could get without climbing into the passenger seat.

"What's going on?" Grace jumped out of the car and slammed the door.

The man jerked his head out of the car, bumping it on the way out. He rubbed the spot he had hit and scowled at her.

"What do you want?" His voice sounded raspy, like that of a three-pack-a-day smoker.

"I'm her sister. A better question is who are *you*?"

Becky hurriedly got out of the car and Grace saw that she was trembling.

"This is, um, Mr. Franklin, a janitor at my school."

Mr. Franklin appeared to have lived a hard life. There were deep creases in his face, and his expression was more wary than a man with a clear conscience should have. He had a receding hairline and his hair was pulled back into a long, thin ponytail. Grace wondered exactly what school official had chosen him to be around students.

"Is there something we can help you with, Mr. Franklin?" Grace asked.

Becky and the man glanced at each other as though sharing a secret.

"He was just telling me about a teachers' in-service on Tuesday," Becky said. "We won't be having any school."

"Thank you, Mr. Franklin," Grace said. "I'm sure my sister appreciates your concern. Have you finished getting groceries, Becky?"

"No. I still need to go to Walmart."

"Me, too." She glanced at the man. "I'll follow you there."

The man stalked off.

The whole scenario bothered her. Becky had been recoiling from the man even before she knew Grace was watching, then had climbed out of the car and more or less jumped to his defense.

"What's going on, Becky?" she asked.

"I already told you." Her sister studied her feet. "He's just a janitor at my school."

Well, who knew? Maybe Becky was telling the truth. Grace had never known her sister to lie. She got back into her car and followed Becky to Walmart, where she really did have a couple of purchases to make. On the way, she repeated the exchange with Becky to her grandmother.

"I know it looks a little odd," Elizabeth said, "but Becky's a pretty good judge of character."

"But what if this is some sleazy guy she met on the Internet? She's only seventeen—just the right age to think she
knows everything—when she doesn't."

"The exact same age you were when you signed up for the
military."

"I thought I was all grown up."

Grandma scraped the last bit of vanilla ice cream out of
her Styrofoam cup. "So does Becky."

Grace found Rose pacing the floor with the baby arching its
back, crying. Claire lay on her side in her bed with her eyes
closed. Three other Amish women dressed in somber-colored
dresses were busy in the kitchen but did not introduce themselves. Since it was not a social call, neither did Grace.

"Has he kept anything down in the time I was gone?"

"No." Rose jiggled the baby up and down. She had faced
him outward, one arm tight around his stomach, the other
arm beneath his bottom. "I've never seen a baby have colic this
bad before. I'm very worried."

"Don't hold him like that, Rose."

"Why not?"

"Didn't Levi tell you what I suspected?"

"No. He just said that you would be back soon and explain
everything to us. He was anxious to get out to the fields."

"Shift him to your shoulder, Rose. He needs to be held in
an upright position as much as possible."

"But this was the way my babies liked to be held."

"Daniel has a special problem." Grace explained what she
knew to the two women and gave Rose the baby sling she had
purchased.

"Make sure you hold him upright for at least thirty minutes after each feeding. Much longer than that if possible.

A carried baby cries less, and crying increases the reflux."

Then she pulled out an infant sleeping wedge from a Walmart bag.

"I've never seen one of those before." Claire was sitting up in bed now, fully engaged.

"It will let Daniel lie safely at an angle, which will help keep the contents of his stomach from flowing the wrong way."

All three of the other Amish women wandered over to watch, speaking softly to one another in German. They handled the wedge and discussed it among themselves.

"Feed him smaller, more frequent meals." Grace pulled a small box of rice cereal out of the bag, which she had also purchased. "And you could try giving him a little formula from time to time with a tiny amount of this in it—maybe a half teaspoon at most."

"What do we owe you?" Claire asked.

"Consider it my baby gift," Grace said.

"If this works," Claire said, "I think you not only saved my life, you may have saved my sanity."

"And mine," Rose echoed.

"The good news is he should grow out of this when his little esophagus matures. The fact that you're nursing him is a plus—it's so much easier on his digestive tract."

"You know all this but you have no children of your own?"

"Not unless you count Grandma," Grace joked.

None of the women so much as cracked a smile. Evidently one didn't joke about one's grandparent in a Swartzentruber household.

"Would you like some pie?" Rose was now carrying Daniel in the sling, and he was already beginning to calm down. "People from Claire's church have brought much food these past few days. We will not be able to eat it all."

"I have to get back," Grace said. "But thank you anyway."

She had carried her medical basket in with her. Now she slung it over her shoulder as she started to leave.

"May I see that?" Claire asked.

"This?" Grace took it off and handed it to her.

"Beautiful work." Claire turned it this way and that. "Who made it?"

"Levi." Grace wondered if she had been unwise bringing it in with her. Would she get Levi into trouble?

Claire fingered it. "I thought it looked like his workmanship."

"He gave it to me while you were still in the hospital." Grace wondered if she had crossed yet another forbidden Amish line in the sand. "I wouldn't take any money for driving him to the hospital. He said this gift was my payment."

She felt Rose's and Claire's eyes boring into her.

"I told a nurse friend about it, and she wants one, too, now," she added lamely.

Claire stroked the basket. "My Levi is a wonderful son," she said. "I pray often that someday he will find a good Amish girl to marry."

What did marriage have to do with a nurse's basket? And was she imagining it, or had Claire just emphasized the phrase "Amish girl"?

"I'll come by tomorrow to check on how you and Daniel are doing," Grace promised.

It wasn't until she was inside the car that she realized neither Rose nor Claire had said a word about wanting her to come back.

The home that Levi entered felt like a different world than the one he had left a few hours earlier. His mother was smiling for the first time in days. Rose was bustling around the kitchen warming what appeared to be a stew for his noon meal. She, too, was smiling. But the biggest change was the fact that his baby brother was no longer crying. He lay peacefully sucking his thumb while lying beside his mother in her bed, upon what appeared to be a triangle-shaped pillow.

Levi could feel the tension of his neck and shoulders relax when he saw that all was well. Everything had changed since early this morning, and he was sure that Grace had helped bring about that change.

"The babe sleeps," he said.

His mother looked up at him, her eyes soft with love. "Yes," she said. "Little Daniel has eaten well and kept it down, thanks to the knowledge of our new neighbor. The poor babe was in terrible pain all along, and we didn't know."

Levi lifted the baby into his arms, careful to keep his tiny body tilted upward as Grace had said. He lifted his brother's shirt and caressed the warm little belly with his fingertips. A smile curved his own lips as he thought how his brother resembled a small, satiated puppy. Having a new baby in a home was one of the nicest feelings in the world—if the babe was happy.

He sat down in one of the kitchen chairs and cradled his little brother against his chest. "This new knowledge is a good thing."

"Yes. Things should get better now," Rose said. "Your new neighbor says she thinks he will soon outgrow this problem."

"Grace Connor carries a very special basket," his mother said.

She let the words hang in the air waiting for a reaction, but Levi weighed his words before he answered. His mother had been young when she had given birth to him, and young when she was widowed. Only seventeen years of age separated them. Because of this, in many ways they had grown up together. There was a strong friendship between them with total honesty. They knew each other well, and he understood exactly what she was asking him. One of the greatest fears an Amish mother had for her son was that he would get caught up in a love relationship with an *Englisch* woman.

For a grown man like Levi, who had already accepted baptism into the Swartzentruber church, even the hint of a relationship with an *Englisch* woman was forbidden.

"Grace Connor saved your life when I went to her for help," he said. "She took the children to Rose's and drove me to Columbus. She bought me water when I could not leave Daniel's side. She refused payment for any of this. Because of all she did for our family, I did not think an ordinary basket was payment enough."

"That is good, then," his mother said. "You paid our debt with the very best you had. She seemed well pleased with your gift, son. She said that a nurse friend is envious and wants one, also."

A feeling of pride filled his body at his mother's words. It pleased him that Grace had liked it well enough to boast of it to a friend.

"I don't want to get into the business of making those," Levi said. "No one would pay me enough to justify the hours I put into it."

He thought he had skillfully avoided his mother's need to know how he felt about Grace Connor. He was wrong.

"Our neighbor is an attractive woman."

For the first time in his life, Levi found himself avoiding an honest exchange with his mother.

"She is too worldly in the way she dresses and acts."

"Yes." His mother seemed satisfied with his answer. "I agree. She is kind, but she is entirely too much of the world."

"Now that I know the baby is better, I will start work in the far field this afternoon."

"Are you hungry?" Rose asked.

"Some food would be good."

As Rose dished out stew and sliced bread, he handed Daniel back to his mother.

"The bishop was here," he said, "while you were asleep."

"That is what Rose told me." His mother checked the baby's diaper and then positioned him over her shoulder. "Do you know what he wanted?"

"He was not pleased when he discovered that Rose was still with us."

His mother glanced at her sister. "I know."

"He says that she is to go home, and he will send Zillah to stay with you."

A frown creased her brow. "Zillah?"

"Yes."

"Do you want Zillah to stay?"

He shook his head. "I have not cared for her since we were scholars together. She was unkind to other girls when she thought no one was looking."

"People change," his mother said.

"I have not yet seen signs of it in her."

"Zillah and you are of marriageable age. If you spend many days beneath the same roof, our people will expect a marriage to be announced. I have heard that the bishop is afraid his daughter will become an *alt Maidel*—an old maid."

"And I believe that is the true reason Bishop Weaver is sending her to stay here."

"I will pray that she chooses not to stay long," Claire said. "I am afraid the bishop will be greatly offended if we send his daughter home before she wishes to go."

"And I will pray, also," Levi said, "with much persistence."

chapter ELEVEN

Levi could see Grace and Becky sitting on Elizabeth's back porch in the swing. They were playing with a kitten, dangling a string of yarn in front of it. It was not his way to spy on his neighbors, but he could see that they were enjoying themselves. Their laughter rang out over the kitten's antics. What a blessing for Elizabeth to have such granddaughters. He wondered if the sound of their laughter wouldn't speed her healing.

He smiled to himself as he watched them. They made a pretty picture together. It was good for sisters to be close, as his mother and Rose had once been. He could remember when Rose had been a daily part of his mother's life. The fact that they had not seen each other for ten years because Rose had decided to become Old Order struck him as unnecessary. The fact that Rose would have to be shunned again after this crisis was over seemed cruel.

He did not understand why they should not have fellowship with a woman as fine as his aunt. It seemed awfully rigid of the bishop to insist that she leave so soon.

There were so many Amish churches that had kind, godly men leading them. Levi envied those districts. But he and his family were bound by geography to Bishop Weaver's church.

It wasn't as though he could hop into a car and drive to a Swartzentruber church he liked better.

By the time he made the next turn and came back over the hill the sisters were gone. As he plowed, his eyes sought for problems that might be developing in Elizabeth's farmhouse or on one of the many outbuildings behind the house. He noticed that a gutter pipe was sagging off the kitchen roof. He should repair it before the next rainstorm.

Before Grace moved in, he would have simply gone over and made the repair. Elizabeth had been good to him and his family, and he tried to watch over her. But things were not as simple now. His people could care less about his helping an elderly neighbor. Even Bishop Weaver would not find fault with that, but now that Grace was there, he would have to be careful not to be seen at her house much.

Each time he came to the fencerow, the one that separated his land from Elizabeth's, that sagging gutter pipe bothered him.

He finished the field, leaving the plow where he had stopped, ready to use again in the morning. Then he took his horses in for a good feed. Today had been a shorter day than he would attempt later in the season, but his horses were like humans in some ways, needing to get their muscles back into condition after a winter of laziness. They would become strong in a few days that he would be able to work them from sunup to sundown with only a few breaks in between.

He drew a bucket of water from the well and poured it into an outdoor basin where he washed before he went inside. It was suppertime and now that little Daniel's belly was not troubling him so much and Rose was presiding in the kitchen, his home would be a pleasant place.

Except—as he approached the open kitchen door, he saw

Zillah sitting at the table, sipping tea and eating a cookie, while Rose stirred something on the stove. The moment she saw him, Zillah jumped to her feet and made a show of helping his aunt.

"Here, let me do that." Zillah grabbed the spoon out of Rose's hand. As he entered, she slyly glanced over her shoulder and pretended to see him for the first time.

"Hello, Levi!"

His mother was sitting up in the rocking chair for the first time since she had been home. He scanned her face trying to read her expression, hoping to see how she was faring with Zillah's presence in the house. Was it tolerable? After one long look had passed between them, she turned away and began to fuss over the blanket she had wrapped around his little brother, and he was no more enlightened than before he had entered the room.

All he knew was that he was grateful that he had built that room for himself over his stepfather's workshop. That is where he would stay until Zillah was gone. He had no intention of sleeping beneath the same roof.

"*Bischt foddich shoffa heit?*" Rose asked.

"Yes," he answered. "I'm done working for today."

Rose wiped her hands on her apron. "Have a seat. I'll dish out the *Buhnesupp.*"

"Bean soup is my favorite, Rose. Thank you for making it."

"The *soup* was no trouble." For the first time since Rose had come, he heard a note of irritation in her voice. Even when little Daniel would not quit crying, his aunt had managed to be patient and steady. Was she simply missing her own family? Or was Zillah already getting on her nerves?

Zillah helped carry some of the dishes to the table, constantly glancing at him from the corner of her eyes. Eventually, when the three of them were seated, they bowed their heads in silent prayer and then Rose stood and dished out a plate for his mother, who remained in her rocker. Rose then took the baby out of Claire's arms so she could eat. Unfortunately, Rose chose to sit down on the bed with Daniel instead of coming back to the table—which left Levi and Zillah sitting at the table alone, across from one another. Like a married couple.

It was worse than awkward. He could think of absolutely nothing to say to this girl . . . and so he ate in silence.

His mother, gracious woman that she was, tried to carry on a polite conversation with Zillah from her rocking chair.

"And how long will your father and mother be able to do without you in their home, Zillah?" Claire asked.

He smiled inwardly at the polite way his mother had chosen to discover how long Zillah would be living beneath their roof.

"Oh, they don't need me right now." Another flirtatious glance at Levi. "My father told me to stay for as long as I want."

If Zillah was as annoying to her father as she was to everyone else, he had no doubt that the bishop would be thrilled to have the girl off his hands for a while. He buttered some bread and concentrated on quickly filling his stomach. The sooner he finished, the sooner he could get up from the table.

"In fact, Rose," Zillah continued, "my father said to tell you that now that I am here, there is no reason for you to stay even one more day. He says that you should be getting back to your own family—and your own church."

He saw Rose bite her lip.

Zillah dished a liberal dollop of mashed potatoes onto her plate and then forked two pieces of beefsteak on top of it. She had already piled her plate high with the green beans and corn that his mother had so laboriously raised, picked, and canned the summer before. There was, he saw, no birdlike appetite here.

Zillah chatted on as though oblivious to the effect she was having on everyone in the room.

"In fact, my father says that Rose should not be here at all." Zillah stuffed a forkful of beefsteak into her mouth. "My father says that since you are Old Order, Rose, we should not even be eating with you."

Rose was pressing her lips together so hard now, they were growing white. The Amish could be a blunt people, and they were definitely an honest people, but they were seldom deliberately rude. Zillah, however, didn't seem to care.

It was the strangest thing. She truly was a beautiful girl. If one just looked at her face and her body, her demure clothing, her perfectly starched prayer *Kapp,* one would think that she was the epitome of modest, lovely, Amish womanhood. But all it took was a few minutes in Zillah's presence, and any man with common sense would run for the hills.

There seemed to be something critical missing from her heart. Levi had picked up on it in third grade, when she had pointed out another little girl's scuffed and oversized shoes, which were obvious hand-me-downs from the child's older brother. Zillah had made fun of her one recess until the little girl cried.

Most Amish children, had they accidentally teased a playmate to the point of tears, would have been crushed and sorry for having caused such pain. But not Zillah. As the other little girl wept, he had seen a self-satisfied smile curl Zillah's mouth, and her eyes had danced with pleasure. The memory of Zillah savoring her deliberate cruelty that day, and on other occasions, made him cringe.

Why on earth she had developed an attachment to him,

he couldn't fathom. But she had, and it had been the bane of his life.

When supper was over, he helped his mother back into bed and got Daniel situated on his little wedge-shaped pillow. Then he went into the kitchen and found Rose elbow deep in dishwater.

"Isn't Zillah supposed to be helping you with that?" he asked.

"She went to the outhouse and hasn't come back yet."

"I'll help you, then."

"Dishwashing is not a man's job."

He picked up a drying cloth and a wet plate. "Nor is it yours to do it all alone."

"I don't mind washing dishes, but I do need to know something. Do you want me to leave, Levi?" Rose said. "Do you feel it is wrong for me to be here?"

"As far as I'm concerned"—Levi picked up another plate and polished it dry—"you could stay here forever. But I know your *Kinner* are missing you."

"Thank you, Levi." Rose sighed with relief. "But what will you do? Zillah doesn't strike me as someone who is willing to take on the task of fully caring for this family, and yet with the bishop's daughter living here I doubt the other churchwomen will see the need to pitch in. Especially since they've already spent so much time here and have so many chores of their own."

"It will be all right. *Maam* will heal. Little Daniel will get stronger. And we will send Zillah back to her father as quickly as possible."

"Be careful, Levi," Rose said. "I don't trust that girl. She looks at you like a hawk looks at a plump chicken."

Levi wasn't thrilled with the comparison, but Rose had gotten her point across.

"I have known Zillah for a long time," Levi said. "I can handle her."

"But you cannot handle what she might say to others about living here. She has her *Kapp* set for you. If you are not careful she will be giving the church the news of your marriage before you even know what's happening."

"Perhaps, but she cannot force me to say the words that will bind me to her."

Rose turned away from the sink and laid one damp hand against Levi's cheek.

"I am so sorry that Abraham was killed. And I would give anything if your mother had not been wounded. There is great evil in the world, and sometimes, no matter how careful we are, or how well we treat our neighbors, that evil will hurt us." She looked deep into his eyes. "But remember that God will somehow manage to turn evil into good for those who love Him. Satan can hurt us, but he cannot destroy us."

"Truly said."

Rose removed the dishcloth from his hand and dried his cheek where she had touched his face. "There are some blessings that have already come, even from this tragedy. I have been allowed to know my sister again, and I have spent time with her children. One of the biggest blessings is that I've gotten reacquainted with you—and you, Levi, are someone worth knowing."

"Only God is worth knowing. I am nothing."

"I know we are a plain people, and I know that we are to be humble people. I also know that there are those among the other Amish orders who make fun of the Swartzentruber sect."

"You mean calling us 'woolly lumps'?" Levi smiled and rubbed his knuckles over his chin. "That does not bother me. I am as yet without a beard."

Rose did not smile in return. Her face was worried. "You are handsome and strong, and you have a valiant heart. You would make some woman a wonderful, good husband. But you deserve a good wife. Don't settle for someone like Zillah. Marriage is too intimate to be shackled to someone who does not make your heart sing."

The door slammed as Zillah walked back into the kitchen. Levi could not help but think how his mother had taught her children to close doors gently to show respect for the house and the inhabitants within.

He thought about Zillah's mother. He did not know the bishop's wife well. She was a quiet woman who rarely spoke, and too often had a sad, faraway look in her eyes. He did not blame the poor woman for being sad—what with living with Bishop Weaver and Zillah her only child. That ghostlike woman would be no match against either of those strong-willed people.

But he was not the bishop's wife, and he would go up against the strong-willed Zillah if it was necessary.

chapter TWELVE

G race wiped her hands on the seat of the most ragged pair of jeans she owned. Elizabeth sat on a folding chair supervising as she worked on the vegetable garden that her grandmother had started back before her heart attack.

"You're planting those lettuce seeds a little too deeply, dear. They barely need a dusting of dirt on them."

"Are you still feeling okay, Grandma? You've had an awfully big day, what with going out for the first time since your surgery, and now this."

"I feel better out here than I did in the house." Elizabeth turned her face to the sky as though soaking up the last rays of the late-afternoon sun. "Your grandfather always joked that I must be solar-powered. I never liked staying inside if I could be out."

"Teaching must have been hard for you."

"On the contrary. It was perfect for me. I had summers off to play outside."

"Even as a little girl I wanted a garden," Grace said, "but Mom wasn't interested. I think moving so much took the desire to plant and watch things grow out of her. She tried not to get too attached to the places where we lived. It feels good now to have my hands in dirt."

"Didn't they have dirt in Afghanistan?"

"Not like this."

She had just covered up the first row when a squad car pulled in to their driveway. A man wearing a sheriff's uniform and a crew cut approached them.

"Hello, Gerald," her grandmother said. "What's brought you out here on this fine spring day? Have you met my granddaughter? Grace, this is Sheriff Newsome."

"No, ma'am. I have not had the pleasure." He took off his hat, a gesture of respect Grace had not seen from any Amish man.

Grace stood up, put her hands on the small of her back, and stretched. "How can I help you, officer?"

He pulled out a small pad and glanced at some writing.

"You're the nurse who was first on the scene at the Shetler home? The one who was with Mrs. Shetler in the hospital when my deputy came by?"

"I am."

"You were also with Levi Troyer that day."

"I took him to Children's Hospital to be with his younger brother."

The sheriff scribbled something on his pad. "Did you know Levi before this?"

"I'd never met the man before."

"Did Levi say anything to you on the ride there? Maybe about enemies the family might have had? Threats they had not told anyone about?"

"Levi is not much of a talker, Sheriff."

"That's the problem." He closed his pad and put it back in his pocket. "None of the Amish are talkers when we're around, even when we're trying to protect them. The Swartzentrubers are the best when it comes to being close-mouthed."

"I wish I could help. Do you have any leads?"

"Not one—and we've been talking to everyone we could. Strange thing—it had been raining the night before, a hard rain. If you noticed, the Shetler farm only has a dirt driveway— good enough for horses and buggies, not so good for cars."

"How is that significant?" Elizabeth asked.

"I was the first one there after the ambulance left. I was able to see Grace's tire tracks and the ambulance's. I could see the hoofprints of Levi's mare."

"But?" Elizabeth cocked an eyebrow.

"There were no other tracks except the ones the children left when they ran for the barn. Whoever killed Abraham came on foot, and they probably came through the fields and backyard."

"On foot?" Grace asked.

"We lost what we think were the murderer's footprints at the creek behind the Shetler house. Couldn't pick them up again. We're afraid whoever did this might be local."

Elizabeth and Grace looked at each other with consternation.

"You ladies need to be real careful for a while until we find this fellow."

After the outside chores had been done, after the kitchen had been cleaned, and after his mother had settled down to sleep with Daniel beside her, Levi moved his few things out of the house and up into his workroom.

A few months earlier, he had created a private space for himself above his stepfather's workshop. It looked as if the babies were going to be coming hard and fast, and so in anticipation of needing quiet from time to time, he had insulated and Sheetrocked and put down proper wood flooring.

Because he had done all the work himself and paid for the supplies, his stepfather had not minded his creating a room where nothing had existed before. There was a cot up there, a couple of chairs, and a table. Most of his specialty weaving supplies were there, also.

Beneath the window was his favorite thing in the room. He had built a low bookcase holding a collection of high school textbooks that he had been reading these past months. He had seen them spilling out of two broken cardboard boxes sitting atop an overflowing Dumpster near a used-book store in Millersburg one day. What had been trash to the used-book store owner had been a treasure trove to him. He would never have deliberately purchased such a collection of books, but it seemed a terrible waste to leave them there to ruin.

On the long ride home, he struggled with his conscience, but his desire for learning held sway. He had carried the boxes straight up to his workroom. There were books on chemistry, geography, calculus, science, world history, geometry, and biology. Such treasures! There was even a thick book on American literature—which had been quite an eye-opener. He especially enjoyed the stories written by a man named Mark Twain and had read them over and over, chuckling at the man's talented use of words.

Of course, all these books were strictly forbidden by his sect. That very fact, to his shame, made the reading of them even sweeter.

He rationalized his self-indulgence with the fact that these textbooks would not be forbidden in an Old Order household. He had even overheard an Old Order teacher, a young man near his age, patiently explaining to a tourist that even though the Amish did not go to school beyond the eighth grade, their learning never stopped. He explained that many studied various subjects on their own, as he himself did in order to become a better teacher.

Levi sometimes thought he would enjoy being a teacher—but not in a Swartzentruber school, where the curriculum was so severely limited. He knew that he would soon be in trouble for trying to supplement the children's education.

The hour or so that he stole from time to time to read these books was a great luxury. It was, in his opinion, his greatest sin: this thirst for knowledge. He was ashamed of this vice. But still, he started a fire in the small woodstove he had installed against the chill of an early-spring evening, lit the oil lamp sitting on the table, and anticipated an enjoyable evening reading.

He was lost in the study of a drawing of the human muscular system when he heard footsteps on the stairwell. He glanced at the clock. It was nearly ten, much too late for the rest of the family to be stirring—unless there was an emergency. Perhaps something else had gone wrong with Daniel, or his mother. Perhaps it was Rose coming to him for help. Before he could get to the door, there was a loud knock.

He answered the door and his jaw dropped.

It was Zillah. The foolish girl had followed him out here.

The first thing he noticed was that she was wearing no prayer *Kapp*. He was seeing her hair unloosed for the first time. She had brushed it to a shimmering gold, and it hung down over her shoulders in waves. She looked stunning in the moonlight.

"May I come in?"

The only thing he could think to say was an abrupt "No!"

Her head jerked back, as though she had been slapped, and her eyes widened in shock. Zillah was not used to being refused, but it took her only an instant to regroup.

"When my father told me I would be living here for a

while, my mother and I spent all day yesterday sewing my *Nacht Rock*. I knew that if I was living here, I would have need of a beautiful new nightdress. It's pink, look." She began to unpin her overdress.

"You need to stop right there, Zillah," he said. "Do not remove one more pin."

Her hands stilled, and she glanced up at him with a confused expression.

He knew she would be wearing a modest new nightgown in a color that was forbidden to wear in public, but he had no desire to see the thing. It was not at all unusual for a mother and daughter to make these special nightdresses together, creating them specifically for the Swartzentruber tradition of *Uneheliche beischlof*—bed courtship—where a girl and a boy would chastely lie in bed together, talking and getting to know each other.

At least that was how it was *supposed* to be and often was, but he knew of a few cases where it had not been so chaste. These things were sometimes talked about in whispers during the young folks' singings. Yet the tradition went back so far with their people that it was seldom questioned by the Swartzentruber sect. The New Order Amish, on the other hand, strictly forbade it. At this moment, Levi was wishing desperately that Zillah and he were New Order Amish.

But this bed courtship, sometimes called bundling, was supposed to take place in the girl's bedroom, not the boy's. For Zillah to come to him like this was completely out of bounds.

"I thought we could talk about our future together," she said.

"We have no future to talk about, Zillah."

"Why not?" This came out as a whine, as though she were a little girl being denied a treat. She even stamped her foot. "I have been waiting on you for a long time, Levi Troyer. Nei-

ther of us is getting any younger. I have shown you every way
I know how that I have picked you for my husband. There is
not one girl in our church my age who is not already married.
Girls younger than me already have three or four babies."

"I am not *in lieb* with you, Zillah. I never have been."

"Why?" she demanded. "Why don't you love me?"

How did one tell a girl that although she was beautiful on
the outside, she was a mess on the inside? This was not something he knew how to do.

"Is it that nurse who came to the funeral?" Zillah demanded. "Do you care for her instead?"

This was going too far. He could not afford for Zillah to
start gossip.

"There is nothing between us. She is only a neighbor."

Zillah thought this over. "I am prettier than her."

He took hold of the door, anxious to close it behind her.
The careful dance he had done around Zillah's fixation on
him had been going on for years and he was sick of it.

"You should leave now, Zillah."

"Never mind about love." Zillah stepped closer and looked
up at him through slanted eyes. "I want you. That should be
enough. I want to bundle with you—even if you don't love
me."

The Swartzentrubers did not allow the tradition of *Rumspringa* for their young. There was no closing of their church's
eyes when a young person chose to run wild. But thanks in
part to the ancient tradition of bed courtship, some babies still
came suspiciously early.

For a moment, in spite of his dislike for Zillah, Levi felt
a wave of desire so strong he knew it must be a direct attack
from Satan. He had never wanted anything to do with Zillah,
but just for a moment he seriously considered ignoring the
consequences and simply doing as she wished.

Zillah read the momentary weakness in his face and her eyes once again took on that sly look he had known since childhood. It was like a splash of cold water. She was planning something—and she being Zillah, it was not good. Giving in to her could very possibly trap him for life. An Amish man did not abandon a woman he had impregnated. A few minutes of pleasure with her could buy him a lifetime of misery.

"No, Zillah." He shook his head and reached for the door. "You need to leave."

She saw that he had closed himself off from her and it made her furious.

"You will be sorry for this," she warned.

"I am certain you are right." He knew she would find some way to punish him. But he also knew that he would be a whole lot sorrier if he did as she wished.

She had stepped inside the room as they had talked. Too late, he realized that his temporary living quarters were open for her perusal.

"What have we here?" she said.

"Please leave, Zillah." He tried to block her view.

She sidestepped him and headed straight to the table where he had been reading. Unfortunately, the biology book was still opened to the pages explaining the human muscular system.

"You are not supposed to own things like this, Levi Troyer." She flipped a few pages. Then her eyes caught the other books on the bookshelf.

"Why, these are all textbooks." The satisfaction in her voice was infuriating. "You have been very *dumm,* my friend. You are going to be in so much trouble!"

He knew that short of physically picking her up and throwing her out, Zillah would not leave until she was good and ready. And when she left, she would have quite a tale to tell her father.

His mind, unbidden, flashed to the great gulf between her and Grace. They were about the same age, and yet Zillah was still not much more than a childish tattletale, and Grace was . . . well, Grace was so much more than Zillah could ever dream of becoming.

"What on earth do you want with all of these?" Zillah ran her fingers along the spines. "Why waste your time?"

Levi had asked himself that a million times. He gave her the only answer he knew. "It feels good to learn new things."

"New things?"

Well, that was the wrong answer. Individuality was a sort of sin to the Swartzentrubers. They dressed alike, drove buggies that looked alike, worshipped alike, cooked alike, and as far as he could tell, they were supposed to think alike. What he had just said could be considered dangerous and divisive.

"All of these are worldly books." Her voice was sanctimonious. "My father will want to know about this."

Levi wasn't about to beg her to keep his books a secret. It was exactly what Zillah wanted him to do, so that she would have something to hold over his head.

"Then tell him."

Zillah realized that she had reached a stalemate. She brushed by him and sashayed down the steps, humming a little tune, carrying toxic information for her father.

And there wasn't a thing in the world Levi could do about it.

chapter THIRTEEN

H e closed the door behind Zillah and prepared for bed by removing all his clothing. It was the same clothing he would wear tomorrow and the day after that until he could take his once-a-week bath.

Swartzentruber men, at least the ones from his church, were forbidden to wear underwear—except for long johns in the winter. Even then, if the long johns were store bought, they had to have the elastic removed before they were acceptable. Nor was he allowed to own any sort of pajamas.

As he lay between the rough sheets, he realized what he had to do. His family had endured enough. He would not be the reason for bringing more trouble down upon his mother's head. And he knew Zillah would most definitely make trouble if she could.

Knowing that he would not get any rest until he rid himself of the forbidden books, he threw back the blankets and dressed. Then he gathered a few pieces of kindling, some matches, an armload of books, and went behind the barn to start a small bonfire. With the barn between him and the house, the fire would not be visible to the women in there. He didn't want to frighten Rose or his mother, and he certainly did not want to give Zillah the satisfaction of knowing what he was doing.

He might as well destroy all the books tonight because the bishop would insist on it after he got an earful from Zillah.

Elizabeth was having a restless night and Grace was heating water for cocoa when she glanced out the kitchen window and saw flames coming from the direction of the Shetlers' barn.

Turning the teakettle down to simmer, she walked out onto the porch to get a better look. There was a definite blaze. Grace couldn't tell if the barn was on fire or if there was some sort of bonfire.

She glanced at one of the clocks in her grandmother's kitchen. It was eleven o'clock, definitely the wrong time to see a fire coming from neighbors who, considering they didn't have electric lights, probably went to bed with the chickens.

She debated whether to call the fire department but decided against it. She was still so new to this area that she did not know if having bonfires late at night might simply be some sort of strange custom the Swartzentrubers practiced.

Hurriedly, she made the cocoa and took it into her grandmother.

"Do the Shetlers ever deliberately set fires late at night?" She sat the cup down on the nightstand. "Be careful, this is hot."

"There's a fire there?"

"It looks like it's behind the barn, but it's a little too far for me to see clearly. Should I call the fire department, or go down and investigate?"

"Normally, I would tell you to call the fire department and the police. Sometimes vandals think it is funny to set an Amish barn on fire. But considering how out-of-whack things have been around there the past few days, it could be something as simple as Levi burning trash because he's behind in his chores."

"I think I'll drive by and check."

"Keep your windows rolled up, your doors locked, and make sure you've got your phone," Grandma said. "After all, there's still a murderer on the loose."

Grace slipped on her shoes, grabbed her keys and cell phone, and, just to be on the safe side, slung the medical basket Levi had made for her over her shoulder. It was best to always go prepared.

As she drew closer to Levi's farm she saw that the barn wasn't on fire. Then she caught sight of Levi throwing something on the fire and decided to stop and make absolutely certain all was well.

She parked away from the house so as to not awaken any of the inhabitants—particularly the hair-trigger crying of Daniel. Levi did not say a word of welcome when she walked over to him. No big surprise there.

"What are you burning?" she asked.

His face was illuminated by the flickering fire. He didn't look up.

"I was afraid something was wrong," she continued when he said nothing. "Grandma said sometimes vandals set fire to Amish barns. Is that true?"

"Sometimes barns burn. I do not know the reasons."

He shifted his weight, obviously waiting for her to leave, but she didn't want to leave. She wanted to know what he was doing, and frankly, she was beginning to enjoy—as her grandmother would say—rattling Levi's chain. Primarily because it was so easy to do.

"I thought you guys went to bed early," she said. "Why couldn't this have waited until tomorrow?"

He didn't reply but tossed something onto the flame—a book.

"Books?" she said. "You're burning books?"

He tossed another volume into the fire.

"Why in the world are you burning books?"

He still didn't answer.

"Look. I'm sorry for being so nosy, and I know I'm as ignorant as dirt about your people's ways, but in my world, you take old books to Goodwill, or a used-book store, or you use them to prop up table legs—but you don't burn them. And you especially don't bother to burn them this late at night! So excuse me if I'm a little confused."

The fire flickered up, and she saw that there was a sizable pile lying at his feet. A new thought struck.

"Are you burning porn, Levi?"

"What's porn?"

"Dirty books."

"No!"

"Well, then, what you're doing doesn't make sense. But then again, not much of what you do does make sense to me."

This, finally, got a rise out of him.

"Our lives might not make sense to you—but at least our tables are built so sturdily they do not require books to prop them up!"

"Was that a joke or an insult?" she asked.

"I was making a point."

"And it was a good one," she said admiringly. "Point taken!"

"It is harder to burn books than I thought," he muttered. "This is going to take a long time."

"What are they about?"

He seemed to be weighing the consequences of talking with her. Finally, he responded.

"History. Science. Mathematics. Biology." He ripped all

of the pages out of one of the books, crumpling them up and tossing them and the book's binding into the flames. The fire leaped up as it consumed the destroyed book. "There. That helped."

"Where did you get them?"

"I found them."

"Where?"

"A bookstore was throwing them away."

"So you got some books for free. That doesn't explain why you are burning them."

"We are forbidden to read worldly books like these."

"Textbooks on math and science are worldly? Why?"

"I do not know." He ran both hands through his sweat-drenched hair. It shoved his bangs off his forehead, revealing a face etched with regret.

There was something terribly wrong here. They were only books—the kind that could be purchased at a thrift store for pocket change. And yet it was obvious that burning these books was a great sacrifice on Levi's part.

The healer inside of her wanted to reach out to him, in spite of the fact that he did not want her here.

"Levi, what happened to make you start burning your books in the middle of the night?"

"An *Englischer* would not understand."

"Maybe not. But you could try me."

In the flickering firelight, she could see that he was weighing the wisdom of taking her into his confidence.

She got a whiff of acrid sweat coming off him. It was not the scent of a man who had simply worked hard all day. She had experienced this particular smell on the battlefield. It was the scent the body gave off when it was under tremendous stress.

"These books mean a great deal to you," she prompted.

"Yes." He nodded. "I have read every word of every one of them. But we Amish have a saying. It is from a line in our hymnal. *'Demut ist de Schonste.'*"

"And that means?"

"'Humility is the best virtue.' Studying these books is not a humble thing to do. I cannot allow myself to become like the *de Hochen,* the proud ones."

"And who are these 'proud ones'?"

"The *Englisch*. No offense."

"None taken."

"I cannot allow the bishop to throw this sin of mine in my mother's face. Not now. Not when she is so weak. None of this was her fault."

"So—if you can't read textbooks, what are you allowed to read?"

"The Bible, but only the German Bible—the one our ancestors read. We are not like the Old Order Amish. Some of them allow *Englisch* translations into their homes."

"That's all you can read? The German Bible? Nothing else?"

He thought for a moment. "We are allowed to read the book about our martyrs and the trials they endured."

"No magazines? No newspapers?"

"Very few."

"You love to read, but you are pretty much forbidden to read."

"It is wrong to love learning so much that I would defy my church's teachings. It is a weakness I should not give in to." He grabbed a shovel and moved the books around on the coals until the fire licked through them more efficiently.

She watched, wondering what sort of hold the leaders must have on their people to be able to deprive hungry minds of learning.

"So—do you read German well?"

"Not well."

"But you speak it."

"I speak Pennsylvania Deutsch. It is not a written language. High German is what our Bible is written in. It is different."

"So if you don't read the language of your Bible all that well, you sort of have to take your bishop's word for what it says."

"I should take the time to read High German better."

"So does that mean that Bishop Weaver is some kind of biblical scholar?"

"An Amish person would never claim to be a Bible scholar—that would be prideful."

"But he reads German well?"

"I don't know."

"So you have no way of knowing if what he is telling you to do is right or not?"

"I do not wish to talk about my bishop anymore, Grace. You are *Englisch*. You will never understand our ways."

She ignored his rebuff.

"I'm just saying—you have no way of knowing, do you? I mean, Bishop Weaver sounds and acts like someone with a pretty dark interpretation of the Scriptures."

He rested his hands on top of his shovel. "Are you a Bible scholar, Grace?"

"Well. No."

"Then you have no idea what you are talking about. You should go home now."

"Maybe I don't know a lot about the ins and outs of your . . . *Ordnung*. Did I pronounce that right?"

"Go home, Grace."

"I'm just saying . . . I could not live like you do, Levi."

"No one is asking you to."

"So, let's talk about something else. How are things in your house? Is everything okay over there?"

"My aunt will be leaving soon," he said. "The bishop has sent his daughter to care for my mother."

She could hear the unhappiness in his voice about the situation, but she didn't pry. She had pried enough for one night.

"Do you mind if I check in on your mom tomorrow?"

He hesitated.

"I won't say anything about tonight."

He seemed to be wrestling with the decision of whether to allow her to come back.

"I'm a nurse, Levi. I just want to make certain her wounds are healing. It doesn't appear that she intends to go to the doctor anytime soon. Besides," she said, "I'm sorry for talking about your bishop the way I did. That was out of line. I won't do it again. It's just that it hurts me to see a friend in pain."

"You may come and check my mother," he said. "But there is something you should know."

"What's that?"

"You and I will never be friends."

She knew she shouldn't be hurt, but his words stung. "I'll check on your mother tomorrow, and I won't speak to you unless spoken to."

"That would be wise," he said. "I am sorry. But we are not like the *Englisch*."

"That's quite an understatement, Levi." She pulled her keys out of her pocket. "I'll leave you to your book burning now."

chapter FOURTEEN

There was a strange hollowness in Levi after Grace left. Having her there beside him, even with all of her questions and arguments, had helped drain away some of the toxins over his confrontation with Zillah.

She had not understood the magnitude of what he was doing or what it meant to him. She did not understand that in many ways he was giving up hope as he threw those books onto the fire. But she had seemed to grieve a little with him anyway. She, too, saw no sense in what he had to do.

Watching her drive away, he realized for the first time that there had always been inside of him, growing stronger ever since Bishop Weaver had been put in as their leader, a small seed of rebellion that from time to time whispered from the depths of his soul that he might choose a different life from the one he was living.

It had not been a strong stirring—not enough to make him truly consider leaving the church—it had only been a thought now and then that would flit through his mind. He didn't have to do this. He could make a change.

He knew that this was one of the reasons he had held on to those books. Deep down he had harbored the notion that someday he could leave if he wanted to—and he would not be completely ignorant if he did.

He would never leave, of course. He could never bring himself to give up his family—and he would have to give up his family if he left the church. His mother would have to shun him just as she had shunned her sister and brother-in-law, as would all the other church members. Many of whom were close kin.

But sometimes he allowed himself to imagine his life as it could be if he were not Swartzentruber.

He stirred the ashes until he was certain that no one could determine what had been burned there. Then he wearily climbed the steps to his room above the workshop and fell into bed.

He knew he reeked of smoke. Many an Old Order Amish man would be standing beneath a warm shower right now, soaping the grime of the day off himself, before putting his clean body between clean sheets. An *Englischman* would think nothing of it at all.

But for Levi to even take a shallow bath in the family's tin tub would involve at least an hour of drawing water from the well and heating it on the stove. And he would be questioned by everyone in his house while doing so because it would be perceived as odd behavior unless it was in preparation for a wedding, a funeral, or a Sunday.

When he did justify taking the time to prepare a bath, he would be expected to share it with the rest of the family—the littlest ones going first, then his mother, and lastly himself.

He loved his mother and his family. He loved the rich earth beneath his feet, and he even enjoyed pitting himself against the weather and insects and all the things that could go wrong in farming—just for the pleasure of harvesting crops that he had planted with his own hands.

He also enjoyed watching a basket grow into something beautiful beneath his hands. He loved the carpentry work he sometimes got to do. But most importantly, he loved the Lord—or at least he tried very hard to. Unfortunately, in his mind, God looked a whole lot like Bishop Weaver.

It was hard to pray to a God who resembled the bishop, but he tried to pray every day anyway.

He knew that if he were a better Amish man he would not be struggling with these thoughts. He would accept his role and his place in life without question. He would find some nice Amish girl and settle down to produce children with her. There were many wonderful Amish women, not at all like Zillah. And yet so far, he had seen no one with whom he was willing to spend the rest of his life. He sometimes wondered why he had never seriously courted anyone, but deep in his heart he knew the answer.

Marriage with an Amish woman would mean that he could never allow himself to even think about leading a different life. He could never pull someone he loved away from the only church she had ever known.

He had often thought about the possibility of following his aunt and uncle in their decision to join the Old Order church. He would be allowed so much more freedom then. In his eyes, the Old Order Amish were quite a modern bunch.

If he and his family were Old Order, he would be allowed to put in a bathroom for his mother. He could use battery-operated flashlights. He could even purchase those amazing Coleman lamps that could illuminate an entire room. The light those things gave out—how bright they were—almost like daylight!

If he were Old Order Amish he could install reflective devices on his buggy that would make traveling much safer for his brothers and sister. If he were Old Order Amish he would be allowed to have a windshield on his buggy to cut the bitter cold in the winter, and he could even install battery-controlled flashing lights for more visibility. If he were Old Order Amish he would be allowed to use a generator that could power tools to make woodworking go so much faster, and he could even use a gasoline-powered weed whacker to make his farm look less overgrown. Oh, and a chainsaw for cutting firewood for the stove—what a luxury that would be!

But having these luxuries would mean he would be banned by all Swartzentrubers. They would tell him that he was going to hell, and for all he knew, they might be right.

Hell was a terrible thing. He clasped his hands beneath his head and stared at the ceiling as he imagined the great abyss that had been described to him during the three- to four-hour-long Sunday services. Hell was for eternity. Hell was a burning lake of fire. Hell was eternal darkness. And no matter how good he was, no matter how hard he tried, no matter how passionate his love for God and Jesus and his fellow man, he could never be sure that he wasn't going there. That was up to God himself.

Those religious people who claimed to know they were going to heaven were an arrogant bunch. Every Swartzentruber man knew that you worked hard, you prayed, and you followed the *Ordnung* to the letter. And if you were very, very lucky, when you died, if you had been good enough, you might go to heaven.

But until then, no one could be certain of their fate.

It was a puzzle, and one that he did not have the knowledge to solve. All he knew was that his best chance of escaping the fires of hell was to be the best Swartzentruber man he could be. For as long as he could stand it. And hopefully that would be enough.

He felt a great weariness descend as he imagined the next fifty or sixty years of his life.

As Grace pulled into her driveway, she saw a flash of something light-colored fleeing into the woods behind the house. She tensed, then forced herself to relax as she realized it was probably nothing more than one of the many white-tailed deer that frequented this area. Deer were thick around here, and they frequently fed at night. Unfortunately, the leftover hair-trigger sensibilities she had developed while dodging bullets in Afghanistan had caused her to be spooked more than once since she had come home by a deer bursting out of a thicket and running into the woods.

The first time it had happened, she and her grandmother were taking a slow stroll around the yard so Elizabeth could get some exercise. Grace had been so startled she had hit the ground, only to glance up and find her grandmother leaning on her cane and watching her with concern. "It's a deer," Elizabeth had said. "It won't hurt you."

Only last night the deer had decimated her grandmother's lilac bushes. Apparently lilacs were quite the deer delicacy.

Still, she hadn't seen whatever it was fleeing into the woods just now all that clearly.

For a moment, her instincts told her to call Sheriff Newsome—but the problem was, she no longer trusted her instincts. It seemed unfair to bother him with something that was probably nothing more than a frightened doe, combined with her own ongoing struggle with battle fatigue. The strange scene of an Amish man conducting a late-night book burning had not done her nerves a bit of good, either.

Yes, it must definitely have been a deer.

She shook off her concern and went inside to check on Grandma, whom she found sleeping with the archaeology book facedown on her stomach. Grace gently lifted it off, hoping not to awaken her. She didn't succeed. Grandma's eyes flew open.

"Is everything all right at the Shetlers'?"

"I suppose."

Grandma pushed herself up until she was propped up against the headboard. She patted the bed. "Come here and tell me."

Grace sat down and described what she had found, recounting most of the conversation she'd had with Levi. "He told me to go home. The last thing he said as I was leaving was that we could not be friends. It really wasn't necessary for him to say that. It was rude when I was only there to help."

"What I'm hearing troubles me," Elizabeth said.

"Why?"

"I know Levi well, and it is not like him to say something like that."

"That's what I'm saying. It wasn't necessary."

"He must be starting to care for you in ways that he shouldn't. He was warning you, for both your sakes, to stay out of his life."

"You're kidding."

"It would be a tragedy, Grace, for him as well as for you if he and you were to begin to care for each other. Levi is wise enough to see that and to stop things before they go any further."

"I've never so much as flirted with him, Grandma. What would give him the idea that I—?"

"If you had flirted, he would have dismissed you and never thought of you again. Unfortunately, instead of a flirt, you came into his life as the fine, strong woman you are. The very kind of woman Levi could fall in love with. How do you feel about him?"

Grace shrugged. "He's Amish."

"And beneath those Amish clothes and that Amish hat, he is one of the finest men I have ever known. You cannot imagine how true he would be to the woman he chose. He would take care of her with the last breath in his body. I'm warning you, Grace, once Levi falls in love, it will be a terrible thing if it is with someone he cannot love for the rest of his life."

Grace was too stirred up to sleep. Grandma's warning had upset her. Why did everything have to be so complicated? Why couldn't she just have a normal, friendly relationship with Levi and his family without all this dark, brooding emotion swirling about her?

She changed into pajamas, went back downstairs, and checked in the refrigerator for a snack. She ended up with yogurt. Then she went into the living room and sat down on the couch, hoping to veg out for a few minutes and not think about anything important.

She clicked on the television, turning the volume down low so it wouldn't disturb Grandma or Becky, and thumbed through the few channels they could get with only an antenna. Either it was not a priority to the cable companies to come out this far, or Grandma simply thought four channels were enough—Grace didn't know.

She turned the volume down even further and sat staring at a talk show host, barely noticing what was happening on the screen. Nothing she saw could erase the image that was emblazoned on her mind of Levi burning his books.

She had been around men all her life. She had eaten with

them, joked with them, fought beside them, and dated some of them. But Levi affected her in a way she couldn't define and after what Grandma had just said, it made her extremely uneasy.

She finished her snack and turned off the TV.

This thing with Levi was messing with her head.

Then she heard her grandmother's quiet, soft voice once again praying aloud.

It hit Grace how often she relied on her own brain and knowledge and strength to figure things out, and how infrequently she relied on talking to God. She realized how often she had comforted herself with the knowledge that her grandmother was praying daily for her. Hearing Elizabeth's voice talking things over with God while she wished for cable television shamed her. It occurred to her that there was absolutely nothing she could do with her time right now that would be more productive or make more sense than to go upstairs and have a long talk with God.

When she got to her bedroom, she knelt on the wooden floor beside her bed. It had been way too long between prayers. The most she had said to God recently were what she thought of as her "over-the-shoulder" prayers—brief flashes of supplication for herself or her family. Those prayers, she knew, were important, but they just didn't carry the emotional satisfaction of a real conversation.

"I'm so sorry, Father." She sighed. "I can't help but wonder why You put up with me, why You keep caring about me when I don't even bother to say good morning to You most of the time. But thank You so much for always being there, ready to listen."

It struck her that her knees were really beginning to hurt her as she knelt upon the hard oak floor. She decided that if her grandmother could pray lying on her back in bed, perhaps it would be okay if she just eased up off her knees and sat on the edge of the bed.

"It's like this, Father. I feel pulled toward Levi in a powerful way, but I don't know why. Besides that, I'm not in real good shape emotionally, and I don't trust my feelings."

She realized that her back was growing uncomfortable with nothing to support it. She scooted over until she could rest her back against the headboard. That was definitely better.

"I'm grateful to be home, Lord, but I can't seem to hear a jet flying low overhead without ducking and taking cover. Sometimes when I fall asleep, I have nightmares. I haven't even told Grandma about them because I don't want her to worry, but I suppose You wouldn't mind if I talked about it with You. I mean—You were there, too. You know what it was like, and no one else around here does. No one else I can talk to about it."

She picked up a pillow and hugged it to her chest.

"Do You remember that night when my friend Derek, the rest of the Dustoff crew, and I flew straight into that valley to pull out those four soldiers? I forget the name of the valley, but I remember those men and how badly they were wounded, and how all of us who went to extract them were disobeying direct orders and didn't care. None of us could bear listening for one more second to the sound of the captain's voice on the ground begging us to come get his wounded men. Frankly, Lord, I didn't care if that coward of a commander we had *did* keep telling us we weren't allowed to go out because the conditions on the ground were 'too hot' for us to fly into. I had to go get those soldiers. I just *had* to, and so did Derek and the rest of the crew."

A hot tear streaked down her cheek. She wiped it away.

"Do You remember how easy that decision was for all of

us? We didn't walk out to the copter, debating whether or not we should disobey orders. We ran! There were soldiers in trouble calling out for us!

"Derek landed us smack in the middle of all that mess, and we got those men out even though the copter took heavy damage. I remember how we landed at Bagram Air Base with smoke pouring out of the engine and hydraulic fluids leaking. Half the base were cheering us because they had heard what that commander had said—and they knew we had made the right decision, even though if the base had been thirty seconds further, we would have had to crash-land 'outside the wire.' But with Derek's nerve and skill, and Your answering our crew's prayers, we made it in. And we saved those soldiers' lives."

Another hot tear slipped down her cheek, and she wiped it away. Its very presence irritated her. She was *not* a crier.

"That's who I am, Father, and that's what I do. I'm the one who goes in, even if there's heavy fire, to save lives. Here in Ohio—even though I know that's where I belong for now— I'm just not sure of who I am."

She laughed a little. "But there's one thing I'm absolutely certain of. I definitely don't have the makings to become an Amish man's wife, and Grandma seems to think that's where I'm headed if I don't forget about Levi real soon."

She slipped into a cross-legged position. "So what am I supposed to do? I can't just ignore the guy—I'm treating his mother. But I know Grandma's right. That is not a man to trifle with. He's too serious, and he's too decent."

She placed the pillow beneath her head and stretched herself full out upon the bed. The longer she talked, the more a tightly wound spring inside of her seemed to uncoil.

"I know Grandma has been praying for me to meet a good man. And frankly, I find it very strange that I spent all that time over in Afghanistan with men who were my age practically coming out my ears—and the only thing I felt toward any of them was friendship. Now I show up here in Holmes County, where the median age of men appears to be about sixty, and I find myself unable to think about anything else except a noncommunicative Swartzentruber who burns books and wears his hair down around his ears." She crossed her hands behind her head. "Unless You have a really good plan up Your sleeve, Lord, none of this makes sense to me."

She closed her eyes. "Of course, not a whole lot You do does make sense to me. I guess that's why You're God and I'm not. I'm really glad I'm not. I much prefer Your being in charge."

It seemed as if she had closed her eyes for only an instant, but she awoke two hours later feeling more refreshed and at peace than she had felt in ages.

The first thing she did was check on Elizabeth, who was sleeping peacefully. Then she went back upstairs.

It seemed a shame not to use the extra energy the nap had given her in a productive way. She decided she would at least make a stab at sorting out a few things in the extra bedroom her grandmother used for storage.

As she considered the best way to start, she noticed, at the top of the stairs, that a small painting that had been propped up on a shelf was gone. It had been nearly hidden by a silk flower arrangement, but it had caught her eye as one of the few decorations her grandmother had that she really liked.

Perhaps Becky had liked it, too, and had taken it into her room.

Grace opened the door to the storage room and discovered it wasn't quite as junky as she remembered. Perhaps Becky had moved things around, but it seemed slightly emptier than the last time she had been in there. Elizabeth had not been in there because she was not allowed to climb steps yet.

One thing she could pinpoint that was missing was an ornate gilded mirror that had hung on one of the walls.

She walked over to the wall and checked. Sure enough, the wallpaper where it had hung was a brighter color—she wasn't just imagining things. Evidently, Becky was redecorating her room and had decided to go shopping in the storage room. Fair enough. Becky was the one who had lived with these things most of her life, not her.

As she looked around the room it occurred to her what an odd mishmash of objects were here—as though a crazy person had decided to go through very ancient Dumpsters. There were old movie posters on the wall, a red plastic radio on a table, quilts with oddly shaped pieces stitched together every which way flung over the bed. A box of old photograph albums lay on the floor. She had glanced at them a few days earlier, and they were of people she had never seen and who bore no resemblance to her family. Some even wore Civil War uniforms, but to her knowledge, none of her ancestors had ever fought in it.

Brushing that thought aside, she picked up a squatty little clock and blew the dust off. Beneath the clock was a small Navajo-type rug. Against the wall were boxes so stuffed with old magazines and comic books that some of the boxes had given way and were now spilling their contents out onto the floor. And then there were the creel baskets, old ones, at least a dozen of them, hanging on the wall.

It was a little too much to take this late at night. Finally tired enough to sleep, she gave a great yawn and headed back down to the couch. She would deal with this another time.

chapter FIFTEEN

L evi awoke the next morning and prepared himself for another day of making a living from the land. He missed his stepfather's help. Last night had taken a toll on him. Four hours of sleep was simply not enough. Even though he was young, the heaviness of his heart this morning made his body feel old.

He dreaded going to the house for breakfast and having to face Zillah, but there was no way around it. Someone would come looking for him if he didn't appear. His aunt was probably already dishing breakfast out onto the table.

He hated that things had become so complicated. The simple life that so many *Englisch* people seemed to think the Amish lived was exceedingly hard to maintain.

After milking their two cows and doing all the other morning chores, he stomped the dirt off his feet and entered the kitchen. The scene he walked into was a pleasant one. Daniel was curled up asleep on his little pillow in the middle of his mother's bed, Rose was frying potatoes and sausage, and Zillah was setting out the peanut-butter-honey spread, but the big surprise was that *Maam* was up and standing at the dry sink, slicing bread. She grimaced when she placed a plate on the table, but she gave him a brave smile before seating herself at the table.

157

"Good morning, my son," she said. "Did you sleep well?"

"Very well." He looked Zillah straight in the eyes as he answered. He didn't want to give her the satisfaction of knowing he had been up half the night.

"Are you sure you slept well?" Zillah asked innocently. "I thought I saw your light burning for quite a while last night. I thought you must be reading."

"I had nothing to read," he replied.

His mother glanced between them.

"Henry is bringing the children this morning," she said brightly. "Rose will be returning home with him."

"I will be glad to see the children again," he said, "but sorry to see you go, Rose."

"I will miss both of you." She pulled the cast-iron skillet from the woodstove and scraped the fried potatoes into a blue bowl. "But I am missing my *Kinner* as well. Besides, now that your mother is feeling better, it is time I leave. I would not want to cause problems in your church by remaining here too long."

"With the children here to help me," his mother said, "I should be fine."

"With me here, you mean," Zillah reminded her.

"Oh, I am sure you will be able to go back to your home soon. Albert and Jesse are good workers. Even little Sarah will be a help."

So—his mother did not want her here, either. That was interesting. It was probably why his mother was trying so hard to pretend to be stronger than she was. Had she known about Zillah's late-night visit to his room?

His uncle Henry wasted no time coming for his wife. Levi heard the buggy just as they were lifting their heads from prayer.

The children burst through the door, and all became chaos

for a short time until they got settled. At four, Sarah was determined to climb into her mother's lap, still swollen from the surgery.

"Come here to me, *Liebe*." Levi lifted Sarah into his own arms. "I have missed you and your brothers. Did you obey your cousin?"

"We did," Albert said. "But it is better to be here. I was worried about the chores."

Levi laughed and ruffled the boy's hair. "Of course you were, little farmer!"

"I saw a bird on their farm that I have never seen before," Jesse informed him.

"If you draw and color a picture of it, perhaps I can name it for you," Levi suggested.

"Hello, Henry," Rose said from across the room.

"It is good to see you again, wife," Henry said.

Levi knew that if his aunt and uncle were *Englisch,* they would probably hug or kiss one another, but he noticed that their eyes lit up when they saw each other. It was good to see a husband and wife still in love.

"Will you soon be ready to go?" Henry asked.

Rose looked around. "I should feed the children first."

"Our daughter has already fed all of us well," Henry said proudly. "She is nearly as good a cook as her mother, but not quite as good I think—not yet."

"And our son-in-law?"

"Staying at the *Haus* with us, helping feed both our livestock and his."

"And our other *Kinner?*"

"Healthy but probably already missing their cousins. They played and worked well together."

"It is a shame," Rose said, shaking her head, "that they will not see each other again so easily."

"It's your own fault," Zillah said archly. "My father says you should not have left our church."

There was a pained silence around the table.

"It was not a decision quickly or easily made," Henry said, calmly and firmly. "You should not speak your mind on something you know little about."

"Boys," Rose said, "your beds are freshly made up for you, and Sarah—you will be sleeping with Zillah."

"No!" The little girl looked at Zillah in alarm.

"Now, Sarah," Rose said, "it is only for a short time."

"No, no, no, no!" She began to scream, and her screams woke the baby, who began to howl.

"Now see what you have done, Sarah," Zillah said angrily. "You have made Daniel cry."

"I've never seen Sarah act like this," *Maam* said.

Zillah stomped over to pick up Daniel. Not yet knowing his need to be held in an upright position, she settled into the rocking chair, plopped him down over her knees, and began to pat his back. He vomited all over the bottom of her dress.

With the exception of dandling other women's babies at church, Zillah had never had the care of younger siblings—unlike so many girls her age. Instead of taking it in stride, she let out a gasp, handed the baby to Rose, and fled upstairs.

"This is not going well," Levi observed.

"Not well at all," Rose agreed, grinning slightly.

"Are you ready to go, wife?" Henry said.

"I'll go get my things," Rose said. "I have already packed."

She came back downstairs in a few minutes. To everyone's surprise, Zillah was directly behind her, clothed in a fresh dress and carrying her own bundle of clothing.

"I want to go home, too," Zillah said.

"Already?" Claire asked.

"Yes. I want to go. Now."

No one said a word of protest.

"I'll ride with you and Rose," Zillah informed Henry.

Henry looked uncomfortable. "Could you take her, Levi? It's a long ride home and if I remember right, Bishop Weaver's place is in the opposite direction."

The last thing Levi wanted to do was spend any more time with Zillah—but he could not turn down his uncle's reasonable request. His uncle's horse was not young. It could handle the five-mile distance, but it would be cruel to make it have to go all the way to Bishop Weaver's and then back. Besides, the fact that Zillah wanted to go home so soon was an enormous blessing. He did not want to give her time to change her mind! For the first time, he was grateful for Daniel's digestive problems.

Grace was surprised to find the children all home again and Rose, Levi, and Zillah gone. Claire made no explanation, but she did send the children upstairs to play after Grace had greeted them.

"Would you like for me to take a look at your incisions?" Grace asked. "I'd feel better if I knew there was no infection. Those bandages have been on there a little longer than they should."

"I would like that," Claire said. "But how much do you charge?"

"What is it with you people?" Grace grumbled. "Levi was determined to pay me for taking him to Columbus, and now you want to pay me for something as simple as making certain you're healing properly." She opened up her medical basket. "I'm not charging anything, okay? Just relax."

"But you're *Englisch*."

"Is that a crime?"

"No." Claire looked puzzled. "It is no crime."

"Look, I know you don't go to the doctor unless you absolutely have to. I know it's an ordeal to hitch up your buggy and go all the way into Millersburg to the hospital. I happen to have the skills to determine if things don't look right, and I have a car to take you to the hospital if it is necessary. Frankly, Claire, I'm here to make certain your kids aren't orphaned on my watch—even if I am *Englisch*."

"So who put antifreeze in your oatmeal this morning?" Claire asked.

Grace looked at her in astonishment. "Where did you hear that?"

"Levi said it yesterday when I was in a bad mood. He said it is a phrase that the *Englisch* use. What is antifreeze?"

"Not something you want to put in your oatmeal." Levi was quoting her? Maybe Grandma was right. Maybe she did need to stay away from him.

"I accept your offer, Grace. Thank you. It was embarrassing having a man doctor deliver Daniel. It is much easier being seen by a woman nurse."

"Nurse practitioner," Grace corrected her automatically as she pulled fresh bandages out of the basket Levi had created for her.

"What did you say?"

"It doesn't matter. Let me help you get undressed."

After completing her examination and replacing the bandages with fresh ones, Grace snapped off her gloves, pleased with what she had seen.

"I'm very impressed," Grace said. "You're healing better and faster than I had hoped. You seem to be in a lot less pain than what I had expected."

"Having my sister here was a great comfort. She took good care of me."

"I'm sure she did." Grace put away her stethoscope. "Now, if you'll just tell me where the bathroom is, I'll wash up."

"We have no bathroom," Claire said. "It is not permitted. But you may wash your hands in the dishwater Rose poured before she left."

Grace had washed up in more primitive situations, but once again, she was puzzled by yet another religious restriction. How could having or not having running water in a home make a difference to one's salvation?

As she dried her hands on a nearby dish towel, she took a good look around the kitchen and noticed something else that was missing besides a sink with faucets.

"Where is your refrigerator?"

"They are forbidden."

"But I saw propane-powered refrigerators at Lehman's Hardware once. Grandma said the Amish use them."

"Yes, but not Swartzentrubers. Our *Ordnung* does not permit refrigeration."

"How can you feed kids without a refrigerator?"

"We just always have."

No running water. An outdoor privy. No electricity. No refrigeration. How did these people manage to survive? Let alone raise healthy children?

"I'm going to take Grandma into town today to pick up a prescription. Is there anything I can get for you?"

"Oh no," Claire said. "You have already been too kind."

"Are you sure? Bread? Milk? Eggs? We always seem to be running out of those at our house."

"Really? *Englisch* people run out of milk, bread, and eggs often?" Claire shook her head with pity. "That is sad."

"Don't you?"

"Seldom." Claire brightened. "Rose made eight fresh loaves of bread yesterday. That will last us several days. I will be well enough to bake my own by then—except women from church will probably continue to come by for a while, so I might not need to."

"What about eggs and milk?"

"We have our two cows, so there is always plenty of fresh cream and milk and butter cooling in the spring *Haus*. And our chickens are laying well. We can hardly eat all the eggs we get. In fact, perhaps you would like to take some home with you. Elizabeth has always liked it when we have an overflow of eggs. She says that our chickens have nice, healthy, orange yolks instead of the pale yellow yolks of store-bought ones. She says it's because our chickens scratch in the dirt for bugs instead of being locked in wire cages being fed nothing but chicken feed. I would not know about that. I have never bought eggs from the store."

"Could I pick you up some canned stuff, then? Food that doesn't need refrigeration, like some Campbell's soups? Rose won't be here to cook for you. Having a few cans of soup on hand when you're not feeling well is nice."

"That is true, but I still have fifty quart jars of beef vegetable soup remaining from the two hundred quarts that I canned last August using up the leftovers from my garden."

The nurse in Grace was finding this conversation extremely interesting. With nutrition like this, no wonder Claire's incision was healing so well.

"How many quarts of produce did you can last summer, total?"

Claire thought for a moment. "Including pears and peaches and cherries from our orchard?"

"Sure."

"And grape juice from our grapes, and tomato juice?"

"Why not?"

"Counting all the apple butter, too—a little over fifteen

hundred quarts. I think there's about three hundred left. That should get us through until our garden and orchard can produce again."

"What about meat?"

"We butchered a pig and a steer and many chickens last fall."

"How did you preserve that?"

"I put up four hundred quarts of cooked meat when the winter got cold enough to butcher. Canning meat makes it very tender." Claire smiled, remembering all the good food she had put up. "That roast beef is handy coming up out of the cellar in the middle of winter. I make noodles and mix it with the beef and gravy and serve it over mashed potatoes. It is *appeditlic*—delicious. The children love that on a cold day. We smoked most of the pork—sausages, hams, and bacon."

Grace was fascinated with the abundance and variety of Claire's pantry.

"Potatoes?"

"Several bushels left in the cellar."

"Apples?"

"Two different varieties in the cellar. Oh, and I have some cabbage and winter squash down there, too."

"Don't you at least have to buy sugar?"

"Not much. Abraham kept bees. We mainly use honey for sweetener."

"Coffee?"

"Not so much. We mostly drink special teas that I make. Clover blossom and sassafras root are my favorites. They are very healing."

"You're making me hungry, Claire."

"I'm sorry. I think we still have some of Rose's fried potatoes left, and there's some sliced bread and jam. Oh, I forgot. I made fifty pints of jam. Most of it from elderberries the children and I picked down by the creek. Elderberries keep colds and sore throats away. Did you know that?"

"No, I did not know that."

"I will go get you some—there are several pints left." Claire started toward the door.

"Some other time, Claire." Grace stopped her. "If you're sure there's nothing that you need—and it certainly sounds like you don't—I'll go ahead and leave. Grandma was getting herself ready for a doctor's appointment when I left. I need to run by the grocery store afterward to pick up a few things and I promised her we could stop at Coblentz afterward and pick up some more fancy chocolates for her. It seems like she's been craving sweets like crazy ever since her surgery."

"Chocolate?" Claire's voice rose.

"Would you like me to bring you some?"

Claire's shy smile said it all.

"A woman who has been through everything you have should most definitely have some chocolate. I'm sorry I didn't think of it sooner."

"Thank you."

Later that day Grace found herself prowling Rodhe's IGA in Millersburg trying to find something to cook for supper, but she couldn't get the idea of Claire's homemade vegetable beef soup out of her mind.

There had been a time when a can of commercially made soup would have been fine with her. Now the only thing she could think about was wishing she knew how to make her own vegetable soup from scratch, just like Claire.

What other changes would she end up making if she continued to hang out with the Amish?

She had a feeling those changes, if they came, would be good ones.

chapter SIXTEEN

Considering everything that had happened, Levi found it a little strange that Zillah seemed in such a good mood, chatting pleasantly with him as they traveled the three miles to her house.

He clucked his tongue, willing his horse to go faster as Zillah talked about the dress material she had purchased for an upcoming wedding in which she would take part. He did not know if she was choosing the subject of weddings deliberately or if the only thing on her mind right now was how good she would look in her new dress.

With his horse team standing idle, Levi did not want to tarry. He needed to get back into the fields as soon as possible.

Ezra Weaver was walking from the barn to the house when Levi brought his horse to a stop. The bishop saw that Zillah was with him, and Levi could tell that he was not pleased to see her being brought back so soon.

"Your mother is feeling better?" the bishop asked.

"Much better," Levi said. "We will be able to manage by ourselves now. My mother did not want to keep Zillah from her work here longer than necessary."

"Does that mean her sister is gone?"

"Rose left with Henry this morning."

"Good." The bishop was visibly pleased. "The babe is doing well?"

"Very well, thank you."

Levi helped Zillah retrieve her things from the back of the buggy and then he set the various bundles on the ground at the bishop's feet. With any luck, he might be able to leave without Zillah causing a scene.

"Is there word from the sheriff?" Bishop Weaver asked.

"I have heard nothing."

There must have been a tinge of bitterness in his voice that the bishop picked up on.

"Vengeance is mine, saith the Lord," the bishop quoted.

"Truly said. There is enough worry in each day now with my stepfather gone."

"You need for me to send men to help?"

Part of Levi wanted to shout, "Yes!" but he did not want to appear weak.

"I can take care of my family."

"Good."

Zillah had evidently tired of the pleasant conversation between her father and Levi. Either that or she was tired of being ignored. Zillah, unlike any other Amish woman Levi had ever known, was seldom happy unless she was the center of attention.

She butted in, her voice high like that of a child tattling to a teacher. "Levi keeps forbidden books in his room, Father."

"Is this true, Levi?" Bishop Weaver asked.

"I have no books in my room, except the Bible."

It was true. Thanks to the bonfire last night, there were no books in his room except his stepfather's German Bible, which he was planning on attempting, once again, to read.

"He is lying, Father." Zillah reminded him of the small,

spoiled girl she used to be. "He does have books in his room. I saw them with my own eyes . . . while I was cleaning."

Levi chose not to correct her. It was fine with him if the bishop believed his daughter's lie that she was cleaning his room.

"He had books on all sorts of forbidden things. There was one that was lying open and it had a picture of a man with no skin on."

"It was a book on biology," Levi tried to explain. "The picture was that of the muscular structure of a human."

The way Zillah had put it made it sound so much worse than it was.

"Did my daughter truly see these things?" the bishop asked.

"Yes," Levi admitted, "but I burned them after your daughter pointed out to me how wrong it was to own such books."

"It should not be up to my daughter to point out your wrongs," Bishop Weaver said. "You are a baptized believer. You should know right from wrong."

"I am very sorry."

"Then that is good. You have confessed your sin to me, and you have rid yourself of those evil things. You are still young and sometimes young people's judgment is not good. That is why you must leave it up to your elders to guide you. We will speak of it no more. There will be no need to confess your wrongdoing to the congregation on Sunday."

"Thank you, Bishop."

"Come along into the *Haus,* Zillah," the bishop said. "Your mother will be glad of your help."

Levi's heart lifted. It was over. He had made it.

And just at that moment, as the bishop and Zillah were headed toward their house, the unthinkable occurred. It was something so terrible that Levi could hardly believe it was happening.

The secret prepaid cell phone that he had purchased at Walmart two days after his stepfather's murder, the cell phone he had paid the clerk to show him how to use, the cell phone he had asked the clerk to program to 911 only, the cell phone he intended for no frivolous use, the cell phone that no one on earth besides the clerk knew that he had, the cell phone to which no one on earth had been given the number—

That forbidden cell phone began to ring. And it rang. And rang.

He had never heard it ring before, and a distant part of himself wondered at the amazing amount of noise the tiny thing could make. The sound pealed out, splitting the quiet of the early morning. And it was not just any normal ringtone— no, it was some sort of rock-and-roll music the young clerk had chosen to program into it, probably as a joke.

Bishop Weaver froze in midstep.

Zillah whirled around, her face lit up with pleasure at his predicament.

Levi scrambled to pull the phone out of the top of his sock where he kept it. He fumbled with it, trying to turn it off. The clerk had shown him which button to push, and he remembered how, but in his nervous haste he felt as though he had sausages for fingers.

Finally, finally, he managed to press the right button, and the thing stopped its screeching. But the damage had been done.

"You keep a telephone in your trousers?" the bishop asked.

"In my sock," Levi said miserably.

"And why do you keep this forbidden instrument upon your person?"

"In case there is another emergency like there was the day my stepfather died. Only for that."

"And you think God is not able to take care of emergencies?"

Levi felt a great bitterness welling up, thinking about his mother lying alone, bleeding, while he raced to Grace's for help. With this cell phone, he could have saved many minutes and would not have had to leave his mother and siblings alone.

"God was not much help the night of my stepfather's murder. It was Grace Connor who came to my family's rescue."

He didn't mean to say it. He was not even aware that he was harboring such thoughts. The words came out of nowhere and sounded blasphemous even to his own ears.

"This is something you will need to repent of. I will expect your confession come Sunday." The bishop frowned so deeply, his shaggy white eyebrows came together. "And you will dispose of that pocket telephone before then."

Levi did not agree to get rid of it—nor did he disagree. He simply clucked to his horse, did a U-turn in the bishop's driveway, and left. Thankfully, he was a mile down the road before the cell phone rang again.

This time, he remembered what the clerk had told him. He pressed the green button and listened to the voice on the other end.

"Susan?" a male voice asked.

"I am not Susan," Levi answered.

"Dwayne?"

He looked at the phone in disbelief before putting it back up to his ear. "I am not Dwayne."

"Who are you anyway?" the man demanded. "And what are you doing answering my wife's cell phone?" Then the voice grew belligerent. "Are you with my wife? Are you in that bar she said she was going with girlfriends? You better leave her alone, buddy, or I'll . . ."

Levi quickly pushed the off button and sat staring at the small telephone that barely took up half the palm of his hand.

He was not Susan, he was not Dwayne, he was not in a bar, and he certainly did not want anyone else's wife. It was, of course, what the *Englisch* called a "wrong number." He knew that, and he hoped the man got the numbers right the next time, and yet it had been upsetting to have someone threaten him when the stranger did not even know him.

The *Englisch* world was much too complicated. He wondered how they dealt with all they had to deal with. His own simple world was complicated enough.

He was so tired of thinking and had gotten so little sleep the night before that he fell asleep in the buggy and dozed most of the way home. Fortunately, his horse knew the back roads as well as he did, and he arrived home safely.

Levi's mother was washing dishes when he came home. Sarah was playing happily at the table with some wooden blocks he had made for her.

"Maam," Levi said, "you should not be up."

"I need to push myself a little," she said. "If I stay in that bed much longer, I'll lose the ability to walk. Did you get Zillah home safely?"

"I did."

"She is a strange one, that girl."

"I have always thought so."

"Sometimes I think some bad-tempered *Englisch* person must have left her on the bishop's doorstep," his mother joked. "And he and his wife were so happy to have a child, they never told us of it."

Daniel stirred and snuffled upon his wedge cushion. Levi went over to check on him. The little guy had just awakened and now gazed up at him with solemn blue eyes. Levi lifted him out of the cradle. The infant was sopping wet. No wonder he was awake!

There were a few clean diapers lying folded upon a cabinet where his aunt had placed them. He made his little brother comfortable with a fresh diaper. This was not a man's work, but it was quickly done, and he doubted it was easy for his mother to bend over right now.

He walked the floor with Daniel's fuzzy head tucked up against his chin. After the scene he had just been through, it gave him comfort to hold the warm little bundle. He was debating whether or not to tell his mother about what had just transpired at the bishop's. He hated to worry her with it, but in the end, he knew she had to be told, and it was best that it came from him.

"Albert and Jesse will be home from school soon and they can help you with the outdoor chores. I have been thinking about how we are to go about our lives now that Abraham is gone. It is time your two brothers rise earlier and help more with the milking—it will free up more time for you to be in the fields. School will be over in a few more days, and Albert is old enough to learn to work the horses now. He can help you."

"Albert is small for ten, *Maam,* and our four Belgians are so large."

"You were only ten when Abraham sent you out with a team."

"I remember. That is why I want to give Albert a couple more years to grow."

A look passed between them.

"You said nothing to me," his mother said. "I thought you were all right with it."

"I did what I had to do," Levi said, "but I don't think it's wise to send a child out to control four large horses. The summer he is twelve, we'll see."

"Our income will be less with Abraham gone, no matter how hard you work, but I can sell some of my quilts if we need to. Timothy's Mary told me after meeting last Sunday that she recently sold one of her quilts to a tourist for eight hundred dollars. Imagine someone spending that much for a quilt! Mine have a little more quilting and tinier stitches than Mary's. They might fetch an even higher price."

Levi listened miserably to his mother's chatting. She was trying to make plans for their family and to be strong for them, even though she had put Abraham in the ground such a short time ago. He hated to bring something else into the house for her to deal with.

"Oh, and my brother Eli came by today with a pot of cabbage and noodles and a strawberry pie that his Martha made for us. That Martha is a good cook. It is on the stove whenever you get hungry."

"What of your wounds?"

"We have had much company while you were taking Zillah home. Not only did Eli stop by, Grace came and checked on me. She put on fresh bandages, and she was very happy with how well I am healing. I don't know why, but she was interested in how much canning I had done last year."

He tried to act nonchalant when he asked, "Did she say if she will be coming back?"

"Grace is a healer," his mother said, knowingly. "She will not be able to stay away."

He kept his face turned away from her, not wanting her to see the mixed emotions that comment created inside of him. Yes, Grace was a healer—one with whom, unfortunately, he was realizing he wished he had the freedom to spend many hours.

"I need to sit down for a bit." His mother dried her hands on a dish towel, walked over to her rocking chair, sat down, and held out her arms. "Give me the babe."

He obediently placed little Daniel into his mother's arms. The baby could already distinguish the difference in smell and feel between him and his mother. Daniel began to root around like the little piglet he was. Levi handed his mother the shawl with which she covered herself whenever she nursed the baby. He busied himself with disposing of the wet diaper while she got herself and the baby modestly positioned.

He had put it off long enough. It was time to tell her.

"Something bad happened when I took Zillah home."

"Oh? *Was in dei Velt is letz?*" His mother's expression was troubled.

"What in the world is wrong?" Levi repeated. "My cell phone rang."

His mother's rocking stopped. "What cell phone?"

"The one I bought to call for help if any other bad thing happened to our family."

He waited for her to get angry, but that had been his stepfather's way—not his mother's.

"I understand," Claire said. "I very much wished to have a phone in my pocket when I was lying on the floor bleeding."

"The bishop thinks I am being rebellious."

"You are not rebellious, but it is his duty to watch over our souls. When he dies, he knows he will be held accountable with a stricter judgment for having had that heavy responsibility laid upon him. What did he say to you?"

"I left before he could say too much."

"You will have to destroy it now that he knows."

"I know."

"Who was it that called you?"

"Someone made a mistake. It was a wrong number."

"Do you know how to use this telephone?"

"Yes."

She rocked a little harder, thinking.

"How do you keep it—what do you call it—charged up?"

"The man at Walmart sold me a small solar-powered charger."

"Did this phone cost much money?"

"About the cost of one of our largest baskets."

"That is a lot to spend for something you'll never get to use." She rocked a little harder. "If you look inside my sewing basket there is a small piece of paper. Rose put it there. It has her telephone number on it. She said if I needed her, I could ask Grace to call and she would come. Please go get it for me."

"Do you need Rose? Is there something wrong that I don't know about?"

"It has only been a few hours, but already I miss her. I would like to use that forbidden phone—before you have to destroy it—to talk to my sister. I want to know if she arrived safely. I want to reassure her that I am all right. I want to tell her the good things Grace said about my recovery. It will lighten her heart. It seems a shame to throw away money on a telephone that was never used."

"That is true."

"In fact, it could even be considered a sin to pay good money for something and not use it."

Levi nodded. "That also is true."

"Is there anyone you wish to talk to, Levi? It is you who will be suffering the discipline of the bishop."

"There is no one."

"Then I will talk to my sister this one time—if she is

within hearing distance of her telephone shanty. Oh, and this evening would you come in a little earlier so that you can do a quick errand for me?"

"Of course. What is it you want?"

"Get one of our round market baskets, go down to the cellar, and fill the basket with two pints of elderberry jelly, two quarts of soup, a jar of those nice white peach halves, and . . . some of those sweet cherries we picked last fall over at the Beachys' farm. Also, some eggs. There are probably several freshly laid today."

"And what am I supposed to do with this basket?"

"Take it to Elizabeth's. After the conversation I had with Grace today, I suspect that girl hasn't the slightest idea how to cook. I'm afraid Elizabeth might be in need of some real nourishment."

chapter SEVENTEEN

The canned soup she had bought for supper was pale, watery, and far too salty.

Just as she had opened the refrigerator, wondering if there was something else she could fix for supper, there was a knock on the back door.

She was still a little nervous about the mysterious intruder who had turned the Shetlers' world upside down, and she approached the door cautiously. Then she saw it was Levi and opened up. He was standing back, holding a basket in his hand, and inspecting something above the porch.

"You have a gutter coming down," he said.

"Really?" Grace stepped outside onto the porch and craned her neck. "I hadn't noticed. I'll have to get someone to fix that."

"I will take care of it while I am here."

"You don't have to do that. You have too much work as it is."

"It won't take long and rain is coming."

"Last night, the weatherman said it would be clear."

"The weatherman is wrong," Levi stated. "There will be rain."

He handed her the large round basket he had been holding.

Grace was delighted. "You made another basket just for me?"

"No. Not especially for you, although you can keep it. This is the kind we sell to the tourists. I think Albert made it—you can look on the bottom later and see if his name is on it. My mother sent this for your grandmother. For some reason, she doubts that you are feeding her properly."

At first, Grace felt a hurtful twinge, then she bit down on a laugh. Claire must have equated her wonder and amazement over the quality of their food supply with a deficiency in Elizabeth's diet. Unfortunately, at least for tonight, Claire wasn't too far off.

Grace looked inside the basket. The rich-looking soup, fresh brown eggs, and ruby red cherries practically took her breath away. Claire had even tucked in a loaf of Rose's fresh bread. She closed her mouth against any protest. This was a feast, and she was hungry.

"Wow!"

"I will get your grandmother's stepladder now," Levi said. "Make sure Elizabeth gets a good helping of that soup. It is very nutritious."

"I will." She glanced up from her hungry perusal of the basket. "Do you need anything else?"

"No. I brought the necessary tools."

Becky still wasn't home from school and Elizabeth was napping. Grace heated the soup, sliced the bread, and ate supper alone—accompanied solely by Levi's knees as she watched him on the stepladder outside her kitchen window.

It was nice to have company—even if it was only Levi's knees.

Finally, just as Levi was finishing up and putting the stepladder away, Becky came home.

"Hi, sis." She lifted the lid of the kettle that Grace had

poured her own tepid soup out of, and Claire's rich soup into. "Smells good."

"It's from Claire."

"Where's Grandma?"

"She's asleep. Where have you been?"

Becky began to stir the soup. "I was studying at the library."

"Oh. Next time, call," Grace said. "I was worried."

"Why didn't you call me if you were worried?"

"I kept getting your voice mail."

"Oops." Becky checked her cell phone. "I had it turned off. I'm really sorry."

"I am finished." Levi stuck his head in the kitchen door. "But I saw something from the top of that ladder you two might like to see."

"Where is it?" Becky asked.

"Down by the fence, not far."

Grace was intrigued. "What is it?"

"I think you will enjoy the surprise."

Intrigued, the two girls followed him across their yard. One of Levi's cows was standing in the newly plowed field. Evidently, it had gotten out of the pasture where Levi usually kept it. Her head was down, and she seemed to be licking something in the weeds.

"She's a bad one for trying to go where she does not belong," Levi said. "Perhaps she was trying to bring you a present."

He climbed over the fence and shoved the high grass away so that Becky and she could see. There on the ground were two little brown and white calves so newborn that they were still wet.

"Twins," Levi said proudly. "I noticed the mother giving birth to them just as I was putting the final screw in."

One of the little things struggled to its feet and wobbled over to its mother, where it received the first nourishment outside of its mother's womb. The other calf was so much smaller and apparently still so weak from the birthing process that it was too wobbly to stand on its own.

"Why is that one so small?" Becky asked.

"It is a runt," Levi said. "Things like this happen when more than one calf is birthed at a time. It should be all right if we take special care of it."

Grace was in awe.

"Would you like to name them?" Levi asked.

"What are they?" Grace asked. "Boys or girls?"

"They are little heifers." When Levi saw the blank look on her face he added, "Girls."

"Twin girls," Grace said. "What about naming them Rose and Claire?"

"I doubt my aunt will be pleased having a cow named after her."

"What about your mother?"

"*Maam* will just be happy to have the income from the price they will bring at auction after they are weaned." He glanced up at the sky. "A storm is coming. I need to get these newborns to the barn. Could one of you help?" He hesitated, looking between Grace and Becky. "It will be a messy job."

"I'm already dressed in old clothes," Grace said. "I'll do it."

"We will need to hurry." Levi lifted the smallest one into her arms.

Even though it was a runt, the calf still weighed upward of twenty-five pounds and it was wet and slippery and it smelled a little funky. Grace tried to grab hold of it as she would a large puppy, but it was the most awkward living thing she had ever tried to hold.

"Here," Levi said, "like this."

He showed her how to hold the calf by hugging it close to her, its nose over the crook of her left arm, the tail end over the crook of the other, and the long legs dangling in between.

"Squeeze your arms tight around it," he instructed.

"Got it." She locked it into her arms by gripping both of her wrists with her hands.

Levi gently lifted the larger one onto his shoulders and then strode off toward his barn with Grace and the mother cow following close behind.

When Grace had volunteered to help Levi get the calf into the barn, she didn't know that she would be putting her life on the line. They were only halfway across the field when she saw lightning streak through the sky far to the south, followed by the ominous growl of thunder. A strong wind began to blow.

"We should hurry!" Levi shouted.

"No kidding!" Grace stumbled over the freshly plowed ground, carrying twenty-five pounds of calf.

Raindrops suddenly splattered the ground in front of her, and a torrential rain hit the barn just as she stumbled through the door. She sank to the dusty floor, the baby calf cradled in her lap. "That was close."

"Thank you. It is best if newborn calves do not get chilled."

"I prefer not to get chilled, too."

"Calves can get pneumonia. I don't think little Rose there could have stood a pelting of cold rain—and she would never have made it to the barn on her own."

"You're naming the weaker one after your aunt?"

"My aunt's feelings will not be hurt." He tossed an old towel to her. "Here. Let me take her while you dry yourself off."

Grace wiped off the front of her shirt while she watched Levi take both calves into a clean stall and rub them down with clean straw. Then he allowed the anxious-acting mother cow to come into the stall with him and her calves.

"Watch," he said as he stood back.

The cow began to lick the smallest one with great thrusts of her rough tongue.

"She certainly wants her babies to be clean," Grace commented. "Reminds me of my mom when she'd give me an emergency spit-bath with her handkerchief right before we went into church."

"Cleanliness isn't the only thing that is happening," Levi said. "The mother's tongue helps stimulate her calf's circulation. Watch."

Sure enough, in a few moments, little Rose struggled to her feet. Levi steadied her just long enough to begin to feed. She became stronger the longer she nursed. Soon, she was bumping her head against the mother cow's udder with as much enthusiasm as her stronger sister.

Grace hung over the walls of the stall, watching. "You're good at this." She tossed him the towel he had given her.

"I have spent a lifetime working with animals." He wiped off the back of his neck.

"You care about them?"

"Very much."

"I've heard that some Amish don't treat their animals well."

"Really?" He looked up at her from where he knelt beside the calves. "I have heard that some *Englisch* allow their pets to starve."

"Unfortunately, that is true."

"Some Amish are kinder to their animals than others, but they are usually cared for, if for no other reason than their financial value."

He exited the stall and fastened it behind him. The sound

of rain on the tin roof was thunderous. Grace stared up at the ceiling. There was no way she was going to be able to leave right now. Even running to Levi's house was out of the question. It would be like running through a giant waterfall. She would be soaked to the skin by a cold rain before she could even reach the porch.

And then there was the problem of lightning . . .

If Levi had stopped to think it through, he never would have asked her to help him take the calf to the barn. He should have carried both calves himself somehow—or carried the weaker one and let the stronger one wobble back on its own.

Now he was virtually imprisoned within his own barn with his lovely neighbor while waiting for the rain to stop. If it were only him here, he would simply brave the rain and go to his house, but he couldn't ask Grace to walk into a deluge.

What was he supposed to do with this *Englisch* woman while he waited? The very woman he had warned that they could not be friends? He had meant it. But somehow, without realizing it, every time he was around her they fell more into a comfortable relationship.

His mother should not have sent him over with that basket of food. Then he would not have seen the cow giving birth in the field. And then he would not have ended up here in this barn with a woman to whom he was not married—and could never be married.

"This is a really big barn." Grace looked around. "And really clean—as far as barns go."

"We use it to host church if our turn comes in the summer."

"And you used it for your stepfather's funeral."

"That is why it is still so clean. My people readied it for us."

Grace didn't seem bothered by the fact that they were out here alone. She wandered over to a large wooden box with a hinged lid in which he stored supplies.

"Do you care if I sit down?" she asked. "It looks as if we're going to be here a while."

It was the only decent place in the whole barn to sit, and it was more than large enough for the two of them. It would look silly if he continued to stand. He didn't know what else to do except sit down beside her. If this were a different barn and a different farm, there would be plenty of square bales of hay to sit upon—but not a Swartzentruber barn. Their hay was loose, as God intended, and it filled the loft.

He would take a seat upon the hard wooden surface of the storage box beside Grace. He was certainly used to sitting upon hard surfaces even if she was not. Every piece of furniture in his home was bare wood, too. No upholstery allowed. Swartzentrubers did not lounge around on couches and overstuffed chairs. Their only concession to physical comfort besides the thin mattresses upon their beds was the cushion his mother was allowed to place upon her rocking chair.

"So," Grace said, "anything you want to talk about while we wait for the rain to stop?"

"There is nothing I want to talk about."

"You prefer silence? I'm good with that." She leaned her head back against the stall.

He tried to do the same. Usually being in the barn during a rainstorm gave him a feeling of peace. But not now. Not with Grace sitting only two feet away from him. Every nerve in his body was on high alert.

He did not expect for her to be able to sustain the silence, but she surprised him. She gave a little sigh of contentment and seemed to be thoroughly enjoying doing nothing more than listening to the rain.

It bothered him that she wasn't saying anything. She was always the one with the questions and the comments. But now that they had all the time in the world to talk, she had decided to go silent on him.

It lasted for a full ten minutes. Still she didn't speak. Finally he could stand it no longer. The rain showed no signs of letting up. It seemed unnatural to sit beside someone and not say anything. Besides, there was one question that had been burning a hole in his mind ever since he had learned of her.

"What was it like for you in Afghanistan?"

She turned to look at him. "You really want to know?"

He thought about it. "Yes. I want to know."

"If you're sure."

"I'm sure."

"Well, it was noisy, and hot, and dangerous." She took a deep breath. "You could never let your guard down—ever. I flew in helicopters that were specially equipped for extracting wounded soldiers out of war zones. Sometimes we got shot at. Sometimes we saved lives. Sometimes we didn't. Many of the wounded soldiers we took out of there were still just kids. And as I fought to save their lives, I was always aware that somewhere back home there was a mother, or a wife, or a husband, or a grandparent, or a child hoping and praying that their soldier would come home safe and sound."

"When Elizabeth gets better, will you go back?"

"Probably."

"Why?"

"Because I'm good at it."

"But can you not stay here? Elizabeth worries about your safety so far away, and Holmes County needs good nurses, too."

"I could stay," she said slowly. "I've even been told that there might be a job for me in the ER at Millersburg."

"Then why would you not want to take that instead?"

There was a long pause. When she spoke, she seemed to be carefully measuring her words. "I think it best that I not stay here much longer."

He looked into her eyes, and the emotion he saw there saddened him. He knew exactly why she was hesitant to take the job in Millersburg. It would not be wise for the two of them to remain neighbors. He had been dead serious when he told her they could not be friends. Already this *Englisch* woman filled too many of his thoughts.

chapter EIGHTEEN

I t had been a long, long day. Church days were always long.
This one had been their Communion, foot-washing Sunday, and it had been held inside the member's home farthest
from Levi's farm.

And it had been made especially long because the bishop
had taken the opportunity to chastise Levi in front of the entire congregation. Even though he had already confessed his
sin the day he had taken Zillah home, Bishop Weaver had felt
the need to dredge up that he had kept his books and then had
informed the people of his cell phone.

Levi had no choice except to publicly confess his wrongdoings and to promise he would no longer indulge in such
forbidden things. No leniency had been given simply because
his stepfather had died recently. Death was a part of life, and
life had to go on, exactly as it had in years past.

At least his mother had not been there. She was not yet
strong enough to endure a three- to four-hour service sitting
on a backless wooden bench. But he had been forced to endure
the humiliation in front of Albert, Jesse, and Sarah, whom he
had taken to church with him.

It had been a long day. In so many ways.

Now it was already getting dark, and he always tried to

avoid being out in the buggy after dark, especially when the children were with him.

"Will we be home soon, *Bruder?*" Jesse asked, fidgeting on the backseat.

All of them were miserable. It had begun to rain, and he had put all the children in the backseat, where they huddled together.

The Swartzentruber sect was not allowed to have windshields on its buggies. Rain, sleet, or snow—they simply endured. Without a windshield, there was little he could do except put the children behind him and try to block the rain with his own body.

"We just turned onto our road. It will not be long now."

Jesse always had ants in his pants, but Levi had to admit this drive had felt particularly lengthy. He should have left earlier, but too many well-meaning people had felt the need to talk with him privately about the books and phone. It was part of their religion to try to keep one another on the straight path. He did not blame them, but it had made him late leaving.

The evening grew even darker as the horse plodded toward home. Levi wished it were just him in the buggy. Sometimes cars came around these curves too fast, and many times they did not see a plain, black Swartzentruber buggy until it was too late. There were so many accidents, and it seemed like there were more every year.

He had once overheard a law official tell someone that he was "sick of scraping Swartzentrubers off the road."

It had made his stomach churn to hear such a thing said, as though his people were nothing more than roadkill. And yet he understood the law official's frustration. He did not understand why his church leaders felt so strongly about not using the reflective triangles on the backs of their buggies, but there were Swartzentruber leaders who had chosen to go to jail rather than accommodate the law.

And so on this dark night, there was nothing protecting his precious little brothers and sister except the hope that God would be merciful and not allow any fast-driving *Englisch* driver to destroy the buggy and their lives.

"How much farther?" Jesse was tired and hungry. A whine had entered his voice.

"Soon. We are almost to the Connors' driveway and then . . ."

Before he could finish the sentence, he heard the sound of a car rushing toward them from behind a blind curve. He slapped the horse's rump with the reins and shouted for it to go faster, hoping to minimize the impact a little by not being quite such a slow-moving target.

He heard the car's brakes slam on and then the terrible sound of a vehicle skidding on the rain-slicked road behind him. The squeal of the tires drowned out everything else in his world. Even as he shouted at the horse, he braced himself for the impact, wondering if this was going to be his last moment on earth.

The sound of the crash was horrific. It took Levi a moment to realize that they had not been hit. And then he realized that somehow he had managed to get Sarah and her brothers out of the backseat and into the front with him, although he had no memory of doing so. His right arm was protectively around his brothers and Sarah was clinging to his neck.

A horn blared behind them as though it were stuck.

Shaken, he pulled Sarah's arms from around his neck, sat her on the seat beside Jesse, and climbed out.

"You children stay where you are. Albert, take the reins. Don't let the horse go anywhere."

The eerie sight that greeted him nearly made his knees buckle.

Grace's red car had plowed headfirst into a large maple tree growing near the road. The car's shattered headlights were still on, and they illuminated the rainy night in a fractured, crazy way.

It was not hard to see what had happened. Grace had deliberately jerked her car into the ditch and had plunged into a tree with so much force that the front of the car had crumpled up like a wad of paper.

Levi headed toward the wreck on a run. If Grace were dead he would never forgive himself. If she were crippled or hurt he would do whatever it took to see that she was cared for. But first he had to find her and see how much damage had been done.

She appeared to be trapped by a balloonlike thing, and she was not moving. Instead of struggling, she was lying completely, deathly still. The steering wheel had been shoved up against her by the tree, and the horn wailed on and on, hurting his ears and hurting his heart.

He did not know much about cars, but he could see that he would not be able to get her out without puncturing that heavy bag that held her trapped. It took every bit of his strength to wrench open the door. Then he pulled out his pocketknife and plunged it into the bag. As it lost air, Grace slumped to her side and began to slowly slide out of the car.

He caught her in his arms before she could tumble out onto the ground.

There was a large cut above her right eye, bleeding and staining her clothes as he clasped her against his chest. The car had traveled up an embankment, and he struggled to keep his balance as he carried her across the ditch and to his buggy.

As he waded through the darkness, the rain pelting him with the sting of needles against his face, he could see exactly why she had so little time to react. His buggy was all but invisible. The few strips of gray reflective tape that he was allowed were no help in the dark. The two kerosene lanterns that he was allowed to hang on his buggy were barely noticeable in the glare of the bright headlights.

Grace, in a split-second decision, had aimed at a line of trees instead of crashing into him. He was so grateful, he was trembling. From the looks of the crumbled nose of her car, he knew that the fragile buggy would have been a pile of matchsticks had she hit it with that much force.

She could not even have known it was him. There were other Swartzentruber families further down the road. There were no distinguishing features on his buggy to indicate who it was arriving home too late from Sunday services. She had nearly killed herself without even knowing for whom she was sacrificing herself. What kind of woman did something like that?

It was awkward climbing into the buggy with her in his arms, but he was so upset over what had happened, he felt as though he could lift the buggy and the horse all by himself if it would mean saving her life.

The thing he feared most was that there could be internal bleeding. He knew that ribs protected the inner organs. He also knew that sometimes there was great trauma if they broke and punctured something. Grace had taken a great blow to the chest. She seemed to be breathing all right, but one could not always tell this quickly if there was damage.

Once again he needed medical help and had no way of asking for it.

If only the bishop had not made him throw away his telephone. There would already be an ambulance on its way.

They would have a safe and fast way to get her to the hospital. Instead all he had was a buggy, a horse, and three children.

"Hurry, Albert," he said. "We must get her home."

Albert knew how to drive the buggy horse as well as any other ten-year-old Amish boy—and that was extremely well.

"Giddyup!" Albert shouted, and once again their driving horse felt the sting of wet reins being slapped across its rump.

The horse took off, jerking Levi against the back of his seat. They were at her house in a few heart-stopping minutes.

"Stay here," he said to the children. "Albert, you and Jesse care for your sister."

He had no doubt that they would obey. Their mother had taught them to respect his authority.

He raced up onto the porch and pounded on the door with his boot. It was a screen door, not particularly well fitted, and it banged with each kick.

No one came to the door.

Holding her body against his with one arm and one knee, he tried the doorknob. It was locked.

Frantically, he cast about in his mind for what to do if no one was home. Then the door swung open.

"Levi!" Elizabeth looked at the precious burden he was carrying. "Oh, dear God, please, no!"

For a moment, he was afraid he was going to have to call for two ambulances when he got inside. The pallor that came over Elizabeth's face was startling, but she managed to hold the door open so that he could carry Grace inside.

"She crashed into a tree," he explained, "to keep from running into us."

"Oh, dear."

He carried her to the flowered couch and laid her gently upon it. The blood from the head wound seeped onto the fabric, making one large red cabbage rose even larger.

"There are cloths in the kitchen," Elizabeth said. "You are faster than I am. Go bring me one. Wet it with cold water."

He ran to the kitchen and grabbed a dish cloth off the counter. He then turned knobs until he had a stream of cold water with which to moisten the cloth. So handy. So incredibly handy not to have to go outside and draw well water.

He wrung the cloth out, went back into the living room, and handed it to Elizabeth, who pressed the cold compress against the cut.

"Should we call an ambulance?" he asked.

"In a moment," Elizabeth said. "Let's see if we can wake her up first. She might not be pleased to discover herself riding along in an ambulance if she's only been knocked out for a few minutes."

Elizabeth took the compress away and examined the wound more closely. The bleeding was lessening, but it had not stopped completely.

Suddenly, Grace's eyes flew open. "What in the . . . ?" She looked around the room, trying to get her bearings. "What happened? And where in the world did you come from, Levi?"

He told her what had happened.

"Do you want to go to the hospital?" Elizabeth asked.

"Give me a minute." Grace tried to sit up. She winced and lay back down. "Somebody help me up."

Levi lifted her to a sitting position.

She explored her rib cage with her fingers. "I don't think any ribs are broken."

"That's good," Elizabeth said.

She wiggled hers toes and fingers. Lifted both legs.

"I think I'm okay, but I'm going to be very sore tomorrow. I don't think I need to go to the hospital."

"That big balloon thing saved your life," Levi said.

"You mean the airbag?" she said.

"Yes—the airbag."

"That's also probably what knocked me out." She wriggled her jaw back and forth. "I don't think any facial bones are broken, but I feel like I've been punched in the face by a professional boxer."

"It is beginning to swell a little," Elizabeth said.

"Where's Becky?"

"She called a little while ago and said she was helping collate a cookbook the women at church are putting together."

"She was supposed to come straight home from church tonight and be here with you," Grace said. "I wouldn't have gone out to pick up that gallon of ice cream you wanted otherwise."

"I told her I was fine and to stay and help."

"What time is it?"

There was a clock just a few feet in front of her on the wall.

"It is after eight," Levi said. "Can you not see the clock?"

"My eyes are still a little blurry."

"Perhaps they will get better if you rest them."

"How is my car?"

"Not good."

"I remember now," she said. "I came around the curve and then suddenly I realized I was going to hit someone. The last thing I remember is heading for the ditch. Did you have the children with you? Are they okay?"

"Because of you, they are fine."

"Where are they?" Grace asked.

"Outside in the buggy."

Elizabeth suddenly sank down into an armchair. Her pallor had returned.

"Go bring me her medication bottles that are beside her bed, Levi," Grace instructed. "All of them. Quickly."

He hurriedly brought the handful of medicine bottles to Grace. "Are these what you want?"

"This one." She selected a bottle of small white pills and shook one out. "Here, Grandma. Put this under your tongue."

Elizabeth did as instructed and he saw the color gradually return to her face.

"I think I need to lie down for a bit," Elizabeth said. "Would you help me into my room, Levi?"

"Of course."

"I'm so sorry to be such a bother," she apologized as he helped her lie down. "I used to be much stronger."

"You will never be a bother." He pulled his mother's quilt up over his old friend. "Now rest."

"I shouldn't leave either of you alone," Levi said when he returned to Grace in the front room. "When do you think your sister will return?"

"She told me two hours ago that she would be home in a few minutes. I wouldn't have left otherwise."

"Then perhaps I should bring the children in and wait until your sister gets home."

"I hate to ask, but that might be a good idea," Grace said. "I'm still feeling a little wonky."

Wonky was not an *Englisch* word he had heard before, but it sounded like a word that well described how she must feel.

When he got to the buggy, Jesse was playing a finger game with Sarah, and Albert was sitting as quietly as a statue, concentrating on making certain that the big horse did not move.

"We need to go into Elizabeth's *Haus* until the sister gets home," he said.

"Is Grace all right?" Albert asked.

"She says she is. I am not so sure."

He tied the horse to a fence post, gathered up the children, and took them inside. Grace still had the dish towel pressed against her head. One eye was beginning to swell shut, but she still had a smile for the children.

"There's a package of Oreo cookies in the kitchen," she told Levi, "if they would like some."

He marveled at the woman. She was bruised and bloody, her car was destroyed, and by the way she squinted her eyes at him he could tell that she was still having trouble focusing—and yet she was concerned for the children.

"There's a gallon of fresh milk in there, too," she said. "The glasses are above the sink."

The children looked up at him with hopeful eyes, but he knew that if he refused they would not complain. They had been taught better than that—unlike so many *Englisch* children he had seen throwing fits in the stores wanting things their parents did not want to purchase for them.

"They have been good children tonight. They may have some cookies," he said. "Can I bring something to you?"

"Honestly, I could really use a hot cup of tea," she said. "If you don't mind. There's a canister on the counter by the stove. While you're making it, I'm going to call the sheriff. They need to know about the wreck."

He found the package of cookies and seated the children around the table. There were napkins in a little container in the middle, and he put one in front of each child, giving them two cookies apiece. Then he put the package back on the counter. There was no reason to allow them to make pigs of themselves.

The children's eyes were wide as they watched him open the door and pull out a plastic gallon of milk. It took a moment to find glasses for the milk. As he searched he saw more dishes than he had ever seen before. He could not imagine what use they had for all of them.

He found three small glasses. They had funny pictures on them that he thought would amuse the children. There was a big-eared mouse wearing clothes with big buttons, a silly-looking duck wearing a blue coat and a hat, and a funny little man with red whiskers, a big hat, and two guns. He put that glass back in the cabinet. The children did not need to see guns on their milk glass. He chose instead a glass with a red-headed woodpecker on it. There was a mischievous look on the woodpecker's face—which he thought very much caught the attitude of some woodpeckers he had watched.

He filled each glass with milk and placed one in front of each child. They automatically bowed their heads and said a silent prayer before they took the first bite.

"These taste good," Jesse said, "but not as good as *Maam*'s."

"Let's not tell Grace that." Levi tousled the little boy's hair.

It was now time to start Grace's tea. He filled the teakettle with water from the faucet and placed it on the electric stove. He twisted knobs until he felt heat emanating from one of the burners, and he set the teakettle on it. Then he searched for a cup. After what Grace had done to keep from harming the children, making tea was the least he could do. In fact, the sight of the children sitting unharmed around the table was so miraculous to him that there was little Grace could ask of him right now that he would not do.

He was a little overwhelmed by the sheer number of mugs from which to choose. He stared at them while waiting for the kettle to boil. He finally selected one covered in gold-colored daisies.

Somehow the daisies reminded him of Grace. They were such a friendly flower, and one that did not need a great deal of care. They thrived in whatever soil they were planted. Like Grace.

He put the teabag in the cup and just as the kettle was

ready to boil he had a crisis. He did not know if *Englisch* people took sugar in their tea or not. He hurried to the living room.

"Do you want sugar?" he asked.

"Tonight—I think it would be a good thing to drink something sweet," she said. "I'm still feeling shaky."

He made the tea and took it in to her. When she touched the cup, she pulled her fingers back quickly. "Hot!"

The cup had not felt that hot to him.

"I'm sorry." He turned it so that he held the bowl of the cup in his hands with the handle held toward her.

She stared at his hands, and then at him. "Doesn't that burn you?" She took the cup from him.

"No." He held his hands out flat and turned them over. His palms were so calloused from work that he had barely felt the heat.

"I have met a lot of people, Levi," she said, blowing gently on the steaming tea, "but never anyone like you."

"And I have never known someone like you."

She took a sip. "But we cannot be friends."

"No." This was one thing about which he was certain. "We cannot be friends."

She held the tea gingerly on her lap. "You do know that this rule your people have against making their buggies visible at night is a form of suicide."

"No. It is God's will."

"You don't believe that," she said. "You don't believe for a minute that it is God's will to put small children at risk. We *Englisch* may do many stupid things, but at least most of us try to protect our children. We put them in car seats and seat belts. You rely entirely on God to be their seat belt as you drive down the road hoping and praying that an *Englischman* will just happen to see your buggy in time to stop. That's just wrong, Levi, and you know it. Those children have no one to protect them except you. It won't be Bishop Weaver who'll grieve for the rest of his life if anything happens to them."

"You do not understand our ways."

"That's a smoke screen you throw up every time you don't know how to answer me, and you know it."

She leaned over to set her teacup on a magazine lying upon the coffee table and winced as she sat back up.

It hurt him to see her in pain, especially since he knew he had inadvertently been the cause of it.

"My grandmother has told me that even the Old Order Amish allow the orange triangle on the back of their buggies. I've even seen several of them with flashing lights. They and the other Amish orders do what they can to give an *Englisch* driver some warning, some help. Do you know what it would have done to me if I had hit your buggy? Do you know what it would have done to me if I had actually hurt one of those precious children or you?"

He saw a flash of fury in her green eyes. It was the first time he had ever seen her truly angry.

"It would have killed me inside," Grace said. "Do you understand what I am saying to you? It would have killed me!"

She leaned back against the couch as though exhausted from the effort to get through to him. "I have spent my life trying to save other people's lives. I have seen soldiers torn apart by bombs deliberately set by other human beings, and I have helped patch those soldiers back together. I've sent them back home to their families missing limbs and eyes—some unable to walk. To see someone as intelligent as you are putting people you love in jeopardy for no other reason than some leader's arbitrary ruling—it's just about more than I can bear."

Now he was getting angry. She had accused him of not caring about his own family.

"I'm sorry if I've hurt you," she said when she saw the pain in his face. "But I would be a coward if I didn't say these things to you."

"You judge us, but you know nothing about us."

"Then explain it to me, Levi!" Her eyes again flashed green fire. "I don't care if you don't have refrigeration or indoor plumbing or wear one suspender or two. I don't care if you want to bump along on steel wheels or glide along on rubber ones. But you need to explain to me why you endanger the people you love simply because you have allowed yourself to be imprisoned by some man-made tradition! Why can't you get it into your head that you live in the United States? Unlike so many people all over the world, you actually have freedom—including the freedom to choose to protect your family by sticking a stupid orange triangle on the back of your buggy!"

He was truly furious now, and yet he knew, deep down, that the reason he was furious was because she was asking the same questions he had asked himself time and time again. He gave her the only answer he could think of.

"Freedom? How can you, a woman from a world that allows you to choose anything you want to wear, or anything you want to drive, understand the freedom of not having to think about styles or colors or vehicles because the community has already made that decision? There is freedom in simplicity, Grace, freedom in unity. And that includes retaining the freedom for our Swartzentruber sect to be allowed to leave our buggies Plain and not be dictated to by a government that is supposed to allow religious freedom."

It was the longest speech he had ever given, the first time he had ever defended his faith to anyone except himself, and he found himself breathing hard from the emotion of it.

She came right back at him.

"Think about who you're talking to, Levi," she said dangerously. "I'm not some prom queen trying to decide what fancy dress to wear. Until a month ago, I was a career military nurse. I wore a uniform. I was told when to go to sleep and when to wake up. I was told what to eat and how to make a bed. On your strictest, most *Ordnung*-fearing days, you have more freedom to choose than I have had over these past several years. But my commanding officer never, ever asked me to put myself in harm's way—unless it was to save the life of another soldier."

"Or to kill some other country's soldier," he shot back.

"Oh, that's right, buddy. Go ahead and pull out the pacifist card. You and your people allow other people to lay their lives on the line keeping this country safe so that you can enjoy the right to live like you want to, and wear what you want to wear, and drive what you want to drive. If it weren't for the men and women in uniform who protect our country, you wouldn't be worrying about whether or not your buggy had a stupid orange triangle on it—you would be trying to figure out a way to keep your children from being forced to bow to Mecca!"

"The Bible says, 'Thou shalt not kill.'"

"Then why the heck was the warrior David a 'man after God's own heart'? Good grief, man. God was talking about murder in the Ten Commandments, not war."

Levi had never had a conversation like this. He was hurt, he was angry, but he was also exhilarated by the rush of intellectual battle.

"If all men lived as we do, there would be no more wars. There would be no need for armies or soldiers. There would be peace."

"You make a good point, Levi—except for one thing."

"What's that?"

"If all men lived as you do—burning your libraries because you're afraid some bishop will disapprove—there would be no hospitals to save the lives of people like your mother. There would be no doctors to save the life of little Daniel. And if all men lived as you do—bathing only once a week—the world would smell a whole lot worse than it does."

Now that stung.

"Are you telling me that I have a bad odor?"

"Not right now. Presumably you bathed before you left for worship this morning. But, Levi, I hate to tell you this, but the last time I was there, your house stunk."

"It was Daniel's diapers. There has been too much rain recently to do laundry."

"Don't blame it on your baby brother."

"Well—your *Haus* smells stuffy and close. There are too many things in here. I can barely breathe."

There was a hesitation—and he thought he might have dealt the final blow—but Grace surprised him by bursting out into a belly laugh. "Boy, you got that right! I'm afraid my grandfather never saw a fishing lure he didn't fall in love with, and I don't think my grandmother ever laid eyes on a butter dish she didn't buy."

The fact that she was laughing at her family's possessions was something he had not expected. He had assumed that *Englisch* people were attached to every knickknack in their homes. Evidently she wasn't.

She grinned at him mischievously, in spite of the shiner she was developing. "That was a great argument, Levi. I enjoyed it. It's the kind of argument that friends might have. But we're not friends, right?"

"No—we are not friends."

"Good," she said complacently. "Because I would hate to have said all those awful things to a friend."

Just then, Sarah tiptoed into the room and whispered into his ear.

"She needs to use the toilet," Levi said.

"Sweetie, just go to the last door at the end of the hall," Grace told the little girl.

"I will have to take her. She won't know how to use an indoor bathroom by herself."

"Go ahead, Levi. Knock yourself out."

"Excuse me?"

"Take your little sister to the bathroom," Grace said. "While you're gone, I'm going to think up some better arguments."

"Please don't," Levi said, ushering his little sister out of the room.

chapter NINETEEN

Levi took Sarah to the bathroom. The commode frightened Sarah and he had to help her hold on. While doing so, his mind raced with arguments to counter anything else Grace might want to bring up. No one had ever talked to him in such a way before, although he suspected a great many *Englischers* thought the rude things that Grace had said.

The thing was, Grace was not trying to be rude. She cared about his family and was genuinely puzzled by the things they did.

It felt strangely exhilarating to use his wits to argue with her. But he knew that in spite of his people's attempts to be godly and separate from the world, they were far from perfect. They worked hard and helped each other. They endured long worship services sitting on hard benches in the name of Jesus. But they were not perfect. There was sometimes much gossip and smallness of mind during their get-togethers. Not all of them were honest. Not all of them were kind.

Could it be possible that what he had been taught was the only way to heaven—wasn't true? Could it be that the restrictions under which he lived were not necessary for God's approval? One thing he did know, and it bothered him, was that it was nearly impossible for an outsider to become Amish, and the few who tried seldom went the distance. After a few years they gave up. It was just too hard.

Had God truly made it necessary to live exactly as he and his family lived in order to be saved?

He didn't know. He only knew that the preachers said that the path to heaven was narrow and few would achieve it. And yet could women as fine as Grace and Elizabeth—both believers in Jesus—miss heaven because they did not live exactly as he lived?

"I'm done," Sarah said.

"Good girl!"

She was fascinated with what happened when he flushed, and he had to stop her from putting her hands into the swirling water.

He adjusted the faucets until the water temperature was just right, and then he held Sarah up by her waist while she played with the soap and water. This was a new experience for her, and she drew out the moment as long as she could.

It felt strange being in Grace's bathroom. There were too many women things and fancy bottles in here for him to feel comfortable. He had to admit, it certainly smelled a whole lot better than his family's outhouse.

"Are you finished?" He turned the water off and helped his little sister dry her hands on a fluffy pink towel.

She held on to his finger as they went out the door, but he saw her glance back over her shoulder at the bathroom.

"I like that place," Sarah said.

Her innocent comment hurt. This Sunday was turning into a day of hurts.

All thoughts of bathrooms and arguments left him when they entered the living room. Standing in the middle of the floor looking down at Grace was one of the largest men he had ever seen—dressed in a sheriff's uniform. He recognized him immediately as Gerald Newsome, the man who had talked with him up in the hayloft the day his stepfather was killed.

His two little brothers were sitting close together on Elizabeth's other couch. Their legs stuck straight out, and their hands were clasped tightly together upon their knees—as though to make certain they stayed absolutely, completely out of trouble.

The sheriff shook his head when he saw him. "Sure would help everyone out if you people would just put that orange triangle on your buggies."

Levi was sick of hearing this. It wasn't as though he had any control over what his church's leaders had decided. He waited stoically for Newsome to say whatever it was he was going to say.

"At least this time I don't have to take anyone to the morgue—but from the looks of that car it's a wonder you didn't get killed, Grace."

"It wasn't Levi's fault." Grace, who ten minutes earlier had been giving him grief about the issue, now flew to his defense. "I should have known better than to drive that fast on a rainy Sunday night. I should have realized there would be buggies returning from church."

"If you say so," the sheriff said. "Well, that pretty much wraps things up. I'll call a wrecker for that car of yours."

"Thanks."

Levi's little brothers' eyes were nearly popping out of their heads being so close to this big sheriff again, close to his uniform and his gun holster. He knew they would not soon forget this moment. Why did the world have to infringe so harshly upon their family? All his people had ever wanted was to be left alone to make a modest living off the land and to worship God as they deemed best. His little brothers had not needed to see that gun on the sheriff's belt.

The sheriff shot a glance at Levi. "It's dark. I'm headed out past your house. Why don't I follow you? It might help us avoid another accident tonight."

As soon as she was alone, Grace lifted herself off the couch and limped over to the window where she watched the sheriff slowly following Levi's buggy down the road. He had turned his flashing lights on, but no siren. If only she had come home a few minutes earlier, she could have avoided this whole thing.

It seemed as though even thinking about it made her head ache. In fact, everything ached. Her face throbbed, and her eye was swollen completely shut.

Grace turned out the lights and made herself as comfortable as possible. She wanted to wait up for Becky, to make certain she got home safe.

A half hour later, she heard her sister's car pulling into the driveway. Becky came through the door, not turning on any lights, feeling her way along the wall and toward the stairs.

"Hi," Grace said from the recesses of the couch.

Becky jumped and gave a little squeal. "You scared me!"

Grace turned on the lamp beside the couch.

Becky gasped when she got a good look at Grace. "Now that really is scary. What happened to your face?"

"I wrapped my car around a tree."

"Are you okay?" Becky dropped onto the couch opposite Grace. "You look awful."

"I'm alive—and so are Levi and his brothers and sister." She told her the whole story.

"Is there anything I can do?" Becky asked.

"It would be heaven to soak in Grandma's big old clawfoot bathtub upstairs."

Becky jumped up. "I'll go start the water running."

Grace gritted her teeth and managed to get up off the couch again. She limped over to the stairwell, grasped the banister, and began to pull herself up step by step. Everything hurt. Everything ached. She wanted to soak in that tub for about a month. She hurt so badly that she broke out into a cold sweat just trying to get her bruised body up to her room. Perhaps she should have asked the sheriff to drive her to the ER.

After all that effort, she managed to make it up only four steps. The long stairwell seemed to stretch on for miles. It would take her forever to go to the top. She was just starting to consider giving up and simply going to bed on the couch when Becky appeared at the top of the stairs.

"Are you okay?" she asked.

"I don't think I can make it up there alone."

Becky hurried down. "Put your arm around my shoulders and I'll help."

When they got to the top of the staircase, Becky prepared an Epsom salts–infused bath and stayed with her until Grace was soaking in it. She set a glass of water and a couple of Tylenol beside her on a chair.

"Do you want me to stay with you?" Becky asked.

"I'll be fine. Nothing's broken, just very bruised."

"I'll sleep on the couch tonight instead of you," Becky said. "You're in no shape to help Grandma if she calls out."

"You have school in the morning."

"So? If Grandma has a bad night, I'll sleep during first period study hall." She grinned. "It won't be the first time and it probably won't be the last."

In the morning, Grace was too sore, at first, even to get out of bed—but after a great deal of willpower, a hot shower, and a little more Tylenol, she was able to go downstairs and fix herself some toast and juice. Little by little, she began to feel better.

Becky wandered in from the living room.

"How did Grandma do last night?" Grace asked.

"She was up a lot. Nothing major, just couldn't seem to settle down until about four o'clock. My guess is that she'll be asleep for a while."

"Thanks for taking care of her for me. I should be able to handle it tonight."

"It's a beautiful day," Becky said. "Do you think you'll be taking your jog?"

"Do I look like I'm up for a jog?"

Becky laughed. "Sorry. I wasn't thinking."

"I'm going to need to get around today and deal with my car situation. I'll have to use Grandma's car. Could you take the school bus?"

Becky wasn't enthusiastic, but she agreed. After she hurried off to catch the bus, Grace eased herself out of the chair. If she still felt this bad tomorrow, she really would go get some X-rays.

With her grandmother still asleep, she went out to the back porch to enjoy the early morning. She glanced over at the little shoe box Becky had fixed for the kitten to sleep in. She decided that having a little kitten to pet was entirely too nice not to take advantage of.

"How are you doing, little one?" she crooned as she lifted it from its box. "Do you mind if I borrow you for a while? You sure did land on your feet when you came to this place."

She couldn't help but think, as she relaxed in the swing, looking out over the beautiful, misty countryside, that in many ways she, too, had landed on her feet in coming here. In spite of all that had transpired, Holmes County, Ohio, was about as close to heaven as Grace thought was possible on this earth.

chapter TWENTY

Six weeks after the killing, there was still some conjecture among the Swartzentruber congregation about who had killed Abraham Shetler, but for the most part, Levi's people did not dwell on such things. Levi decided it was probably because the Amish had endured too much over the centuries not to have learned the wisdom of accepting harsh reality and then moving on. Instead of pondering whether or not justice would be served, they worked. Always they worked. There were fields to plant, livestock to care for, children to tend, and quilts to sew.

Life went on. And those like Levi and his family, who had experienced great loss, were expected to do exactly what everyone else did in the Amish community who faced hard things—endure.

It would be a waste of time, in their minds, for Levi to attempt to investigate on his own, because there was no recourse even if he did discover who had violated his family. The Amish did not go to court. They did not seek vengeance. They did not retaliate.

Instead, they scratched out a living with horses and hand tools . . . and they went to church.

If the law officials never found out who it was, even if the murderer went unpunished, Levi knew that he and his family would go on just as they always had.

In many ways it was best. Ignoring the evil in the world helped a man focus on what was truly important: getting the best yield of corn, weaving his baskets just a little tighter than others, and taking the time to rub linseed oil once again into his mother's wooden floors.

When everyday life was a study in weather patterns and survival, there was not much time left over for vengeance.

After processing the milk from this morning, he planned to get ahead on cutting out the wooden bottoms and lids that they used in the larger baskets. These could hold two or three quilts apiece and were favorites among the tourists.

It was raining again. He had never experienced such a wet spring. His cousin Timothy had walked from the third farm over to keep him company. Two sets of hands made his work that much faster. Tomorrow, he would go help Timothy clean out his gutters—and so would continue the back-and-forth that made it possible for them both to make a living without having to hire help.

They were making great progress, and the stack of wooden lids was nearly high enough to begin the sanding and staining, when he glanced out the workshop window and saw a familiar buggy and horse trot up his driveway.

He was surprised to see the bishop so early in the morning. Whatever Ezra Weaver had come for must have great importance. As the bishop's buggy got closer, he saw that Zillah was with him. Could it be an early social call to see his mother?

"Have you done anything else wrong lately?" Timothy teased. "Something bad enough to cause Bishop Weaver to leave the comfort of his home this rainy morning?"

"Perhaps the bishop is coming to see you," Levi shot back.

"With Zillah along, it could be anything. That girl would tattle on the rain for making too much noise on her rooftop."

The bishop drew his horse to a stop in front of the workshop.

Levi stepped outside to see what the bishop wanted, but he stayed beneath the eaves so as not to get wet.

The bishop's face was grim and Zillah wouldn't meet his eyes, which was ominous. He searched his mind for something that his family or he might have done wrong, but his conscience was clear. He had confessed everything and made amends in front of the church. His poor mother certainly had not done anything except try to recuperate and care for the children.

The bishop got out of the buggy and went around to the other side, where he helped his daughter down. Levi wondered about this. Zillah was healthy enough to spring out of the buggy by herself and always had as far as he had seen.

"Come in out of the rain." Levi held the door open for them.

As they entered, even though there were always a few chairs scattered about for visitors, neither Zillah nor her father sat down.

The bishop did not bother to even glance at Timothy. Instead, he focused his formidable gaze on Levi.

Zillah still would not meet his eyes, even though she was standing only a few feet away. This definitely did not bode well.

Timothy, sensing trouble, sidled closer to the open workshop door. It was obvious that he wanted to bolt but didn't want to leave Levi to face the bishop alone.

"How can I help you?" Levi asked. The bishop's behavior was very odd, even for him. But on his most pessimistic day, he would never have guessed what was coming next.

"You and Zillah are to be wed in three weeks' time," the bishop stated.

Levi was stunned. Timothy made a small "oof" sound, as though someone had hit him in the stomach.

Bishop Weaver put one hand up as though to ward off any questions or comments Levi might have.

"That will give us time to make the announcement next Sunday. The marriage will take place the following Thursday."

"Why?" Levi felt as befuddled as a newborn colt.

"You know why!" The bishop sounded as though he were spewing venom.

"I do not know why!" Levi said. "Marrying your daughter is the last thing I would ever want to do."

He saw pain flash through the bishop's eyes, and then they simmered with anger.

"You should have thought of that before you got her with child!"

He was even more dumbfounded. "Zillah is with child?"

"She is."

"But I did not get her with child."

"She has already told me what happened. The two of you bundled the one night she was here, and it got out of hand. Things like that happen sometimes between young people. It can be confessed and forgiven."

Levi glanced at Timothy, whose mouth was hanging open.

"We did not bundle," Levi said.

"I know for a fact that you did," the bishop argued. "You as much as told me so yourself. You said that you rid yourself of those books because she had seen them and chastised you for them, like the proper bishop's daughter she is. Zillah was in your *Kammer*—your bedroom. You cannot deny it."

"She was in my room, and she wanted to bundle, but I refused."

If Levi thought the bishop was angry before, he had been mistaken. The bishop's eyes positively blazed at this comment.

Zillah glanced up at him from beneath her demure black bonnet. "Oh, Levi," she said. "You cannot abandon me now— not after all the things you said to me about how we would spend the rest of our lives together."

Her lie made him clench his teeth in frustration. He had always known Zillah was manipulative, but he never dreamed she would go to these lengths to get back at him.

"Your daughter is lying, Bishop."

The bishop's fists clenched. Levi saw that it was everything the man could do not to punch him in the face. He was certain that if they were not a nonviolent people, he would be stretched out on the ground by now.

His guess was that Zillah really was pregnant. He could not imagine an Amish girl putting herself through this kind of humiliation if she wasn't. It occurred to him that this might have happened with someone who would not marry her, and she had decided to use it to snare someone who would.

In fact, perhaps that was what had been behind her request to bundle with him. Perhaps she had been desperately trying to trick someone who would be a good provider for her and the baby.

But he was not the child's father. That was a fact. He was simply the man she was trying to maneuver, through her father, into marrying her. First babies that took less than nine months to arrive were not unheard of, nor spoken much about, but it was most definitely expected that the boy and girl would get married as soon as possible.

He had no way to convince the bishop that he had not been intimate with his daughter except his own word. And that word was now pitted against hers.

"I will not allow my daughter to be disgraced because of your slick ways," the bishop said. "I have had my eye on you for some time, and I have seen how restless you are. I was not surprised when you admitted that you owned forbidden books, or when you admitted to purchasing a pocket telephone. You confessed these wrongdoings not only to me but the rest of the church. Do you think that they are going to take your word over my daughter's now?"

"I don't know what the church will believe or not believe. I only know the truth. The truth is that I am not the child's father."

"I think you should give this up now, Levi, before you humiliate yourself any further." The bishop attempted to make his voice sound reasonable. "We will publish your wedding announcement this coming Sunday. Her mother and I will somehow get a wedding together, which will take place two Thursdays from now. It is May, and not the time for weddings, but you have given us no choice in choosing a date."

"But I did not do anything!"

"That is what you say, but my daughter tells me differently. You should pray that God will reconcile your heart to being a good and faithful husband to the innocent girl you sinned against."

Levi did not know what to do. There was no way on earth he was going to shackle himself for life to Zillah.

How did one prove a negative?

He had heard that in the promiscuous *Englisch* world there was a test they could do to determine whether or not a child belonged to a man. He had no idea how to go about having it done. His guess was that he would have to wait until the child was born to obtain a piece of paper that would prove that he was not the father.

Nine months was a long time to wait to be exonerated.

He knew he was capable of loving a child that was not his own, but he was not capable of living with Zillah day in and day out for the rest of his life. And it would be for the rest of his life. Amish did not divorce. It would be like receiving a lifetime prison sentence.

"I will pray," he answered. "I will pray that the father of Zillah's child will come forward and make things right, but it would be wrong for me to confess to a sin that I did not commit."

He saw Zillah's eyes dart to her father. It was the first loss of confidence he'd seen in her since the conversation began. Her gamble had failed. She had underestimated how desperately he did not want to marry her. Evidently she did not have another plan to fall back on.

Unfortunately, neither did he.

The joy Levi had taken in the contemplation of the day's work ahead had evaporated. The only thing left inside him now was a deep dread. The bishop was not someone to give up easily, nor was Zillah. Within the narrow bounds of their Amish culture, he had never seen her ask for anything that she had not received. Zillah did not have to wait as long for a new dress. The shoes she wore were always a little more expensive than the other girls'. Even as a young girl, she had her own buggy cart and a pretty pony to pull it.

Only children were rare among the Swartzentrubers and so he did not know what was normal behavior for one. But he had a strong suspicion that being an only child living with a weak mother and a father who wielded too much power had ruined this girl.

Zillah and her father got back into the buggy. The bishop was so angry he actually whipped his horse as they shot out of the driveway. Levi was sorry that he had caused the horse needless pain, but it was not something over which he had control.

When Zillah and her father had departed, Timothy looked at Levi with great sympathy. "I would not want to walk in your shoes, my friend. *Gut Gleek,* good luck."

In the distance, she could see Levi behind a horse-drawn machine that she supposed was a planter of some kind. It was a comfort just knowing he was out there. Even though they were not "friends," she knew he would do whatever he could if she needed him—not because of any affection for her, but because of who he was.

As he got closer, she waved. He did not wave back, but she thought she saw him tip his head in her direction. With the reins in his hand, that was probably the best she would get.

The swing was cushioned, and there were comfortable pillows on it. She leaned back against them and pulled out the paperback novel the nurse had given her grandmother. There was just a little more to go and she thought she could get it finished during her grandmother's nap time. Scooping up the gray kitten, which had turned out to be quite a sweetheart, she lay back against the cushions and began to read.

There must have been something about the relaxing feel of being on the porch, or the feel of a rare sunny day, or perhaps the feel of a warm, cozy kitten curled up on her stomach, but as soon as she finished the novel, she fell into a deep sleep.

"Are you all right?" Levi was standing over her, his shirt sleeves rolled up, his straw hat tipped back on his head. What skin showed was bronzed by the sun.

Surprised, she jerked upright. The lurid novel slid off her lap onto the floor and the kitten scrambled to keep from falling.

"I'm sorry," he said. "I didn't want to disturb you, but you've been asleep for a very long time and I thought maybe something was wrong."

"Have a seat, Levi." She used her foot to surreptitiously move the novel underneath the swing, hopefully out of his line of vision. "You look like you could use some shade."

"Actually, I have shade back there with my horses." He pointed to one lone tree that had been allowed to remain in the middle of the cleared field. Grace had wondered why that tree had been left. Now she knew. "But it won't hurt if my horses rest a few minutes longer."

"Have you eaten?" She looked at her watch.

"Yes. You did not move the whole time I ate. That is why I came over."

He bent over and ran a finger over the kitten she was holding. "Where did you get this little one?"

"He's one of Becky's strays." Grace held the kitten up for him to admire. "If there's any sort of crippled or abandoned animal on the place, she'll find it and worry over it until it gets better. I've never known anyone more tenderhearted."

"I saw her cry over a baby robin once that fell out of its nest too soon."

"What did she do?"

He smiled. "After she spent the better part of her summer vacation catching bugs all day every day, I don't think she envied the life of a mama bird."

"Did it live?"

"It did. I was surprised."

She expected him to leave now that he had discovered there was nothing wrong, but he didn't. Instead, he sat down on a chair beside the swing.

"Won't you get into trouble for being here?" she asked.

"I am already in *Druwwel*— in trouble."

She could tell by the sound of his voice that he was not joking. "What's wrong, Levi?"

He stared at the edge of the porch roof. "You have another downspout coming loose."

"There are a lot of things on this old house that are coming loose. What's wrong?"

"I will fix the downspout for you."

"You don't have to do that, Levi. What's wrong?"

"I will fix it."

There was a long silence while Levi surveyed her property. "Your barn is in need of repair and some of those outbuildings should be torn down. The lumber could be put to better use. All sorts of unwanted things could be nesting within them."

She wondered if this was his attempt at small talk—or was he, perhaps, in economic trouble and simply looking for work?

"Do you need a job, Levi?"

"No." He chuckled mirthlessly. "One thing I do not need is more work."

"I didn't think so."

Another silence ensued while she waited to see what it was that Levi wanted. She had no idea what was going on, but she didn't think it was normal behavior for an Amish farmer to come to an *Englisch* woman's house and sit on the porch in the middle of a spring day for no particular reason.

"You are a nurse," he said.

So it was a medical question. She could deal with that. "What do you need to know?"

"It is embarrassing." He removed his hat and stared down at it. "It is hard for me to ask."

"I doubt you can possibly come up with a medical question that will embarrass me."

"I hope that is true." Then he dropped a bombshell. "Is it possible to prove who a child's father is before it is born?"

Of all the questions Levi might have asked, this had to be the very last one she was expecting. "Yes, but it is risky."

"How is it risky?"

"A needle has to be inserted into the woman's stomach. Amnio fluid has to be drawn out. Sometimes the procedure can cause a miscarriage."

Levi sighed and stared out over the hills. "There is a quail's nest in that field. I saw it in time to plow around it. There should be a nice covey there soon."

"Did you get someone pregnant, Levi?"

His eyes were clouded with worry. "No, but Zillah has accused me of fathering a child with her. The bishop is demanding that we marry."

This shook her. "Is there any chance you are the father?"

"None whatsoever."

"Do you want to marry her?"

His eyes locked onto hers. "Never."

Grace believed him. Levi was too honorable a man to put himself in the position of accidentally needing to marry some girl with whom he was not in love.

"What will happen if you refuse? Could you be banned?"

"I could be banned by putting rubber wheels on my buggy instead of steel ones." His voice held a tinge of bitterness. "What do you think?"

"I think that unless Zillah recants or someone else steps forward to take responsibility for this child, you are going to have a rough time over the next nine months."

"I think so, too."

"After a child is born," Grace said, "paternity is easy to establish. It only takes a gentle mouth swab from the baby to get enough DNA."

"Nine months of the *Meidung*—the ban—is a long time."

"I have heard that the Amish aren't so strict these days," Grace said. "At least not as strict as a few years ago."

"That is true for the Old Order Amish," he said. "But a strictly enforced *Meidung* is one of the reasons the Swartzentrubers left the Old Order in the first place. Our leaders felt that the other Amish were becoming too lenient."

Grace tickled under the kitten's neck until it rolled over onto its back. "Is being shunned bad enough that you would be willing to marry Zillah to avoid it?"

"I could not bear it." His voice was thick with emotion. "My life with Zillah would be a bitter one."

"Then perhaps you will have to endure the ban for only nine months."

"I have doubts that Zillah or her father will allow the test even after the baby is born."

Levi's head was down and he was staring at the straw hat dangling from his fingers. She had never seen him look so dejected.

"You can get a court order for that sort of thing, Levi."

There was a flicker of humor in his eyes as he glanced up at her. "Our people do not go to court. Not unless it is something that affects the Amish community as a whole."

"Have you told your mother what Zillah is accusing you of?"

"It is not a conversation I want to have. Mothers and sons should not have to discuss such things together."

"Claire needs to know—before someone else tells her."

His sigh was so deep, it sounded as though it had been drawn up from the soles of his feet. "I will talk to her."

Levi glanced over at his horses. "I must get back. They are getting restless. We are expecting rain again tonight and they sense it."

Without thinking, Grace laid a hand on his arm. "Levi?"

His body tensed beneath her touch. "Yes?"

She yanked her hand away as though she had touched something hot. "If there's any way I can help, please tell me."

"Thank you, Grace." He scratched behind the kitten's ears again before he stood. "I might need your help before this is over. The next nine months will be a hard time."

Even under the circumstances, as he left the porch he was able to turn and give her a mischievous grin. "Now that I'm leaving, you can get back to reading that book you did not want me to see."

chapter TWENTY-ONE

I t rained the day after the bishop and Zillah came to call.
And it rained the day after that.

It rained for a full week with little letup.

The rich ground soaked up the water until it could not hold one more drop. Farmers watched their fields in despair.

Those who had managed to get their crops in saw the rain wash away the topsoil from the precious seeds they had planted. Crows pounced upon exposed kernels and with raucous calls gobbled them up. In the places where the corn had managed to sprout, the winged gluttons tugged the tender shoots out of the ground and feasted on the sprouting corn.

What struggling crops the crows did not eat, the deer did. The graceful animals materialized in early-morning mists— virtual eating machines that munched any growing thing they could consume before a distraught farmer or his dogs chased them away.

A feeling of bleakness descended up the county as tourists gave up and melted back to their homes, disappointed that the lovely countryside they had hoped to see had been replaced by a dreary landscape in which even the spring flowers were depressed looking and forlorn.

The engorged earth vomited up rivulets in unexpected

places. The rivulets turned into streams where there had never been streams before. The streams made their way into small creek beds, turning little creeks into raging rivers. Then the rivers spread out into shallow lakes, turning thousands of acres of farmland into untillable swamp.

Because of the turmoil his family had been in in the first part of May, Levi was behind in everything. In a way, it had worked to his advantage. His crops were not hurt as badly as some. He had plowed the fields, spread manure, and purchased seed at the local feedstore, but he had managed to plant only one oat field so far. For a while, with his mother once again presiding in her own kitchen, it had felt almost as though life were getting back to some semblance of normal.

Until it continued to rain.

He watched from a window of his workshop, making plans on how to try to salvage what was left of this planting season. For every day he was delayed in getting his corn crop in, he knew he could lose up to two bushels of corn per acre. If the rain did not stop soon, there would be no reason left to plant.

Grace was getting ready to go for her morning run. It was drizzling, but she was determined not to let that hold her back. She had jogged through much worse than this during basic training.

She was doing her stretches on the porch when she heard something down by the river behind their house. It sounded like an animal of some kind in distress. She stopped stretching and trotted down to the swollen creek bed to see what the problem was.

The river was much closer to the house than it had been before the rains began. It had overflowed its banks and now engulfed most of her grandmother's back pasture. Fortunately, there was nothing in her grandmother's pasture. As she followed the sound, she saw that some of Levi's fence had been shoved down or torn away by the floodwater. And there, standing on a small hillock in the middle of the river, was little Rose the calf, bawling for its mother.

As it stood there, she could see that the hillock was being washed away in small chunks as the floodwaters rose, and now the poor thing had only a tiny area on which to stand. Its cries were pitiful and she didn't know what to do for it. Then Grace heard a bellowing and saw that the mother cow was standing near the river's edge calling to its calf. She couldn't see the other calf, little Claire, and wondered if it had been swept away while its twin managed to get a foothold on land. But that bit of land was going to be underwater soon.

The hillock wasn't far from the waterline. Maybe eight feet total. It couldn't possibly be all that deep, she reasoned. Her shoes, shorts, and tank top were already sopping wet. It appeared to her that she could probably walk over, pick up the calf, and deposit it back with its mother in less than five minutes. She doubted the water would come up any further than her knees, and she would hate it if Levi lost this calf, especially since it looked as if he might have already lost the other one.

She glanced toward his house. It might be better to go tell him, but the little thing might fall off its dwindling perch by the time she could get there and back. Levi wouldn't say anything, but he would probably wonder why she didn't just get the calf herself instead of being a wimp and walking all that way to get him.

The water was cold, but she didn't intend to be in it long. She eased into it and slowly made her way toward the calf. She was correct in thinking it would come up only to her knees—at least for a few feet. The problem was, she was on a steeper incline than she realized, and by the time she reached the calf, she was almost up to her chest in swiftly flowing water.

It was getting a little scary, but she didn't want to stop now—not when she was so close. She managed to gather the young animal into her arms, except it wasn't quite as little anymore. It had gained enough weight that it was a struggle even to carry it, let alone carry it through swift water. Just as she had almost made it to the water's edge, the little calf, anxious to get back to its mother, kicked hard and flung itself out of her arms. It landed in the shallow water, scrambled a bit, and managed to make its way onto solid ground.

Its forward thrust against her chest as it leaped from her arms, combined with the slick mud beneath her feet, made Grace lose her footing. She windmilled for a moment, desperately trying to regain her balance before falling backward into the river.

Even in the time it had taken her to wade in to get the calf, the rain had increased in intensity, and the river had continued to rise. With the weird currents swirling around her, she had to fight to get her head out of the water. She spluttered and gasped for air before she realized that the flooded river was carrying her farther away from the water's edge.

She almost felt as though she were being swept out to sea, so strong was the current. Grace could swim, but it had not been her strongest skill during basic training. The current was now swirling her around and around, and she couldn't seem to get her bearings or her breath as it tumbled her farther and farther down the river.

She knew better than to go swimming in floodwaters. No one was that stupid. It definitely had not been her intention. Regardless, the fact was that now, for the first time since she had decided to rescue the calf, she realized that she could drown out here and no one would know.

• • •

The mother cow had gotten into the wrong pasture again. Livestock was like that. Each one had a different personality. Some, like people, had to go their own way. The twin calves' Jersey mother had always had some maverick in her. She gave rich milk, but to her, the grass was always greener on the other side of the fence. With the fence torn down by the floodwaters, she had managed to lead her calves into a terrible mess.

He had heard the calf bawling for its mother, seen the problem, and returned to the barn for a rope to tie around a tree and himself before he went in after it. Floodwaters could be tricky.

When he came out of the barn, Grace was headed down to the river. At first he had been amused when he saw her standing at the edge of the water, obviously worrying about the calf. That was so like the woman. Give her someone or something in distress, and she was there. When he saw her wading into the river, he shouted for her to stop, but with the sound of the bawling cow and calf and the rush of water, she did not hear him.

Now she was fighting for her life and he was running harder than he had ever run before, hoping somehow to save her. As he ran, he removed his shirt, pulling it up over his head, and flung it away.

Having a river flowing through a farm had many advantages. It made a natural place for livestock to drink. It helped keep the fields adjacent to it moist, and it could amuse a small boy for hours. Timothy and Levi had grown up horsing around in this river, and in the process both had become skilled swimmers. It was one of the few luxuries he had as a child—a river and parents who let him swim in it when his chores were finished.

He knew he would need every bit of that skill to rescue

Grace. She was starting to panic now—he could tell by the choppy, awkward strokes she was making. Both of them drowning if he went in after her was a real possibility, but the idea of not going in after her was simply not an option. As she floundered about, he sprinted toward a spot several feet beyond where she was. At the water's edge, he dragged off his boots, dove headfirst into the muddy, churning water, and fought his way toward her.

Grace was struggling to keep her face above the water. She had given up on actually swimming—the best she could do under these circumstances was to dog-paddle like crazy, just to keep from drowning. She already had fought so hard, and the water was so cold, that her limbs were growing heavy. She didn't know if she had enough strength left. The current had carried her into the middle of the river, and it seemed to have no intention of letting her go.

And then suddenly, Levi was beside her in the rushing water.

"Don't be afraid," he said. "I've got you."

She had thought she was in good shape, but he was so much stronger than she and a much better swimmer. He was also wise enough not to fight the river now that he was with her. Instead of muscling his way across, he used the current to help propel them at an angle toward the river's edge. With him beside her, the panic subsided, her courage returned—and with courage came renewed strength.

The biggest problem was dodging the trees and other debris that the flood had ripped up and was carrying away like some sort of macabre trophy. Between the rain and the floodwaters, she barely knew which way was up—except that she had Levi beside her.

"You can do this," he said.

It seemed to take an eternity, but the edge of the floodwaters got closer and closer until eventually their feet were on slippery, water-covered grass, and then finally they collapsed upon solid ground.

It was then that she began to shake. She was so chilled that her teeth began to chatter. They had floated at least a mile from their homes. Nothing looked familiar. She could not see a road. The only thing that spoke of human habitation was a field where three round bales of hay lay moldering in the rain.

"Come." Levi held out his hand.

At one time, two of the bales had been covered in large tarps. Those tarps had long ago been ripped partially off by wind and rain. While Grace stood shivering with her arms wrapped around her waist, Levi hurriedly dug a depression deep into the side of one of the bales of hay. Then he lined the large, concave hole with a faded tarp he had torn the rest of the way off.

"Crawl in here, Grace. There is warmth in the center of this old hay."

She managed to curl up in a sort of fetal position while he ripped the other tarp off and climbed into the depression beside her, dragging the second tarp up over them, completely over their heads, shielding them from the rain that continued to pour down.

The hay did have a sort of warmth to it—she supposed it was probably from decomposition—but although it kept the rain off, the tarp wasn't much of a cover when it came to warmth. She couldn't stop shivering.

"Come here." Levi gathered her to his chest, warming her with his own body. She didn't care where the heat came from if it would just make her feel like a human instead of a popsicle. The nurse in her knew that she was very close to hypothermia, and that if Levi hadn't rescued her and created this makeshift nest for her, she would not have survived.

The shivering continued. Her teeth were chattering so hard she was half afraid they would shatter.

His skin was warm and smooth, and his heartbeat strong as she shivered against him. He rubbed her arms, creating friction, trying to get the circulation moving. Finally, finally, the shaking began to subside.

"Better?" Levi asked as the rain drummed upon the tarp above their heads.

"A little."

"All of this trouble for a small calf?"

"It looked so pitiful."

"And who looks pitiful now?" He lifted a strand of hair away from her face.

The chattering of her teeth began to ease up. "I'm more than pitiful. I'm half dead. Hypothermia is no joke."

Her body gave another involuntary shudder.

"Your lips are blue."

"Wonderful. It's my favorite color."

"But not a healthy color."

"No. Not healthy at all."

Beneath the tarp, even with the rain pounding upon them, she could see that he was looking at her with an intensity she had never seen in his eyes before.

"I think we need to do something about that."

He dipped his head toward her, just enough to give her the sweetest kiss she could ever have imagined. It took her breath away. She had no idea what to say when it was over.

He drew back and traced her mouth with his fingers and then he kissed her again. This one sent shock waves all the way to her toes.

Suddenly, she was no longer cold. She was getting very, very warm.

"We can't do this, Levi."

He pulled away from her and lay back with his wrist over his eyes. "I know."

The rain continued to drum on the tarp.

"I thought I had lost you when I saw you struggling in the water. Then here you were beside me, alive. I was not thinking straight."

"It's okay," she tried to reassure him.

"No. It is very much *not* okay."

As she lay there, trying to assess the damage that had been done to her heart, and his, the rain finally ceased. She pushed the tarp away from her face and sat up. The sun had broken through and the air had warmed up just enough that she thought she might be able to walk home without freezing.

"We have sunshine," she said as he continued to lie there with his wrist over his eyes. "Look."

Levi did not admire the sunshine with her. Instead, he sat up and looked straight at her. "Against my will and better judgment, I have come to care too much for you."

And then he folded up one of the tarps and put it around her shoulders like a shawl, keeping her warm as they walked home.

Their walk was a quiet one, each deep in his or her own thoughts. Both of them were unwilling, or unable, to verbalize those thoughts.

They found Levi's collarless shirt, which he pulled on over his head, leaving the two buttons at the neck hole unbuttoned. Then they found his boots at the edge of the creek and he put them on. Grace was still wearing her running shoes, which squished every time she took a step.

"Are you still planning on going running?" he asked.

"I think I've gotten my exercise in for the day."

"The flooding has done much damage."

She wondered if he meant to the fields or to them. She was still shattered by the revelation that he cared for her.

"Yes, it has."

"Mother cow is happy." He pointed to a corner in the field where she and both calves huddled together.

"That's good."

When they arrived at the place where she had fallen in, the place where they would part ways, he leaned against a fence post as though he needed the extra support.

"If I allow myself to care for you, Grace, in the way a man should care for a woman, it would mean leaving my church and my family. I would never be allowed inside my mother's home again. I would not be allowed to talk with my brothers or my little sister. Ever. Practically all of my *Freindschaft*—my extended family—would also shun me. It is a harsh rule, but it is a necessary one."

"I understand, Levi."

"I doubt that. I'm not sure even I understand. I just know that I cannot put my family through the *Meidung* just because I fell for an *Englisch* woman."

For some reason, that stung. "I'm not just an *Englisch* woman, Levi." She placed the flat of her hand against her chest. "I am me. And who I am is a pretty good deal. I've never asked you to leave your family. I've never asked you for anything. The only thing I have ever tried to do is be a good neighbor and a friend."

"Do you care for me?"

She looked down at the ground and mulled his question over. It would be a kindness to make this man's life easier. "No, Levi. I don't."

He placed two fingers beneath her chin and tipped her

face up until he could see her eyes. And then he asked again. "Do you care for me?"

She gave a great sigh as she gave up on convincing him of a lie. "Yes, Levi. I'm afraid that I care for you a great deal."

He nodded as though having gotten the answer he expected.

"Now that we know this, we must never be alone together again."

chapter TWENTY-TWO

L evi grasped the reins of his buggy so tightly, his knuckles were white. His mother sat beside him with little Daniel in her arms. The other children rode silently in the back. Everyone, except for Daniel and Sarah, was struck dumb by what had just happened.

He had known this might happen. He had even known that in all probability it would happen. But he had not expected it to happen with such speed and finality. The bishop had not even allowed him the grace period other members had received before him.

He had been formally banned by his church. The word *banned* in connection with himself felt so strange. He was one of the last people in the world he had ever expected to experience it.

Even his own mother was not supposed to be allowed to have anything to do with him, the bishop had reminded them, unless he recanted and confessed his "sin." It went without saying that the bishop expected the confession to be a prelude to making things "right" with Zillah.

He had refused and had continued to assert his innocence. Zillah had tearfully continued to claim that he was the father of her unborn child. The bishop glanced between him and his daughter and came down firmly on the side of his daughter.

Zillah did an excellent job of acting the part of the wronged, humiliated girl. In all probability, she had been wronged—but it hadn't been by him, and no pressure his church and bishop could put on him would cause him to recant.

Levi could see the doubt in the eyes of the other members. He knew that many did not particularly like Zillah. There had been too many small cruelties on her part down through the years, cruelties that her father had never witnessed. But no one, including himself, knew of any other man in Zillah's life. Everyone knew that she had spent a night beneath his mother's roof. Everyone knew that she had described the inside of his bedroom to her father. There were few secrets within an Amish church.

Being accused of walking away from his responsibilities after what appeared to be an obvious sin was so against his nature that he barely knew how to feel about being accused of it.

Every emotion conceivable had coursed through his body when the bishop had publicly condemned him. Humiliation, shock, anger. He had expected to feel all of those things if it ever came to this. But the emotion he had not anticipated was the feeling of total loss and abandonment.

It had been the strangest thing to look at the sea of faces, people he had spent most of his life among, people he cared deeply about—many of them his own relatives—to look into their gentle, loving faces and see them begin to close down against him. He watched as they deliberately shut him out of their lives.

The *Meidung* was a powerful weapon. It was designed not as punishment, as many outsiders thought, but as a way to keep a beloved church member from going to hell.

The *Meidung* was such an exacting tool that well over

ninety percent of young Swartzentrubers stayed within its fold. The alternative—that of becoming a non-person to nearly everyone they had ever known—was simply too great a price to pay just to own a transistor radio or to put a windshield into one's buggy.

The *Meidung* was so powerful that he could already feel the effect it was beginning to have on his own mother.

"I did not do this thing that Zillah accuses me of." Because of the topic, and the humiliation his family had just endured, he stared straight ahead, unable to look his mother in the eyes.

This was all deeply embarrassing for both of them. Mothers and sons did not talk about such things. Mothers and daughters did not talk of such things, either, if they could possibly help it. Levi resented Zillah for many things right now, one of which was forcing him and his mother to have such an awkward and painful conversation.

"I saw Zillah go to your room." Claire seemed unable to look at him directly. "I did not see her leave. Sometimes"—she hesitated to put her thoughts into words—"young men do not have the discipline they should."

"You were very ill, *Maam*. Did you stay at the window and watch?"

"I did not." Her voice broke. "With all my heart I wish I had. Then I could tell the bishop that with my own eyes I saw her leaving and he would have to believe me."

This time he looked straight at her. "Have you ever known me to tell you an untruth?"

"No. Never."

"I am telling you the truth. I would never put myself in a position where I might have to marry Zillah."

"I believe you. And there are probably others in our church who believe you." She sighed. "But innocent or not, the fact remains that you have been put under the ban by one of God's own servants. The rest of us have no choice but to observe the bishop's decision."

"Including you?" He could not believe that his own mother could turn away from him. She was the gentlest, most loving person he had ever known. Unlike other mothers, she had never swatted his bottom or shaken him. He had thought, up until this moment, that his mother would be firmly on his side until she drew her last breath.

"Er set nat sa agnie fulussa cause Gott fulusst nat sa agnie!" Levi said.

"'One should not abandon one's own because God does not abandon His own'?" Claire looked as though he had struck her. "Do you think I am abandoning you? I have no choice but to uphold the ban. I have other children to protect. If I do not practice this *Meidung,* I will be in danger of being shunned myself. I will not be allowed to take the children with me to church. My friends will not speak to me when we meet. Our income will suffer because no one will come to me for herbs or healing. They will not buy the crops of our fields, nor the baskets I take to market. The only hope we have of surviving is if I support this *Meidung.*"

An anger welled up within him so great that, for the first time in his life, he knew what it was to hate.

He did not hate the bishop. He knew the burden that had been put on that man. The burden of taking souls to heaven with him was a wearying one.

He did not hate Zillah, although he certainly did not like the girl.

He did not hate his church. They were simply doing what they had done for centuries.

He was not angry at God. His heavenly Father had not caused Zillah to make this accusation.

And he could never hate his mother. She would follow the

bishop's directive because she was being forced to, but at least in her heart she believed in him and that gave him strength.

The only person on earth he hated right now was the man who had shot his stepfather and wounded his mother. Whoever had done this terrible deed had stolen more than his stepfather's life. That person had stolen the peace that had once been theirs. He longed for a time when the greatest concern his family had was whether or not it would rain before they could get all the hay in, or whether or not the hens laid enough eggs. A discussion of whether one of the plow horses might be going lame could take up an entire dinner conversation. Talking about crops, or how many quarts of tomatoes his mother had canned that day—these were the kinds of things that his family and he had talked and thought about before evil had walked into the door of their home and destroyed their lives.

He looked down at his hands holding the reins. He was a bigger man than most Amish. His hands were large and strong. Muscles corded his forearms. He had never known a sick day in his life, nor had he ever faced a challenge that he could not meet.

He had used these hands to plant seedlings and train horses, and in a pinch he had diapered babies. He had been grateful for his good mind, his strong body, and the skill that God had put into these hands.

And now, for the first time in his life, he knew the desire to take these hands and crush the life out of the man who had caused the ruination of him and his family.

But he had to extinguish this hatred. He came from a pacifist people. This belief was so deep that Levi had known many Amish to literally turn the other cheek when attacked. Many had gone to jail rather than go to war.

His people had allowed themselves to be burned at the

stake because of their belief. Through him ran the blood of martyrs.

That thought helped him realize that his own *Meidung* was nothing compared to what others had endured, his ancestors who had also been innocent.

And yet he still felt disoriented and worried about the future. He simply did not know how not to be Amish. He did not know how to live apart from his church and family.

In many ways, he reminded himself of one of his stepfather's honeybees.

His family had always kept a few beehives on their farm. Not only did the bees help pollinate their fruit trees and plants, but also the harvesting of their honey brought a great savings in the cost of sweeteners for the household—if one did not mind a few stings. He had always been fascinated by the creatures who lived out their short lives taking care of their community's needs.

There were the warrior bees, the soldiers guarding the entrance, who were ready at all times to give up their lives in defense of the hive. Then there were the honeybees, who worked nonstop building the honeycomb, the structure in which the precious honey was stored and the eggs laid by the ponderous queen bee.

Each bee had a specific role that it fulfilled perfectly. Some tended the nursery of bee larvae, some gathered pollen, some gathered nectar, and some simply wriggled their bodies for warmth or used their wings to air-condition the hive, keeping it at a steady temperature regardless of the weather.

The Amish community was similar. Everyone had work to do, important work, even the children or the very old. Everyone worked for the common good. Every Amish person's thought was for the survival of his or her family, and of the religious community.

But a honeybee was not equipped to survive on its own.

That's what made the *Meidung* so terrible. The Amish had survived through the ages because of their network of support. He had known only three or four Swartzentrubers who had attempted to leave the church. It had been a sad sight. Like the honeybee, they were not equipped to live apart from their church community. Unless they found an *Englisch* or ex-Amish person willing to help them learn the intricacies of the *Englisch* world, they were doomed to failure, as well as being easy prey for unscrupulous people.

"Will the bishop allow me to live in the room above the workshop?" he asked.

"I have known of one other case like this," Claire said. "The person was allowed to live on the property and continue to farm, but the rest of the family could have no contact with him."

"Then I will stay and farm. I will support our family. But you . . ." He felt his throat closing up at the thought. "You must obey the *Meidung*."

"How will you feed yourself? I won't even be allowed to cook for you."

"I had a mother who had the wisdom to teach me how to cook a few things when I was a boy." He smiled grimly at her. "I will survive."

They rode the rest of the way in silence.

It was the first Sunday Grace had gone to church since she had arrived in Holmes County. Becky had insisted on staying home with Elizabeth this morning and letting Grace take a turn.

"What are people wearing at your church these days?" she called into Becky's bedroom.

"Clothes," Becky replied.

"What kind of clothes? Skirts, dresses, jeans . . . Do I have to wear my hair in a bun?"

"Excuse me?" Becky said.

"I was joking." She rummaged through her closet. "I have uniforms, nurse's scrubs, a few jeans and T-shirts, a few casual blouses and sweaters, and one lone black skirt. But what I don't have is a church dress. It wasn't exactly required on base."

Becky came in and checked out her sister's sparse closet. She pulled out a pair of tan slacks, a coral shell, and a matching thin cardigan.

"What about this?" She held the outfit up for Grace's inspection.

"I thought about that, but I don't have any shoes that match the slacks."

"I do," Becky said, "and we wear the same size. Is a tan low heel okay?"

"Perfect."

Grace had not taken time to get a haircut in the weeks since she had been here. Her hair, though still short, was the longest it had been in recent memory. After scrunching her hair with gel, putting on earrings, and getting dressed in the outfit Becky had chosen, she looked in the mirror and for the first time in a long time saw a true civilian.

This was a softer, more feminine look than what she was used to, and she liked it.

She wondered if Levi would like it, too. Not that she would be seeing him today. Or that it mattered what he thought of how she dressed.

"You look lovely, dear," Elizabeth said as Grace sat down beside her at the breakfast table.

Grace poured herself a bowl of granola. "Are you sure you and Becky don't want to go?"

"I am sure that I *would* like to go," Elizabeth answered. "I would just love to worship with my church family today—but you have no idea how many people I'll have to talk to after services when I show up. I've been gone so long, everyone will want to hug me. People with colds will insist on kissing me and I'll be too nice to keep them from it. I have just about enough stamina to worship God, but I don't yet have the stamina to withstand the fellowship!"

"I'll give them your best," Grace said.

"Please do, and tell them I'll see them soon."

The church in Millersburg that Grace headed to was the same one that Elizabeth had attended for years. She took notes as the preacher spoke, sang a few hymns she had never heard before, and afterward enjoyed getting to meet many of her grandmother's friends, all of whom were thrilled that Elizabeth was feeling better.

Grace was thoroughly enjoying herself until the minister, a tall, white-haired man, asked how Becky's prison ministry was going.

Prison ministry?

"My sister has never mentioned a prison ministry to me," Grace said. "Is this something Becky's been doing alone, or is the whole church involved?"

"Some members of the church are participating—not all," he said. "We try to obey the Scriptures about visiting those who are in prison by having an active letter-writing ministry. We partner with the prison chaplain and have been able to minister to many hungry souls behind bars."

"How nice," she murmured.

She said her good-byes and drove home, all the while

turning over the possible implications of a teenaged girl having a letter-writing "prison ministry." There was no way she was going to let this pass. The very idea of Becky writing to a hardened criminal worried her.

Becky had made scrambled eggs, turkey ham, and sliced tomatoes for lunch. All three were ready to eat as soon as Grace came through the door.

"How was it?" Elizabeth asked after she had blessed the food.

"Nice." Grace ladled some scrambled eggs onto her plate. "There are some sweet people there, but you were right about fellowship. Those people do love to stand around and talk. It took me a while to get out of there, everyone wanted to know details about how you were doing."

"Did Bill Jones try to kiss you?"

"Which one is Bill Jones?"

"He's a gentleman in his nineties whom everyone adores. He's been the treasurer there for about sixty years."

"Oh, yes—he's the one who asked if I had any leftover Afghanistan money for him."

Elizabeth nodded. "Bill has quite a collection of foreign money."

"I'll take him some next time I go."

"Oh, he would love that." Elizabeth took a bite of turkey ham. "Is this low-fat, Becky?"

"It is. The doctor said this was what you needed to be eating."

"I don't think God ever intended for turkey to pretend to be ham." Elizabeth took a close look at the turkey. "But never mind."

"I think it tastes okay," Grace said. "No worse than what we got back at camp. Oh, by the way"—she glanced at Becky—"the preacher asked me how your prison ministry was going. I didn't know what to tell him." She cut a tomato slice in half. "Who have you been writing to?"

Becky's fork paused in midair. "Nobody lately."

"What do you mean?"

"With Grandma sick and trying to keep up in school, I didn't have a lot of time." She shrugged. "Besides, I didn't like doing it much. Snail mail is a pain. A few of the older people at church really put a lot of time and thought into it, though."

Grace couldn't help but smile. The answer was exactly the kind most seventeen-year-olds would give. Stationery, pens, and stamps were things of the past. If it were something that couldn't be texted or tweeted, then forget it.

They finished their lunch, and Becky offered to do dishes while Grace went upstairs to change. As she passed a window on her way to her bedroom, she heard the back door slam and saw her sister carrying the remains of their lunch outside. Becky had been feeding a small stray dog she found hiding in the woods lately. The poor thing had been so abused, Becky said, that it was too afraid to come close to the house. She had taken to carrying any leftovers they had out to the edge of the woods for it to eat.

Grace watched her sister disappear behind the cluster of outbuildings that had once been part of the working farm this place had functioned as before her grandmother purchased it. There was a corncrib and various storage buildings crammed with old farm implements, an old outhouse and smokehouse, a tumbledown barn that was starting to lean. In her estimation, those old buildings really should be removed someday soon. She was already dreading mowing around them.

A few moments later, Becky came upstairs and leaned against her door frame. "Do you mind if I go to evening services tonight?"

"Sure," Grace answered. "I'll be happy to stay home with Grandma."

"I'll probably stay after to help put spiral binding on the cookbooks the ladies have been putting together. Those cookbooks are going to be really nice."

Becky and Elizabeth had mentioned the cookbooks several times in the past, but Grace didn't remember hearing about their purpose. "How is the church planning on using the money they get from the sales?"

Becky's eyes lit up. "Some of the men are going to Honduras to build one-room houses for people who are so poor they are living in little tentlike things they make with sheets and sticks. I saw pictures. It was so pitiful. We hope to make enough to pay for at least some of the materials. We have enough preorders to build two so far!"

"Put me down for a cookbook, then. In fact, make it two. I'll give one to Claire."

"Sure thing."

After Becky left, Grace finished changing clothes. Her little sister had turned into such a sweetheart. She had never known a seventeen-year-old who was more thoughtful of other people.

She was intensely relieved that Becky had lost interest in her "prison ministry." A girl who was so tenderhearted that she fussed over stray animals and tried to raise funds for homeless people in Honduras had absolutely no business getting involved—even if it was only snail mail letters—with hardened criminals.

chapter TWENTY-THREE

L evi entered the outdoor cellar that an ancestor of his step-father's had carved into the small rise behind the house. It smelled of damp earth, apples, and bins of potatoes. It was a pleasant scent. One of his favorite chores as a child had been to carry his mother's quarts of produce down here and place them neatly on the shelves.

He lit the overhead lamp and sniffed the air for the scent of cucumbers—the telltale smell that warned of the presence of copperheads who sometimes mistook the cellar for a nice, quiet den. But the only scent within that hillock was of earth.

Tomorrow he would take the buggy into town and purchase food for himself, food that would be separate from the rest of the household's. But for now he was just hungry, and his sweat and toil had gone into the growing of this food. He had no problem with helping himself to it, and he knew his mother would have no problem with it.

It was going to be very lonely for a while, but as long as he had access to the land and his workshop and his horses and his farm equipment, he would survive.

Not for a moment did he consider finding a job in one of the factories that employed so many of the Old and New Order Amish. He was a Swartzentruber and Swartzentrubers farmed—if they were blessed enough to have land to farm. If he could hang on long enough, perhaps Zillah would have a change of heart, tell the truth, and the bishop would allow him back into the church.

His eyes caught on a jar of home-canned tomato juice and he felt a sudden craving for it. With no supper beneath his belt, he was ravenous. He screwed off the lid and drank deep of the sun-ripened richness.

Albert, Jesse, and he had all worked together, putting the tomato plants into the ground, watering them, and then mounding the dirt up around the tiny roots. Even little Sarah had been given a job. She had toddled around with a little tin cup happily pouring water into the holes that her brothers dug. They had made a small fuss over what a good job she was doing, and she had been proud of herself for being a productive part of the family.

She had stood there in her tiny dress and work apron, barefoot, her little toes digging into the ground, frowning as she concentrated on pouring just the right amount of water for her brothers. The picture was as clear and crisp in his mind as a snapshot from a tourist's camera.

But the tourist's camera could never show the years of tradition and family togetherness that this portrayed. The Amish worked. It was part of their identity. And they worked together. With help from one another, they raised giant, sturdy barns, houses large enough to hold as many as seventeen children under one roof, houses that were large enough that once or twice a year the partitions could be removed and a congregation of two hundred people could be fitted into rooms that had been designed with that very purpose in mind.

As someone now shunned, he would not be allowed to participate in the barn raising that would be taking place

next Saturday at John Yoder's farm. He would not be allowed the joyful camaraderie among the men as they pooled
their strength and knowledge together to create the sturdy
structure that would make it possible for the young couple to
make a living with the small dairy herd that John planned to
accumulate.

As someone who had been banned, he would not be allowed to attend the wedding next Thursday morning of his
good friend Gabriel. It was going to be a happy event. Gabriel
and his wife-to-be, Amanda, had been courting longer than
most because she had been helping care for an ill mother who
had recently passed on. Amanda had fulfilled her responsibilities well and was respected by the entire community because
of her faithfulness. Gabriel was respected for his restraint as
he had waited for his wife-to-be to fulfill her obligation as a
dutiful daughter.

Gabriel and Levi had talked about the upcoming wedding
on their last fishing trip together.

Until the ban was lifted—assuming it ever was—there
would be no more fishing trips. There would be no more
easy conversation between him and his childhood friends.
He could not play the tricks on the young couple that were
customary in their group.

He would not be allowed to join in the men's singing
while the women washed dishes after the wedding dinner
and began preparations for supper. He would not be allowed
to stand around with the other men dressed in their Sunday
clothes, discussing everything from the weather to the price of
milk to the latest calf born on someone's farm.

He finished the quart of tomato juice, carefully closed the
cellar door behind him, mounted the stone steps, and went
to the well, where he drew a bucket of water, rinsed out the
Mason jar, and sat it on his mother's back porch.

She would have need of it soon enough when she began her canning again.

He went back up to his room, sat down on his bed, and looked at the empty bookshelves. He had burned his books for nothing. In the end he had been banned anyway. He now wondered what to do with the long evening that stretched before him.

Normally, he would spend Sunday evening in the front room of the house, playing some silly game with his little brothers and sister, entertaining them while his mother cleaned up the kitchen from the evening meal. He might work on a basket once the children became occupied with a game of their own, and in the past, he would discuss the next day's work with his stepfather.

But not tonight. Or the following nights. So many long evenings stretched out before him. He couldn't even go visit a friend. He did not have any friends who were not part of his church. After today, he would not be welcome in any of their homes—even those homes that he had sweated and strained to help build.

Tonight he had no heart for weaving or any other kind of work. He sat at his table, as the room grew darker, and he wondered how he would live the rest of his life.

chapter TWENTY-FOUR

"**G**ood report today, Grandma." Grace looked both ways, waiting for the traffic to clear before pulling out of the parking lot after Elizabeth's doctor visit. "I'm really happy with how well you're doing."

"Me, too," Elizabeth said. "But do we have to go home immediately?"

"Where do you want to go? For more ice cream?"

"That would be lovely, but while we're in Millersburg I was wondering if we could go to the Antique Emporium. It's just a couple of doors down from the Millersburg Hotel and I just love that store. Could we go in and browse a bit?"

"You aren't on the prowl for more butter dishes, are you?"

"I probably won't buy a thing. I just enjoy going in there and seeing all the pretty things. The woman who owns the place has quite a knack for displaying the merchandise."

Grace had no particular desire to go look at antiques, especially since she sometimes felt as if she were already living in an antiques store. In her opinion, all Elizabeth would have to do is slap some price stickers on things and people wouldn't be able to tell the difference between her house and a hundred other old homes that had been turned into stores.

But if going to the Antique Emporium would help

Grandma feel she was getting her life back, Grace was all for it.

"Sometimes, if you're lucky," Grandma said, "you can get a parking spot right in front of the store. Oh, and afterward, could we go to Mrs. Yoder's restaurant for the buffet? I've been daydreaming about her custard pie."

"When we get back to Mt. Hope, if you're still feeling strong enough, I'd be delighted to take you to Mrs. Yoder's."

Grace was indeed lucky. There was a parking place right in front of the store. As she ushered Elizabeth into the Antique Emporium, she was surprised at how much larger it was inside than how it appeared out front. One room opened into the next and the next. A pleasant mix of new things and old were artfully displayed. Along one wall, beside ancient kitchen utensils, was a display of unique small purses, locally made. In another corner stood a giant wheel upon which someone was apparently engaged in weaving a round rag rug. A staircase ran up the side of the store, with a sign inviting guests to the second story. Across from the staircase was a room that appeared to be entirely given over to used books.

"This is nice!" Grace said.

Elizabeth grinned, pleased at her appreciation of the place. "I told you so."

The woman behind the counter was engaged in a cheerful conversation with a customer over an old scrub board.

"We're closing in a half hour, but go ahead and look all you want," the woman said when she saw them. "Upstairs is also filled with some lovely items." She went back to her discussion with the customer.

Grace got engrossed in the handmade cloth purses. She disliked carrying large purses and these had been cunningly made to fit onto a belt and yet look stylish. She checked the tag. Not a bad price, and made by someone right here in

Holmes County. She gave the Antique Emporium points for selling locally made items.

She thought one of those purses might make a nice present for Becky's upcoming birthday but wanted Elizabeth's opinion before making her decision. She found out that her grandmother had taken root in front of a display of antique toys.

"What did you find?" she asked. "Something you used to play with when you were a kid?"

"No." Elizabeth's voice sounded strange. "I've found something that belongs to me."

"What are you talking about?"

Elizabeth carefully lifted a toy from the shelf in front of her. "This mechanized monkey. Your grandfather bought it for me over forty years ago. I never sold it and I never gave it away."

"How can you tell for sure that it's yours?"

"See this mark?" Her grandmother turned it over. "That's where your father bit into it when he was a toddler." She flipped a little switch and the monkey began to clang the two cymbals together and pull back its lips in a grimace.

"Kind of scary, isn't it?" Elizabeth said. "Your dad was a fearless little guy. I could never decide if he had tried to use the monkey as a teething toy or was simply attacking it. I put it up high where he couldn't reach it after that."

Grace noticed a price tag dangling from the monkey's wrist. "Two hundred dollars?"

"It's worth more," Elizabeth said. "Because the box is with it. With the box it's worth closer to three hundred." She set the monkey down. "How could this toy have gotten here?"

"I have no earthly idea, Grandma. Let's look around and see if there is anything else of yours. Maybe this is just a freak coincidence. Perhaps someone else's kid tried to take a bite out of their monkey, too."

"Perhaps," Elizabeth said, "but I doubt it."

Grace stayed at her grandmother's side as they looked around. She hoped there wouldn't be any more surprises. She hoped there was nothing going on here except a huge coincidence. And then she heard her grandmother gasp.

"What is it?"

"Two of your grandfather's prize fishing lures." She pointed to where they were hanging on the wall. "It was awkward to display them as they were, so I paid Abraham to make that particular shadow box for them. This is no coincidence."

Grace looked at the price and her jaw dropped. "You've got to be kidding. These things are worth that much?"

"I told you we knew what we were doing."

The proprietor finished her conversation with the other customer and came to check on them. She had a pleasant face and softly curled hair. It struck Grace that she was the kind of woman who would look equally at home running an antiques store, sitting behind a library desk, or teaching a kindergarten class.

"Can I help you ladies with anything?"

Elizabeth took charge of the conversation. "My husband used to collect fishing lures, and I'm very interested in these two in this shadow box. Could you tell me where they came from?"

"Actually, I got that piece quite recently. A darling teenaged girl came in. Such a pretty girl. She had some items her grandmother wanted her to sell. The poor old thing is bedridden and is subsisting on Social Security. I bought a couple of items to help out, even though I don't usually purchase things from people who just walk through the door."

"You have a lovely store." Elizabeth had grown pale. "But I think I need to get home. Grace, I'm starting to feel a little tired."

"My grandmother had heart surgery recently," Grace explained. "This was her first shopping trip and I think we've tired her out."

"Can I get you anything?" the woman asked. "Water? An aspirin? A chair?"

"Thank you, but we're parked right in front. I think all she really needs is to get home and rest."

The owner walked them to the door and held it open while Grace helped Elizabeth into the car.

"Funny that we should be talking about that girl right now," the woman said. "Your car is almost identical to the one she drove. I think it belonged to her uncle."

"Her uncle?" Elizabeth and Grace both spoke at once.

"Yes." The proprietor looked perplexed. "The man who was with her. He carried in a small painting that I decided not to buy. The girl said he was her uncle."

"Did this man, this 'uncle,' by any chance have a long ponytail?" Grace asked.

"Why, yes. What makes you ask?"

"It's a long story. Right now I just need to get my grandmother home."

"I don't feel like stopping at Mrs. Yoder's anymore," Elizabeth told Grace after they had settled themselves in the car.

"Trust me." Grace's fingers gripped the steering wheel so hard her knuckles turned white. "I completely understand."

Becky had already been home and was gone again by the time Grace and Elizabeth got home. She had left a note for them saying that she had fed the kitten and done her homework, and a girlfriend was picking her up to go to an early movie over in New Philadelphia.

It was thoughtful of Becky to leave a note, especially since it was starting to get dark, and they would have worried about her. Unfortunately, Grace didn't know if they could believe a word she said anymore—except she was fairly certain Becky was telling the truth about feeding the kitten. Apart from that, who knew what the girl might be up to?

Grace dialed Becky's cell phone. She was itching to have it out with her little sister, but the call went straight to voice mail. Becky had either deliberately turned the phone off or she had let her battery die. She also had conveniently failed to mention the name of the girlfriend with whom she was supposedly going to the movies, so there was no real good way to check up on her.

It struck her that Becky had been keeping her door closed recently, something she hadn't been doing when Grace had first arrived. She had been careful to respect Becky's privacy. But no more. She was going to turn Becky's room inside out. Something bad was going on and she wouldn't stop until she found out what.

"Do you suppose it's drugs?" Elizabeth asked. "Usually when teenagers steal from their family it is because of drug addiction, and yet I've seen no signs of substance abuse in Becky. I've been careful to watch for the signs. I taught school entirely too long to be naïve about what kids get into."

"I think it's more likely that she's supporting a boyfriend's habit. Evidently a boyfriend who is old enough to be her father."

"Do you think it might be that man she said was a janitor?"

"That's the one I'm suspecting."

"Oh, dear." Elizabeth picked up the telephone book. "Well, it's easy enough to find out. Do you remember the man's name?"

"Becky introduced him as Mr. Franklin."

Elizabeth dialed a number. "I should have done this

earlier—except that Becky has never lied to me. I just assumed she was telling us the truth about that man. Hello? Is Superintendent Allen there?"

A few moments later, when Elizabeth hung up, she looked as though she had aged ten years. "There is no Mr. Franklin or anyone of that man's description working as a janitor. Becky has been lying to us, Grace."

"Maybe it's a blessing Becky isn't here right now after all. I'm going to tear her room apart. I want to see if I can find something that will shed some light on what's happening."

"I wish I could help you. Maybe I could climb those stairs after all."

"You've already had enough excitement for one day, Grandma. In fact, it might be a good idea if you laid down and rested."

"I'm too upset to rest. How about I look around here on this main floor to see if anything else is missing? See if my granddaughter has stolen anything else from me!"

"I'm so sorry this is happening, Grandma."

"I'm sorry, too." Elizabeth patted her on the shoulder. "But I've endured worse. We'll get through this."

Becky's room was more orderly than Grace had expected. The last time she had glanced in, the floor was littered with the flotsam and jetsam of a teenager's life.

Then Becky had taken to keeping the door closed.

Now it was almost military in its precision. Even the bed was carefully made. Was this Becky's way of trying to regain control of her life when everything else was out of control?

Grace realized now that she didn't know her sister at all except that she was a very good actress. Anything could be happening in Becky's life right now.

• • •

It was Levi's second evening of being shunned. During the day, he had not felt so alone because of his horses and the other livestock with whom he had one-sided conversations while he worked. He had not felt alone when he went to town for groceries—at least the store clerk had spoken to him. But tonight, he was not doing so well.

He tried to read his stepfather's Bible, but the friendly language he spoke on a daily basis was not the same language of this Bible. The High German words were ponderous and difficult for him to understand.

He closed it back up in frustration.

He wished that he just could go to sleep and make everything go away, then awaken from this nightmare. But he doubted he would sleep at all tonight.

He paced the floor, nervous, wishing there were something to do or someplace to go. The room that he had constructed and been so pleased with now seemed small and confining. Plain beyond belief. Being Plain didn't matter when one was with one's family and friends. Children and other loved ones were all the decoration that an Amish home ever needed. But now, the room felt as bare as a prison cell.

An *Englisch* person would watch television, he supposed. Or listen to music. Or read a novel. Or tinker with some small hobby. Or even just go for a drive. Perhaps they would even drive to a town that had a place where those big pictures were shown. What did the *Englisch* call them? Oh, yes, *movies*.

Levi had seen television sets when he had gone into Millersburg to Walmart. He had been mesmerized for a few seconds in front of the big screen with the big faces talking to each other. There were people sitting around at a beach on that screen. Some of the words the people on the screen said embarrassed him. And he had been shocked at the scantily clad bodies.

He had paused there for only a moment because he knew that the sight of an Amish man gaping at the wall of televisions would be amusing to any *Englisch* person who happened by. And he also had Jesse with him—Jesse who was already too susceptible to trouble. He got out of there as quickly as possible and never allowed himself to be drawn to that department again.

The question he was pondering for the umpteenth time today was how one could be Amish alone. He concluded that, like those social creatures the honeybees, one couldn't.

An anger began to smolder within him once again. What good was there in trying to follow all the rules and obey everything that the *Ordnung* decreed from boyhood, if one could be shoved out of the religious community by one vindictive, lying girl?

Through his window he could see the lights on in Grace's house. It seemed unusually lit up. He grabbed his bird-watching binoculars and trained them on the house. He was right. Every light in the house was blazing. Usually just a couple of lights were on.

That many lights on in a house could mean problems. The only time he had ever seen it lit up like that was the night the ambulance had come for Elizabeth.

On the night that he burned his books, Grace had come running because she was afraid there was trouble and wanted to help. When his mother had been shot, Grace had come running.

That's what neighbors did for one another in this community, whether they were Amish or *Englisch*.

It could be that Grace and Elizabeth and Becky had decided, for reasons inconceivable to him, to do their spring cleaning on a Monday evening and had turned on every light in the house. He hoped that was all that was happening. However, he had

an excuse now to do something besides walk the floors of this
room. He would take Angel Dancer and go investigate.

The Connor women had not banned him from their
lives—and from what he knew of them, they never would.

Becky's laptop, Grace discovered, was password protected,
and Grace did not know how to get around that.

Instead, she went through every drawer, ran her hand between the mattress and box springs, checked under the bed,
looked in the jewelry box, checked the backpack that Becky
used for school. There was nothing the least bit suspicious
anywhere. In fact, she didn't really know what she was looking for.

She went through the closet and looked behind the
clothes. Then she dragged a chair over to the shelf in the top
of Becky's closet.

It was stacked neatly with shoe boxes. It took her a while
to open them, and all she found were shoes. Until she opened
a box that had been shoved far into a back corner, in which
there was a stack of letters. Her heart sank when she saw that
the return address was from a prison in Ohio. She lifted the
box down and with trembling fingers peeled off the rubber
band that had been holding the letters together. Could these
hold a clue to the mystery behind Becky's lies?

The first few letters on top were fairly innocuous. The man
described his life in prison. And Becky had evidently described
hers here at home. Unfortunately, it appeared that Becky had
described her life in entirely too much detail. Grace could tell
because of his responses to things that Becky had revealed.

He told her that she was the only person in the world who
cared about him. Strong words for a girl who had such a tender heart that she could not resist taking in strays.

Grace skipped to the middle of the stack of letters, and they grew more passionate. Now he was telling Becky how beautiful she was and how much all the other men had admired the pictures she had sent him.

Grace felt sick at the thought of prisoners leering at a picture of her innocent, trusting sister.

She skipped to the final letter. The date was recent. Two days before Grace arrived home.

I have just heard that they are letting me out early. The prison is overcrowded and since I'm so close to finishing my time, I am one of the lucky ones being released. When I get out, we'll finally get to see each other face to face.

I can't wait until I can see you again, sweet Becky.

Again? When had he seen her before? Had Becky gone to see him in prison? This correspondence was infinitely more than Becky had indicated. Exactly how far had her sister's relationship with the older guy gone? Obviously, it had gone far enough to cause her to lie and steal. Grace folded the letter back up carefully. She placed it back into the envelope and put the envelope back in the stack of letters. She placed the stack inside the shoe box and put the shoe box back on the top shelf. She smoothed the rumpled place on the bed where she had sat while she read the letters, and she closed the bedroom door gently behind her.

Then she raced to the bathroom, knelt in front of the commode, and was violently ill.

Levi knocked and knocked. At first no one came to the door, and then Elizabeth opened it.

"Oh, Levi. Thank goodness you're here!"

Elizabeth grabbed him by the arm and pulled him into the house. To his surprise, she was trembling.

"What's wrong?" he asked.

"It's Grace." Elizabeth tugged him over to the staircase. "Listen."

From upstairs he heard the sound of retching and sobbing.

"The doctor told me I am not supposed to climb stairs." Elizabeth wrung her hands. "But I was just about to go up anyway. I've never heard Grace sound like this. Will you go see what's happening up there?"

The sound of Grace crying was enough to draw him to her, even if Elizabeth had not been there to ask him. What could make that strong woman cry enough to throw up? It must be a terrible thing.

"Grace?" he called as he reached the top of the stairs.

Another round of vomiting.

He followed the sound to a small bathroom at the end of the hallway. And there he found Grace on her knees in front of the commode. He knelt beside her and laid his hand on her back.

"My mother has herbs for stomachache. I can go back and get some."

Grace shook her head.

"You do not have a stomachache?"

Grace shook her head again. And then she began heaving again. But there was nothing left to come up.

He saw that there were paper cups on the bathroom sink. He filled and handed one to her.

It seemed to help a little—to break the spell. She stopped crying, flushed the toilet, and shakily got to her feet, sipping the water Levi gave her.

"Tell me how to help you," he said.

Her eyes were red and swollen and filled with such a terrible sadness. He did what many other people would have done under the circumstances. He simply gathered her into his arms and held her. Just as he would if it were little Sarah or Albert or Jesse who was crying and needed comforting.

She buried her face in his chest almost as though the one thing on earth she had to hold on to was him. Her arms went around his waist and her tears dampened the front of his shirt.

He had not anticipated this seeming so right, for the smell of her hair and the warmth of her body to feel as though she had been meant from the beginning of time to be his.

He could have stood there forever holding her, absorbing her into his heart, but he knew he could not.

He kissed the top of her head and held her at arm's length. He lifted her chin and looked into her eyes. "What caused this?"

Grace didn't answer. She turned away from him, grabbed a washcloth, wet it with cold water, and, while leaning against the sink, held it against her swollen eyes. "Does this mean we're friends now?"

Under normal circumstances, he might have chuckled at Grace's little joke. But this time, Grace was not joking. Her voice was dead serious—and after all they had been through together, so was his.

"Yes, Grace." He brushed her hair out of her eyes. "We are friends now."

chapter TWENTY-FIVE

Grace could not believe that she had just cried her eyes out in the arms of an Amish farmer while standing in the middle of her grandma's upstairs bathroom. He had been right to break the embrace. Otherwise she might have clung to him forever.

"When did you get here?" She folded the washcloth and laid it on the sink. "How did you know to come?"

"I saw too many electric lights on and thought Elizabeth or you might be in trouble."

"I'm not the one in trouble," she said. "It's my sister. I think she's in very, very deep trouble."

He frowned. "What has happened?"

"Let's go downstairs first. Grandma needs to know what I just found, too. Is she okay?"

"She's worried about you," he said. "She sent me up here to see if I could help."

"Well," she said, smiling, "you did. Thanks."

"Is everything okay?" Elizabeth was standing at the foot of the stairs. Her face was pinched with worry.

"Sit down, Grandma," Grace said. "I think I've found out at least part of what's been going on with Becky."

Elizabeth sank into an armchair. "Tell me."

With Levi sitting on the opposite couch, she did.

"All I can say," Elizabeth commented when Grace was finished, "is what an incredibly inconvenient time this is for me to have heart issues."

"If you hadn't had the heart attack, I would probably still be in Afghanistan," Grace pointed out. "At least I'm here now, and this thing with Becky would have happened anyway. It had nothing to do with either of us."

"That's true."

"I am still wondering, why do you have all the lights on?" Levi asked. "It is very bright in here."

"Grandma and I were checking every room in the house to make an inventory of possessions. We found out today that Becky has been secretly taking things and selling them to an antiques dealer. Possibly more than one antiques dealer. This is the first chance we've had to go through everything without her being here. Frankly, the last thing on our minds tonight was saving electricity."

"Do you know the name of this man she has been writing?"

"Owen Peterson. That name is burned into my mind. I even have his prisoner ID number memorized. It was written on every envelope."

"I'm sorry this has happened to your family."

"I apologize for keeping you here so long. I know being here can cause trouble for you with your church."

There was a long silence. And then Levi, a man who rarely smiled, let out a laugh. She was dumbfounded.

"I don't understand," she said. "Why are you laughing?"

"I don't think I can get in any worse trouble with my church than I already am. Bishop Weaver put me under the *Meidung* yesterday."

"Good heavens!" Elizabeth was aghast. "You are being

shunned? Already? Isn't there supposed to be a grace period?"

"Is this because of what Zillah accused you of?" Grace asked.

"No, not because of what Zillah accused me of. I am being shunned because I refuse to confess and ask forgiveness for my great sin."

"Is Zillah banned, also?" Grace asked.

"No."

"Well, that hardly seems fair."

"Actually, in my people's eyes, it is very fair. Zillah has confessed her sin and asked forgiveness from the church. She is now, in their eyes, in a right relationship with both the church and God."

"But she's lying," Elizabeth pointed out.

"My church does not know that."

"What will you do, Levi?" Grace asked. "Your family and your church are your life."

"I'll learn to live alone. I'll work my fields. And I'll wait."

Levi mounted Angel Dancer. He was very concerned for the Connor family, but there was little he could do. He was certain, though, that it had at least comforted her to have someone to talk to.

It was very late, but he did not feel like going back to his room yet. Tonight had that balmy feel of certain spring evenings where everything seemed possible. There was the music of the little frogs up by the pond, and a whip-poor-will sang in the distance. He didn't feel tired at all anymore. The rawness of his upset over being shunned had begun to ease. It was still a great, aching void in his life, but he felt less lonely after spending a short time this evening with his neighbors. At least they believed him over Zillah. Without question.

Instead of heading home he decided to ride farther down the road, just for the pleasure of breathing in the honeysuckle-scented night air. He allowed himself the luxury of thinking about Grace, every nuance of her voice and face. He allowed himself to remember the feel of Grace's arms around his waist. He even allowed himself to dwell upon the feel of kissing her the day she almost drowned.

These heady feelings he was allowing himself to savor were as close to experiencing a *Rumspringa* as he had ever come. Content in his work, wanting to be a good example for his younger siblings, he had never felt the need for a "running around" time—until now.

Speaking of *Rumspringa*—it occurred to him as he rode past Grace's fields, fields that had lain fallow now for the past two years—that he could even purchase an automobile and experience the sensation of driving if he wanted to. There was nothing to lose anymore. He had already lost!

A car.

So many times in the dead of winter riding against the cold wind in his buggy with no windshield, bundled up against the cold but feeling the chill wind seeping down into his bones, no matter how warmly he dressed, he would be passed by cars.

Sometimes he would think about how warm it must be in those cars. And how there was probably music playing. And how nice it would be to drive along in warmth and comfort. He would think about how easy it would be to simply park that car when he got to his destination. How he wouldn't have to wipe down a car to make certain the sweat didn't freeze on its body, or find water for it, or make sure there was feed for it. A car was sometimes a great temptation to a young Amish man.

Yes. At least for tonight, he would allow himself to think about forbidden things.

· · ·

Levi had left, and Grandma was in bed. Grace lay on the couch staring up at the dark ceiling, wondering just exactly how foolish Becky had been with this man.

She heard a car stop outside. Becky and her girlfriend were home from the movies. Supposedly. At least that's where Becky had said she was going. Grace intended to let her sister go straight up to her bedroom tonight. There would be no questions. Why bother? They would serve no purpose because Grace no longer believed a word her sister said.

Levi rode Angel Dancer into his barn, put her in a stall, and headed toward his room above the workshop. His mother surprised him by opening her door and shouting at him.

"Levi! Come. Now!"

He headed toward the house at a dead run. Claire Shetler rarely raised her voice, and unless she was wrestling a colicky baby, she never, ever stayed up past ten o'clock. It was nearly eleven o'clock now. She wasn't supposed to even talk to him, let alone allow him inside her house. Something was terribly wrong.

"What is it, *Maam*?"

"It is Jesse. We have been waiting and waiting for you to come home."

"Is he hurt?"

"No. But only by the grace of God."

He walked into a scene that he could never have imagined. At his mother's kitchen table the glow of an oil lamp cast its shadows upon both Albert and Jesse, who sat very still. They looked utterly cowed and frightened.

"What has happened here?" he asked.

"Tell him, Jesse," his mother said. "Tell him what you have done."

Jesse was shaking.

"Tell me what you have done," Levi said.

"I—I found a gun."

Levi's heart nearly stopped. The image of this small, mischievous boy with a gun in his hand was a horrific picture. Anything could have happened. "Where did you find this gun?"

"In the tall weeds by the fence. I was climbing the apple tree and I looked down and I saw it."

"And then what did you do?"

"I brought it home."

"And?"

"I hid it under my bed."

Levi glanced at Albert, who looked equally upset. "Did you know of this?"

Albert nodded.

"Did you boys think it was a toy?"

Both of them shook their heads.

"Then why did you do this thing? Why did you not come and get me or *Maam*?"

"*Er heaet gut, awwer er hicht schlecht,*" Claire said. "Your brother hears well, but he obeys poorly!"

Jesse now had tears streaming down his face. "We wanted to have it with us if the bad man came back."

Levi closed his eyes, absorbing the pain this statement caused. How frightened the little boys had been to do such a terrible thing. It broke his heart. "You were going to shoot the bad man with the gun you found?"

Both of them nodded. Jesse hiccuped a sob.

"Where is this gun?"

The boys pointed at the dry sink where his mother's tin breadbox sat.

"I put it in there until you came home," Claire said. "I did not know what to do with it." She glanced at her two small sons. "Or them."

He opened the breadbox and drew out the gun. He knew that fingerprints were important to police officers, but he didn't think it was possible for it to have any fingerprints left on it. Not after it had lain in the weather for many days. Not after it had been handled by two small boys and his mother.

He opened up the chamber and counted three bullets left in a six-bullet gun. There was every chance that this was the weapon that had killed his stepfather.

It was a miracle from God that the boys had managed not to kill themselves.

"What will we do?" Claire asked.

"I will take this up to the Connors' first thing tomorrow morning, and they will call the sheriff."

"No. I don't want you to wait until then. I don't want that thing beneath my roof for one more night."

"It is late."

"I don't care." She shuddered. "This thing should not be here. I don't want it here."

"Then I will take it to the Connors' now." He pulled a paper sack from a handful his mother had stashed in a cabinet and carefully put the gun inside of it.

"You boys know you did wrong by not taking *Maam* or me to the gun? You know you should never have touched it?"

Once again, the two little boys nodded. Jesse wiped his nose on his sleeve.

"You know that we are not a people of violence, and yet you hid it anyway. This is a grave thing you have done," Levi said. "I think the two of you will be cleaning out that long fencerow tomorrow with hand scythes in the hot sun while you think about what you have done."

"That's all?" Jesse acted as if he could not believe his ears.

"If it were any other time, under any other circumstances that you found this weapon and hid it from us, the consequences would be severe. But we have all been through so much, I understand your fear. You should go to bed now and plan an early morning. It will take nearly all day to finish clearing the fencerow."

"Yes." His mother affirmed Levi's words. "You heard your brother. *Die Zeit fer in Bett is nau!* The time to go to bed is now."

The two trudged off, but just before they got to the stairs, Jesse turned around. His chin was quivering and his voice sounded as though he were holding back more tears.

"Will you come and sleep here with us tonight, *Bruder?* When you are here, I feel safe."

Levi looked a question at his mother.

She nodded.

"I will, but just for tonight."

As soon as they left, she sat down at the table, put her face in her hands, and broke down for the first time since the funeral. "Why can't the *Englisch* leave us alone? We do them no harm. We ask nothing from anyone except our own people. And now I find my boys with a weapon hidden beneath their bed—it is too much!"

"Shhh." Levi patted her shoulder. "It is all right. Perhaps finding this gun will help the sheriff find out who did this terrible thing."

"Then go quickly. My children need to know that their father's killer is not lurking about waiting to jump out at them."

He knew that Angel Dancer would be surprised to be taken out of her stall again so late. He held the reins one-handed, the paper-sack-wrapped weapon in his other hand. And as he rode, he thanked God that He had spared the children.

All the lights were out, and he hated to rouse anyone, but his mother was right. They did not need to keep this gun beneath their roof for even one more night.

Grace was the one who answered the door. She was wearing a T-shirt and sweatpants and her hair was mussed.

"You were asleep," he said. "I am sorry I woke you—but I have something the sheriff will want to see."

"You are certain this is your revolver, Elizabeth?" Sheriff Newsome said.

"Absolutely certain. It belonged to my husband, who was a history teacher. His favorite era was the Wild West during the late 1800s. This is a U.S. Cavalry Colt, the kind used by General Custer at the Battle of the Little Bighorn. My husband bought it nearly forty years ago. This one, which is particularly rare, was worth around ten thousand dollars the last time I checked."

"Antique or not, it's the same caliber weapon that was used for the Shetler murder. Do either of you know how it ended up in their yard?"

"Not a clue," Grace said.

"It was in a drawer in an upstairs bedroom," Elizabeth said. "It's been months since I even looked at it."

"Where is your sister?" the sheriff asked.

"Upstairs, asleep."

"Would you go get her?"

When Grace opened Becky's door, she was not asleep. She was still completely dressed and seated at a dressing table looking into a mirror. She wasn't taking off makeup, or brushing her hair. She was simply staring into her own sad eyes. She didn't even turn around. Little Tabby was on her lap, and she was stroking the kitten, over and over.

"The sheriff is downstairs," Grace said. "He wants to talk to you."

"What does he want?" Becky continued to stroke the kitten.

"Jesse found Grandpa's old revolver in the weeds behind their house. The sheriff thinks it was the murder weapon."

"Grandpa's gun?"

"Grandma's already identified it, and she should know."

The pallor on Becky's face was instantaneous.

"Here, take care of Tabby for me." She handed the kitten to Grace. "When all this is over, I just want you to know—I did the best I could."

"What do you mean?" Grace felt sick.

Becky kissed her on the cheek. "Just remember."

The sheriff seemed to fill the room when they arrived at the bottom of the stairs.

"Where were you the morning of the murder, Becky?" he asked.

Becky didn't answer. Her head was down. Her long, dark hair created a sort of curtain that hid her face.

Grace pushed her sister's hair back. "Where were you that morning, Becky?"

"School," Becky said in an unsure voice.

"No, you weren't," Sheriff Newsome said. "We already checked. You were truant that morning."

Elizabeth gasped. "Becky, where were you?"

Becky didn't answer.

"With the gun coming from this house, and your lying about where you were, I need to take you in for questioning," Sheriff Newsome said. He looked at Elizabeth and Grace. "She's a minor, so one of you will need to come along. Will that be you, Miss Connor?"

"No," Elizabeth said. "It will be both of us."

chapter TWENTY-SIX

From atop Angel Dancer, Levi watched the sheriff's car depart with Becky in the backseat. He could hardly believe how crazy life had become.

Becky could not possibly be the killer—if that had been the sheriff's thinking. He had watched that girl cry over a wren with a broken wing. When she first moved in with her grandmother, he had seen her try to put a smashed earthworm together with a bandage. Her tenderness with her grandmother had impressed even his own people, who knew what it was to care for family members.

There was nothing he could do. It was in the hands of the sheriff now. He made a clicking sound with his mouth and urged his horse toward home. He needed to get to bed. Tomorrow was supposed to be a clear day, he desperately needed to get his planting finished, and he needed to oversee his brothers' work along the fencerow. The earth and the seasons did not wait for people to get their problems worked out.

Grace put the kitten back in its box on the screened-in back porch. While Elizabeth changed out of her nightgown, Grace ran upstairs and grabbed the shoe box full of letters to take with her to the sheriff's office. She did not know if they would help, but she hoped they might shed some light. She was worried about her sister, and about her grandmother. Elizabeth had already withstood burying a husband, a son, and a daughter-in-law, as well as triple bypass surgery. She did not need to watch a granddaughter being questioned about the possibility of being involved in a murder. But Grace knew there was no way her grandmother would stay behind.

What had Becky meant when she told her that she had done the best she could?

When they arrived at the county sheriff's, they found Becky sitting in a chair in his office. Sheriff Newsome was doing paperwork while he waited for Grace and Elizabeth to arrive.

Elizabeth went straight to Becky, sat down beside her, and grabbed her hand.

"It will be okay, sweetie," Elizabeth said, patting Becky's hand.

Grace wasn't so sure.

"I just found these today, Sheriff." She placed the shoe box on the desk. "I thought they might have something in them that would help."

"You went through my room?" Becky said.

"I did, and from what I've seen and heard tonight, I had good reason."

The sheriff glanced at the return address. "Owen Peterson? I remember him. He was a foster kid we arrested a couple years ago on drug charges."

Elizabeth gave a small groan. "You *are* involved with drugs!"

"No! I've never touched them," Becky said.

"That's the man I saw with you at Troyer's, isn't it?" Grace said.

Becky began to sniffle.

The sheriff had been typing on the computer. Now he turned the screen around so Grace could see.

"Is this the man you saw with her?"

Grace found herself looking into the eyes of a young man in his twenties. He wasn't someone she would exactly describe as clean cut, but he didn't look like a killer. And he certainly wasn't the man she had seen talking to Becky. She also doubted that Becky would try to pass this kid off as her uncle.

"The man I saw was at least fifteen years older."

The sheriff turned the screen back around.

"It says here that Owen Peterson was just released from prison a few weeks ago. It looks like he's made all his appointments with his probation officer." The sheriff hit a few more keys. "Hmm. That's interesting."

"What?"

"The home address they have on record is yours."

"What?" Grace looked at her sister. "What have you done, Becky?"

The sheriff thumbed through the letters. "You have been a very foolish girl. Whatever possessed you to write to an inmate?"

"It was something people at my church were doing," she mumbled.

"Why is his address the same as yours?"

Becky shrugged.

"This isn't a game, child." The sheriff leaned forward, both elbows on his desk. "This isn't a movie. This is real life. A man has died and right now I'm looking at you as a possible accomplice to a murder. If you don't talk to us right now, you could be facing serious jail time. The courts aren't nearly as lenient with minors as they used to be. You have to tell us what you know."

Becky's shoulders slumped and she began to cry. "I was just trying to help."

"Who were you trying to help?" the sheriff asked.

"Owen."

"Why were you trying to help Owen?"

Becky's nose was running. Grace saw a tissue box, grabbed a few, and handed the tissues to her sister, then squatted down in front of Becky so they would be eye to eye. "Just tell us the truth, Becky."

The sheriff tried again. "Why is Owen's address the same as yours?"

Becky wiped her nose. "Because he's living there."

"Where?" Elizabeth exclaimed.

"In the old smokehouse."

"For how long?" Grace asked.

"Weeks."

"Why?"

"Because he was my friend."

"What do you mean he was your 'friend'?" Grace asked. "You mean you became friends with him after you started writing to him?"

Becky gave a great sigh. "No. We were friends before. There was a big boy who picked on us little kids when I first moved here. He was really mean. Then Owen got placed in a foster home close by and started riding the bus. He was a senior and he made the big boy stop. I was the smallest kid on the bus and Owen always watched out for me. I heard he was in prison, and when they started the prison ministry thing, I decided to write to him."

"I remember your telling me about that foster kid who helped you," Grace said, "but I didn't remember his name. And I didn't know he was in prison."

"You were always gone," Becky said.

"Start at the beginning, Becky," the sheriff said. "And tell us everything."

Once Becky started talking, it was as if a dam had broken. She told about the hard life Owen had lived, bouncing from one foster home to another. How he had sold drugs, but had had a jailhouse conversion in prison and was clean now. She explained that he had nowhere else to go except a halfway house for prisoners that was badly run and known for its brutality. Owen wasn't a violent man. He had needed an address to give his probation officer, and she offered one to him—along with a dry place to sleep.

It was such a Becky kind of thing to do.

"Is this true?" Grace asked. "Are our halfway houses that bad?"

"Some are better than others." Sheriff Newsome checked the computer again. "I see that the one Owen was scheduled to go to has a bad reputation, but, then, some pretty nasty guys end up there."

"Becky has always taken in strays," Elizabeth told the sheriff. "Cats, dogs, turtles, damaged birds. Looks like she found another stray to save." She shook her head in disbelief.

"What happens now?" Grace asked.

"We need to find Peterson and bring him in for questioning. He may not have anything at all to do with the murder, but with his prison record and proximity to the Shetlers' house, he is definitely someone I want to talk with."

Becky shook her head. "He didn't have anything to do with it."

"You don't know that," Grace said.

"Yes I do. Owen would never hurt anyone."

"Nearly every criminal I have ever known," the sheriff said, "had a girlfriend or a mother who said that. They were almost always wrong."

"I'm not his girlfriend."

"Then why have you been selling Grandma's things?" Grace asked.

Becky's eyes widened. "You know about that?"

"Oh, yeah. You want to explain it?"

"Can I have another tissue first?"

Grace handed her one and Becky blew her nose loudly. "Okay, then. Owen owed a guy some money from before he was arrested. The man's name is Frank Skraggs and he's really mean. He'd been waiting for Owen to get out of prison so he could collect. Owen didn't have the money. Frank beat him up because of it."

"How much did he owe?" Grace asked.

"Ten thousand dollars. It was something to do with when Owen was dealing drugs."

"That's why you've been selling my things?" Elizabeth asked. "To give money to some ex–drug dealer to protect an ex-convict?"

"I was going to pay you back, Grandma. Honest."

"We've already established that you were not in school," the sheriff interrupted. "Where were you the morning of the murder?"

"I picked up Owen and took him to check in with his probation officer. He was scared to miss even one appointment."

"What time was the appointment?"

"Eleven."

"That would have given him plenty of time to rob and shoot the Shetlers. Were you in on that, Becky? Did you know what had happened?"

"I didn't. If I had known Frank was part of it, I would have told you, I swear. But I didn't even know about Frank until a few days later. Owen never said a word about the murder."

"Tell us more about this Skraggs guy." The sheriff drummed a pencil on his desk.

"As long as he got enough money every week, he promised not to hurt anybody. I gave Owen everything I had in my savings account, but it wasn't enough. I thought if I could sell some things and give him the money, Frank would go away."

"Why in the world didn't you tell me?" Grace asked. "I could have helped you."

"You would have gone straight to the sheriff's department, and Owen would have gone back to jail if his probation officer found out that he was having contact with a felon. Plus, Frank said he would hurt anyone we told. I believed him. I never knew where he lived, or when he would show up. Sometimes he would send threatening text messages to me, saying that he was watching me, and I could tell he really was. Besides, if I had told you about Owen, I know you wouldn't have let him stay and he didn't have anywhere else to go."

"Is Owen the reason you told us you were taking food to a stray dog that lived in the woods?"

"Yes." She nodded miserably.

"Allowing children to write to criminals . . ." The sheriff shook his head. "I'm a religious man, and I understand the Scripture about visiting people in prison, but sometimes I think the church should pay a little more attention to being as 'wise as serpents' instead of putting so much emphasis on being as 'gentle as doves.'" He shook his finger at Becky. "There truly is evil in the world, young lady—and a lot of that evil, thanks to a whole lot of people like me who put their lives on the line, is behind bars. I have no problem with prison ministries, except when it involves people like you who are young and easily manipulated."

"But Owen wasn't just some sleazy prisoner," Becky said hotly. "He was a good guy!"

"How much have you given him so far?" Grace asked.

"Counting my college savings account, about six thousand dollars," Becky said. "I had to go to a lot of antique stores. It's harder to sell antiques than I realized."

"How did you even know which things were worth anything?"

"I think I can answer that," Elizabeth said. "A few weeks before I got sick, I had an expert come in to evaluate some items. I knew I might have a few things that were valuable, but I didn't know how valuable. My husband and I just bought things that we liked and enjoyed, but it turned out we had better taste than I realized. When the evaluator finished going through everything, Becky and I found out that our little collections were worth around a hundred thousand dollars."

"You've got to be kidding!" Grace exclaimed. "Why didn't you tell me?"

"I was going to." Grandma shrugged. "But I had plans to have an auction when I got better, and sell most of it off. I have enjoyed my things, and they hold a lot of memories, but I didn't want to be one of those people who die and leave a house stuffed full of possessions that their children have to sort through. Plus, I wanted to do what good I could with the money while I was still alive."

"That's terrific," Grace said. "But I still don't understand why you didn't tell me."

"It was a private joke between Becky and me. We thought it would be funny to see the look on your face when what you kept calling 'clutter' brought in enough money for a trip around the world, or a college education, or any number of things that would be more fun than staring at a bunch of dusty antiques. It sounds a little foolish now," Elizabeth said, "but I guess I was just anticipating the look of surprise on your face when you found out."

"When did you take all this stuff out of the house, Becky?" Grace said. "We were usually there. We would have seen you."

"I always knew when you would be taking Grandma to a doctor's appointment. I would plan to come back after you left."

The sheriff had been typing something into his computer while listening to Becky. He turned the screen toward them.

"Is this the man?" he asked.

"That's Frank," she answered.

Grace recognized the person Becky had introduced as the janitor.

The sheriff turned the screen back around and stared thoughtfully at Skraggs's face.

"What has he done?" Grace asked.

"You name it, he's done it," he said. "There's a good chance Becky actually might have saved your life by doling out money each week. Some of these guys—the really nutso ones—can almost read your mind. They are such good liars themselves, they can practically smell a lie coming from someone else. In my opinion, this guy would have had no moral problem with wiping out your whole family."

"Do you think Skraggs had something to do with the Shetler murder?" Grace asked.

"I have no idea. I don't want to go around trying to pin that killing on every stranger that enters Holmes County—but I've already sent the gun to the lab and we should hear something soon. I'm hoping that whoever shot Abraham and Claire didn't remember to wipe his fingerprints off the bullets."

"I still don't understand," Grace said. "Why is someone like Frank Skraggs even out?"

"A good lawyer, a lenient parole board, time off for good

behavior, prison overcrowding—you name it. There's all kinds of reasons these guys get out."

The sheriff leaned back against his desk and crossed his arms. "I want to go find this Owen Peterson and bring him in for questioning. I want the three of you to stay here until I do."

"May I come with you?" Grace asked.

"Why?"

"There are a lot of outbuildings behind Grandma's house. The weeds are high and thick, and finding the right building won't be easy. Make enough noise opening and closing doors, and Owen might hear you and run off into the woods. I know exactly where the smokehouse is, and I can lead you straight to it."

"That's a good point, but there's always the chance he might be armed."

"I'm ex-military, Sheriff. I know how to defend myself and I don't scare easily."

The sheriff steepled his fingers and considered. "Well, we are short-staffed tonight."

Levi felt uneasy. It wasn't the *Meidung,* and it wasn't the scene with the sheriff and Becky. It was something else. Something he couldn't put his finger on, and it was definitely keeping him awake.

He paced through the house, unable to settle down, looking out each window. He checked the boys' room. Albert was carefully tucked beneath the covers, lying flat on his back. His eyes were closed and his breathing was steady. He slept so carefully, he would barely have to straighten the covers of his side of the bed when he awoke to make it tidy.

Jesse lay sprawled out, taking up most of the space on

the full-sized bed the two boys shared. His pillow had been pushed to the floor and his covers were in total disarray. Jesse slept like he lived. Too much energy, too much movement, too much curiosity, and so much potential. Life would not be easy for Jesse, but it would be interesting.

Levi picked the pillow up, placed it beneath Jesse's head, and rearranged the little flayed-out limbs until they lay beneath the covers. Then he smoothed back the boy's sweaty bangs and placed a kiss on his forehead.

Jesse opened his eyes. "Is that you, *Bruder?*"

"Yes. It's me. Go back to sleep now."

"I am glad you are here," Jesse said sleepily. He yawned, closed his eyes, and fell back to sleep.

"Gute Nacht, ihr meine Lieben," Levi whispered. "Good night, my loved ones."

He entered his little sister's room. Her prayer *Kapp* was gone, and her baby-fine blond hair was unpinned and unbraided. She looked like a tiny angel lying there. He ran his fingers gently through her soft curls.

What lengths would he go to in order to protect this child? Was there anything he wouldn't do to save her if she or her brothers were threatened?

As he stood on guard between these innocent children and a possible threat, he knew in his heart that he could never stand aside and watch passively while someone hurt one of them. He knew that he would protect these children with his life.

These were not the thoughts of a proper, God-fearing Amish man. A good Swartzentruber would leave everything in the hands of God.

He wanted to have that kind of faith, but deep down he knew that if any of the people beneath this roof were in mortal danger, he would take it into his own hands to protect them.

God help him, he couldn't be any other way.

He knew in that instant, as he watched the shadow of the moon dance upon his baby sister's sleeping form, as he watched her curls moving in the gentle breeze that came through the open window, he would never be able to change.

He went into his old bedroom. It was a corner room, with a window on each side. One window overlooked the back of their property. The barn and some of the outbuildings could be seen from the other. The air felt stuffy in his old room, and he opened a window to let in a breeze.

Tomorrow morning would come very early. He lay down on top of the coverlet, fully clothed, and tried to relax. Perhaps he could at least doze a little before morning came.

He tried hard, but he could not relax. It seemed as though every muscle in his body was clenched like a fist, and he didn't know why.

And then he heard a nervous whinny from within the barn where he had put Angel Dancer, and then another, louder one.

Something was upsetting her.

He hoped it was nothing. He hoped it was just a stray dog or cat that had wandered into Angel Dancer's stall.

Looking out the window that faced the barn, he didn't see anything. Then Angel Dancer whinnied again and kicked the wall of her stall. She was definitely upset.

Angel Dancer was too valuable and intelligent an animal to overreact.

High above the kitchen door—so high the children could not easily reach it—was the loaded hunting rifle that Abraham had kept ready to protect his chickens and livestock from predators. Levi went down to the kitchen, grabbed the gun, and went outside to investigate.

chapter TWENTY-SEVEN

Grace led the sheriff behind Elizabeth's old barn, past the tumbledown corncrib, the unused outhouse, and the old chicken house. The sheriff pointed his flashlight downward and motioned for her to look. There was a break in the tall grass, the beginnings of a path. Quietly they approached the smokehouse. There was a faint light spilling out through various cracks.

"Owen Peterson?" The sheriff drew his gun. "If you're in there, come out. This is the county sheriff."

Grace held her breath.

The door opened, and a disheveled, lanky young man came out with his hands up.

"Are you Peterson?" the sheriff asked.

The man nodded. Grace thought if she had ever seen a deer-in-the-headlights look in someone's eyes, it was Owen's.

"What do you want?" the boy asked. "I've kept every appointment with my probation officer. I haven't done anything wrong."

"I just need you to come down to the station with me for questioning. We're not charging you with anything."

"Okay." Owen was skinny and scared looking. "I guess. Can I put my hands down now?"

The sheriff frisked him for weapons. "Yes. You can put your hands down now."

As the sheriff took Owen back to the car, Grace looked inside the small building where the original owners had once smoked their hams. It hadn't been used in decades. It was about ten feet by ten feet, but Owen had made a small home for himself. It had been swept clear of dirt and spiderwebs. There was a blow-up mattress in one corner of the floor with a sleeping bag on it. Becky had evidently managed to find an old table somewhere, and a chair with one rung missing. A few cans of food were stacked on the table, along with a half-empty bag of Doritos. The only light was from an old oil lamp. There were a few articles of clothing folded neatly beside his bed and a large container of water and a wash pan with a washcloth folded beside it.

Her guess was that everything except the mattress had been scrounged by either him or Becky from various outbuildings.

Everything was as neat and clean as possible. But the thing that broke her heart, and helped her understand why Becky had felt it was necessary to help him, was the open Bible lying on the table. The Bible had seen much use. A yellow highlighting pen lay, with its cap off, between the pages.

She put the cap back on, blew out the lamp, and closed the door behind her. It was time to go. She would deal with the pitifulness of this scene later.

Levi had just stepped into the darkened barn door when he saw a match flare and got a glimpse of a man's face. The man lit a lantern that Levi kept hanging in the barn for doing chores in the dark, early hours.

"You don't actually plan on using that peashooter on me, do you, Amish?" he calmly asked.

All Levi could see now was a shadowy form backing into the darkest corner of the barn.

"What do you want?" Levi asked.

"I'm looking for something that belongs to me."

"Why are you looking for it in my barn?"

"Well," the man drawled, "that would probably be because I dropped it somewhere around here."

A chill ran up Levi's spine. It didn't take a genius to realize that the thing this man was looking for was the handgun his little brothers had found.

"You should leave now." Levi cocked the rifle. It was only a .22, but it was an automatic. He wished he had thought to see how many bullets were in the chamber before leaving the kitchen.

"And here I thought you Amish didn't believe in guns."

The man had somehow circled around and was behind him now. Levi whirled just as something solid knocked into him and his rifle went skittering off into the dust. The fall caused the cocked rifle to fire one round and it reverberated throughout the barn. He tried to get up, but the man's hands gripped him around his neck.

"You should have left well enough alone, Amish, and stayed inside. I was just trying to find the gun I dropped. I was too drunk that night to remember whether or not I had wiped my prints off." He chuckled as though amused by his own incompetence, even as he struggled to squeeze the life out of Levi. "And believe me—my fingerprints are on all kinds of cops' computer files."

Levi did not know how to get this man's hands off his neck. He writhed in the dust of his own barn with the man's long fingers wrapped like steel bands around his throat. He grappled at the man's arms and wrists, trying to yank them away, trying to dislodge them long enough to gasp for air—

but the man held doggedly on, his fingers immovable, strangling him to death.

Levi knew no fancy moves, he had no idea how to fight this man, but what he did have was a lifetime of hard physical labor. He grappled at the man's hands and finally managed to wedge two fingers beneath his palms.

Whether it was from the anger of knowing that this was the man who had tried to destroy his family, or whether it was a gift from God, he didn't know, but suddenly he found the strength to tear the man's hands away from his throat.

He felt a violent urge as he flipped the man over onto his back and pinned him to the earth. Levi was no fighter, but he had wrestled calves, wrangled horses, and forked tons of hay into the mow of his barn. He held the man, bucking and kicking, against the floor.

The fight upset Angel Dancer, who whinnied and stamped against the inside of the stall while Levi struggled to decide what to do next. He knew now that his strength was superior to the man's. He knew that he could probably crush the life from this man's body with his bare hands.

And he wanted to. Oh, how he wanted to!

In his mind he saw images of his mother lying in the hospital, pale and shaken.

Images of his newborn baby brother in that incubator.

Images of Albert, Jesse, and little Sarah crying in the hayloft while their mother bled in an upstairs bedroom.

Jesse's and Albert's faces when they told him they had hidden the gun because they were afraid.

Images of his family's peaceful life being left in shreds because of this man's greed.

"Levi?"

He heard a familiar voice—Jesse!

"*Bruder?* Are you okay?"

The rifle shot. Jesse had awakened because of the rifle shot. Jesse—always such a restless, light sleeper.

"Bring me that rope." Levi nodded toward one looped over a nail in the barn wall. "Quick."

Jesse didn't hesitate. He ran to get the rope.

Levi's attention was diverted by his brother for only a split second, but his grasp loosened a fraction, just enough to give the man the opening he needed. He twisted like an eel beneath Levi, freed himself, and lunged for the rifle lying discarded on the ground. He had it in his hands before Levi could stop him.

Jesse had already returned to Levi's side. The now useless rope dangled from his hands.

It was probably simply a trick of the light, but Levi would have sworn that the man's eyes glittered like an animal's as he sighted down the rifle barrel.

"This gun's not much, but if you take one step toward me," the man said, "I'll shoot the boy."

Levi saw the muzzle of the rifle lower until it pointed directly at Jesse. And then he saw a crazy half smile spread over the man's face—an expression that Levi had never seen on a human before. It looked as though the man was looking forward to pulling the trigger. Relishing it. As if shooting people were a sport.

If he had ever doubted that there was true insanity in the world, that doubt disappeared.

Grace was getting into the sheriff's car when she heard a shot coming from Levi's farm. It could be Levi scaring off a fox or coyote, or it could be something more sinister.

She and the sheriff looked at each other. He had heard the gunshot, too.

"Get out of the squad car, son," the sheriff said.

"What?" Owen looked totally confused.

"Just get out—and don't run away. I'm coming back for you later. Remember, you're not under arrest. We just need to talk with you."

The boy got out.

The sheriff turned to Grace. "You're military-trained in weaponry?"

"I'm a nurse, but I did well on the rifle range in basic."

"You know how to handle a shotgun?"

"Yes, sir."

He backed out of her driveway and jammed his foot down on the accelerator.

Without giving thought to his own safety, Levi lunged toward the man, closing the distance between them at a full run. His headlong rush caught the man by surprise, but he still reacted in time to get off two shots that tore into Levi's shoulder.

Levi felt the fire go through his body, but his only thought was to stop this man from hurting Jesse.

He fell against him, taking him down by the sheer force and weight of his body. The blow knocked the rifle out of the man's grasp. Two seconds later, Levi had the man's arms locked behind him. Without having to say a word, Jesse was already beside him, placing the rope in his hand.

Levi wound the rope around the man's hands, and then both of his feet, hog-tying him as he would a calf.

The man lay cursing on the ground. He reminded Levi of a wounded snake as he writhed in the dust, and he hoped with all his heart that Jesse would not remember the bad words streaming from the man's mouth.

By the grace of God, it was finished—and he had not even

struck the man except to knock him to the ground with his own body. He had absorbed the bullets into himself rather than allowing Jesse to be harmed.

He yanked on the end of the rope binding the man's hands and feet, giving it one more cinch. He could feel the dizziness coming and he did not want to lose consciousness until he made certain that Jesse would no longer be at risk. Then he sank to the ground.

At that moment, the big sheriff came through the door with his gun drawn—and Grace directly behind him holding a shotgun.

"Not again!" Grace knelt beside him, held her hand pressed tight against the wound in his shoulder, and flipped open her cell phone with the other.

The last thing he remembered was thinking that he really needed to get one of those things. A man never knew when he might need one—for an emergency.

"Is my *Bruder* going to be okay?" Jesse's voice was unsteady.

"Come here, sweetheart," she said. "Do you suppose you could give me a hug? I could sure use one right now."

The little boy didn't hesitate. He flew toward her. She held him with her left arm while she pressed down on Levi's wound with her right hand.

"Better?" she asked the little boy.

He nodded.

"It's over now. This man will never hurt anyone again," the sheriff said. "Your brother is very brave."

"Now go get your *Maam,*" Grace said. "I think she will want to know what has happened."

A few moments later Claire arrived wearing a long, plain nightgown. Her prayer *Kapp* was missing, her hair was plaited down her back. Grace was impressed with the woman's relative calm under the circumstances.

"How is he?" she asked anxiously.

"I'm pretty sure he'll be fine, Claire," Grace said. "Where's Daniel?"

"Jesse is watching him." She stared at the man lying trussed up on the ground. "Is that the man who shot my Levi?"

"Evidently," the sheriff said.

"And killed my Abraham?"

"I'm pretty sure it's the same guy."

Claire walked over and squatted down beside Skraggs. "Why did you do these terrible things?"

Grace hoped nothing too vile would come out of the man's mouth. It didn't. He simply lay in the dirt, glaring at Claire, and then he spat at her.

Claire calmly wiped the spittle off her arm, stood up, and said the harshest thing Grace had ever heard her utter.

"I am glad my Levi knows how to tie such strong knots!"

chapter TWENTY-EIGHT

"**I**s Levi going to be okay?" Becky asked when she picked up Grace at Pomerene Hospital at dawn the next day.

Grace snapped on her seat belt. "By the grace of God, he is."

Becky backed out of the parking spot. "Are you mad at me?"

"'Mad' isn't a strong enough word, Becky," Grace said. "I'm positively furious at you."

"Because I gave Owen a place to stay?"

"No!" Grace slapped the seat. "That I can understand. I even understand trying to help him get enough money together to keep a killer at bay. What I'm furious about is that you kept all this from me."

"You heard what the sheriff said." Becky waited for traffic to clear, then pulled out onto the highway. "Frank might truly have hurt you."

"He's wrong about that." Grace sank back into her seat, exhausted from a night of watching and worrying over Levi. "I can take care of myself. You should have told me."

"Okay, so I made some stupid decisions. If I could do it over, I would make different ones. I was just doing the best I knew how. Can you ever forgive me?"

"I honestly don't know yet." Grace rummaged around in

her purse. "Do you have a mint? I feel as if my mouth is filled with cotton."

"There's some Tic Tacs in Grandma's glove compartment." Grace shook some out into her hand. "You want one?"

"Thanks." Becky popped one into her mouth without taking her eyes off the road.

"What happened while I was at the hospital?" Grace asked. "What did the sheriff do with Owen and Frank?"

"Frank's in jail. The sheriff said they found a couple of his fingerprints on the bullets. The sheriff said he was glad Grandma wasn't in the habit of keeping it already loaded, or it would have been harder to connect Frank to the murder."

"What did he do about Owen?"

"The sheriff found a better temporary home for Owen than Grandma's smokehouse."

"Where's that?"

"Some Old Order Amish man is giving Owen a place to stay in exchange for some work. Owen isn't thrilled about getting up at four in the morning to put mechanical milkers on a herd of dairy cows, but he's doing it."

Grace sucked on the mint for a moment. "You'd better slow down. It's too foggy to drive the speed limit. There are too many buggies on the roads in the morning."

Becky obediently eased her foot off the accelerator.

"There's one thing I don't understand," Grace said. "Why did Skraggs need to use you to sell Grandma's things? Why didn't he just back a truck up, clean us out, and head to the next state?"

"He said everyone would be suspicious of him, but no one would suspect me because I'm just the sweet, innocent little granddaughter."

"Are you trying to be funny?"

"No. It's the truth. That's what Frank said."

"I still don't understand what Frank was doing at the Shetlers' in the first place. How did he know there would be auction money there? He didn't strike me as the kind of man to spend a lot of time hanging out at livestock auctions."

"I found out only last night." Becky swerved slightly to avoid a buggy and horses trotting along in the early-morning mist. "The murder happened on a Thursday morning. I didn't know about Frank yet, and Owen didn't want to get me involved. On the other hand, he didn't have so much as a dime to give to Frank. On Wednesday, Owen had seen Abraham take a young horse to the weekly auction in Mt. Hope. He knew they would bring back cash and since the Amish are supposed to be nonviolent, he told Frank about it, thinking it would be a way of making Frank happy without anyone getting hurt."

"Was Owen with Frank when he shot Abraham?"

"No. He didn't even know Frank had the gun until afterward, when Frank started bragging about how he had shot Abraham and Claire. He said that's when he realized Frank was crazy. Owen said he was scared stiff of the man. There's something seriously wrong with Skraggs."

Grace made a sound of disgust. "You think?"

"You really aren't going to forgive me for a while, are you?"

"Nope." Grace pointed. "Watch out. There's another buggy."

Becky swerved. "Gosh, they're thick this morning."

"It's early," Grace said. "And it's a workday."

"So many bicycles, too. Sometimes I wonder if Holmes County doesn't have more bicycles than any other county in the United States. Even the Amish girls ride bikes to work." Becky tapped her fingers on the steering wheel. "Maybe I should get a job."

"You're going to have to if you're going to pay Grandma back for the things you sold."

"I took only the things she had told me I could have when she died."

"She's not dead yet, Becky!" Grace huffed. "Although I'm surprised this mess you made didn't kill her."

"I said I was sorry!"

"Yes, but it's going to take a while before either one of us completely trusts you again."

"I know."

"What I don't understand is how Frank managed to get the gun in the first place. Did you give it to him?"

"Of course not! He found it in Grandma's house."

"Skraggs was in our house?"

"Oh, yeah," Becky said. "The first time I ever saw him, he was inside the house going through Grandma's stuff and I surprised him. I about had a heart attack. He promised to stay out as long as I was giving him regular cash payments."

"It gives me the creeps to know that he was going through our stuff!" Grace said.

"Are you ready to forgive me yet?"

"No." Grace stared out the window for a few minutes. "What is the sheriff going to do to you?"

"I'll have to testify, but the sheriff said he wasn't going to charge me with anything except being young and stupid."

"Nothing?"

"The only thing I had done illegally was sell some of Grandma's things. The sheriff asked her if she wanted to press charges and she said that since I was her ride home, she'd rather not."

"Sounds like her," Grace said. "By the way, I saw the place where Owen was staying."

"Sad, wasn't it?"

"Very."

"He was going to leave. He had found a job at one of the cheese-processing plants and was supposed to start next Monday. As soon as he got Frank paid off, he was going to find a place to rent."

"You'll need to go apologize to Claire and Levi for bringing this tragedy into their lives."

"I'm really dreading that. But honestly, I was just trying to help. I never in a million years thought giving a friend a place to sleep would turn into this. Have you forgiven me yet?"

"Will you ever be dumb enough to do something like this again?"

"Not in a million years."

Grace hesitated a moment. "I'll work on it."

chapter TWENTY-NINE

"**Y**ou should not be here," Levi said as his mother brought soup and fresh-baked rolls to his room above the workshop. "The bishop would not approve."

"Well, then we will be even, because I do not much approve of the bishop."

"Maam!" He could hardly believe that his gentle mother had said such a thing. In their world, this was skirting very close to blasphemy.

"I will not shun my own son who has done nothing wrong." She set the tray of food on his table. "Never again."

"What? You will be disciplined if the bishop finds out."

"The bishop is not God"—Claire put her hands on her hips—"and his daughter is not with child!"

This was surprising news to Levi. "How do you know?"

"I am not blind. I have helped deliver too many babies and watched too many women in the early stages of pregnancy. You can take my word on it. That girl is not carrying a child."

"Does the bishop know?"

"Ezra Weaver is blind when it comes to his only daughter."

"If you're right," Levi mused, "and she's not pregnant, she'll have to tell the bishop and her mother sometime."

"Not necessarily," Claire said.

"What do you mean?"

"She could always pretend that she 'lost' the baby." Claire shrugged. "Zillah is good at pretending."

"She is."

His mother looked around the sparsely furnished room. "Is there anything else you need?"

"Only for this shoulder to heal so that I can get back to work. I'm worried about getting the rest of the planting finished."

"You chose a good time to get shot," Claire teased. "It has been too wet to work the soil."

"Truly said."

His mother glanced out the window. "Oh. Here comes Grace. She's carrying something." She busied herself setting out the rolls, soup, and silverware on the table. "Sometimes I wish Grace were Amish." She shot a glance at him. "I think you sometimes wish for this, too?"

"I don't wish for that. Grace would not be who she is if she were not *Englisch*."

There was a knock on the door. Claire opened it and Grace stepped in. In addition to her medical basket, she was carrying a cake. Levi's heart leaped when he saw her—and it wasn't because of the cake.

"Hi, Claire," Grace said. "The children said you were over here. How is our patient this morning?"

"Complaining, as usual, about not being able to work," Claire boasted. "My Levi does not know how to rest."

"I know."

"How is your grandmother?" Claire asked.

"Feeling so much better that she baked this morning. It's the first time since her surgery that she's felt strong enough. She wanted me to bring this to Levi. She said she remembers his liking this when he was little." She placed the cake on the table beside the tray that Claire had carried in. "Orange cake with dark chocolate frosting. Do you remember this, Levi?"

"Of course. It was your grandfather's favorite," Levi said. "Sometimes when she was especially missing him, she would bake this and we would eat it together while she told me stories about him."

"I'm sure that was a comfort to her."

Levi smiled. "It was also a comfort to a little boy's belly."

Suddenly there was a disturbance in the yard.

"*Maam!*" Albert called. "*Maam!* Daniel is crying!"

"Enjoy your food." Claire patted him on the leg. "I will be back soon."

Once Claire was gone, Grace came over and placed a hand against his forehead. "No fever. How are you feeling?"

"*De ganz dog rum hocka macht em faul.*"

"And that means?"

"Sitting all day makes one lazy." He shrugged. "It's something my stepfather used to say."

"Perhaps, but a little rest has agreed with you. Your color is better than yesterday."

"I've had a good nurse."

Grace removed his bandages and pulled fresh ones out of her medical basket.

"You have done too much of this for our family lately," he said as he watched.

"You're right." She was intent on her work. "Your family needs to break the habit of standing in front of bullets."

"I was not standing."

"I know." She grinned. "You were like a mad bull charging that man."

"He was threatening Jesse. I was not thinking straight."

"If you had been a soldier, you would get a medal for what you did."

"I don't want medals. I only want my family to be safe."

She sat on the edge of the bed while she put on the fresh bandages. After she finished taping them she pulled off her gloves and started to rise, but he grabbed her wrist and held it.

"Don't go."

She sat quietly beside him. It felt good just to have her near. She smelled like wild roses. It was a surprisingly old-fashioned smell—not a scent he would have expected a modern woman like Grace to choose.

Now that he was feeling better, everything within him wanted to pull her close. To hold her near him for the rest of his life. He could see the longing in her eyes for him as well.

"We are alone," Grace said. "And we shouldn't be. I need to go."

"Yes." He sighed as he released her. "You need to go."

She placed the palm of her hand against his cheek for a brief caress before she arose.

"You may start moving around more, but please take it easy, Levi. Don't use your shoulder for anything heavy. You don't want to tear something that has begun to heal."

"I'll be careful," Levi promised.

"I'm going into Millersburg today to try to repurchase the things that Becky sold to that antiques store owner," Grace said.

"Like that toy monkey you told me about?"

"Especially that one." She reached for the door. "Before I go, is there anything I can pick up for you while I'm in town?"

"There is one thing I've been wishing I had."

"What's that?"

He smiled. "Do you own a library card, Grace?"

"Not yet, but I can get one. Why?"

"I would very much appreciate it if you would." He pulled a small list from his pocket. "My people have a saying—*Di mai glond, di mai fuguddled*—'The more learned, the more confused.' Since it is impossible for me to get into any more trouble with the bishop than I already am, and since I am already very confused, here's a list of topics I would like to learn about if the library has any books on them."

Grace took the list. "I'll be more than happy to do that for you, Levi."

He did not understand why Grace had tears in her eyes when she left.

chapter THIRTY

I t was yet another drizzly morning. It seemed as though the sun had rarely shown its face throughout the entire month of May. Levi thought how well the weather had mirrored his emotions through these past turbulent weeks. Now it was the middle of June and every farmer in the state was desperately hoping the rain would go away so their fields would have a chance to recuperate.

Today he was repairing harnesses inside his workshop. His wounds had healed well, and although his shoulder was stiff, it was nothing that he could not live with. He would have endured much worse than a couple of gunshot wounds to save his little brother's life.

The close call with Skraggs had brought out a serious side to Jesse that Levi was saddened to see. He hoped Jesse would recover quickly and once again be a carefree little boy.

He wondered what Grace was doing this morning. Grace was on his mind almost constantly these days. She had come every day to dress his wound or to bring him some new library books, or something special to eat. It had been painful to forfeit her daily visits once he had healed enough that there was no more reason for her to come to see him.

But in spite of everything he had been through, the ban was not lifted. If anything, he was under even more suspicion now. Amish people did not fight. And he had.

He knew that whether or not an Amish could defend himself or his family was a question that most Amish men pondered from time to time. Most dealt with it by simply praying that God would never put them in such a situation.

But he had been put in that situation and he had discovered that it was impossible for him to even stand back and allow someone he loved to be hurt.

This was deeply troubling.

Knowing this about himself, could he in all good conscience remain Swartzentruber? Could he remain Amish at all?

He had gone from being panicked about being placed under the *Meidung* to being almost grateful for the relative isolation in which he had been living the past few weeks. The ban had left him with much time to think.

He loved being part of a community of believers. He loved being held within the strong network of extended family and friends. He didn't mind at all wearing the simple clothing of the Swartzentrubers, and he could live the rest of his life without electricity or even running water.

But he was afraid he would never again be able to respect Bishop Weaver's leadership. The unquestioning love and affection he had always held for his church was eroding.

He did not expect to see anyone today and was surprised when he heard a buggy in his driveway.

He had a lapful of harness, so he didn't bother to get up. He figured whoever it was had probably come to see his mother about something, perhaps some illness that needed one of Claire's herbs or tinctures. Now that she was well, her work as a healer was picking up.

He was surprised when the door to his workshop opened and even more surprised when he saw that it was Bishop Weaver.

His hands stilled as he waited to see what the bishop wanted. Perhaps to try to convince him one more time to marry his daughter now that he had a good taste of the ban.

The bishop had aged in the few weeks since Levi had seen him. His beard was grayer. The lines around his eyes and mouth looked deeper. Levi's heart went out to the man—in spite of his own pain—because he knew it must be a terrible thing to be reminded of his unmarried daughter's pregnancy, false though it was, every time he looked at her.

Bishop Weaver took his hat off and shook the raindrops off it. Then he wearily sat down.

Levi waited. It was not his place to initiate the conversation.

The bishop stared at the floor as though gathering his thoughts, and then he slowly raised his head and looked him straight in the eyes.

"The burden of being a bishop is a heavy one," he said, "and it is not a position I ever wanted."

He brushed the wet hat with his fingers and wiped them on his equally wet pants legs.

"I know it is a heavy responsibility," Levi agreed. He forced himself not to say more—he might say something he would regret. Much better to be quiet and let the bishop speak.

"If I am allowed to go to heaven," the bishop said, "I know I will be judged with a much heavier judgment than those who did not serve as leaders. It is a job I have taken seriously and I have done the best I knew to do. It is not an easy task to be the one who is constantly trying to hold back the reins when some of my people want to try new things. I was afraid that if I ever loosened my grip, our church would become as liberal as the other Amish orders."

Levi was surprised to hear the bishop's voice choke with emotion.

He wished he could take this great burden off the man, but he simply could not. This was something that Bishop Weaver would have to bear on his own.

He was stunned at the man's next words.

"I have done you a great injustice," the bishop said. He handed Levi a rain-splattered envelope.

"My wife found this in Zillah's bedroom this morning," the bishop said. "I came here as soon as I could harness my team."

Levi allowed the broken harness to fall to the floor as he reached for the envelope. It was lavender with a faint background of pansies—girl's stationery. Amish girls loved to write letters to one another. The ownership of pretty stationery was one of the few luxuries they were allowed.

On the front of the envelope it simply said "*Maam* and *Daed*," written in what looked to be hurriedly scribbled handwriting.

He pulled the single page out of the envelope and opened it.

"Are you sure you want me to read this?" he asked.

Bishop Weaver nodded.

The letter was short and to the point.

I am leaving home. Me and my new boyfriend are going far away. You will not be able to find me. Do not waste your time trying. I am sick of being Amish and I am going to break every commandment I can. My boyfriend has a car and money.

Zillah

P.S. Don't worry about your grandchild. I'm not pregnant.

Levi experienced many emotions reading the letter with the rain pounding down upon the workshop roof and a broken man sitting across from him.

He felt his soul open up at the freedom he now had. Freedom to be exonerated. Freedom to be accepted back into the bosom of the church. Freedom to walk in and out of his mother's home. Freedom to take Communion with the rest of the church with no cloud of suspicion hanging over his head.

But his heart ached for the man rubbing the brim of his black hat between his fingers, staring at floorboards, ashamed to meet his eyes.

He folded the letter and carefully fitted it back inside the envelope. Then he handed it back to the bishop.

"It is not your fault," Levi said, trying to comfort the grieving man. "It was never your fault."

"My wife and I will continue to pray for our daughter's soul. We will not try to find her. She has made it clear that she will resist any efforts to bring her back. I am afraid that Satan has gotten a terrible hold of her. We will pray that she will someday realize what she has done and ask for forgiveness not only for running away, but for what she put you and our church through by accusing you."

"Which we will give," Levi said.

"Yes." The bishop nodded. "Which we will always give—as God commanded."

Levi felt a great pity for the man before him, enough pity that he could honestly say, "I will pray daily that Zillah's heart will change and that she will come back to you and to the Lord."

"I will put the word out that the *Meidung* has been lifted and announce it at meeting," the bishop said. "I would be grateful if you could forgive me for believing my daughter over you."

"You are forgiven," Levi said. "I know the position Zillah placed you in."

"Thank you, Levi."

There was nothing else to say. The discussion of crops or livestock illnesses would not be appropriate, not after the *Hertza-laeht*—the awful heartache that the letter had brought upon the bishop and his wife.

As Levi watched the broken man leave, he had a strong suspicion that Ezra Weaver was going to be a much humbler and more compassionate bishop from this point on. The church would greatly benefit from that compassion. Then Levi put on his hat and walked across the driveway to have a long talk with his mother.

The kitchen was warm and welcoming when he arrived. It smelled of good things baking in the wood cookstove. His mother was checking something in the oven when he came through the door. A worried frown creased her forehead.

"What did the bishop want?"

"Zillah ran off with someone and left a note saying that she's not coming back. She also said that she had lied about being with child."

Claire's face was exultant. "I knew it!"

"I'm welcome back into the church. The bishop apologized. He is very sorry for not believing me."

She began pulling loaves of bread out of the oven and setting them on the table. "Then you will be able to go to meeting with us Sunday. That is wonderful."

He sat down at his mother's table. "I am not going back this Sunday."

She dropped the last pan of bread on the table, shocked. "Why not?"

"There are some things I want to do first."

"Like what?"

"For one thing, I was thinking that you and the children might like to pay a visit to Rose and Henry while the bishop is still ashamed of what he did."

"It is forbidden."

"Yes, but wouldn't it be nice if it were not?"

The rain had once again subsided, but every day seemed to bring at least a small shower or two—just enough to keep the fields in quagmires. When the sun finally found its way back to them, Levi knew that every farmer in Holmes County would be out with his team from sunrise to sundown, trying to make up for lost time.

He had woven a few baskets to add to the ones already stored in the workshop. On Wednesday, his mother packed up the children and all the baskets, adding several quarts of apple butter from her cellar, and drove the buggy to Mt. Hope to the livestock and produce auction. This was something they could do regardless of the weather. Beneath the roof of a giant barn near the auction, people bought and sold everything from live plants, to honey, to used kitchenware.

When she returned, his mother told him that she and the children had set their baskets out beside the man selling bundles of rhubarb and waited.

They came home with an empty buggy and money to support their family for several more weeks. Claire said that Daniel had been quite the center of attention as tourist women stopped to make a fuss over him—and ended up buying a basket and, in some instances, a quart or two of her good apple butter.

In the meantime, Levi had been devouring the books Grace brought him, books on agriculture, solar energy, astronomy, hydroponics, greenhouses, ornithology, geometry, basic physics, and geography.

For the first time in his life he had the freedom to feed his mind the knowledge it craved—and he feasted.

But along with the new knowledge came a spiritual struggle. The time of forced isolation he had endured had ended up being a sort of sanctuary for his soul. He had prayed harder and thought more deeply than ever before, and what he was thinking both frightened and beckoned to him.

He desperately wanted someone to talk to about what was on his mind, but it could not be his mother—not yet. She would become upset and defensive, afraid that she was going to lose her oldest son to the world. It could not be Grace. When he was around Grace, he did not have a clear head. The one person he knew that he could speak his heart to was the woman who had befriended him when he was still a young boy—Elizabeth.

Although Angel Dancer would have loved the exercise, he chose not to ride her to the Connors'. He was afraid he would tear his still-tender shoulder while mounting or dismounting. Instead, he walked, hoping he would have a chance to talk to Elizabeth alone.

Grace's car was gone when he arrived, but Elizabeth was sitting on the back porch in her swing, reading her Bible, as he had seen her do so many times before. This was the place in her house that he liked the best. It had a panoramic view of their fields and made a comfortable place for two old friends to sit and visit. He remembered the hours they had spent here together when he was a child while she had told him stories and taught him much about the natural world from her books.

If Elizabeth had been less sensitive to their culture, he would never have been allowed to come here. He had always been grateful to her for having overcome his mother and step-father's suspicions of allowing an *Englisch* person into his life.

"Levi!" Her face lit up when she saw him. "You're feeling better."

"Yes. You are looking stronger, also."

"Have you come to see Grace about something? I'm afraid she and Becky are gone."

"I'm glad they are not here." He sat down in the swing beside her. "I would like to talk to you alone."

"Oh?" Elizabeth closed her Bible and folded her hands upon it. "What do you want to talk about, Levi?"

It took courage for him to begin. It felt as though a piece of yarn from a sweater had come loose during his weeks of the *Meidung*. He feared that once he began to tug on it, it would start unraveling until the sweater was completely gone. This was a frightening thought because that particular sweater—although at times rather itchy—had provided a great deal of warmth to him over the years. He was afraid that if he opened his mouth and said the words he had come here to say, his whole life would come unraveled. But he spoke anyway.

"I am thinking of leaving my church."

"Oh, dear." Elizabeth heaved a great sigh. "Does this have anything to do with my granddaughter?"

"No."

She cocked an eyebrow. "Are you retaliating against your church for shunning you?"

"No. This is between God and me alone."

"Then what did you want to ask me?"

"Do you think I will go to hell if I leave the Swartzentruber church?"

Elizabeth acted startled by his question. "Well, of course not!"

"How do you know that for sure?"

"I've never interfered with your beliefs in any way, Levi."

Elizabeth seemed troubled. "Are you certain you want to know what I think?"

"Very much so."

"You're really sure you want to hear this?"

"I'm sure."

"Well, then." Elizabeth gazed out over the fields. "I've sat here on my porch and watched you and Abraham plow your land for many years. I've always enjoyed that—the image of a good farmer caring for the earth God had given him. But it has also saddened me."

He thought this was an odd way to answer his question about whether or not he was going to hell. "In what way were you saddened by watching us tend our fields?"

"Four enormous horses pulling one plow, right?"

"Our Belgians are large. Yes."

"I've watched you rest your horses beneath the shade of that tree where you sometimes eat your lunch. I've seen you check their harnesses to make certain nothing was rubbing or hurting them in any way. I've admired how you check their hooves and pry stones out long before they could become lame. Sometimes I've even heard you talking to them. I couldn't understand the words you used, but your voice sounded soothing, as though you truly cared about them."

"That is what a farmer does." Levi wondered what she was getting at. "A good farmer takes care of his animals."

"And when you get them back to the barn, I'm guessing that you feed them with the best that you have."

"I try to take good care of my horses."

"Apart from their earthly financial value, Levi, why do you take such pains with them?"

"Because they are my responsibility . . . and I care about them."

She nodded, as though that was the answer she had

expected. "So—would you ever put a big, heavy yoke on one of those horses, hitch it to your biggest plow, weigh it down with boulders, stand on top of it, and whip the horse to make it pull?"

"Never! You know me better than that."

"Every time I've watched you working your fields with your horses, one Scripture always leaps into my mind— Matthew 11:28–30. Are you familiar with it?"

"No."

"Jesus understood exactly how hard this life was, what a struggle it would be to get through. In the scene I'm describing, He is talking to His followers—some of whom are no doubt exhausted by the heaviness of this life—and His heart is full of love for them. What He says to them is, in my opinion, one of the most beautiful passages in the Bible."

Levi's curiosity was definitely piqued. "And what is that?"

"Jesus says, 'Come to Me, all you who are weary and burdened, and I will give you rest. Take My yoke upon you and learn from Me, for I am gentle and humble in heart, and you will find rest for your souls.'"

Levi felt not only his heart but even his body respond to the peace of that language. "That Scripture is very beautiful."

"Ah, but the very best is the Scripture that follows that one. It's my favorite verse in the whole Bible. Do you want to hear it?"

"Most definitely."

"'For My yoke is easy and My burden is light.'"

He drew a deep breath, absorbing and memorizing those words.

"The Lord I read about is not cruel, Levi. He came specifically to help us carry our burden, not load us up with so many rules and regulations that we stagger beneath the load, always

living in terror of breaking even one. When you truly understand this, everything changes—the yoke becomes so much
easier, and the burden becomes so very light."

This was not a Scripture that had ever been emphasized
in his Swartzentruber church. The idea of an easy burden
and a light yoke was against everything he had ever been
taught. He was surprised at how starved he felt for these
words.

"How?" he asked. "How does the burden become easy
and light?"

"Because instead of living your life constantly beneath the
heavy weight of fear"—Elizabeth caressed the worn, leather
binding of her Bible—"you find yourself serving out of sheer
gratitude. A relationship built on acceptance, forgiveness, and
love is an easy yoke to carry indeed."

"The yoke I have carried has been very heavy."

"I know, Levi. I've watched."

My yoke is easy and My burden is light.

He savored these healing words. All those years of trying
to be good enough. All those years of wondering if he were
doing everything he could to keep from going to hell. All
those years of not knowing if he would ever manage to make
it to heaven.

My yoke is easy and My burden is light.

Those nine words were like a drink of cold, pure water
after a day spent haying in a hot field. Those nine words
cooled his feverish soul. His heart told him that God had
never, ever meant for him to be that poor horse wearing a
heavy yoke, pulling a plow with boulders piled on it, being
whipped for not pulling harder.

Elizabeth was right. If Jesus had been a farmer, He would
be the kind of farmer who would give His horses a good

feed when they were hungry and cool water when they were thirsty, and let them rest beneath the shade of a tree when they were tired.

Levi had not cried since the first whipping that Abraham had given him after Abraham married Levi's mother. He had disciplined himself to shove the need to cry deep inside. But now, he broke down and wept.

Elizabeth sat very still, saying nothing, keeping him company while he grieved.

He heard Grace's car pull in. This was one time he did not want to see her—not with his eyes red from weeping.

"I should go." He stood to leave.

"I'm not going to speak of this conversation with Grace," Elizabeth said. "That is your choice—when you have decided for sure what you want to do."

"Thank you."

"Are you still trying to work your way through your step-father's German Bible?" Elizabeth asked.

"I am."

Elizabeth smiled. "And how is that going for you?"

"A little better with practice, but it is still difficult."

She handed him the Bible she had been reading when he had arrived. "This is written in everyday English. Read it yourself. Come to your own conclusions about whether or not God is going to reject you if you aren't Swartzentruber. You are not ten years old anymore. Your stepfather can't burn your book this time."

Levi took the volume into his hands. It was thick and well thumbed. "But this is yours."

"I have at least five others lying about," Elizabeth said. "Now go."

"I will treasure this, my friend."

"I'd rather you wear it out from use."

Elizabeth had never hugged him, but this time she did—and he needed it. He felt as if he were setting out on a long journey as he departed through the back way, holding a forbidden English translation of the Bible.

The very fact that it was forbidden would make the reading of it all the sweeter.

chapter THIRTY-ONE

"I'm truly happy for Levi," Grace said as she sprinkled some lettuce seed inside the depression she had made in the earth. The rains had washed away the lettuce bed she had created earlier in the spring, and they were replanting. "Honest, I am. He loves his people. Being shunned was a terrible thing for him. Now he's able to be a part of the life he's always known again. That's the way it should be."

"I'm happy for him, too," Elizabeth said. "You're sprinkling those seeds a little thick, don't you think? They like enough space to breathe."

Grace was doing her best to be excited about Levi's exoneration. Now that he had been welcomed back into the Swartzentruber community with open arms, she rarely saw him—which she knew was how it should be.

"Have you talked with him lately?" Elizabeth asked.

"No. Now that both he and Claire are well, I don't have any reason to go over there. I haven't seen him since he dropped off those library books a couple of weeks ago."

"Did he ask you to get him more?"

"No. He said he wouldn't need for me to get him any more—from now on."

"Ah," Elizabeth said. "Then he has gone back to his church completely. I had wondered if he would."

"I think he's probably sworn off ever being around *Englisch* women ever again," Grace said. "He probably got a belly full of us considering what our family put him through."

"You know, I'm actually looking forward to the auction we're having next week." Elizabeth deliberately turned the subject away from Levi, and Grace was grateful. Talking about Levi was hard for her. She would rather think about something else entirely.

"Are you sure? I'd think it would be sad to see so many memories being sold."

"Perhaps, but they are my memories, not yours. I don't want the two of you having to make a lot of decisions about what to keep and what to give away one day when I'm gone. Plus, I wouldn't mind doing some traveling again. Want to float down the Nile with me come autumn?"

"How about we visit Niagara Falls or the Grand Canyon instead? I like the idea of staying within the United States. I think I've seen enough of the world for a while."

"You are no fun at all, Grace," Elizabeth teased. "Are you certain you don't want to float down the Nile with me while exotic men feed us grapes?"

"I don't think that's quite how it works, Grandma."

"Don't put so much dirt over those seeds, Grace. Lettuce needs just a light dusting."

"Got it."

As she worked, she thought about Levi. She was determined not to grieve over the fact that he had once again embraced the church of his ancestors. It was how it should be. It would be cruel for him to have to pull away from those little brothers and sister of his. All along, she had known the day would come when they would go back to being just nodding acquaintances again.

Grace knew that she would soon have to decide whether to go back to her life in the military or see if there was still an opening at the local hospital. Once again, she was torn.

In her heart, she wanted to stay here in Holmes County. She loved the beauty and the gentler pace. She enjoyed being with Becky and Elizabeth. She just didn't know how hard it would be on her having Levi living just down the road.

The rainy season they had endured had finally ended. The sun had come out, and everything that could grow was doing so at top speed.

Elizabeth had recently decided that she wanted fresh eggs like the Shetlers' and had insisted that Grace and Becky purchase chicken wire. Together, the three of them had managed to turn one of the ramshackle outbuildings into a workable chicken coop. It wasn't pretty, but she did have some hens now. Hopes were high in their house that the chickens would start laying soon. Levi had pointed out, however, the day he dropped off the library books, that three of their "hens" were roosters. This was news. The chickens had all looked the same to her.

Grandma had rented out her tillable acres to a non-Amish neighbor. Although she would have preferred to have Levi use them, he had enough on his hands. Levi was working in his fields practically from sunup to sundown now that the rain had ceased.

Grace wondered how long before she would see some lovely Amish girl at his side when he drove his buggy past their house. That girl would be a lucky person indeed.

The little church in Millersburg her grandmother and Becky attended had become a home to her. It was not the most exciting church, but the people were kind and the minister's lessons sometimes spoke to her. Excitement was not something she craved these days. What with her previous work at Bagram Air Base and the past few weeks dealing with family crises, she had experienced enough excitement to last her a lifetime.

"Now for the onion sets," Elizabeth said. "You'll need to pack the earth around them firmly."

Grace had just finished planting the onions, and Elizabeth had gone inside to get them some iced tea, when Grace heard horses coming down the road.

She looked up and saw Levi on Angel Dancer. He was leading another mare behind him. On some errand to an Amish friend, she supposed. She walked over to the garden hose and rinsed off her hands. The cool water felt good against her skin. She also got a long drink of water and splashed some on her face.

There was a time when she would never have bothered to savor such things, but some profound changes had occurred within her since she had moved to Amish country. She had deliberately slowed her pace until she could sometimes almost hear the rhythms of the earth. She still woke early, but instead of immediately going off on her run, she would sit on the back porch awhile, listening—really listening—to the symphony of birds celebrating the sunrise.

The question was, at the end of the summer, would she go back to Afghanistan or would she stay and make a life for herself here?

Tell me what to do, Lord. Do I leave? Do I stay? I'll do whatever you say—if you'll just tell me for sure which way to go.

As Levi drew closer to her house, she wondered where he was going with the other horse. It was not one she had ever seen before.

She ran her wet hands through her hair. It still hadn't been cut since she had moved here. There had just been too much going on in her life to worry about finding a hairdresser and making an appointment. It was getting ragged and was in bad need of a trim. Perhaps she should let it grow so she could just pull it back into a ponytail. That was a simple hairstyle, and she had a great hunger for simplicity these days.

Grace sat down on a large stone, with her muddy gardening boots stretched out in front of her, closed her eyes, and relished the feeling of the sun on her face as she tried to ignore the sound of Levi's horses coming up the hill.

The horses grew closer, and then they were no longer on the road. Instead, their hooves clattered on gravel.

Her eyes flew open at the realization that Levi was coming up their driveway.

"Want to go riding?" He offered no explanation for his sudden appearance.

She stood up and brushed gardening dirt off her bottom. "I have no earthly idea how to ride a horse, Levi."

"It won't be hard to learn. This is *en guta Gaul*—a good horse—and she is very gentle."

"Where did you get her?"

"I traded some carpentry work for her. Go stand on the porch," he said. "I'll bring her around to you."

As Grace obeyed, Levi dismounted and brought the horse over to her until it was no effort at all to swing her leg over the saddle. He adjusted the stirrups until they were exactly the right length for her legs.

"Just hold on to the saddle horn for now," he said, "and try not to fall off. I'll lead her until you get used to the feel of it."

Grace had no idea where they were going, nor did she care. It simply felt good being with Levi again. Her grandmother heard their voices and came out onto the back porch. Grandma waved as they rode past. "Don't fall off!" she yelled.

"I'm not promising anything!" Grace called. She was afraid to let go of the saddle horn long enough to wave back.

She was happy to be with Levi, of course, but she wished she had a nice sturdy seat belt as she tried to accustom herself to the rolling motion of the horse. Every now and then, Levi would look back and check to see how she was doing. At one point, the mare she was riding looked back as though she, too, were unsure of Grace's ability to stay seated.

They crossed a field and then followed a small path for a short distance until they came to the rise on top of a hill.

"Whoa." Levi brought both horses to a stop.

She found herself gazing out over one of the most stunning landscapes she had ever seen.

"It's beautiful!" She eased her death grip on the saddle horn and relaxed slightly. The horse stamped its foot at a horsefly and she grabbed hold again for dear life.

"I thought you would like this," Levi said. "That's why I got the horse for you. Sometimes it is good to see the world from the back of a horse. A person can see more clearly when they travel slowly."

"You got this horse for me? Why?"

"You have taken good care of me and my family and I wanted to give you something."

Oh. This ride was nothing more than his expressing gratitude for her nursing skill. She should have known. The Amish paid their debts one way or another, and he had already given her two baskets.

And then he said something so shocking, she really did come close to falling off the horse.

"I'm leaving my church, Grace."

If a lightning bolt had struck the ground beside her, she couldn't have been more surprised. The reality of what this would do to his family staggered her.

"Levi, you can't do that. It would kill your mother and Jesse as well as Albert and Sarah. This last ban was hard enough on them. To never be able to see you again—you just can't do that to them."

"I'm not. My mother is leaving the Swartzentruber church, also."

Grace was thunderstruck. The idea of his mother leaving her church was practically incomprehensible. A woman who had been so obedient to her church as to shun her own son— how could she leave now?

"What in the world has happened?"

"*Maam* is not happy with our bishop and she misses her sister. She will be making her kneeling vow in Henry and Rose's Old Order Amish church. She and the children will be attending with my aunt and her family from this Sunday on."

It took her a moment to process all the implications of this. Rose and Claire could visit as much as they wanted once again. How wonderful!

"It is maybe not the best solution, but it is the solution she chose," he said. "Rose and Henry's church does not ban those who become members of other conservative Christian churches."

"What do you mean by 'solution'?"

"I've heard that there is a community church a few miles from here that has Mennonite roots. It has become a place where not only *Englisch* Christians are welcome but those who have left the Amish tradition can also feel comfortable. As you *Englisch* might say, this church does not have as many 'bells and whistles' as some. But once my mother becomes Old Order, it will not be expected of her to shun me. I have visited that church, and I have talked at length with the former bishop. They are trying very hard to follow Jesus' teachings. I would like to attend there. If I do, she and my brothers and sister will be allowed to treat me exactly as they always have."

"Oh, Levi! I'm so glad you found a solution! But you loved your church. This must have been a terrible decision to have to make."

"I still love my church, but for several weeks it didn't feel like my church loved me all that much. Zillah would not be pleased to know that in trying to hurt me, she did me a great favor. That dark time when my people turned their backs on me was necessary to make me rethink many things that I had never before questioned."

He turned to look at her, and in his eyes she saw the struggle that he had waged in making this decision. "I have to leave them, Grace. I am no longer able to accept the Swartzentruber *Ordnung* in my heart, and I won't pretend."

"How can I help you?" she asked.

He dismounted, walked over, and lifted his arms up to help her slide down off her horse. "Well, for one thing, I could definitely use a friend."

"You've got it, Levi. For as long as you need."

"In case you were wondering . . . this was between God and me. You did not cause this. It would have eventually happened even if you were not in my life."

"Thank you for telling me that."

"I have known for a while that I was not a good Swartzentruber." He turned her around and pointed her in the direction of the pond shimmering below them. "I have stood on this hill and looked at that pond. I have drawn diagrams in my mind about how simple it would be to bring a pipeline down to my mother's house and put in gravity-fed running water for my family. I have often longed to be able to use something besides oil lamps to read by. I have dreamed of bathing at the end of every day, instead of having to take the time to draw and heat water from the well. I have rebelled over and over within my

heart against not having the safety and convenience of a telephone, and I have become very frustrated with a church that
will not allow me to use a simple orange triangle to protect the
lives of my little brothers and sister. But that night in the barn,
when I realized that I truly wanted to hurt another human, I
knew that I was no longer Swartzentruber."

"But you didn't hurt him."

"By the grace of God, I did not. But the realization that I
was capable of wanting to shook me."

"You are a good man, Levi."

"No, my feet are very much made of clay. Right now, all
I am is a bewildered ex–Amish man who is trying to decide
how to live in an *Englisch* world without losing all the valuable things my people have taught me."

"What things are you afraid of losing?"

"Let's sit down." He led her to a giant oak tree on top of
the hill. They sat with their backs against the tree while their
horses contentedly cropped grass.

Levi plucked a blade of grass and began to shred it. "Many
young people who leave our church go completely wild once
they are gone. It is as though they have been reined in for so
long that when they leave, there are not enough drugs and
alcohol and fast cars in the world to satisfy them. Some are
eventually like prodigal sons. When they are completely
beaten by the world, they come back. But I am not a prodigal.
I am not running away. I value what I learned in my Amish
home."

He dropped the blade of grass, took her hand in his, and
entwined her fingers with his own. "I think there is wisdom
in raising children who do not see the world through the window of a television or computer. There is wisdom in teaching
children how to work and how to respect their elders. There
is strength in families living close enough to help one another,

and I have seen the power of what can be accomplished when a man and a woman make a covenant to love and support each other for the rest of their lives—and then honor that covenant."

"I agree with all of that."

"I would like to make such a covenant with you—if you would—but before that, I need to learn more about being *Englisch*."

Grace could hardly believe what she had just heard. Was that a proposal?

"If we were both Swartzentrubers and marrying within the church," he said, "hundreds of people would come to our wedding. But ours will be much smaller. Oh, and one more thing. Even though I will be banned from any Swartzentruber home, you will not. If some of my people needed your knowledge and skill, I would take it as a great favor if you would help them. Many of them are so poor, and they suffer rather than ask for medical help."

It *was* a proposal!

"That's no problem, but let me get something clear. Are you asking me to marry you, Levi Troyer?"

"No."

Her bubble of happiness deflated. "Okay, now I'm confused."

"I'm not asking you to marry me. I am asking you to wait for me. I have so much to do and so much to learn. I would not be much of a husband to you for a while."

"What is it that you want to do?"

"Things that you do without a second thought. It feels as if I am entering a different country from the one where I have always lived. I need to learn how to walk into a barber's shop and ask for a haircut—I don't even know what to tell them to do. I need to learn how to purchase *Englisch* clothes. I went to the Walmart in Millersburg and I tried, but the variety of clothes was so overwhelming that I didn't buy anything. I need to learn how to look up a phone number in a telephone book. I want to get my own library card, and I want to learn how to drive a car. I also want to purchase one. I hear that it is not lawful to own a car without insurance, and I have no idea how to go about getting that. There are so many things to learn. I don't think I can concentrate on courting you, farming, caring for my family, and reinventing my entire life all at the same time."

"There is no need to court me," Grace said, "but it sounds as though it is going to be a very long time before we can marry."

"A few months. Our people usually get married in the fall, after the harvest is safely in the barns and all the canning is finished. I'm thinking early November would be good. Does that sound all right to you?"

"November is fine."

"I'm glad."

Grace couldn't decide quite how she felt about all this. She was thrilled that Levi apparently wanted to spend the rest of his life with her, but this conversation seemed awfully . . . unemotional.

"So," she said, "it sure sounds like you have everything planned. Have you given any thought to where we will live?"

"I want to build a *Daadi-haus* onto your grandmother's house—if Elizabeth likes the idea. We can live in it until she needs it, or until the children come. My people seldom allow someone to go into a nursing home, so they build small houses attached to the larger house for the grandfather or grandmother to live in. Elizabeth is better now, but someday she will need care and I would be honored to help you care for her. I also want our children to have the gift of knowing her."

"You're willing to accept the electricity of my grand-mother's home?"

He grinned. "I've always been a little envious of the bright lights your family gets to read by."

"You've really thought this through, haven't you, Levi? I guess there's nothing left for me to decide." Grace was strangely unhappy. This was supposed to be one of the big-gest moments of her life—and yet the conversation felt flat and unsatisfying.

"I've said something wrong?"

"No. You've said nothing wrong. Everything you said is fine. It's what you have not said that bothers me."

He looked puzzled. "I don't understand."

"You have not told me that you love me."

"Oh. That."

"Yes. That."

"You are so *Englisch*." He brought her hand up to his lips and kissed it. "You do not understand."

"Then explain it to me, Levi."

"I will tell you I love you as many times as you want, and I will mean it. But my people's way of showing their love does not lie in saying mushy words. I will be telling you that I love you with everything I do. When I am building your grandmother's *Daadi-haus,* I will be telling you that I love you. When I fix the roof, I will be telling you that I love you. When I carry something that is too heavy for you, when I take you to see the tiny hummingbird's nest I have found, when I walk the floor with our babies so that you can rest, when I help you bring up our children in the Lord, when I live my life in com-plete faithfulness to you . . . I will be saying that I love you."

Tears welled up in her eyes. She knew every word he had spoken was as true as his loyal heart.

"I love you, Levi."

"I know." He kissed her on the nose. "You have spoken your love for me over and over with your actions." He kissed her on the forehead. "With every book you brought me when I was sick." He kissed her on the cheek. "When you wrecked your car to avoid hitting us." He kissed her on the other cheek. "When you came to the barn, ready to fight Frank Skraggs for me." He kissed her chin. "When you nearly drowned trying to save my little calf."

He pulled away and devoured her with his eyes. "You did not have to say the words. I already knew. You had said them to me a hundred times in a hundred different ways."

She was ready for his kiss when it came. And she was ready for the good life they would build together.

The Lord had spoken loud and clear.

Discussion Questions—
An Uncommon Grace

1. Many people admire what they perceive as the "simple life" of the Amish. After reading *An Uncommon Grace,* do you think their life is more or less complicated than your own? How?

2. One of the themes of this book was the ingrained work ethic of the Amish. In most Amish households, children are taught to work from the time they are two years old. In your opinion, is this a good or bad thing? Why?

3. Something that impresses many people who spend time with the Amish are the calm, polite manners of even the smallest Amish children. I observed a four-year-old happily amusing herself with a handful of small stones for hours while her mother and I chatted beside a campfire. What cultural influences, if any, do you think might impact the children's behavior?

4. The Amish go to church only every other Sunday. The "off" Sunday is a day for rest and/or visits between friends and family. If you are part of a church community, do you think this practice would have a positive or negative effect upon your family and your church? Why?

5. The Amish support one-room private schools for their children that go up to only the eighth grade. Their curriculum is simple and basic. The children seldom, if ever, have homework. Many teachers have no more education than their students, and yet as a group, these children

consistently score at or above national testing averages. Why do you think this is? If you are a parent, are you envious of this option, or do you think it's detrimental for the children to have such a limited scholastic experience?

6. In Holmes County, a large number of Amish homes have a small *Daadi-haus* attached for the grandparents to live in. It is extremely rare for them to use a nursing home. What is your opinion about this choice from the standpoint of each of the three generations usually involved?

7. Being a neighbor to the Amish sometimes means being available for small favors of everything from the use of a telephone to transporting members in emergency situations. Some people, like Elizabeth and Grace, embrace the culture and value the friendship. Others, in real life, find it annoying. Would you want to have Amish neighbors? Why?

8. In the final scene, Levi says that he needs to learn how to be *Englisch* before he can be a good husband to Grace. What things do you foresee his needing to overcome before they can marry?

9. If you were doing premarital counseling with Grace and Levi, what cultural, emotional, and financial problems would you prepare them to deal with as they build a life together?

10. Both the Mennonite and Amish churches are rooted in the persecution they endured five hundred years ago when they refused infant baptism and insisted on adult baptism only. Many were burned at the stake for this belief. What doctrinal beliefs, if any, do you personally hold that you would be willing to die for?

A Conversation with Serena B. Miller

1. **What was the most challenging part of writing _An Uncommon Grace_?**

   Researching the Swartzentrubers. The Old Order Amish are a hospitable people and relatively easy to engage in conversations about their faith and practices. There is also a great deal written about the Old Order Amish and other less conservative Amish sects. However, the Swartzentrubers, in general, are much more closed to outsiders. That was definitely a challenge.

2. **On your website, www.serenabmiller.com, you share that while doing research an Amish father told you, "Nothing is forbidden." You said that his family read one of your books and gave you an "enthusiastic nod of approval." In the story Bishop Weaver has quite the opposite temperament toward outsiders, like Grace and even Aunt Rose. Is Bishop Weaver's character based on any resistance toward you during your research?**

   To clarify your question, on that particular night, the Amish father had agreed to allow me to ask questions, but I kept trying so hard not to ask anything that might be considered rude or offensive, that I kept apologizing for each question. He was kind enough to put me entirely at my ease by saying that I could ask him anything I wanted, that no question was forbidden. He said he simply wanted to make certain the information I wrote about his people was accurate.

I have personally never experienced anything but kindness and patience among the Amish. Even the few Swartzentruber Amish I have met have been kind, although much more reticent about talking about their faith.

The personality of Bishop Weaver was actually based on a non-Amish minister whom I once knew. However, I have heard of extremely rigid and dictatorial bishops. In that case, sometimes an entire family will sell their home and move to a different location rather than be under that particular bishop's thumb. I think that most Amish bishops are good men who are simply trying to do the best they can in a position that they neither asked for nor wanted. As I pointed out in the last part of the book, the mantle of responsibility that a bishop accepts is extremely heavy and it is for life.

3. **Your previous novel, *Love Finds You in Sugarcreek, Ohio,* centers on Rachel Troyer, her three Amish aunts, and a mysterious stranger who comes to Sugarcreek looking for refuge. What inspired you to write another story about the Amish community?**

Purely selfish reasons. I really enjoy and respect these people. I love their humor, their gentleness, and their wonderful children. I love sitting at the kitchen table with the women after the dishes are done, talking about small domestic matters by the light of a kerosene lamp. I love the peace I feel in their homes. I treasure their friendship. I almost always learn something important that I can apply to my own life. Writing this book gave me a good excuse to spend more time with my friends.

4. A very interesting theme in the book is the divide not only between the Amish and the *Englisch* but also within the Amish community itself. Was there a particular experience you observed that led you to further explore this aspect of Amish life?

I was talking with a Holmes County law enforcement officer about some of the challenges of working among the Amish. He was a kind man who took his job of protecting the public seriously. The first thing he mentioned was the heartbreak of buggy/car crashes. He said that many wrecks could be avoided if the Swartzentrubers would simply agree to make their buggies more visible. He said that those unadorned black buggies were almost impossible to see on a dark night. Then he made a statement that gave me chills. He said, "I wish they would agree to put the reflective triangles on the back of their buggies, just to give us some warning. I'm so tired of scraping Swartzentrubers up off the road." Until that moment, I had no idea such a sect existed. It was at that point I began to study these people who would rather go to jail than allow the red triangle—which they consider decorative—on their buggies.

5. If you could take one aspect of Amish life to incorporate into your own life or contemporary society as a whole, what would it be?

A friend who makes her living driving a van for the Amish told me once that she was convinced Amish children were, on the whole, the happiest children on earth. From what I've seen, I have to agree. I've spent days at a time in my Amish friends' homes—and the children are a delight. They are more respectful, not only toward adults but also toward one another. I've never seen so much as a good squabble between them. They also have longer attention spans and can play quietly for hours. I attribute this to four things: (1) The lack of television and electronic devices. (2) The almost nonexistent divorce rate. (3) The work ethic taught each child from the age of two. (4) The peace of knowing there is an extended network of family and church members ready to help if any need arises.

6. Grace and Levi are such opposite characters and exemplify distinct personality types. Was it difficult to make the switch in perspectives while writing?

No. By the time I began to write the story, their personalities were so firmly entrenched in my mind that it was not difficult at all. In fact, that was the part I most enjoyed—the switching back and forth and seeing the various situations through entirely different eyes.

7. Elizabeth works as a perfect liaison between Grace and the Amish community. How did her character come about?

When I first began writing the book, Elizabeth wasn't even alive. I had intended for Grace to come home to inherit her grandmother's house—along with the responsibility of a younger sister. But as I wrote the story, her grandmother became such a strong personality, I had no choice but to bring her onto the page. Once there, Elizabeth practically wrote herself. There were so many things she said and did that surprised me. For instance, toward the end, when Levi comes to talk with her about the possibility of leaving his church, I had an entirely different speech planned for her to give. The problem was, Elizabeth had no intention of giving that speech. She had her own ideas—and they were much better than mine. I know it sounds weird, but characters really do sometimes take over the writing—and when that happens, it's wise to simply say thank you and accept the gift.

8. **Levi envies small luxuries in *Englisch* life, such as battery-powered flashlights and windshield wipers, while Grace admires the simple pleasures of Amish living, such as fresh food ingredients and homemade vegetable stock. Would you say that these desires played a role in drawing the two characters toward each other?**

Oh, yes. That was a major part of their attraction to each other. Also, in spite of the differences of their outward appearances and lives, they had many similar traits. Both were highly intelligent, both were compassionate and courageous, and both felt passionately loyal to their families and to God. Add to that the fact that both envied many things about each other's lives—it made a perfect place for them to eventually meet in the middle.

9. **You keep a journal on your website. Have you always kept a journal? Do you try to write every day?**

I've kept a journal for most of my married life. I began it when I went on a mission trip and was afraid that if anything happened to me, my two-year-old son would never really know who I was, what I believed, or how much I loved him. It started out as a letter to him, and then I just never stopped. At last count, I had about fifteen notebooks I've filled to someday be read by my kids and grandkids.

And yes, unless I am terribly ill, or there is a major family crisis, I do write every day. Some days I accomplish more than others, but there are few days in which I don't write at least a thousand words—which is approximately four to five pages.

10. Where is your favorite place to write? To read?

I don't have a favorite place to write anymore. Over the years, I have trained myself to write anywhere, anyplace, and anytime. When my husband was very ill this past year, I wrote the biggest part of one novel on yellow legal pads beside his hospital bed. I recently told my sister that if necessary, I think I could write a chapter on a roll of toilet paper, with eyebrow pencil, in a crowded waiting room. She laughed, but I was serious.

Favorite place to read? Absolutely the best place in the world to read is on my front porch, overlooking these gorgeous southern Ohio hills, with my sweet rescued hound dog lying next to me and a glass of iced tea close at hand. That's my idea of heaven on earth. Actually, that's a pretty sweet place to write, too.

11. What else are you working on? Can readers expect to hear more from Grace and Levi?

How could I possibly abandon Grace and Levi? The next Amish book will be a love story about two entirely different characters, but Grace and Levi will definitely show up. I don't think it will be telling too much if I say that I intend to bring a very special man into the life of Levi's valiant widowed mother.